"Knapp's intense debut is a ... takes the familiar zombie story down a radically new path. . . .[His] writing is sharp, and his fast and furious plot twists keep the pages turning. . . . Fans of zombie fiction and readers looking for a good thrill will find it here." —*Publishers Weekly*

"Will appeal to readers who like Jonathan Maberry's zombie thriller, *Patient Zero*, and fans of gritty SF author Richard K. Morgan (*Altered Carbon*) will enjoy it as well. Highly recommended." —*Library Journal*

"There are many strong points to Knapp's story, the best being his reimagining of the zombie tale. . . . This is a very unique and excellently plotted debut." —*Sacramento Book Review*

"An intriguing futuristic Americana thriller. . . . The story line is action-packed with the zombie concept fresh. . . . Fans will appreciate this entertaining look at the future." —*Midwest Book Review*

"The dialog is strong and believable. . . . The plot hums along, moving briskly but repeatedly dodging the obvious next twist. And the conceit Knapp is playing with here is a fascinating one, and bigger than one book can hold. Hopefully the next one in the series will be up soon, because I want to know what happens next." —The Green Man Review

continued . . .

"A good blend of urban fantasy and sci-fi mixed. It's a very original idea with the concept of zombies that keeps you on the edge of your seat. . . . I'm looking forward to more!" —Night Owl Romance

"This impressive debut incorporates futuristic technology, fantasy, zombielike creatures, mystery, danger, and intrigue. It's a dark and gritty, complex story, full of intense excitement and suspense. With the creepy feeling of zombie horror, this fantastic mystery thriller will satisfy any genre fan." —SciFiChick.com

"An awesome science fiction ride. . . . Knapp manages to keep the tension high throughout the story. . . . The plot has twists you won't see coming, with an ending to match. I can't wait to see what happens next." —Sci-Fi Fan Letter

"*State of Decay* takes all the familiar tropes of zombie fiction and gives them a real world spin that is both convincing and plausible. . . . Knapp's writing style *is* really interesting. He manages to pull you into the story very easily and manages to convey a lot of ideas very quickly. . . . Thumbs up." —Fantasy & Sci-Fi Lovin' Book Reviews

ELEMENT ZERO

James Knapp

A ROC BOOK

ROC

Published by New American Library, a division of
Penguin Group (USA) Inc., 375 Hudson Street,
New York, New York 10014, USA
Penguin Group (Canada), 90 Eglinton Avenue East, Suite 700, Toronto,
Ontario M4P 2Y3, Canada (a division of Pearson Penguin Canada Inc.)
Penguin Books Ltd., 80 Strand, London WC2R 0RL, England
Penguin Ireland, 25 St. Stephen's Green, Dublin 2,
Ireland (a division of Penguin Books Ltd.)
Penguin Group (Australia), 250 Camberwell Road, Camberwell, Victoria 3124,
Australia (a division of Pearson Australia Group Pty. Ltd.)
Penguin Books India Pvt. Ltd., 11 Community Centre, Panchsheel Park,
New Delhi - 110 017, India
Penguin Group (NZ), 67 Apollo Drive, Rosedale, North Shore 0632,
New Zealand (a division of Pearson New Zealand Ltd.)
Penguin Books (South Africa) (Pty.) Ltd., 24 Sturdee Avenue,
Rosebank, Johannesburg 2196, South Africa

Penguin Books Ltd., Registered Offices:
80 Strand, London WC2R 0RL, England

First published by Roc, an imprint of New American Library,
a division of Penguin Group (USA) Inc.

First Printing, April 2011
10 9 8 7 6 5 4 3 2 1

For Kim

ACKNOWLEDGMENTS

I would like to acknowledge the following people:

Kim, who puts up with the many, many hours I spend writing.

Jessica, who puts up with my endless (occasionally last-minute) adjustments, and who helped make this book, and this series, the best it could be.

Jack, who is far more savvy than I, and who tells it like it is.

And my parents, who are both rocks—not everyone can say that.

This series wouldn't have been possible without all of their help.

1

Resurrection

Nico Wachalowski—Restaurant District

It was warm inside the noodle house, and the window to my left was fogged at the corners. The place was crowded, full of bodies and the blanket of conversation that bled through the noise screen at my table. It looked, as far as I could remember, the same as it had five years ago. The only difference was that this time I was alone.

The last clouds of steam drifted up from the bowl of ramen that sat untouched in front of me as I looked out onto the street. It was dark, and the snow had piled up. Streams of people wrapped in coats and scarves moved down the narrow sidewalk between the restaurant and a snowbank that had reached waist height. At the intersection vehicles idled, big flakes beginning to accumulate on their hoods and roofs, while a crowd trudged down the crosswalk. To see it then, it was hard to believe any of it had ever happened.

The permanent dark spot swam in front of my eyes as I stared out the window. The brain scans always came up green, but sometimes I thought that spot had grown larger over the past five years. The damage had made me immune to a type of mind control I hadn't even known existed before then, but I wondered if there wouldn't eventually be a price to pay for that. One more, on a growing stack.

My eyes wandered to the other side of the table, where the chair sat empty. I found myself wishing I had used my JZI to record our last conversation. Too much had happened since then. Now when I thought of her, I saw her moonlit eyes staring out from the shadows of their sockets. Her warm, full lips had turned bloodless and cold. My memories of her were fading, replaced with the face of her revivor.

Did I choose the wrong side, Faye? I knew what she'd say now. When she came back, the person she'd been was lost. Now she worked directly with Samuel Fawkes, the same revivor that had her killed, and that fact didn't even seem to faze her. Now, like Fawkes, she believed any cost was acceptable if it meant destroying their enemies. It didn't matter that I found myself sitting in that camp, however uncomfortably. I knew where she stood now, but I wondered what she would have thought back then.

Five years ago, when I first met Zoe Ott, I found it hard to believe she had the power to alter people's memories, and maybe even see the future. Even after I experienced it firsthand, it was hard to believe. Later, when I traced that first string of terrorist attacks back to Fawkes, and he told me that Zoe wasn't unique, that there were hundreds or even thousands just like her, it didn't seem possible. Now Zoe had been whisked away somewhere, out of my reach, and I was working alongside that very group because they offered something no one else could—the chance to stamp out Fawkes. The difference was that I was doing it to protect the city. They were doing it to protect themselves, and I knew it.

I'd told myself early on that it was a means to an end—that I'd address the threat they posed after they had helped me stop Fawkes. As the years went by, though, it became clearer that Fawkes might actually be right about one thing: he might be the only one in a position to stop them, but to do it he would destroy the city, and everyone inside it.

Did I choose the wrong side?

The food in front of me was getting cold, but I wasn't hungry. I don't know why I'd come back to that place, what I thought I'd find, but it was the last time I'd seen her alive. We'd been apart so long, but her quick hug and the smell of her had brought it all back in an instant. All the reasons I'd had for staying away evaporated, and I'd never been able to get them back. It was a chance to change things, to fix things, but I didn't. No matter how many times I played back that meeting in my mind, it kept coming up the same, and there was nothing I could do about it.

I sighed, leaving my breath on the cold window glass. The trip had been a waste of time I didn't have. Whatever I was looking for wasn't there. All that was there was an empty chair where Faye might have been if I'd done things differently.

Every day that passed was another day lost. It had already been three years since Fawkes had stolen the next-gen revivor prototype Huma. That was three years of distribution, and with the ability to create potential soldiers with a simple injection, we had no way of knowing where his numbers were currently at. We assumed he was administering the injections the same way he had before, to third-tier citizens through free clinics, but so far our canvassing hadn't turned up anything. I'd personally visited more than I could count, and found no sign of Fawkes anywhere. He'd lived under our radar for far too long, and he had his thumb on a button that could claim thousands of lives whenever he wanted. For all I knew, half the people sitting around me were among them.

I have to get out of here.

I was just about to push my chair back, to get up, pay my bill, and leave when someone stepped close to the table and spoke from inside the noise screen.

"Was there a problem with your order?" It was a young Asian man in a black, frog-closured shirt. He'd served me when I first came in.

"No problem," I said. "I just need to settle up."

"No charge," he said.

"Really," I told him. "The food was fine, I just—"

"I remember you."

I took a closer look at the boy, but he didn't look familiar. He noticed the orange flicker in my pupils as I ran his face against my list of past contacts, and smiled slightly.

"You won't find me in your system," he said. He was right.

"Where do you know me from, then?" I asked.

He looked out the window, out onto the street, toward the intersection where the line of vehicles had begun to move forward again.

"The revivor stood right there," he said, pointing. He was looking at the spot where, five years ago, the van had stopped and the revivor stepped out, strapped with explosives. I could still see its face and the way it looked around almost curiously when I tried to contact it over the JZI. I remembered its stony stare as it pinpointed the source of the transmission and made eye contact with me.

Time to wake up, Agent Wachalowski. At the time, I'd had no idea what it meant.

"I waited on you that day," the boy said. "You and your lady friend."

"Oh." I didn't remember him at all.

"I didn't see the bomb at first. By the time I did, you had run outside to confront the revivor."

He stared out at that spot. His face was calm, but his eyes were intense.

"You want to sit down?" I asked him. He glanced back at the front to make sure no one would see him; then he took the seat across from me.

"It was hard to see what happened after the explosion," he said. "I thought maybe you died that day. I'm glad you didn't."

"Me too."

He looked out the window again and watched the people stream past.

"We had run out of green onions in the kitchen," he said. "My mother had run across the street to buy some, to get us through lunch. Coming back, she was caught in the blast and killed. She was fifty-one."

"I'm sorry to hear that."

"Thank you," he said. "I remember that day so clearly. You know? I saw her, on the other side of the street just before it happened. You had raised your badge, and the revivor looked at you. Your lady friend tried to pull you away, and my mother watched as you suddenly turned and pushed the woman down behind a delivery truck. I knew the explosion was coming then. I opened the door and shouted to my mother, but she didn't hear me."

He wanted answers. He wanted to make some kind of sense out of why the whole thing happened, but even if I could tell him everything I knew, I didn't think it would help much. The truth was that while I'd never forget the attack that day, it was just one of many and it was already in my rearview mirror. The threats kept piling up, eclipsing the ones before them.

"You really got to me that day," the boy said. "I thought if I had been you, or someone like you, at least I might have had a chance to save her. I was determined that when I was old enough, I'd enlist, but my father needed me here, and as you can see . . ." He shrugged.

I wished I could tell him that we'd at least gotten the ones responsible, but he knew we hadn't. Samuel Fawkes's main target, Motoko Ai, controlled much of the media through the Central Media Communications Tower and its mogul, Robin Raphael, but even they couldn't cover up things completely. Only a small handful of people knew the truth, but our investigation was too big to keep invisible. Something big was still brewing out there, and everyone knew it. Whispers of mass arrests and secret detention centers kept circulating. It was starting to happen faster than Motoko's people could keep up with.

"We almost went out of business back then," the boy said. "A lot of places on the strip were struggling and the damage was too much for them to absorb. No one wanted to come here after what happened. It made no sense that there would be a second random attack in the same spot, but people were afraid."

He pointed again out onto the street.

"But when you look at it now," he said, "it's like it never happened. Right? We all came together in the aftermath. We helped each other. The damage was repaired, the streets are clean now, and everyone is open for business. Some are even better now after rebuilding, and there's something here that wasn't here before. Like a bond. You know? Now if a stranger or a tourist were to come here, they would never even guess what happened right there."

I hadn't really thought of it that way. I hadn't thought much about the area at all since then. As I watched the dark spot in front of my eyes drift across the falling snow, I knew there had to be stories just like his all throughout the city. Had I begun to lose touch? That had been both Fawkes's and Ai's mistake.

The thing was, though, that the kid didn't know everything. He had gotten caught in the crossfire of a conventional bombing that didn't really even have anything to do with him. If Fawkes had pulled off his plan three years prior, there would have been at least three nuclear detonations in the heart of the city, one for each of Ai's strongholds. How long would it take to bounce back from that?

I opened my mouth to say something when my phone buzzed inside my jacket pocket. I took it out and saw the name VAN OFFO flash on the LCD.

A year ago, Alain Van Offo became my partner. The assignment came from high up, and he reported privately to Alice Hsieh. Motoko and her people knew they couldn't directly control my mind anymore, but they still had him shadow me. Van Offo was a good agent, but he was one of them and he never pretended to be anything else. Like all of them, he controlled the minds of the people around us as a matter of course. Sometimes he had a good reason for it. Sometimes he didn't. I dropped the phone back into my coat pocket without answering.

"You're busy," the boy said. "I should go."

"I wish there was something I could tell you," I said.

He waved his hand. "Maybe it's stupid, but I wanted to tell you that we are okay. I wanted to tell you that even though you couldn't stop the bomb that day, we are persevering. We're strong. If another attack comes, we will overcome that too. If my mother was alive to see us still here, she would be very happy. You know?"

"It isn't stupid. And thanks."

Someone yelled across the restaurant in Chinese, and he glanced back before getting up.

"No charge for the food," he said.

"Thanks again."

"When you find the prick that did it, though, kill him for us."

He wormed his way away from my table and back through the crowd.

"I'll do that."

Incoming call. The words flashed in the air between me and the empty chair across the table. It was Van Offo. Whatever he wanted had to be important.

Call accepted.

Wachalowski here.

You didn't answer your phone.

I know that. What do you want?

The data sweeps just got a hit. They think it's related to revivor tech.

Where?

Black Rock train yard.

I brought up details on the location and found it off the projects of Dandridge. The satellite photos showed that a big chunk of it was out of commission. A graveyard of retired freight carriers sat half-buried in the snow, waiting for the scrap heap.

It looks abandoned.

A flyby picked up heat and a big electrical signature. Magnetic scan suggests at least one heavy-duty lock. Someone's there.

Got it.

I browsed through the satellite footage and the more I did, the more convinced I became that we were dealing with Fawkes. Since he'd gotten out of stasis and rejoined the living, we knew he'd disappeared somewhere inside the UAC. That meant sticking to places no one wanted to go. Even when he'd directed things from his box on the other side of the planet, that had been his MO. The city's underbelly was big, bigger than it should have been. It was easy to get lost in, and he knew that.

Who were they communicating with? I asked.

They were unable to track the remote location, so we're going in. SWAT is assembling now. Get back here.

Understood. I'm on my way.

I got up and made my way to the front door, a little bell ringing as I pushed it open and stepped out onto the sidewalk. The temperature had dropped and the snow was picking up. I joined the flow of foot traffic and started back toward the garage to get my car.

Any one of these people, I thought as I walked among them. Any number of them could be carrying the Huma injection. How many would Fawkes feel he needed before he decided to go ahead with whatever his plan was?

At the intersection, the light had changed again and I stood with the rest, waiting while snow began to blanket the vehicles that piled up along the side street in front of us. The spot where the revivor had stood was less than ten feet away from me.

The kid was right, though. The wound had healed, and you couldn't tell. The city had been bruised but not beaten.

So far.

Calliope Flax—Bridgeway Towers Apartments, Unit #1042

Every night, it was the same goddamned dream.

The faces and the voices changed, and even the body I looked out of changed, but it was the same place every time.

I was strapped to a gurney while guys in rubber suits pushed me down a hall. I could see and hear, but I couldn't move. A door crashed open and they took me through to some big warehouse or hangar. Sheets of heavy plastic, some specked with blood, hung from hooks to screen off work areas, and I could see metal tanks with heavy hatches down there, fingers and palms pressed against glass ports. More guys in those hooded suits moved through the rows, and in an open spot in the middle, dirty naked people were on their knees, their necks chained to metal posts.

They wheeled me through and shoved open one of the plastic sheets. The space inside was full of equipment—an oxygen tank and trays of probes and wires. Shapes in white coats stood over me. One prepped a hypo, and I felt it prick my bicep.

"Is he ready?" someone asked.

He? I thought.

"Yes, proceed."

Someone pressed a plastic mask to my face. Cold air went up my nose and things went blurry. One of them moved a bright light over me as they crowded around. Another one of them used a pair of shears to cut down the middle of my shirt, then leaned in with a fistful of long needles.

Who I was in the dream seemed to change. This time my chest was smooth, with no hair, but it belonged to a guy. I felt a sharp prick as the first needle went in. An old man's hand pushed it through the skin, then stuck a wire to the other end. Then he stuck the next one in, and the next.

Thoughts that weren't mine ran through my head: how it wasn't my fault and I didn't know why I was there. I didn't know who the people were. No one would talk to me.

The doc leaned in and shone a light in my eye. In back of him, hands pushed a big piece of hardware over my chest. I could make out a big tube with a glass lens in it as they adjusted the rig until it was aimed at my heart.

"Clear," someone said.

There was a loud snap, and a low hum came from the tube. My hairs stood on end. The needles that stuck out of me shook a little, and a sick feeling dropped into my gut.

"Steady . . ."

"Initiating stasis field."

There was another snap, and pain bolted through my chest. My eyes rolled, and bile burned up my throat. The docs faded, and the lights went out. . . .

I jerked awake in bed and grabbed my chest. My heart pounded under my hand, and I wiped the sweat off my face. Static hissed in my ears, that white noise in the back of my head that never stopped.

"Fucking thing . . ."

The dream was real; that was the worst part. Nico called it passive feedback. It started after the tanker. I was dead for more than two minutes out there, and I didn't turn revivor, but it was close. He shocked my heart and brought me back, but the static kicked in then, background noise from the other Huma carriers—Fawkes's little army. Every time we grabbed one of them and took them wherever it was they went, later I'd have the dream.

That receiver in their heads, in my head, waited day in and day out for Fawkes to give the order. When he did, that would be it; dead and back again in under a minute. For most of them. Not for me. At least, that was the plan.

In the dark, I heard my phone beep.

What time is it?

Before I'd shipped out, eight was early, but in boot camp, I found out what early was. I marched and ran drills before sunup like a robot, and hated every second. Two months in, though, I got used to it. Six months in, I learned to like it. Over there, it was the only time of day that wasn't like a furnace. By eight it was hot as hell, and the sun never let up—no clouds, no rain, just dust, sweat, and bugs.

I yawned and rolled over. I wondered for the millionth time where that place in the dream was. Where they took the carriers we found and what they did with them.

It was still dark out, but down on the street the traffic was gearing up. I grabbed my phone and checked the time: 4:38 a.m. It beeped again.

The screen said SINGH, RIDDHI. I flipped it open.

"What the fuck do you want, Singh?"

"Rise and shine, soldier," he said. He sounded up. I pushed the covers away and sat on the edge of the bed.

"You're an asshole. You know that?"

"Yeah, I know."

Singh was part of my squad at Stillwell Corps. After the rat's nest Nico stirred up two years back, the UAC got hard-core about home defense. Stillwell took the bid to watch the streets and got big, quick. Word got out they wanted firsts—ex-military types looking for action—and just like that I doubled my pay, with the full package thrown in. I got to soldier again, and found out I'd missed it. On the record, we watched for terrorist threats. Off the record, we spent most of our time on one threat: Heinlein's little field test gone wrong.

"Get to the point, Singh."

"We found another hot spot."

Hot spot. That was Singh-speak for Huma carriers, the M10-positive, third-tier dregs.

"So tell Ramirez," I said.

"I did. He said to call you."

Singh always found them first. He never went in— that was me—but Singh found them first.

"How do you track the damn things?" I asked.

"I'm just that good."

"You're full of shit."

"You got the biceps; I got the brains."

I made a fist. That was a nerve I didn't like touched.

"I'm going to pound the fuck out of you, Singh," I said, but my heart wasn't in it.

"Promises. You want the location?"

"More than life."

The data came in and I laid it over the map. The mark was close to Bullrich.

"What a shock," I said.

"How's that?"

I zoomed in. There were three, from the look of it. They were in Pyt-Yahk. The Pit. Great.

"You know the area?" he asked.

"I know it."

"How long you need?"

"It depends. I'm on it. Anything else?"

"That's it."

"Then screw you, and I'll see you later."

"You know, Ramirez uses you because he thinks you're the best," he said.

"Yeah, right."

"Seriously, you've got a sixth sense for finding them once you're in there. You—"

I hung up on him. I was still sitting on the edge of the bed when the alarm went off. I killed it and got up.

My dead hand was cool on my face when I rubbed my eyes, but at least the twitch was gone; all part of the Stillwell package. In the two years since the tanker went down, Heinlein's new toy went public. The easy way out was easier than ever, and it made Heinlein a fuck-ton more cash. Those veins were full of Heinlein-approved, version M10 nanoblood now, which was pretty much the same as Huma—newer and better. No more twitching, no more numbness or tingling. It almost felt real.

They could even upgrade it remotely from Heinlein, so no more stints in the drainage chair. It was worth it for that alone.

I got out of bed and called my guy Yavlinski in Bull-rich. It took a few tries, but he picked up.

"Flax, what the hell?" He sounded half-dead.

"We got three in the Pit."

"What the hell time is it?"

"If you want to keep getting paid, Yavlinski, it's time for you to get up."

He sighed and swore under his breath.

"Where?"

"Open your ears—the fucking Pit."

He swore again.

"You hear me?"

"Yeah, I heard you."

"I got a lead, but I need to narrow it down. Any of your guys call anything in?"

"Not today."

"My info says there're three together. One of your guys has them somewhere."

"If he does, he's probably waiting until the goddamn sun comes up to call me," he said.

"Yeah, well I'm not."

He grumbled some more, but he got the message.

"I'll call you back." He hung up.

It was easier a year back, but you learn to spot trouble when you're third tier, and they spotted it. No one knew why, but word got out: they're rounding up thirds. The ones that got rounded up didn't come back. When an outsider came in and sniffed around, they scattered like roaches.

I fell back on paid snitches. Yavlinski knew everyone because he dealt in every kind of smack there was, plus black-market meds. With most folks steering clear of the free clinics now, he was the closest thing to health care a lot of them had. That put him in the know, and he liked money enough to run the side racket of kickbacks for each verified carrier he sent my way. I gave him the clinic names and patient lists, and he had his dealers track them down. If he found a real carrier or helped me catch one Singh picked up, Stillwell paid me, I paid Yavlinski, and he paid his guys. Everyone was happy. Except the ones that got rounded up.

I flicked on the light in the bathroom and brushed my

teeth. My new place was a step up from the last, and a long way from Bullrich. It had hot water all the time, AC in the summer, and steady heat in the winter. I had five rooms all to myself. Not bad for a third from Bullrich.

I had some time before I got a call back. I worked out, then hit the shower. I let the steam build, then got wet and lathered up.

I was older, but my body was still lean and hard. A few more scars, but except for the hand, I still looked like I did in my fight days. I ran my hands over my scalp and laced my fingers across the back of my neck. Behind my ear, I felt the scar under my thumb.

One night about a year ago, Nico showed up at my place. He told me to get in the car and not to ask questions. He took me somewhere where a guy put me under and I woke up with the scar. A new piece of tech showed up on the JZI. They couldn't dig out Huma's kill switch, but the shunt would keep it from going off, when the time came. That was the plan. He kept the whole thing off the record. He never said anything else about it, and neither did I, but I thought he made some kind of devil's deal that night.

Seriously, you've got a sixth sense for finding them once you're in there....

Singh and the rest of them didn't know that I could hear them. Whenever one turned, I picked it up. The closer I was, the louder it got. If they ever found out, they'd round me up too, right alongside the rest of them.

I'd just toweled off when the call came back.

"Flax, I got them."

"Where?"

"The Pit, like you said. One of my guys picked them up late last night. He'll meet you there."

He sent the coordinates to my GPS. The spot was deeper in than Singh thought, but not too far off.

"Got it."

"The guy wants dope, on top of the credits."

"It's a good thing I know you, then."

I hung up.

Those guys were always after more, but the fact was they worked cheap, and it was Stillwell's dime. I'd have the deal done and the targets trucked out in time for lunch.

Part of me didn't like it, but it was what it was. Every one of them I picked up was one more revivor off the street. They'd kept the average Joe in the dark so far, but behind the scenes no one sugarcoated it; it was coming, and when it did, anything was better than that many jacks tearing up the city.

Anything.

Zoe Ott—The Blue Oyster Bar

"Another drink?"

I looked up from the heavy rocks glass I'd been idly turning on a cocktail napkin. The bartender had come over and was smiling down at me. He was handsome and dressed to the nines. He smiled and his eyes were flirtatious, but it was all an act; he was just sucking up. Underneath, I could tell he looked down on me. When I went out these days, it was always to fancy, upscale places like the Blue Oyster, but I hated them all.

"Just keep them coming," I said. I looked out the window to my right and saw snow falling on the sidewalk outside. In the glass, I could see my faint reflection, and my eyelids had gotten heavy. I looked the part; my clothes cost more than some people's cars, and a diamond solitaire hung just under the Ouroboros tattoo whose red eye stared from over my jugular, where the snake swallowed his tail. My hair was pulled back in a tight bun, speared through with silver chopsticks. I looked as good as I supposed I could look, but the drinking was getting away from me again. I hoped the guy showed up soon so I could just get it over with and go home.

The bartender kept up the smile and nodded, then walked away. I watched the snow come down until I saw his hand put a fresh napkin in front of me, then put a new rocks glass, half-filled with ouzo, on top of it. He took the empty one away as I picked up the new glass and swallowed half of it.

While I waited, I tried to remember how many people I'd killed. I always remembered the first one all those years ago because it was an accident, and I always remembered Ted because he deserved it, but after that it got fuzzy. Ai had taught me a lot over the past year, and directing that particular ability was one of the most important, probably. No more accidents, and no more guesswork. When it had to be done, I could do it quickly, easily, and painlessly.

"You ought to slow down," a man said as he passed. I looked up and saw an older guy with gray hair and a gold watch stop near my table and grin. He was doing the fatherly thing, I guess. Or maybe he had a fetish for weirdos. There was interest brewing around his head; I could sense it, but I couldn't tell what his game was.

"Go away."

"Troubles?" he asked. Was this guy for real? The guy I was waiting for came in every Friday around seven. He stayed for one drink, then went home to his wife. It was almost seven now. I didn't have time for this.

The room got brighter as I looked into his eyes, and patterns of color appeared around his head. His smile dropped a notch and his eyes got stupid.

"Come here," I said. He came closer, and I waved for him to lean in. "What do you want?"

"Nothing, I—"

"Did someone send you?"

Genuine confusion rippled through the pattern of colors. "No."

"Do you know who I am?"

"No, you just . . . You looked lonely," he said.

I focused on the little ebbs and flows of his mind but didn't see anything like sympathy. What I saw in there didn't have anything to do with me. He didn't think I looked lonely. He thought I looked pathetic and that I might be an easy mark. He was the one who was lonely.

"You're barking up the wrong tree," I told him. "Walk away, and forget you ever thought to come over here."

I pushed, and his eyelids drooped. He nodded.

"You understand?" I asked.

"Yes."

"Smile, then walk away."

I let him go. He smiled. I smiled back. He walked away. It was a good thing too, because just then, Marcus Landers walked into the bar.

He walked in, comfortable and easy. He was known there, and he knew everyone. People smiled and waved and he waved back. He signaled toward the bar, and the bartender started pouring him the usual scotch and soda. He didn't even notice the weird redhead who he'd never seen there before.

This one was a politician of some kind. I wasn't sure exactly what it was he did, but he was making a huge deal about unnecessary search and seizure. He was stirring up a lot of media attention around the search for the Huma carriers, and he was smart enough to know he had to go independent, off the CMC's grid, to do it. Ai and the others had done a good job of sweeping it under the rug so far, but it was time to stem this one at the source.

He was a piece of work, anyway; for all his screaming, the only reason he could walk into a place like the one we were in was because he used a contact inside the FBI to funnel money impounded from weapon-smuggling rings into private, offshore accounts. He was a liar, and a thief too.

On a more personal level, he had a year-old assault

record for punching his wife in the face after a domestic dispute. That was all I really cared about. That right there was enough for me to sign on for the job.

I watched him approach the bar and take the drink. He started talking to a pretty brunet with big tits who was not his wife. He kept glancing down at her cleavage like she was blind. There was no way she didn't notice, but she didn't seem to care.

Get a good eyeful, jerk.

He stayed for one drink, like he always did. Then he made a big, showy good-bye, like anyone there really cared whether he lived or died, as long as he kept buying drinks. He leaned forward to the woman with the big tits like he might hug her or kiss her, but he didn't do either. He turned and left the bar, stepping out onto the sidewalk.

In the dim light, no one noticed my eyes change as I stared at Mr. Landers through the window. As he bundled himself against the wind, I saw the colors, that strange signature of his consciousness, bloom around his head. The patterns there looked content, like he was a guy on top of the world. I burrowed deeper, to where other patterns swirled—righteous anger, ambition, and fear of getting caught—then entered his mind. It was as easy as slipping into a warm bath.

He stopped suddenly, perking up as he sensed me.

Hello, Mr. Landers.

His face went pale and he started to look around, until I made him relax. He stood there as people streamed around him.

I want you to do something for me, I told him.

He wasn't equipped to resist me. Actually, he was one of the easier ones I'd come up against during the past year. His mind was easy to influence, and what I wanted him to do was hardly anything at all.

Outside, he nodded, still not even aware I was there watching him. His eyes looked a little unfocused as he stepped to the curb and waited. Snow drifted down and collected in his hair and on the shoulders of his coat while he breathed slow and steady. He stayed like that, between the bumper and grille of two parked cars, until I saw what I was looking for.

The oncoming driver was already speeding. It took only a very small push to make him accelerate. Landers didn't even look over as the engine gunned and tires chirped on the wet blacktop.

Now, Mr. Landers.

He knew, I think. Right at the last second he knew, and I felt him resist, but it didn't work. He took a single, well-timed step backward off the curb and into the street. The crash made everyone in the bar jump. The driver stomped on the brakes, dragging Mr. Landers for several yards before slamming into the rear end of the vehicle ahead of him. Blood rained across the snowbank piled up next to the sidewalk as his body was crushed.

Someone outside screamed. People crowded around the accident, some of them using their phones to take pictures. I saw the bartender pick up a handset and dial as his customers began flocking to the window.

I just sat for a minute and waited. If Landers somehow survived, I was supposed to finish him off. But when I tried to sense him, he wasn't there. Mission accomplished.

I paid my tab, and then without making eye contact with anyone, I left the bar.

Faye Dasalia—Treatment Inflow Pipe

I swam through cold, black water at near-freezing temperatures, through the narrow pipe that seemed to have no end.

The only light came from my own eyes, and even my night vision could barely make out what lay ahead of me. The rumble of the treatment plant's centrifuge had faded behind me a long time ago. The sounds of the street and underground metro were lost through the tons of concrete above me. The only sound that far down was the electric hum from inside my chest.

Three hours had passed since I entered the pipe, and my body temperature was far below normal, even for me. The void that yawned beneath my field of memories seemed very wide, very deep, and very close. With nowhere else to look, I stared into it while fear buzzed in some disused part of my brain.

Will this finally be the day? I wondered as I felt my mind sink further, through the lights of my memories and toward the dark. *Will this be the day that I finally die?*

Faye, you should be almost there. Do you see anything?

The words appeared in the dark and floated there, as I watched a seam in the pipe pass by me. It was Fawkes, contacting me from the surface. I scanned ahead for movement but didn't spot anything.

No sign yet.

Lev had been three hours in when we lost him. Whatever he'd encountered, it had to be close. I left a circuit open, hoping he would pick it up, but so far there'd been nothing.

How are you holding up? Fawkes asked.

Fine.

It had been one year since Samuel awoke, since he stopped being just a voice in the dark. He walked now, and talked here with form and presence. He'd been part of my life for a long time, but now he seemed real to me in a way he never had been before. Before the tanker sank into the ocean, he'd left stasis and stepped into the real world, where he was both more and less vulnerable. He had one more plan, one more chance to stop them. Whatever happened, it would be over soon.

A signal lit up at the edge of my sight. Sonar had picked up movement down the pipe in front of me.

Wait, I've got something.

A gray shape appeared from out of the blackness. Metallic ticks vibrated through the cold pipe as the shape changed position.

What is it? Fawkes asked.

It was dense, and maybe a third of my size. I scanned it and found electrical current.

It's mechanical.

I tuned the sonar, creating an image. Up ahead was a layer of sediment, and just past that was some kind of small machine with many spindly legs. It used a sensor to probe ahead of it as it scuttled through the pipe.

There's some kind of servo down here. Stand by.

The servo reached out with a wire-thin claw and poked through the sediment in front of it, kicking up small, fleshy cubes.

Faye. The word flashed in the dark in front of my face. Lev had picked up the circuit. He was still down here somewhere.

Lev, where are you?

Just ahead. Don't approach the servo yet.

The robot scuttled forward, kicking up more of the soft, uniform cubes. I watched them float back down to the bottom.

It's revivor flesh, I thought. The pieces were Lev's remains.

What happened? I asked.

It's some kind of maintenance 'bot, he said. *It must be designed to carve up blockage. It came up behind me and severed my spine before I could stop it. I've kept it from the rest of me, but I can't continue the mission.*

I strained my eyes through the dark, and there, maybe twenty feet or so in the distance, I could just make out his eyes. They shifted in the darkness, staring, I thought, into his personal void.

How do I get past it? I asked.

Watch the claw, but your best bet is probably to just grab it. It's not designed for combat, and it's not heavily shielded; you should be able to penetrate its skin.

Understood.

The servo moved through the chunks, heading in my direction. When it locked on, it moved surprisingly fast; a claw brushed my face as I lunged and grabbed the leg at its base. Through the water I heard the whir of motors as it tried to pull away.

The cutter flashed in front of me a few times as its little legs scrambled, trying to make a retreat. I found a seam in the thing's outer chassis and placed my free palm on it. I fired my bayonet and it punched through, into its electronics.

The robot jerked in my hand and my body seized as a jolt of electricity passed through it. The current arced from my back and down the pipe as I turned the bayonet. I heard a metallic crunch; then the servo stopped moving.

I retracted the blade and dropped the machine. Pushing through the chunks of flesh, I stirred up fingers and toes until the water cleared on the other side. I swam close to what was left of Lev Prutsko.

I'm here, Lev.

His eyes had dimmed in the dark. All he had left was his torso and one arm. His gaze stopped shifting around and he made eye contact with me.

I'm glad it was you who came, he said.

Glad?

I think so, he said. *Yes.*

Over the channel we shared, he began to stream something, a thin trickle of embers, over to me. It was one of his memories. When the stream ebbed out and died, he signaled for me to lean closer to him. I moved in until our faces nearly touched.

He never expected me to make it, he said. *I knew that. Whoever goes down this pipe is expendable. Did he tell you?*

I had suspected it, but I shook my head.

There's a lot he doesn't tell you, Lev said.

He doesn't trust me?

You shouldn't have told him about what you remembered.

We hadn't spoken of that in a long time. After reanimation, memories that had been erased would return. It's why Ai feared us. But long ago when I awoke on the tanker, one particular memory had returned—a piece of the puzzle that never quite fit. As a detective, I'd processed one of them, a woman named Noelle Hyde. Back then, she'd tried to kill Fawkes, but she wasn't ordered to; it was just the opposite. They'd killed her for what she'd done.

They didn't want Fawkes dead, I said to Lev.

They lie. He thinks you give too much consideration to their motives.

I know what I saw. At the time, I thought they feared something else, something besides Fawkes stripping them from power.

Lev's eyes just watched me from the murky darkness.

I still think that, I said. Lev managed a nod.

Maybe they do.

"... *It will start here, but it won't end here* ..." Ai had said once. "*Fawkes will destroy this city, and then one by one, the rest will begin to fall.* ..."

They need to be stopped, I said, *but he should have listened.*

There's a lot he doesn't tell you. Just remember that.

I will.

Do you want to continue your existence?

I think so.

You think?

The darkness that waits for me, I told him, *it's the only thing left that really scares me. I don't want it to take me. I'm not ready for it to take me, not yet.*

You may come to terms with that someday, he said.

Have you?

A long time ago. He will shut you down, you know. Someday soon.

I know.

I wish I could stop it, he said.

You do?

Yes.

I moved closer to him and hoped he could see my face. Using our private channel, I told him something I hadn't told anyone else.

I found a way to sever his command spoke.

He didn't respond right away. The shunt I'd fashioned over the years would work—I didn't doubt that—but Fawkes's reaction, if he knew, would be extreme. It would mean the end not just for me, but everyone on Fawkes's network who knew of it.

Will you run, then? he asked.

Under my tongue, I felt the small glass capsule. Lev would have had one as well.

Do you still have the Leichenesser? I asked.

No. I swallowed it in the struggle.

I placed one hand on the side of his cold face and the other over his Adam's apple. Peering through his flesh, I found his command nodes.

Good-bye, Lev.

Good-bye, Faye.

The blade pushed through his skin and into his spine. With a small twist, the command connections snapped. The circuit between us dropped as black blood bloomed out into the cold water, blotting out the light from his eyes even as they faded, and went dark.

Alone, I brought up the memory he gave me. With no pathways associated with it, it wouldn't last very long. I wanted to see it before it decayed.

I looked into it and saw myself, alive. From the subtle distortion, I knew he'd been looking through a Light Warping field as he stood and watched me. I was in my apartment. My skin had color, and I still had hair. Real blood still pulsed through my veins, and I could almost sense sadness in my eyes.

This is the night I was killed.

The heat in my veins stood out as he'd watched me and monitored the steady beat of my heart. He kept tabs on a second heartbeat as well; my old partner, Doyle Shanks, was there with me.

Target Shanks is here. The words appeared in the air, and though I realized he'd been talking to Fawkes, his stare remained fixed on me and not on Doyle Shanks.

Kill them both, came the reply, but Lev had hesitated.

I can remove the target and leave the other, he offered.

Kill them both, came the reply, and the memory scattered. The ember, Lev's last thought, faded away, gone forever. I didn't look back as I swam on ahead.

Fawkes, I'm through.

Good. The perimeter is roughly five hundred meters ahead.

From the security perimeter's edge, it would be a half mile. Well past the point of no return, I swam on. Eventually, I saw a broadcast message from the surface far above:

You are entering a restricted area. No unauthorized communications are permitted in or out from this point forward. No unauthorized scans, visual, audio, or data recordings are permitted beyond this point. No unauthorized personnel, or authorized personnel with a security clearance of less than 3, are permitted beyond this point by order of the UAC Government. . . .

The words scrolled by in the dark, but they didn't concern me. It was a stock message, given to all visitors. They had no way to detect my presence, and if they did, I'd get more than a warning.

. . . by continuing, you forfeit your right to refuse any and all searches, including of your vehicle, its contents, and your person, up to and including full internal scanning. Any property including identification may be confiscated at the guard's discretion and held for an indeterminate period of time. Failure to comply with security will result in action up to and including lethal force. . . .

It took thirty minutes to close the distance. The pipe ended abruptly, and a connecting pipe led toward the surface. That muted pang of anxiety faded, and the dark void receded, just a little.

I'm at the junction.

I looked up into the dark. According to the blueprints, the pipe was a straight shot up to the surface. I pushed off the cold metal and began to swim upward. The water pressure eased the higher I went, until I came to a ninety-degree bend. The pipe was running across the tarmac now.

. . . entering a restricted area. No unauthorized communications are permitted in or out from this point forward. No unauthorized scans, visual, audio, or data recordings are permitted beyond this point. . . .

The words warped and then winked out. As part of the security protocol, my communication node had been shut down.

I swam, measuring the distance, then stopped. I snapped open my left arm and took the handheld arc cutter from inside. When my hand rejoined, I placed it on the pipe, feeling the cold metal in front of my face.

The cutter hissed as I carved out a circle three feet in

diameter. I lowered the plug down into the water, and dim light seeped through the hole. I turned off the night vision and looked up through the surface of the water at what looked like ceiling struts high above me. I reached up and gripped the edges of the hole, cold air chilling the skin of my exposed hands, then pulled down until my head broke the surface.

I slipped through and lowered myself to the floor. I was in a huge hangar where a fleet of large vehicles hunkered. Over on the opposite side of the room, a large glass window looked into an office, but the lights were out inside. I listened, but I didn't hear anyone.

I stood, naked, and surveyed my location. I saw twenty or so large trucks parked inside. The pipe ran along the base of one wall. Crouching, I followed it to its exit point, and through a grimy window I saw it continue across the tarmac to a large water tower in the distance. Snow was falling, large flakes swirling in the wind.

The tower held four thousand gallons of water used as coolant down in the processing plant. Every six months it was flushed through the pipeline to the water-treatment plant, where I began my journey. The large silo stood several hundred meters out in back of the main plant, directly across from a storage depot. That depot was my target.

I found the door and stepped out into the snow. The lock clicked shut behind me, and a gust of freezing air whipped over me. I saw no guards or cameras. The security system on the tarmac keyed off heat signatures, which made me effectively invisible. I kept to the shadows and moved fast. At the depot's back entrance I found a plain metal door with a scanner next to it. I pulled a small, tightly rolled magnetic strip out from under an incision in my scalp. Unrolling it, I held it to the scanner until it beeped and the LED turned green.

Ice flaked down onto my back as I pushed open the door. The facility was dark and filled with metal boxes. Each box was the size of a human body, stacked and awaiting shipment. Each had a lot number and a shipping code, and was stamped with a certification:

PRODUCT OF HEINLEIN INDUSTRIES

I followed the map Fawkes had provided and crept down one of the rows all the way to the end of the shipping bay, where a single doorway stood. I stepped through, down a long, dark corridor, to an annex designated SST, for Series Seven Testing.

The magnetic strip got me through the door and into a refrigerated locker where wheeled metal racks were assembled in rows. Rows of revivors hung from hooks on each rack, their arms and legs dangling.

There were ten revivors to each of the racks, dormant, but ready for reanimation. Counting down by date and time, I found the rack that would be processed that morning. I lifted the first revivor off its metal hook and hoisted it down onto the concrete floor. I spit out the glass capsule and slipped it into the corpse's open mouth, down between its rear molars. I struck him beneath the jaw and heard the capsule crunch.

Mist boiled from between the revivor's lips, and a few seconds later his face melted like hot wax. Teeth and bone collapsed and oozed into the hole as I stood and stepped back to a safe distance. His chest sank in on itself, followed by the rest of him, as the substance consumed the necrotized flesh. When its job was done, it turned upon itself. All it left behind were revivor hardware and a cloud of thin white mist that was already being pulled through the vents. I took the tag that had been around his wrist. I slipped it around my own, then hid the bayonet and revivor nodes behind an equipment rack.

The bodies swayed on their hooks as I pulled myself into the empty slot. The hook pierced my skin and I eased myself down until it dug into the bone of my skull. Carefully, I released the bar above me and let myself hang. In another minute, the bodies were still.

Using the trigger Fawkes had given me, I made myself go dormant. The light from my eyes flickered and then went out. If our contacts there were right, I would reawaken in the next few hours.

Until that time, I would sleep.

Nico Wachalowski—Black Rock Train Yard

The morning sun had just begun to turn the sliver of sky above us to a dull gray, and in front of us, the train yard's floodlights were blurred in the fog. The chain-link gate that led into it hung open, pressed into a bank of dirty snow. On the other side, derelict monorail cars were lined up in a long row, half-buried and covered in ice.

Agent Van Offo stood to my left, working the electronic manifest with a stylus. A yard worker leaned against the guard station's metal siding and stared at the head of his cigarette.

We're at the entrance, I told the SWAT leader.

Roger that. Our teams are in position.

"I've got it," Van Offo said. He held up the tablet to show the grid, with one of the cars called out. "Right there; that's the source."

The train car was stored with a block of others, abandoned along the brick-faced rear of the yard. I zoomed in and saw that the snow had been cleared away from the hitch and the door above it. I glanced back at Van Offo.

You see that?

I see it.

"Thanks," he said to the yard worker, and handed the tablet back to him. The man took it without looking up. Van Offo stood in front of him and stared for a few seconds. In the gray light, I saw the brown of his eyes turn black.

"Go back inside," he said in a low voice. "Sit at your desk and go to sleep."

The man nodded. He flicked the cigarette, half-smoked, into the snow and lumbered through the door, into the guard station.

"You look thoughtful," Van Offo said. His eyes, always half-closed, peered over his large nose as snow collected on the shoulders of his coat. He couldn't control my thoughts any longer, but he could still sense them. He didn't know exactly what was going through my head, but he was good at filling in those blanks. It was easy to see, sometimes, why Fawkes hated them.

"Come on," I said. "We're moving in."

Snow drifted down and had just begun to cover the boot tracks that branched off from the rusted metal gate. Several sets headed off between the rusting hulks. I followed them in.

Rail cars loomed on either side. The outsides were weathered, seams stained with rust. In the distance I saw oil drums, their rims scorched and covered with soot. Past that, beyond the perimeter, the huge shadow of the Central Media Communications Tower loomed over the city.

The tracks led down a frozen gray slick that ducked between two cars a few hundred feet away. I drew my gun and started down the path. Van Offo followed.

Wachalowski, this is SWAT leader. The area is secured. We're waiting on your word to move in.

The satellite showed thermal activity in the yard. I could see the two teams as hot spots on the map. Van

Offo and I were two orange points in a field of gray. All signatures converged on the far end of the yard, where a single car stood out from the rest, a pattern of shifting red and yellow among the cold, dark shapes around it.

There, I said. Van Offo nodded.

On the visual feed, I watched SWAT creep down the rows of rusted metal. Their optics floated in the shadows as they made their way toward the target.

Wachalowski, Van Offo said. He pointed at the trail in the snow. Sets of animal tracks trailed alongside the others.

SWAT, we've got dog tracks here, I said. *Computer counts at least four different sets.*

Roger.

I broke from the trail and moved between the car and the weathered brick wall beside it. I stopped a hundred yards south of the target, then zoomed in for a better look. The snow had gotten heavier, making it harder to see.

Anything? Van Offo asked. My breath trailed in the cold as I swept over the area. The wall of the car was too thick and too far away for the backscatter to penetrate, but I could pick out several cameras mounted on the outside of it.

They've got security feeds set up, I said.

We see them, SWAT said. *Ready to cut their power on your mark.*

An LED on the rear door flipped from red to green, and the latch turned.

Wait.

The door slid open and someone stepped out. It was a man with thick black hair and a surgical mask tied over his face. Over his clothes, he wore a black rubber apron.

One of the suspects just came out. Hold position.

The man walked out into the snow and the apron left a trail of black drops. He moved to the side of the car and turned away from the camera. Steam drifted up from in front of him as he started to urinate. From inside, someone barked in Russian. The translator scrolled text at the bottom of my periphery.

Clean it all up! Set the charges, and let's get the fuck out of here!

You get that, SWAT?

Roger that. Team, watch for explosives.

I turned to Van Offo.

Can you lure him away from there? He nodded.

I turned back to the man, and watched as the stream of urine stopped suddenly. His head perked up, like he'd heard something.

They'll see him on the camera, Van Offo said.

That's fine.

The man swayed on his feet for a moment. He zipped up, and stood there like he wasn't sure what to do.

"Come on," Van Offo whispered under his breath. I zoomed in on the man, and watched his eyelids droop. Van Offo had him.

The man in the apron took a single step back. He turned toward us, and I heard a soft pop as his body jerked suddenly. Blood jetted from one ear, and left a red scribble in the snow.

What was that? The SWAT leader asked. It wasn't a gunshot. One of Fawkes's kill switches had detected Van Offo's interference and gone off. If the others weren't alerted, they would be soon.

Cut the power. Move in now.

The man's body crumpled to the ground as the floodlights went out with a loud snap. The LEDs on the storage units went dark as boots tromped through the snow. I closed in on the body, Van Offo close behind me.

"Get that door open!" the SWAT leader shouted.

The magnetic lock had powered down with the bolt still in place. One of them slammed a metal crank into the key and released it manually. Snow drifted down as another officer moved in and heaved open the door.

It was halfway open when a bright flash filled the opening and the force from an explosion inside the car blew the door off its track. It struck the SWAT officer and hurled him back onto the ice. Through the ringing in my ears I could make out shouting, as firelight flickered behind the tinted glass of the train car's windows.

Get that fire out, the SWAT leader said. A team moved in and I followed close behind them. Flames raged behind thick black smoke inside the car, as one of the men slung a douser through the doorway and it thumped in the small space.

The flames died as a huff of hot air and smoke blew through the opening.

How many inside? the SWAT leader asked. The smoke was still too thick to enter the car, but using the backscatter I could make out two male figures inside. They looked dead, but something in there was still moving. A shape slunk below the smoke level, close to the floor.

There's something in—

A dark shape lunged out of the smoke. A male revivor collided with the closest officer, one arm trailing behind it on a cord of sinew. Half its face was obliterated, and one moonlit eye stared from the blackened mess.

"Revivor!"

The officer went down with the thing on top of him. Smoke drifted from the revivor as it clamped its gray, meaty fingers around the man's throat.

I fired a burst into the back of its skull, and black fluid splashed across the fresh snow. A rifle shot slammed into its chest, and it let go. The officer shoved the body to one side and got back up.

Something heavy landed on my back. I slipped on the

ice and fell as it came down on top of me. Coarse hair brushed my neck, and rank-smelling breath huffed over the side of my face.

I twisted onto my back and saw a dog baring sharp yellow teeth. I got one arm between us as it went for my throat, and clamped down instead on the body armor covering my forearm. Its paws dug into my chest as it thrashed its head and growled.

A shot went off near me as several shapes leapt, trailing smoke, out of the storage car. As I struggled I saw two more dogs, large huskies, hit the ground and scramble on the ice. Exposed ribs stuck out where the hide had been blown off of one, and another was missing a back leg. Growls, punctuated by loud barking, sent clouds of breath through the frigid air, and I saw moonlight yellow in one set of eyes.

I pushed myself to my knees as the dog on top of me continued to thrash. The weight of it pulled me down again, and claws raked my face. I pushed the barrel of my gun into its flank and pulled the trigger three times. It let go, but didn't go down. It snapped its jaws as I pulled away, and saliva flecked my face.

I put a shot through one of its eyes, and it staggered and fell. I peered through the hide and saw components clustered along its spine.

They're reanimated, I broadcast. *Destroy those dogs.*

One of the officers fired, and the dog nearest him jerked and went down. The third lunged and clamped its jaws down on the man's calf, thrashing as the rifle went off three more times.

A bullet tore through the animal's side and it went limp. The SWAT officer pried the jaws free and let it fall.

Hold your fire.

The last shot echoed off, and the yard got quiet. The remains of the revivor lay crumpled in the snow, along with the three dogs and the SWAT member who got caught in the blast. Nothing else moved from the direction of the car.

A few feet away, the body of the man in the black apron lay face down in the snow. I used the backscatter to scan into the bloody hole in his ear, and saw traces of shrapnel that had been pushed from the inside out.

"That's Fawkes's work," Van Offo said.

I looked over the body. The only thing the man had on him was a drugstore cell phone. It was clean; no numbers were stored. I pulled the ID from it and fed it back to Alice Hsieh back at headquarters.

Alice, we're at the site. I need a number run from a cell phone we recovered. Can you trace the last circuit?

Hang on.

The SWAT leader was calling in an EMT, his breath blowing plumes as he barked into the radio. I put in for a biohazard team to come impound the revivors.

Got it, Alice said. *I was able to go back twenty-four hours. One call only; someone named Harold Deatherage.*

Thanks.

"Last call went to a guy named Harold Deatherage," I told Van Offo. He shook his head.

"Do you know that name?" he asked.

"No."

"The car is clear!" a voice shouted. I looked through the thinning smoke and switched to a thermal filter. There was nothing living left inside, and no active revivor signatures.

I waved smoke away as I crossed to the entrance and through the doorway. The inside of the car was a mess of twisted metal and broken wire cages. There were remains scattered through the car, but it was hard to separate them all out. Some were canine; I could see singed fur and pointed teeth buried in the mess.

A human leg and two misshapen arms were sprawled among other, unidentifiable pieces.

Near the back of the car were several scorched gurneys. I could make out frayed wire and a broken housing for electronics, along with an IV rack that was bent in half. Some kind of test had been run there, but there was no way to know for sure what they'd been doing without a forensic reconstruction. Van Offo crept through the debris behind me and surveyed the scene.

"Why dogs?" he asked.

"You got me."

In theory, anything with a brain could be revived, but the bottom line was that a real dog was cheaper and easier to maintain. It didn't make sense.

Out at the edge of the yard I saw the first group of camera eyes gathering, recording everything they could see. A van pulled up behind them while I watched. In twenty minutes the place was going to be mobbed.

Alice, this was definitely Fawkes. We're going to need a forensics team down here. They were able to blow the inside of the unit, but I think we can salvage something from it. We need DNA identification on two bodies, and put a rush on that revivor impound; this is too public.

Understood.

I looked around the car. The broken shells of computer terminals were scattered in the wreckage, along with a second gurney. When I scanned the floor, I could make out surgical tools. The head of a dog lay a foot from its body, eyes staring up at me.

Run Deatherage's name. See if anything comes up.

I'm on it.

The SWAT leader appeared at the doorway behind us and leaned in.

"Agent, it looks like the techs picked up a transmission just before the explosion," he said.

"What kind of transmission?"

"Some kind of large transfer. We think it was a core dump, to save the data before they blew the place."

"They get a destination?"

He nodded.

"A copy?"

"No."

Alice, it looks like they did some kind of backup or core dump before they blew the place. We've got a destination.

Where? I checked the SWAT channel. When I saw the name, I grit my teeth.

Mother of Mercy. It was a clinic downtown.

Isn't that facility on our list? she asked.

Yes. We'd been there several times to pull records and hadn't even marked the place as suspicious. I'd been there once myself. Things were slipping through the cracks.

Forensics will clean up the storage site. Take SWAT and get over there. Let me know what you find.

I looked at Van Offo. "You heard the woman."

"Mother of Mercy," he said. There was a strange look in his eye.

"Problem?"

"No."

Back outside, the wind gusted. Grit and snow pelted the side of the train car. Van Offo looked out at the revivor's remains, its shirt flapping in the breeze.

"Let's go."

You have one job now, he told me early on. *Manpower, equipment, funds . . . anything you need, you'll get.*

He was right. I got everything I needed. As long as in the end I put Fawkes down for good, nothing else mattered. Obstacles disappeared. Any footage taken from any camera that put the investigation in a bad light disappeared. If it did air, it was pulled. They were willing to search anyplace and detain anyone. None of it got me any closer to Fawkes.

I climbed back through the wreckage, back out into the cold. Van Offo followed, staring out through the snow as he turned over in his mind whatever divination he'd just received that he wouldn't, or maybe couldn't, share.

2

BREACH

Zoe Ott—Stillwell Corps Base

It was warm in the car, and as Penny sped down the street, the snow that streaked past the windshield was almost hypnotic. Penny rode low in the driver's seat, head bobbing in time with the beat as she whipped down the sharply curved ramp, apparently able to see even though I couldn't. I hated Penny's music at first, but it had grown on me, and as the bass beat in my chest, I caught my own head bobbing a little.

I offered her my flask as red dots of light appeared in the dark up ahead. She waved one hand no, so I nestled back into the big leather seat and I took a long pull off it myself while panels on the dashboard lit up. A holographic display blinked on an inch in front of the glass of the windshield, and the computer highlighted the red dots down the road in front of us. Penny's fingers tapped at the dash console, and the words BLOCKING SCAN appeared there.

When they realized the scan was blocked, they'd call;

this was the fifth time we'd been there, and they did it every time. The place had a ton of security, and no one got in without being checked out, but it didn't have to be on the record. Not for us.

The video panel lit up and a good-looking guy with a crew cut and a Stillwell Corps uniform appeared. He looked at us, and Penny gave him a little wave while he verified our faces. He said something I couldn't hear over the music, and a light next to the display turned green. He nodded at us, and the screen went dark.

The snow stopped abruptly as we blew into the tunnel, the tube lights fixed on top snaking off into the distance like three big, white worms. Text began scrolling across the bottom of the windshield, warning about stuff like security clearance, vehicle search and seizure, and other things that sounded even worse. We didn't have to worry about any of that. The people who counted knew we were coming; in fact, they dreaded it. No one was going to search us or detain us—they wouldn't dare. We were special messengers sent by Ai herself, and I was Element One, the grand savior of everyone who stood against Fawkes.

A jeep and an unmarked black car with tinted windows passed by us going the other way inside the tunnel, before we came out into the huge, underground lot. Penny made her way toward the side entrance they liked us to use. Two armed guards stood to either side of it as she pulled in and killed the music in time to hear the tires chirp. The two men stood like statues in the headlights while I took one last swig from the flask.

"All right," Penny said. "Let's do this; I need a real drink already."

As soon as we pulled up I sensed something was missing. The buzz that came from the research lab's busiest brain wasn't there. I'd seen him only once in person, some scientist on permanent loan from Heinlein. He'd

worked on Huma, so it made sense he'd be our best hope
to sabotage it. He was an older, ugly Chinese man with
thinning hair and spots on his skin. He had a cool aura,
though. It was complex, with a million focused points,
and in between it all his colors roiled like a storm. They
reminded me of how Nico's used to look, and thinking
about that made me a little sad. Penny patted my arm.

"No Chen," she said. She noticed it too.

I was about to get out when the door between the two
guards opened and an older man in a suit stepped out.
I immediately recognized the square face, and the gray
military cut. I took an extra mouthful of ouzo and swallowed hard before stowing the flask in my suit-jacket
pocket next to where the pistol was strapped.

"General Osterhagen," Penny whistled. "That's not
good."

"Why not?"

"He's got bad news. He wants to make sure no one
glosses over it."

His face looked serious, like it always did, but Penny
was right: there was something about the soft light of
his consciousness that was grim and determined. Behind
the thin white halo that surrounded it and behind the
layers of his thought I saw worry, and that worried me.

Osterhagen didn't look especially intimidating. In
fact, if you didn't know anything about him, you'd think
he just looked like somebody's grandfather. I knew
plenty about him, though, and that included all the men
he killed when he was in the service, and all the ones he
killed once he was out. He'd actually killed men with his
bare hands, but when you looked at those calm blue patterns that usually made up his aura, you'd never guess
that any of it bothered him, ever. He didn't scare or
worry easily.

Penny killed the engine, and as we got out, I could see
she'd noticed it too. We walked up to him and he held

out his hand. First Penny shook it, then I did. His hand was hard, and he always squeezed a little too tight, but even though I hated touching people, I'd learned to give him my best shake. It was one of those things that mattered to him.

"General," Penny said, throwing him a wink, "if I'd known you were going to be here, I'd have dressed up."

Penny was dressed up; we both were whenever we visited the Stillwell Corps research facility. She flirted as a matter of course, with men and women, but there never seemed to be much interest behind it. Osterhagen, as usual, completely ignored it.

"I thought I'd give you a tour of the lab tonight," he said. "There's something I want you two to see."

"Sounds great," she said. "Let's do it."

In reality, she was actually really excited to see the lab, and so was I. Ai had sent us before to get what she called an unfiltered report, but so far they'd drawn the line at letting us walk around inside the work area and see what was going on. Ai never pushed it, so I assumed Osterhagen had let her view it remotely or walked her through himself, but I'd always been curious. The lab was where they took all the Huma-infected subjects they'd been able to find. I'd never actually seen one. Not that I knew of anyway.

The guards straightened up even more as he passed back by them and opened the door. We followed him in, and they brought up the rear as the door slammed shut behind us.

The hallway behind the door was long and led directly to the wing where the research took place. No one ever saw us come or go except the guards and the skittish scientist type named Moses who usually met us. There was no Moses, this time. Osterhagen turned back and I saw orange light flicker in the darks of his eyes, like I used to see with Nico sometimes, way back when.

As soon as it happened, the two guards peeled off and left through the next door we passed, leaving the three of us alone.

"So where's your man?" Penny asked. "Chen?"

"Mr. Chen is not currently on the base."

"Why not?"

"He is off shift."

"Hey, it's not like we're coming down to the wire or anything," she said, offhand. The general scowled.

"I know that better than you," he said. "His team works in twenty-four hour shifts. He can't be here all the time."

"Fair enough."

"You seen the map lately?" he asked. He meant the computer model that kept track of all the recorded visions we'd been adding in over the years. It looked a little like a space nebula or something, a colorful ring around a dark center. A bright point where thousands and thousands of visions converged on the rim of the void like a star. That point signified some horrible holocaust, after which there was just a big nothing. Since not all recorded visions were completely certain, the nebula changed subtly over time. No matter what we did, though, it still hadn't changed in the only way that mattered. The star was still there, and so was the void on the other side of it.

"Of course," Penny said. "What's bugging you?"

"Whatever is going to happen, it's going to happen soon," he said.

"What makes you say that?" she asked. She asked it like she wasn't sure she believed him, but Ai had said the same thing to us. We'd figured out that no one ever saw anything that occurred after their lifetime—that's what made that big, blank spot so scary—but aside from that, it did mean that one way or another, time was running out.

"You think we can still change this thing?" he asked

over his shoulder. "That one day, something we do will make that big, empty space light up like the rest of the map, and the bright spot fade away?"

"That's the point, isn't it?" she asked.

"Yes ma'am. That's the point."

I was worried before, but now he had me really worried. I'd never heard him like that before. He usually got on my back for talking like that; he was more of a win-at-all-costs kind of guy. He didn't like what he called my defeatist attitude.

"Does this mean you weren't able to make the virus work?" I asked.

Everyone knew by now that Fawkes had stolen Heinlein Industries' prototype revivor model, Huma, three years back, and that he'd been using it ever since. No one really believed we'd ever find all the people infected with the Huma prototype before Fawkes finally activated them. The virus was somehow supposed to get on to their network and shut all of those infected back down again once they all came back to life. Test subjects were hard to find, though, and with them all still inactive, it was slow going. Sometimes I wondered if they'd be able to pull it off at all, but the more time that passed, the more hope was pinned on that solution. If the virus didn't work, we were in big trouble.

"It works," he said.

"Then—"

"Cell phones and other personal electronics off, please," he said. We were standing at an unmarked door with a badge scanner mounted next to it.

"Is this it?" Penny asked.

"Yes."

We shut off our gadgets, and Osterhagen waved his badge at the scanner, which turned green and made a heavy bolt pop behind the thick metal. He opened it and waved us inside.

The lab wasn't anything like what I expected, and from the look on Penny's face, it seemed like she felt the same way. I thought there would be rows and rows of computer equipment and guys in white lab coats, but mostly I thought I'd see revivors. I expected to see lots of them, but I didn't see any. The scientists, if that's what they were, looked more like soldiers, and none of them wore white lab coats. They all worked behind thick, clear plastic sheets that hung from the ceiling, and they all had on hazmat suits. They walked up and down metal walkways where heavy metal hatches were fixed to the wall. Each hatch had a thick panel of glass in the middle so you could see in, but all I saw was darkness.

I thought it would be sterile and high-tech, but it was dirty and looked more like a prison than a lab. I could see dried blood spatter on some of the plastic sheeting. The air smelled a little like rot.

"There are an estimated ten to eleven thousand carriers of the Huma prototype out there right now," Osterhagen said. "We've managed to find less than four hundred of them, in a little over three years. That's using aggressive tactics."

"He has a limited supply of the proto—" Penny began.

"That's an assumption," he said, cutting her off. "We can't afford to make that assumption here. Here, we have to prepare for the worst-case scenario, and even if the carriers number half of what we estimate, the amount of carnage those things will be able to cause is not something you could imagine, I don't think."

"I don't have to imagine it," I said. "I've seen it, remember?"

He signaled, and two of the soldier-scientists approached one of the hatches, each one flashing their badge at a separate scanner. LEDs on the scanners lit up green as something thudded through the floor, and I saw a black man's hand, fingers splayed wide, press against the glass port in the door. It left a streak of something greasy and brown as it pawed at the smooth surface.

"What you're going to see is a demonstration of the virus," Osterhagen said. "I want you to see it for yourselves so you can let Ai know what you saw."

The soldiers opened the hatch, and one of them stuck a cattle prod through the opening. Sparks lit up the inside and threw shadows of a body as it jerked and fell to the floor. Two more men dragged a dirty, naked man out from inside and hauled him up between them. His head lolled against a thick leather collar around his neck. The front of the collar had a heavy metal ring attached.

His toes dragged on the floor behind him as they carried him to a metal post that was about two feet high and dropped him in front of it. The one with the cattle prod came back and used a short chain to hitch the man's collar to the post. A few rows down, more soldiers dragged out three more captives, two women and one man. All of their bodies were covered in bruises, mostly down the front of them.

"That's lividity," Osterhagen said offhand, "in case you were wondering."

I wasn't. They chained up the other three to posts facing the first one. I counted more than twenty posts total.

"In order for the nodes to form, death has to occur," he said. "Huma stays dormant in a living system and doesn't begin to initialize until after death. Once the reanimation is complete, they join a common network. They also join a command network, if one exists. Currently one doesn't, but that's okay. The full-mesh connection between them is the one we want."

I remembered hearing some of what he said before. That's part of what made the new revivors different from the old ones; the old ones had command connections back to whoever was controlling them, but not to each other. The new ones all had a connection to every other one, plus the control connection. I wasn't completely sure why that was important, but as long as this worked, I didn't care.

"Subjects secured," a voice said over the intercom.

"Roger that," another voice answered. "Implanting virus."

"Transfer successful."

A big screen lit up along the far wall down where the soldiers were, and a countdown started to tick off from twenty-one seconds.

"It takes twenty-one seconds for the virus to initialize and spread," Osterhagen said.

"That's kind of a long time," Penny said. It didn't sound like very long to me, but the general nodded.

"Too long. We need to get it down."

The timer fell to zero, and then, just like that, all four of the test subjects went facedown against the metal posts they were chained to. None of them moved.

"Test complete," a voice said.

"That's it?" I asked.

"That's it," the general said. "The engineering behind this was massive, even with Heinlein's help. But at the end of the day, yes, that's it. The virus was implanted in the single subject by accessing its communication node, then spread to the others on its network, causing full shutdown of all four subjects."

I looked down through the window as soldiers approached the bodies. I saw one of them stick a big needle into the back of the first subject's neck, and check something on a small screen.

"Complete deanimation in all subjects," a voice said. "Test successful."

"If we didn't keep them isolated," Osterhagen said, "that would have shut every last one of them down."

"That's . . . good, isn't it?" I asked.

"Twenty seconds is still too long," he said. "When Fawkes makes his move, he'll have a command spoke in place to each one of them. When there's this big an intrusion into the systems of any one of them, he'll get an alert for sure. Twenty seconds is more than long enough for him to cut the source of the virus off the network."

"How long has this been ready?" Penny asked.

"We got a confirmed reaction four months ago. In another four, if we get four, we'll have the init time down low enough that even Fawkes won't be able to react fast enough."

"That's . . . good, then, isn't it?" I asked again. It sounded like he was saying all he had to do was put the virus in any one of the carriers and he'd wipe out Fawkes's whole army. He only needed one, and he had hundreds of them.

"No," he said. "That's what you need to tell Ai."

He looked back down at the bodies lying on the floor, their necks bent at sharp angles as they hung from the chains.

"What I said before about the map," he said, "I believed it too, just like you."

"Believed what?" Penny asked.

"That at some point we'd find some keystone, some strategy that would erase the event from the system and light up the void at its center. I believed that, but now we're coming down to the wire, and I don't know anymore."

"Changes in the database don't happen overnight," Penny said. "You know that. Give it time for new entries to have some kind of impact."

"We can agree, I think," Osterhagen said, "that there are only three ways to stop these things. The first is to issue the shutdown code from the command source, but since that's Fawkes and he assigned that code, it's a safe bet that's not going to happen. The second is to use this virus, or something like it, to infect their network. The third is to slug it out with them on the ground. Can we agree on that?"

"Sure," Penny said.

"Until four months ago, option three was the only one we had. . . . But four months ago, the second option became a reality. That's four months that it's existed at least in some form. That's long enough for new entries to impact the database."

I got it then, finally. Penny got it too.

"It didn't change," I said. "Over the four months, it didn't change."

"It changed," Osterhagen said. "The creation of the virus did alter the outcome. Several chains of possibility fell off, while others disappeared completely."

On a screen beside him, he brought up two views of the map, and at first glance, the nebulae pictured in both looked identical. He started zooming in to different areas, and Penny watched with a lot of interest as he started explaining what exactly changed and why, and what he thought it meant. As usual, when he did this, the two of them kind of shut me out. But to be fair, I usually didn't follow them.

I got everything I needed from what he said and the way the colors coursed behind that thin white halo when he said it. The problem wasn't that the change was smaller than they'd hoped for or expected.

The problem was that things hadn't gotten better; they'd gotten worse.

Calliope Flax—Pyt-Yahk District, Bullrich Heights

If Bullrich was the ass end of the city, Pyt-Yahk District was the ass end of Bullrich. No one in their right mind who wasn't stuck there ever went into the Pit, not even the cops. No one gave a shit about that place or anyone in it.

I took my bike down a back alley, over frozen trash and slush. It was cold, but I smelled smoke, and when wind blew down the street, a pocket of warm air hit me. A group of them were holed up somewhere close.

The alley came out in an open lot where fires burned in metal drums. The dregs sat in groups, hunkered down in layers of old clothes, coats, and blankets. Bloodshot eyes and hairy faces looked up and watched me pass. They were off the grid—no IDs, no homes, no names, nothing. As far as the rest of the world cared, they didn't exist. They were nobodies. It's why Fawkes picked them.

I cruised through the drum fires and slapped-up shelters. Over the wind, in the back of my head the static changed. Part of it got a little louder. At least one of them was around somewhere.

The GPS was useless that deep inside. The streets were overrun. Shacks were set up, sheet metal and plastic tied with wire. Side streets were blocked off with plywood and chain-link fence. I switched to the locator. As long as Yavlinski kept his phone on, I'd find him.

Hey, Wachalowski. He usually wanted a tip when I found one, but he didn't answer.

Nico, pick up. Nothing.

Asshole.

I didn't work for him, but I kept him in the loop even though it was behind Stillwell's back. If it wasn't for Nico, I'd probably be holed up with those hobos right now. Five years back, he jumped into a real fire to save my ass. A year back, he did it again. If he told me to drag every last one of those dregs out of there and drop them on his doorstep, I'd do it—for free.

My front tire nicked an empty can and spun it into the leg of an old trash bin as I turned down a narrow alley. The signal source was from down there. I ducked a rusted fire escape and came out the other side into another lot that they'd turned into a back-alley shelter.

A bunch of bums looked over when I brought the bike in. The engine backfired when I cut it, and the pop put them on edge. Yavlinski was somewhere in there.

Yavlinski, I'm here, I texted. *Where are you?*

He stepped out of the crowd from over near a wall covered in spray paint, wrapped in that huge coat of his. He was older, maybe Nico's age, but there were more miles on him. There were three other guys with him, all scrawny with bad teeth.

"About time," he said.

"You got three?" I asked. One of the three guys opened his mouth, but Yavlinski cut him off.

"Four," he said.

"Let's see them."

"Let's see the stuff first," the third bum said. Yavlinski reached into his coat and pulled out a plastic bag. He held it up so the guy could see the Zombie Maker. When he reached for it, I snatched it away and held it in my fist.

"That's mine. Show me what I came here for, and it's yours."

"Fucking slut," he muttered under his breath.

"In there," Yavlinski said. He pointed to a rusted metal door at the far end of the alley, and I walked the bike down after him. At the end, he shoved open the door for me.

"You first," I said.

I held the door and the four of them went in. There was light from a fire inside. It came from a doorway on the other side of what used to be a diner. The tables and chairs were gone, and the floor was covered in grime. Anything worth shit got stripped a long time ago.

From the light spilling through the doorway, I saw a shadow move. Yavlinski headed toward it. I parked the bike, armed it, and followed him.

Nico, pick up. When I sent the message, the link bounced, then cut out.

Goddamn it. What the fuck was he doing?

The four walked past a guy who stood guard next to an electric lamp, to a heavy metal door with chipped blue paint. Yavlinski banged on it twice with his fist, and a bolt turned from inside.

He opened the door and we went in. As soon as I was through the door, the static picked up. At least one of the guys they were holding was for real. To my right, a big ape sat on a stool with a shotgun across his lap. There were four guys on the floor against the far wall. At least one was a junkie, and two of them looked sick. One of them looked up when we came in. The rest just stared at the floor.

"Now you give me the bag, you ugly slut," Yavlinski's guy said.

"You'll get paid when I say you get paid."

His eyes flashed and his lip curled. The rest glared over at me as I walked up to the first guy in the row and nudged him with the toe of my boot.

"You, get up."

It took him a second, but he got on his feet and leaned back against the wall. His breath reeked.

"Hold out your arm. Either one."

He put out his right one. His dirty hand shook as I pushed the sleeve back from his wrist. There were needle tracks there. I took the tester out of my jacket and flipped the guard off.

He didn't flinch when I stuck him. The tester sucked in a drop of blood and the screen lit up. The strip at the base turned red. He was a carrier. I pointed to the corner of the room.

"Over there." He shuffled over and sat back down while I popped out the sample and stowed it in my pocket. I swapped the needle and moved to the next one. When I was done, I had three on one side of the room, and one on the other.

Singh, pick up.

I'm here. What did you find?

Three total. You got my position?

I see you. We're sending in a retrieval squad now. Ten minutes.

I cut the link, then turned to Yavlinski and the rest.

"I got hits on these three. Not that one. That one can go."

The one who was clean looked around the room. He took a step toward the door, but the guy with the shotgun tensed up.

"Not so fast," he said.

"I said, he's clean. Let him go." Yavlinski's guys got twitchy. The one that did the talking looked pissed.

"What the fuck?"

"You got three. You get paid for three."

"We got four."

"You got three. That one came up green. Now let him the fuck out."

"Hey, fuck you. This is what you wanted, right? Pay up."

"You'll get your shit once the pickup is done. That's the deal."

He looked at Yavlinski, then back at me. He was trouble. I could tell by his eyes. I stowed the tester inside my jacket and curled my fingers through the brass knuckles there.

"How about I kill them and you, and fucking take the shi—"

I turned around and threw a right cross. The brass slammed into his jaw and broke it. A mouthful of blood and spit hit the wall next to him, and he went down like a rock. The rest of them jumped back, but none of them came at me. The guy with the shotgun didn't point it at me—yet.

"Goddamn it . . ." the guy on the floor growled. He got up on his hands and knees, blood dripping out of his mouth and nose. I stomped my boot down on his ear and he went down in the dust and stayed down.

"You guys take it easy and everyone gets paid," I said. "You want to fuck around? I tagged all your mugs when I came in, and a Stillwell unit is on its way here right now. You keep this shit up, and if I don't bury you assholes, then they'll come in here and kill your fucking grandkids. You get me?"

They got me. The guy with the gun nodded.

"That one goes," I said, pointing to the one who came up green. This time they let him leave. Once he was out the door, he took off.

I checked out the other three. The static that crackled in the back of my skull was making my head hurt. Ten minutes was a long time to stew in that shithole. Yavlinski joined me and leaned in close.

"Just give them what they want," he said. "You got what you came for."

"They do the pickup. I pay you, you pay them. That's how it works." He sighed, and I caught a whiff of vodka.

"Sometimes I think you have a death wish."

A call came in, flagged red. It was an alert from Stillwell. I picked up.

Flax, this is Singh. Forget the pickup, get out—

Out of nowhere, the static turned to a feedback whine that shot through my head. It hit me like a freight train. I saw Yavlinski's eyes go wide as I reeled back. The brass slipped off my fingers and clanged on the floor as the shriek got louder.

Yavlinski's mouth moved, but I couldn't hear. My legs went out from under me. The room spun, and I went down on my back on the cold, hard floor. Garbage puked out of my JZI. The three guys in the corner jerked and started to fall. Behind me, I heard the door open, and someone ran out.

The carriers fell. Their bodies hit the floor near my feet. The last thing I saw was Yavlinski as he came down on his side a foot away from me.

What the—

A vein in Yavlinski's eye turned black. It popped, and black spots bled through the white of it.

Huma.

I got it then: the fucker had finally done it. We were too late. After two years, Fawkes dropped the ax. The inhibitor was a wash. I was going down with the rest of them. Yavlinski's ugly face was the last thing I was ever going to see.

The light popped and went out.

Nico Wachalowski—Mother of Mercy Clinic

Fog drifted across the clinic's lot as I pulled in next to a bank of snow pushed against a twisted chain-link fence. Van Offo watched the entrance with a flat orange glow behind his pupils, as a strip of fabric, part of a shirt, maybe, flapped from a coil of razor wire out back. The building face was covered in graffiti and darkened by years of smog. I'd seen too many places like it in the past year.

I cut the engine. A gust of wind blew powdery snow across the windshield and made the clinic's metal door rattle in its frame. Through the window, I saw the waiting area was full.

"Let's go," I said. But Van Offo didn't move. He leaned back and watched the door through half-closed eyelids. His mood had taken a turn since we left the train yard. He stared at the entrance to the clinic, but not at the people crowded inside. He had that far-off look he got when he saw something else, something only he could see. It was the same look Zoe used to get.

"You know something?" I asked him. He shrugged.

Orange light flickered softly behind his pupils. He had a secure connection open through his JZI, like he always did. The others watched and listened with him.

"Van Offo, if there's something I need to know—"

The orange light went out and his eyes cleared. He'd killed the connection and left us alone in the car.

"The team is still getting into position," he said. "You mind if I smoke?"

"Knock yourself out."

He pulled one of his black cigarillos from his pocket and lit it. The tobacco crackled as he took a long drag, and smoke drifted from his nostrils. He clenched the end between his teeth and fished a business card out of his wallet, then scribbled something on the back. He handed it over to me, under his palm.

"What's this?" I flipped it over. He'd written a phone number there, and under it he'd written a name:

ZOE OTT

"That was not easy to get," he said.

"Is she still in the city?" I asked him.

He nodded. "She is."

I watched him smoke for a minute.

"Is she safe?"

He looked amused as he blew smoke through a crack in the window.

"You think you know something about that woman, Nico, but you don't."

"I know she needs help."

"Not from you. She could kill you where you sit and not even mean to. She's seen things almost no one else has seen. Trust me—she's bigger than both of us."

"Then why give me this? Why now?"

"Because the end is nigh," he said, and he smiled, but eyes were serious.

Van Offo, and those like him, had alluded to something like that before, but the way he said it made me uneasy. It didn't sound like theory or rhetoric just then.

"When?"

He blew smoke from his nose. "Soon."

"Will the city be destroyed?"

"The city? This city is just a drop in the bucket, I'm afraid."

"What does that mean?"

"It means Motoko doesn't tell you everything."

"Then you tell me."

"Let's just say that if what we've seen is true, I'll be glad to not be around for it."

"Around for what, Al? What did you see?"

"A point past which there is no more future to look into," he said. "Once Fawkes pulls the trigger, that's it. Somehow he triggers a global event. I don't know how. Wiping out this city is just the beginning."

I stared at him, and when he saw the look on my face he smiled weakly.

"Never mind," he said. "Just do your job. Maybe all this is a lie, to get you to do what we want. Right?"

Motoko Ai was a liar, that much I knew, but I knew Van Offo too and he believed what he'd told me. I could see it in his eyes.

"Ai told me I kill Fawkes," I said.

"Maybe that will stop this and maybe it won't. Motoko thinks we can still fix things, but I wonder."

"If killing him doesn't stop it, then what will?"

He tapped the business card with Zoe's name on it. "How?"

"I don't know," he said. He looked toward the clinic entrance again with that odd expression on his face. "Something she said once. She suspects she will be involved, or that's what she said."

"Was she drunk when she said it?"

"Of course."

"What do you think?"

"I don't think anything can stop it."

He spoke offhandedly, but he was serious. The bad feeling I had got worse. I stowed the card in my jacket pocket.

For the first time, I realized there might be more to

Van Offo than I'd thought. I knew how his superiors operated. They didn't want me contacting Zoe, and he'd gone against them by giving me that number. It put him at a big risk.

"You know," he said. "You two have something in common."

"Yeah? What's that?"

"An obsession with what you'll never have."

He stubbed out the cigarillo and waved away the smoke.

"Get your affairs in order," he said. "Before it's too late."

"What about you?"

"I just did."

Wachalowski, the team is in position at the rear entrance. Local law is moving in to cordon the block.

Understood.

"I have to reestablish the connection now," Van Offo said.

"Al—"

The orange light flickered back on behind his pupils, and he held up one hand. I stopped talking. He wouldn't answer, and there wasn't time anyway.

Stand by, I told SWAT. *We're going inside.*

I opened the door and climbed out of the car. The air was bitter cold, and at street level, it was barely brighter than night. The clinic kept three lights on over a rusted sign that read MOTHER OF MERCY. As we approached, I saw a bullet scar in the brick and two more dimples in the metal doorframe.

I pushed open the clinic door and stepped through. The waiting room was even more crowded than it looked from the lot. Every chair was filled, and many stood to wait their turn. The receptionist sat behind a pane of bulletproof glass. She busied herself on a computer and didn't look up when we came in.

"The end is nigh."

He believed it. On some level I'd always thought it was a scare tactic, a way to manipulate me when the usual methods failed, but I looked at the people in front of me and I couldn't help but wonder, *Is this all for nothing*?

I closed the distance to the receptionist station, and faces began to turn toward us. Some showed concern, others fear. They were poor, and most were homeless. They didn't need any more trouble than they already had.

The woman at the desk looked up as we approached the glass. She looked us both over.

"What is it this time?" she asked. Her voice came through a barely functioning speaker fixed in the glass pane. I held up my badge so she could see it.

"I'm sorry," I said, "but you know the drill."

She frowned, but reached under the desktop. The door to the examination area buzzed and the bolt opened.

"Don't you have anything better to do than hassle us?" she asked. But right at that second, I didn't have a good answer for her.

"Get your affairs in order, before it's too late."

I opened the door and Van Offo followed me through. It bolted again behind us.

"I'm calling my supervisor. . . ." she began, but her voice trailed off. Al reached across and switched off the speaker to the waiting area. He leaned in close to her and spoke in a low voice.

"That won't be necessary. Just relax and wait here."

I opened a connection to their computer system and began sifting through their logs as I looked down the short hallway that connected the reception area to the rest of the clinic. A man with a grizzled beard and a frost-bitten face sat in a chair, a blood pressure cuff around his right arm. The nurse attending to him didn't look up from the gauge as she pumped the rubber bladder. A doctor stood nearby, and he frowned when he saw us.

"Can I help you?" he asked, but stopped short as two SWAT officers crept in from a side hallway. His eyes widened.

"Calm down," Van Offo said. The man's eyes relaxed but remained wary. "Everyone stay calm and quiet."

"Sir, we've tracked a suspicious data stream to this site," I said to him. "We have reason to think—"

"What do you mean 'suspicious data stream'?" the man asked. "Look at this place . . ."

His voice fizzled in midsentence as Van Offo approached him.

"Sleep."

His eyelids fluttered and closed. He wobbled on his feet a little, and Van Offo steadied him.

"We know there is someone else here," he said to the man. "Where are they?"

The man's face changed then. The look of confusion had been an act, and when it fell away there was anger in his eyes.

"You're too late," he said in a low voice. Several staff members glanced nervously at us, not sure what to make of what they were seeing.

"What makes you say that?" Van Offo asked.

"They're not coming back," he said. "I heard them."

"Answer me," Van Offo said. "Where are they? Don't lie."

I processed the last of the system's logs and found that no significant data had been stored in their system in the past twenty four hours.

"It's not here," I said.

"It's here somewhere."

I looked around and saw confusion and fear. Whatever Fawkes's men were up to, these people didn't know anything about it.

Except the man Van Offo had. He knew. Even while being controlled, there was a spark in his eye and I could tell he'd been converted, in more ways than one.

SWAT, have you found anything? I asked.

Not yet. We've got the perimeter secured.

I signaled to the two officers to check the examination rooms. They moved down the hall and began opening doors. From one, I heard a woman gasp.

Van Offo's pupils dilated as he stared at the doctor, who began to speak in a slow, quiet voice.

"The basement," he said.

"Basement?"

Even while his face remained slack, I could see the intensity in his eyes. The man wrestled with something internally, but as many had before him, he failed. His eyes became sleepy and docile.

It always unnerved me to see it. It was eerie how quickly people could be made to abandon their beliefs. Al was particularly good at it.

"The basement level is flooded," a woman said, not understanding. "It hasn't been used in years."

"What's down there?" I asked her.

"Look," she said. "I know it's out of code, but it's locked up. We don't use it. This place serves—"

"How do we access the lower level?" Van Offo asked the doctor. He pointed down the hall robotically toward a wall of metal shelving stacked with boxes.

SWAT, this place has a basement level that wasn't on the schematic. We're headed down.

Got it.

"Come on," I said. Van Offo and the officers followed as I passed the examination rooms and shoved the rack aside. There was a door behind it, secured with a heavy padlock. Several more SWAT members approached from the connecting hallway.

"Open it," I said. One of them used an arc cutter to slice through the lock, and it trailed smoke as it thumped to the floor. He flipped open the latch.

I opened the door and started down. Flashlight beams swept the stairs in front of me to a landing where a heavy metal door had been mounted in the concrete. I pushed on it, but it didn't budge. When I scanned the edges, I picked up a magnetic field.

"It's got a magnetic lock," I said. There were no hinges and no release mechanism on our side of it. When I tried to peer through the metal, I found it was shielded. Whoever set this up wasn't anyone from the clinic. The door had been installed from the inside, to keep people out.

SWAT leader, can your guys open this? I asked.

Yeah.

One of his team moved in and pressed a metal tool to the doorjamb. A panel lit up on one side, and the hairs on my arms stood up. The feed from my JZI warped briefly and I heard the bolt release from inside the door. He shoved it open with a metallic creak.

Beyond the door, a concrete corridor extended into the dark. There was an electric switchbox mounted on the wall to the right. I flipped it, and electric light flickered on from above. Wires ran along the floor to noise screens that were mounted crudely along the ceiling.

There's something down here. We're moving in.

Understood.

Up ahead, a doorway opened into a large cellar where a dim light flickered. As we neared it, my heel dropped down into a foot of icy water. Laser points swam over the glassy surface as the splash echoed down the tunnel.

"Help us," a voice called from the cellar. It was a scream, but it was muted, so I barely heard it. I drew my gun and signaled to the others.

Watch for civilians.

"Help," the faint voice screamed again.

"No one can hear you," another muffled voice yelled back.

We stepped through the doorway at the end of the hall, SWAT moving in behind me. I passed through the noise screen and the faint screams jumped to full volume.

"—one! Anyone! Help us!"

There were a series of wire metal cages set up on the concrete floor against the far wall. In each one, a person sat shivering in several inches of water. When a flashlight beam moved over them, they squinted and covered their eyes. More noise screens hummed from the ceiling.

A thin man in a wool coat and with acne scars on his face stood outside the cages, holding in each hand a large, insulated alligator clip that trailed thick cables. Many of the wire cages had clips already attached to the frames.

"Hold it!" I shouted, aiming my gun. He turned to look at me, but his expression didn't change. He connected the clips to the cage nearest him while the woman inside stared.

"I said, 'freeze'!"

He stepped away from the cage and held up his hands.

"It's done," he called out. I looked around but didn't see anyone else with him. Two SWAT officers sloshed through the water toward him, rifles trained on him. He knelt down with a splash as one officer bound his wrists behind his back with a zip cord.

"Just do it!" he yelled.

"Shut up," I said.

Alice, we're at Mother of Mercy. We've got human captives here—five men, five women. You getting this?

I see it.

I scanned the pockmarked man's face and found him

in the system. His name was Rafe Pena, arrested in the past for drug and weapons transport, and assault.

"Oh," a woman whispered. "Oh, it's the police. . . . Thank God. Thank God, it's the police. . . ."

Computer equipment hummed on the surfaces of a series of workbenches set up along the right wall. LEDs flashed in the shadows. On the other side of the room, a series of gurneys were set up with IV racks. I could make out blotches of dried blood on the bedding. Surgical tools lay in trays, and behind them, hanging on the concrete wall, were larger blades: bone saws, a machete, and even an ax.

"What is all this?" I asked. Rafe kept his eyes down and didn't answer.

"Who are you working for, Rafe?" I asked.

"Fuck you."

"You're just a thug. Who set this up? Who's paying you?"

"Get us out," another voice said. Someone shook the wall of one of the cages. "Get us out of here!"

"Stay calm," I said. "You're safe now. We're going to get you out."

The rattle got more intense. It was a shirtless, skinny man with brown skin and a shaved head. Tattoos covered his shoulders and chest. His fingers were bloody as he gripped the wire, and his eyes were wild.

"Sir, calm down." I looked around for a way to open the cages. Each one was fitted with an electronic lock. I followed the cables from the alligator clips and saw them merge with other bundles of cable that ran under the water.

"Check that out," I told the officer. I shined a flashlight beam on the metal base of the nearest cage, where a young woman sat, hugging her knees and shivering in the filthy water.

The cables ran up the sides of each cage and into a breaker box on the wall behind them.

"Do it now!" Rafe screamed. He was talking to someone besides us, someone who could throw the electrical switch remotely.

"Kill that breaker!" I said. One of the officers moved toward it and pried it open as I scanned around the edges of the ceiling. There were cameras mounted there behind the foam paneling. Someone was watching us.

The man rattled the cage again and pounded his fist against the side.

"Get me out of here!" he screamed. "Get me the fuck out of here now!"

Van Offo sloshed through the water toward him, and I grabbed his arm.

"If those go live, we'll all fry," I told him. "Wait until we get the power—"

He shook free and continued toward the cage.

"Van Offo!"

"Calm down," Van Offo said to the man.

"Fuck you! Get me out of here!"

"I said be calm. Sleep."

"Fuck you!"

I looked over and caught a glimpse of Van Offo's face, blank with surprise. The lights flickered, and a woman screamed.

"Get me out of here!"

"Someone shut him up!"

I crossed to the cages and checked the electrical box—a major current was running through it from a shielded cable.

"Here," I said. The officer with the arc cutter used it to sever the connection, sending sparks down onto the surface of the water. The current to the cages went out.

"Get me out of here!"

"Van Offo, do something with him!"

"I can't," he said. There was disbelief and fear on his face.

A phone rang loudly in the small space, and for a minute even the man in the cage got quiet.

"Where's that coming from?" I asked. After a few seconds, it rang again.

I swept the flashlight along the walls until I found a heavy black handset mounted there. It rang a third time.

As I waded through the water toward it, I started a trace on the clinic's outgoing circuits. I grabbed the handset and pulled it free from the receiver.

"Hello?"

"Are you with the FBI?" a man's voice asked.

"Who is this?"

"You don't look like regular cops."

"I'm Special Agent Wachalowski. Who is this?"

"I made a terrible mistake," the man said.

"What kind of mistake?"

SWAT had begun cutting through the locks to free the prisoners. The bald man had been sedated and was being pulled out carefully. Some retreated to the backs of the cages, not sure what was happening. One didn't move at all. When the officer shined a light in her face, she didn't respond.

"You have to stop them," the man said.

"Stop who? What is this place?" I asked him.

"I was supposed to put them down," he said. "I thought I could do it. . . . What have I done?"

"Sir, tell me what this place is. Did you bring these people here?"

"It would be a mercy . . . but I can't do it."

"Sir—"

There was a loud bang from back upstairs. Someone screamed, and footsteps began to move across the floor above us.

"MacReady was right . . . we should have listened—" the man said; then the line cut out.

MacReady. I knew that name. A man named Bob MacReady worked at Heinlein Industries. He'd helped me in the past. Was that who he meant?

"Did you get a trace?" Van Offo asked. I shook my head. The call had been rerouted somewhere down the line. The 'bot couldn't track it before the link failed.

"All right, get these people—"

Something heavy crashed across the floor overhead. There was another scream, and then shouting. The ceiling above us began to rumble with many heavy footsteps.

"What the hell's going on up there?" one of the officers asked.

SWAT leader, what's your situation? There was no answer. The racket upstairs got louder until it sounded like they'd fall through on top of us. Back down the concrete tunnel, the metal door banged open.

SWAT, what's your status?

A switch snapped from down the hall, and the lights in the tunnel went out. The shuffle of many footsteps began to echo toward us before splashing into the water.

"What the hell is that?" an officer asked. The laser sights began to drift around the now dark doorway.

I looked at Van Offo and he looked back, his eyes determined. He held his weapon in one fist, the knuckles white.

"Get back, away from the door!" I said; then a figure shambled into view there, with a gang of others close behind.

They were men and women, mobbed together. I saw filthy coats and greasy hair as they stumbled through the opening and sloshed through the water toward us. I recognized them. They'd been in the waiting room when we first came in.

The receptionist from the front desk squeezed through the pack and stumbled into the room, swinging a revolver in one fist.

"Gun!"

Her eyes were wide, and when the flashlight beam hit them, I could see black splotches that had formed in the whites. A light flashed from behind her pupils as she pointed the gun and fired. Van Offo clutched the side of his neck and went down into the water. A laser sight appeared on the woman's forehead as a single shot blew out the back of her head.

By then, twenty more had crowded into the room with another twenty behind them, blocking the only way out. One of them flipped the breaker switch, and the lights inside the basement went out.

The room erupted into a racket of screams, splashes, and gunfire. Muzzle flashes lit up the dark as SWAT fired on the crowd, but there wasn't enough time; they closed in and were on us.

Van Offo, are you okay? Do you read me? He didn't respond.

Someone went down in the water, then a body collided with me and I stumbled back into the dark. I crashed into a gurney and heard surgical equipment splash into the water.

Alice, we need backup.

On its way, Wachalowski. What's your status?

Bodies moved all around me as I picked myself up out of the icy water. Adjusting the light filter on my optics, I saw the clash had filled the whole room. I couldn't tell who was who.

We need backup now.

Wachalowski, Van Offo just dropped. What's your status?

I looked around but couldn't find him.

Al, are you still with me?

He didn't respond. I flipped to the backscatter to try to ID him from the JZI in his head, and the whole place lit up. In and among the zippers and tooth fillings, I saw clusters of nodes and filaments coiled at the base of almost every skull.

They're revivors. All of them—the people from the waiting room, even the body of the receptionist—were revivors. The components stood out in sharp relief in the darkness, moving crazily through the room around me. My heart dropped as I realized what I'd seen.

Huma.

Alice, the—

Something struck my head hard, and everything flashed white for a second. When I tried to take a step, my leg gave out and I fell down into the cold water.

Wachalowski, goddamn it, what is your status?

I popped two stims and a surge of adrenaline pulsed through my body. I tried to push through the crowd, but there were too many of them. I popped another stim as they forced me back down. The back of my head hit the floor and I saw stars.

As they closed in, I managed to get my gun out in front of me. A figure loomed above with something gripped in both hands. It lifted the handle over its shoulder, and I made out the head of the ax I'd seen mounted on the wall.

I fired, but the shot went wild. The revivor behind it pitched back, and the one in front brought the ax down.

There was a hard impact at my right shoulder. Something hot spattered my face. I tried to pull the trigger again, but nothing happened. The cold water that lapped around my neck turned warm.

Alice . . .

Wachalowski, local police and the military are scrambling. A team is on its way. Hang in there.

My heart pounded in my ears. I kicked with one leg

and heard air huff as my heel struck something solid. Warning codes streamed by in the darkness in front of me. The impact came again. The pain in my arm, beyond my shoulder, disappeared.

I'm going to die. . . .

Blackness rushed in. The sounds of the struggle muted, then faded. The faces hanging over me were swallowed by the darkness.

Wachalowski, do you read me? Help is on the way.

The screams disappeared. The warning messages stopped, and everything got quiet.

". . . the end is nigh . . ."

It was the last thing I remember thinking. The chaos around me seemed far away. It was happening somewhere else. In my mind, all I saw was Van Offo's face as he said the words, and the look in his eye that told me it was true.

"When?"

Wachalowski, do you read—

"Soon . . ."

3

HOT ZONE

Faye Dasalia—Heinlein Industries, Pratsky Building

The darkness was reluctant to let me go. With no need for sleep, it had been a long time since I'd been under. The last time had been almost two years ago, and I remembered I'd found it peaceful. This time, though, something felt wrong.

Reanimation occurred without a hitch; energy began to course through my body, and the blood thinned in my veins. My mind, however, awoke to a dark void. Usually I could sense all of my memories, assembled like a field of stars beneath me. And far below that, in the cold depths of space, that dark hole pulled gently at me and waited. This time my memories were gone, and I was face-to-face with oblivion.

My memories were still there, just far above me. My mind had sunk below them, to the bottom, where I'd one day disappear. Even so close, I could see no end to it, but its gentle tug was more insistent now. It held me with millions of tiny black threads, drawing me slowly inside. I had always feared that void, but I found myself unable to resist. It was almost hypnotic.

"What's the problem?" a voice asked. It was a man's voice, from somewhere close to me. Impulses began to fire through my brain as it processed the signals, breaking me out of my trance. I felt my mind float back up, until those black threads stretched taut, then finally broke. The void released me, but it seemed reluctant. As I floated back through the field of memories, it seemed to deliver a wordless promise.

Soon.

"What's the problem?" the voice asked again. This time, another answered.

"The name on the tag doesn't match the signature."

Energy trickled down the length of my spine and bled through my arms and legs. It began to gather where my heart had been, pooling and growing stronger. Muscle tissue began to reactivate, and I curled my fingers closed.

"Let me see," the first voice said.

"Jesus, this one took a beating," a third voice said. "Looks like an old stab wound to the chest, and five, maybe six bullet holes. Look at the size of those entry wounds."

"According to the tag—"

"The tag's wrong. Run the signature."

I became aware that I was lying prone, with several figures positioned around me, and I heard the white noise of electronics. Something sharp and cold probed the back of my neck.

"What's the matter?" the woman asked.

"There's something strange about these wounds."

"Is it a gen seven?"

"Yes. According to the signature, her name was . . . Faye Dasalia."

"She was a police detective," one of them said. "Maybe she got shot in the line of duty."

"I don't think so. Look right there. . . . Were those grafts revivor flesh?"

No one spoke for a moment, but I could sense them crowding in around me.

"I think these wounds happened after reanimation."

"Maybe it's back from the field?"

"These haven't gone out yet."

"Get it hooked up and let's pull the memory."

"Cognizance variant is very narrow," the woman said. "Look at the date. It must have been one of the last before the injunction."

"MacReady's team will want a look at this one. Dump its core and let's get it to T-Five."

One of the figures leaned over my body, and I felt the probe slip through into my spine. My body went rigid as the probe turned live and found the socket to my main control node. All of my systems lit up, and the probe began to take inventory.

"It's definitely been in the field," someone said. "We've got quite a few custom modules here."

"Flush all that. Just take the memory buffers."

The probe cycled through my different packages, schematics flashing by behind my eyelids. The custom software modules raised some eyebrows, but the extra hardware put them all on edge.

"The Leichenesser capsule's been removed," one of them said.

"It's got some kind of custom hardware fitted in with the bayonet too."

"I've got a second bayonet here, in the other arm."

"Stop the scan."

The probe tapped into my memory buffer and opened a connection. When it did, the virus there executed. It took control of the link and then flooded the circuit. The code quickly propagated through the lab, then pushed through onto the rest of the network. Address registers scrolled by as it isolated their security and began to shut it down. A Klaxon sounded but was quickly cut off as the first module went dark in my display.

"What the hell was that?"

"Stop the scan!"

Voices rose outside the room. The intrusion on the network was spotted as they lost their connections to the outside.

"The system's not responding," one of the men said. His fingers worked a console to my right.

"Then pull the probe!" the woman snapped.

Slowly, I opened my eyes. Three people stood around me: an older, gray-haired man with a thick beard; a broad-shouldered black man with a large belly; and a gaunt-looking woman who kept her long, thin hair in a ponytail. Probes stuck out of my chest like pins in a pincushion, and readouts streamed on a bank of monitors.

The old man had reached for the probe in my neck, but stopped when my hand and forearm split apart. The blade deployed with a loud bang, and he froze, the tip an inch from his throat. He raised his hands so I could see them.

"Deanimate it!" the woman snapped.

The tray creaked as I sat up. Wires connected to the probes in my chest pulled taut, then the needles clattered to the floor. The virus branched out, infecting all of their security protocols. It disabled the cameras, motion detectors, heat sensors, everything. The lethal current running through the perimeter fence faded, then died. The gates unlocked and opened. I placed my bare feet on the cold tile floor as behind me the door to the lab opened, and the three technicians looked past me, toward it.

"Ang, Dulari," the woman said. "Shut that thing down!"

As she spoke, her pupils dilated, and I fired the injector from my arm. The thin tube whipped through the air, and the needle lodged in the side of her neck. She slapped the spot with one hand, but the needle was already gone. As I watched, the orange glow in her rib cage that pulsed so frantically began to slow down. Her legs gave out, and as she started to fall, the bearded man caught her, his eyes wide with shock.

"She's alive," I told him.

"Ang, what are you doing?" the second man demanded.

Two of my three contacts had arrived. Ang Chen, a Chinese man with a dour face, and Dulari Shaddrah, a Pakistani woman whom I suspected might have been beautiful, stepped fully into the room. Dulari put one warm hand on my shoulder. Ang approached the men, a pistol in his hand.

"Back against the wall," he told them.

"Hold still," Dulari said in my ear. She carefully removed the probe from my neck, and I felt the circuit cut. I pulled the remaining needles from my chest as she handed me a bag. It contained clothes that had been folded neatly.

"Why did the perimeter go down?" I asked. "You have control of the transmitter array now."

Dulari smiled weakly. "Don't worry about that."

I looked around, but the third man I was supposed to meet was not with them.

"Where's Deatherage?" I asked.

"We can't find him," she said.

"What do you mean, you can't find him?"

"Security logs show he used his badge at the entrance," Chen said, "but no one's seen him."

"Chen, this is insane," the older man said. "What the hell is going on?"

"Put her down," Chen said. The man lowered the unconscious woman to the floor.

"She's not breathing," he said.

"The neurotoxin is not lethal," I said. I opened the bag and began to get dressed. The clothes were plain and a reasonable fit. I thought they might have belonged to Dulari.

"Why'd you dose her?" Chen asked me.

"She's one of them. She was attempting to influence you."

He nodded.

"Wait. Stop," the black man said. He looked past Ang and Dulari at me. "Where did you come from?"

"Just stay here," I said. "Stay here and don't make trouble."

"I know you're one of ours," he continued. "I also know that one bayonet is standard for the sevens, not two. Those injectors aren't standard either. Where did you come from?"

"Listen to me: stay in here, and don't make trouble."

"Do as she says," Chen said. The man stared at the pistol.

"What are you going to do?" he asked. "What is this all about?"

As he spoke, what might have been understanding dawned on the second man's face. I saw his mouth part.

"You're one of Samuel's," he said.

Before I could answer him, I saw an image of Heinlein's satellite, the defense system that was known as The Eye, flicker onto the display in front of me. As I watched, its nodes were all called out and scanned. One by one, they began to go inactive. I turned back to Dulari.

"The virus," I said. "It's—"

"I know."

Someone shouted from down the hallway outside, where I heard many footsteps tromping closer. The last of the nodes on my display went dark. The Eye had gone inactive. The tarmac surrounding Heinlein Industries was no longer protected.

"Someone's taken control of the defense satellite!" a voice shouted. "We're wide open; it's some kind of attack!"

"Dulari, what is this?" She didn't answer, and looked away.

"Chen . . . what have you done?" the black man asked. "What the hell have you two done?"

"Shaddrah, get them out of here," Chen said.

The men stared as Dulari drew a pistol. She motioned toward the door.

Just then, it opened and another man stuck his head in. His eyes were wide.

"Guys, we have multiple vehicles approaching the complex," he said. "We need to . . ."

He saw the guns and trailed off.

"What is going on out there?" the older man asked him.

"Sir, we have confirmation on a wide-scale broadcast of a Huma activation sequence."

"An activation sequence? From where?"

"It looks like it might have been sourced from the Stillwell compound. Someone with high security clearance snuck in a stealth program that bounced it off a communications satellite maybe twenty minutes ago."

"What?"

"It gets worse—someone's inside our system, as well. Campus security has been totally compromised. We're completely unprotected."

"He did it," the black man whispered. "That madman really did it."

"Shaddrah, get them out of here," Chen said.

"You heard him," Dulari said. "Come on, let's go."

Dulari, I said over a private connection. *Why are vehicles approaching? Is he coming here?*

I'm sorry, Faye. I thought you knew.
Knew what?

She looked back and met my eye before she closed the door behind them.

Chen stood over the woman on the floor and watched the shallow rise and fall of her chest.

"Who is she?" I asked.

"Greta Creigh," he said.

"Do you know her?"

"I do, yes," he said. "I thought I did. You're sure about what you saw? She's one of them?"

"Yes."

"One hundred percent sure?"

"Yes."

He aimed the pistol and fired. The shot slammed through the lab as the bullet blew out the top of the woman's head in a mess of blood, gristle, and hair.

He stared at the results for a moment, and then, without changing his expression, he fired again.

Calliope Flax — Pyt-Yahk District, Bullrich Heights

Initialize node 23948. Inception time 21720202091103.
Current version: 010000064013C.
Current instruction set(s) pending.
Outstanding message. Urgent. Please respond.

The words flickered in the dark when I came to. The ground was hard and cold under me, and I smelled blood. My dead hand tingled. It wasn't supposed to do that anymore.

Urgent. Please respond.

I opened my eyes. I was facing a concrete wall with a bloodstain on it. There was a big splatter on the floor under that, with a broken tooth in it. Yavlinski was gone.

Urgent. Please—

I pulled up the message. It was from Singh.

Fawkes pulled the trigger. Call in. I sent a confirmation back, then tried to get Wachalowski on the JZI, but there was some kind of hold on his line.

Great. My muscles were stiff, but I could move. Nothing felt broken when I sat up. My brass knuckles were on the floor a few feet away. I grabbed them and stuffed them in my jacket pocket with the other set.

My hand still had pins and needles. I flexed the gray fingers and they worked, but they were stiff and slow. The static in my head had turned to a steady whine.

If my clock was right, I'd been down over an hour. I checked my pockets, and the bag of Zombie was still there. The brass knuckles, the gun . . . it was all still there. The room was empty.

I got up and limped through the door, back the way I'd come in. My bike was still there, the alarm panel red. Someone tried to heist it but couldn't get it started. They must have left in a hurry.

I walked it back toward the metal door that led outside. When I pushed it open I saw light but no people. The lot was empty. Wind blew snow across the blacktop, and a cardboard cup with blood spatter on it rolled past.

Wachalowski, pick up.

I ran diags and they came up clean, mostly. My body checked out okay, but my head hurt like a bitch. The ringing in my ears wouldn't let up.

I looked around. Cinders glowed in the metal drums, but the people were all gone. I made my way over to one of the tarps they'd set up and pulled open the flap. Someone's shit was in there, but he was long gone. I let the tarp go and the wind blew it shut. I listened, but didn't hear any voices—just wind and the flap of plastic.

I straddled the bike and kick-started it. The engine turned over, and I headed back the way I'd come in. I didn't pass anyone in the alleys. When I got to the main road, it was full of cars, but they all just sat there. None of them moved.

Nico, pick up, goddamn it.

Up ahead, a store window had been smashed, and the sidewalk was covered in broken glass. In the street to my left, a car's doors hung open and the windshield was caved in. Shell casings lay on the sidewalk next to it, and the snowbank was stained red.

I looked down the street. A long strip of bloody cloth blew in the wind, snagged on a car antenna. A lot of car doors were open. I saw broken glass and trash where people had dropped their shit and run. There were footprints in the snow, between cars and up and down the sidewalks. A few car lengths down, a black armored truck had jumped the curb and crashed into the side of a building. Way down the street, a trail of smoke rose from somewhere I couldn't see. In the street, between the cars, a few guys stood with their backs to me. They didn't move as the wind whipped through their coats.

"Hey!" I called. They didn't answer. Down the street I saw a few more. None of them moved.

Flax, this is Singh. You copy?

I copy.

Shit. I was starting to think you were dead.

What the hell happened?

Fawkes happened. He activated the carriers an hour ago. Where are you?

Still in the Pit.

That's a hot zone. You want to get out of there right away.

No shit.

That area was hit hard. There are a lot of revivors still in there.

How many we looking at?

No numbers yet, but thousands. Can you get back to base?

The streets were blocked. Back the other way, I could

barely make out the flash of blues and reds on the other side of an old, rusted bridge.

I'll manage.

Good. You okay?

I'm fine.

"Hey, you!" I called to the guys in the street. They still didn't move.

Wait, I told Singh. *I might have some survivors.*

Be careful.

I took the bike closer, in between the abandoned cars. I pulled up next to the three men.

"Hey, what are you, fucking deaf?" I asked, but by then I could see.

Shit.

The three guys had blood down the front of their shirts and pants. It was smeared around their mouths and beaded up on the ends of their fingers. Black spots bled through the whites of their eyes. They were Huma carriers, revivors, but the signal I usually picked up from them wasn't there.

I looked down the street and saw more of them. Some leaned into cars; others were down on the ground. None of them moved.

Singh, I've got hostiles down here—

Cal, just get out of there.

No, listen. Something's up. They're not moving.

What are they doing?

Nothing. They're just standing there. Hold on.

I scanned the closest of the three and picked up a lot of wireless traffic. It was the same for the rest.

They're all getting some kind of major data dump, I said.

What kind of data dump?

Hold on. The eyes of the closest one were moving around, just barely. As I watched my hand twitched, and a string of garbage code rolled past one corner of my eye. I'd seen this all before.

I know what it is, I told Singh.

You want to share?

That steady screech in the back of my head was because code was coming in. The blood in my hand was picking up the change too; that's why it was tingling again. I looked up and down the street at the frozen bodies. They were all stuck in standby; Heinlein was upgrading them.

Is Heinlein pushing something down from central? I asked.

Pushing what?

I don't know. But the jacks used to do this in the field when a control-module update came down from the satellite.

The shutdown virus is based on the prototype, Cal. Heinlein wouldn't go messing with that even if they could.

I'm telling you—someone's sending something down because I'm getting it too—I can feel it.

I'll look into it. You just get the hell out of there.

I watched them as the wind blew over them. None of them blinked while they were blasted with snow. The closest one's eyes just kept up that slight jitter as the bloodstained shirt flapped around his bony, scabby body.

Roger that.

I took the bike past them and back to the sidewalk. There was more blood on the snow just ahead. A hand, short a little finger, poked out from under a car. There was a big bite mark in the meat of the thumb.

Nico was still offline. I hated talking to that asshole Van Offo, but he was my next-best bet. I tried his line, and he picked up.

Van Offo here.

It's Flax.

Miss Flax. I was going to contact you.

I didn't like the sound of that. I hated him, and he knew it. We had only one thing in common.

Where's Nico?

He's safe.

My fist tightened on the throttle. I wasn't in the mood for that twerp's bullshit runaround.

I didn't ask if he was safe. I asked where he was.

He's at the VA hospital—that's what I was going to—

What happened?

Don't worry. He's alive.

I asked what the fuck happened to him.

I can't give you any more details than that right now. I'm waiting to hear myself—

Where the hell were you during all this?

I was being shot. We were attacked while following a lead. He saved my life.

"Goddamn it!"

I kicked the car next to me and the taillight crunched under the heel of my boot.

I don't care about your life, you motherfucker!

I know.

What hospital?

The streets are blocked. You won't get there. Listen to me, Cal—

Fuck you.

I cut the connection.

Singh, I'm on my way but I need your help.

What do you need?

Work your mojo and find out what hospital Agent Nico Wachalowski is checked into. Find out his status. I want to know everything.

You got it, Cal.

I heard a voice shriek then, just over the idling engine. I looked around, but I didn't see anyone. Wind blew snow across the street, and when it died down, I heard it again.

Thanks, Singh.

Whoever it was, they were close. I cut the engine and listened. It was hard to make anything out over the wind, but it was definitely a person.

"Hello?" I called. I looked around for any movement. "Hello? Is anyone here?"

A voice called back. I couldn't make the words out, but it came from a girl.

I turned on a thermal filter and swept the area. Up ahead, in the middle of the cold, I saw a red-orange glow from the rear of the crashed armored truck.

I closed in and parked the bike ten feet away. The truck was unmarked and painted black. The front end had smashed through the brick face and the doors hung open. The rear plate was marked with the letters MIL.

Military vehicle. I climbed off the bike and stepped closer. There was an emblem in the corner of the back window.

STILLWELL CORPS. It was one of ours.

I looked around the side and saw a revivor up front, standing frozen. It still had the driver by the wrists, blood smeared down the front of its face. The driver hung there by his arms, limp. His head lolled, blood running down over his face. His throat had been torn open, and the snow at their feet was red.

"Hello?" a voice called from the back of the truck. It was female, with some kind of accent. "Who's there?"

I grabbed the handle to the back door and pulled, but it was locked.

"I'm not here to hurt you. Come on, open up!" I said. I thumped the door with my fist.

"Who are you?" the voice asked from inside. The accent was Russian, maybe. I looked through the bulletproof glass and caught a glimpse of what looked like a kid.

"I'm not dead. How's that? Open the damn door."

I heard the bolt let go, and pulled the door open. When I did, a rank smell blew out.

There was a girl back there, some street teen with a dirty face and ratty hair. She wasn't alone.

The back of the truck was filled with bodies. They were all naked, and stacked along the sides in metal trays. The crash had thrown them so that arms and legs hung over the sides. Blue fingers and toes stuck out in the air. A couple had spilled out onto the floor, and one's neck had been slashed on a sharp edge of the rack, and blood covered the floor. The girl knelt on the floor, her knees and hands red.

"Get me out of here," she said. Her hands shook.

The whole back smelled like BO and decomp. The bodies were scrawny and scabby. They had to be thirds, people they'd pulled off the streets.

"Please . . . get me out of here . . ."

All the way back, a window looked into the cab. The dash and the windshield were splashed with blood. On the seat was an electronic manifest, the screen spattered with red.

This is the retrieval team. They were here to pick up the carriers I'd tagged.

"What happened here?" I asked.

"I don't know . . . everyone just . . . fell down. When they got back up . . ."

"How'd you get in here?"

"It was already crashed. Men with guns got out."

"What men?"

"Men in uniform. They tried to hold them, the dead ones, off, but there were too many. They took them."

There were some footprints in the snow behind the truck. Some blood, and shell casings too. Except for the driver, though, there were no bodies.

"Took them where?"

She shook her head.

"Okay, I get it." Her eyes were wide and she shook, still kneeling down in the blood. "Come on, get out of there."

"Are they . . .?"

"Those things in there with you could still get back up," I said. " Let's go."

She crawled out in a hurry and stuck near me.

"We're getting out of here. What's your name?"

"Vika."

"You'll be okay, Vika. Follow me."

I took her back to the bike and she got on behind me. She put her arms around my waist and laced her fingers as I kick-started the engine.

"Hold on," I said.

She squeezed tighter as the rear tire kicked up snow and I took us through the wreckage.

Zoe Ott—Main Drag

Back in the car, I saw Penny was rattled. She didn't turn the music back on, and she didn't call Ai, either. When I offered her the flask again, she grabbed it and took a big swallow. Then she drove to a bar.

Things got a little fuzzy after that. We didn't talk about what the general said, or what we saw in the lab. We didn't talk at all until maybe three drinks in, and even then we didn't talk about anything serious. She didn't flirt with the bartender or punch up any music. She just drank until she got to the point where she could laugh, but even then, her eyes looked worried.

At some point we stopped at a liquor store, because I spilled ouzo while trying to refill the flask, and Penny was drinking grappa straight out of a long-necked bottle while she sped down the street. Then she did turn the music back on, louder than before, like she was daring someone to pull her over and give us a hard time. By then I didn't care. By then I was having fun, and I was glad to forget about the whole thing, at least for the night.

A cop on a motorcycle pulled up alongside us and matched our speed, the reflective faceplate of his helmet turned to look down at Penny. She took a long swallow from the bottle while he watched, then looked over at him as snow spit past the window. A few seconds later, he slowed down and peeled off.

The incoming-call light came up on the dash for the third time. The ID said it came from Stillwell Corps. Penny took one last swig from the bottle and stabbed the stereo button with her finger, cutting off the music. She answered the call, but they'd already disconnected.

"At least they got it working, right?" I offered.

Penny wasn't biting. She shook her head. "The point of all this," she said, "the only point of all this is to change that future. Literally nothing else matters."

"I know."

"An attack here and there, even by that many revivors, that all heals," she said. "Not that big, empty nothing. We have to fix it."

"I know."

"If an infinite number of times everything dies, then there have to be an infinite number of times we get out of it. We have to figure this out. The turn's coming up fast."

"I know," I said, not really understanding her completely.

"Do you?" she asked. "Do you have any idea what I've . . ." She trailed off and took another drink from the bottle. I tipped back the flask and swallowed, past tasting it.

Like the map they used to chart it, I didn't understand the future as well as some of us did. I knew what

Ai believed, and that the visions weren't so much looks into our actual future as they were bleed over from what she called alternate possibilities. I knew there were an infinite number of those possibilities, and that meant an infinite number were almost identical to ours. She thought we could see into them, and that their present was our future. They were all almost the same, and some pitched off the cliff into nothing, while others somehow avoided it.

At least that was what she thought. I don't think she really knew. Not for sure. All I understood was that we wanted to be one of the ones that avoided it, whatever "it" was. The dark void that no one could see into meant we were on the wrong path. We were making mistakes, the same mistakes as the rest. Was the virus a dead end? Was that the mistake?

"Look at it this way," I said. "Even if this plays out a million times and everyone is wiped out every time, we could still make it, right? We could be on the right path."

"No one sees past the end of their own life. You know that."

"But we don't know that for sure. If what we see comes from somewhere else, couldn't it just be that they all die, but we live?"

Penny opened her mouth to answer, then closed it again. She smiled, and for a second the worry left her eyes.

"You know, I think that might actually be deep," she said.

"Hey, it could be true," I said. "Admit it: you don't really know."

"Ai—"

"Ai is amazing, but come on, at the end of the day she's just a person like you or me."

"She's not like you or me."

"Penny, she isn't a god or anything."

"What is this insolence?" she asked. She was kind of kidding but kind of not.

"I'm just saying, she's a person, she makes mistakes just like everybody else, and she doesn't know everything."

"Then you think she's wrong about all this?"

"No, but—"

"Because if she's wrong about this, then what the hell is it we're trying to do here?"

"Fix it," I said, getting annoyed. "Fix everything. That's why we sneak around messing with everybody's head, so we can fix everything, because we know everything, and everyone else is a bunch of stupid sheep—"

"Hey, you can't make an omelet without breaking some eggs."

"Yeah, well, just because you break a bunch of eggs doesn't mean you get an omelet either."

Her knuckles turned white on the steering wheel as she took another swig from the bottle. She was drinking more than usual, a lot more. If I hadn't been so drunk myself, I'd have probably thought more about the fact that although she wasn't any bigger than me, I'd seen Penny break men's fingers. I'd seen her stab people and shoot people.

"I think you're talking some dangerous talk," she said.

"I think you're drunk."

"I think *you're* drunk. I think you're always drunk."

"Screw you, Penny." I growled. That was crossing a line. She wasn't allowed to bring that up. "My drinking is not a problem."

"Who do you think you're talking to?" she snapped back. "Do you know how many times I've held your hair while you puked your guts out?"

There were actually tears in the corners of her eyes.

That was something I'd never seen before, but I kept going.

"If you didn't, they'd probably throw you out on the street," I said. My face was hot and my hand had made a fist around the neck of the flask. "Just like they did with what's-her-face—"

"She had a name!" Penny shouted. I didn't think I'd ever heard her do that either. It actually stopped me cold for a second.

Before me and before Penny, Ai had pinned her hopes on some girl named Noelle Hyde as the one that was going to save the world. She didn't work out so good, though, and so from what I could get, they had to kill her. Penny never talked about her. I never really thought much about if they knew each other or how much or for how long. I could tell by her face that this time it was me who crossed the line, and opened my mouth to maybe take it back or something, but it was too late.

"She had a name," she said in a low voice. Every muscle in her body looked tense, like she wanted to break my neck or something.

She wouldn't, though. Even if she tried, she wouldn't be able to. I was no match for her physically, but if I had to, I could make her stop. If I wanted to, I could kill her.

"I know," I said. I was breathing hard.

"Sometimes you keep talking when you really should just shut up," she said.

Heat rushed up my neck, and I was just about to lay into her when the screen on the dash lit up again with an incoming call. This time it was from Ai.

Penny frowned, and we glared at each other, but when Ai called, you didn't keep her waiting. Penny took a deep breath and answered.

Ai's face appeared on the screen. Her eyelids were half-closed, like when she was concentrating, and her

pupils were dilated. The prominent vein on the right side
of her neck bulged, and every few seconds she twitched,
just barely. She'd drugged herself like she sometimes
did to enhance her abilities, and she looked like she was
tripping hard this time.

"Where are you two? What is your exact location?"
she asked. I closed my eyes for a second and when I concentrated, I could sense her. She was reaching out from
the top of Alto Do Mundo to find us. Something was
wrong.

"We left the Stillwell base," Penny said. "We're
headed back now."

"You left the Stillwell base nearly two hours ago," Ai
said, still staring into space. "Listen to me carefully: forget whatever you're fighting about and—"

"She started it—" I said, and before the last word
even got out of my mouth, I felt her reach into my head.
She reached right through the anger and the drunken-
ness, and it was like a cold hand grabbed some primal
part of me and made my body jump. Penny jumped in
the seat next to me, her mouth stuck open.

"Don't ever interrupt me," Ai said. "Listen, and do
what I say. You're both in danger—"

Penny could still drive, but that didn't change the fact
that she was drunk and about as distracted as you could
get. Her reflexes were good, but even she wasn't fast
enough to react when a man appeared in the headlights
in front of us.

For a second, everything seemed to slow down so
much that it almost stopped. I could see Ai's big lips
move as she kept talking, but all I could hear was a sort
of dull, white noise as Penny cut the wheel and the car
tilted on its suspension. Through the windshield, big
flakes of snow drifted toward us, past the man in the
street. He was dirty and bundled in filthy clothes that
hung from his scrawny frame. His cheeks were hollow,

and through his parted lips I could see teeth that were yellow and brown.

He looked up from the headlights that bore down on him. He looked right through the glass, right at me, and I could see black spots that branched through the whites of his wide eyes. They followed me as the car began to veer, and he just stood there like he was completely unaware of what was happening.

You're in terrible danger, I felt Ai's presence say from where it sat in the back of my mind. She was calling us, calling us to come back home. She wanted us to come quickly, and I could feel the urgency building up inside me.

I didn't think; I just reached out to the man in the street the same way Ai was reaching out to me. Certain minds were easier to control than others. If a mind was receptive enough, I could reach across the city and touch it, but from a few feet away I could push almost anyone. If I could snap him out of his trance and make him move, then he might have enough time.

The inside of the car got bright as my pupils opened all the way and the light from the dash and the headlights swallowed up almost everything except the man's face and those strange, blotchy eyes. I concentrated on him, looking for the swirling colors of his consciousness and the bright electric bands underneath that controlled everything. I focused on him as hard as I could as we bore down on him, but instead of the aura that should have been there, I pushed through into nothing but a black void. It was like stepping off the side of a cliff into a huge, bottomless pit.

He's dead, I thought. Where his thoughts should have been, there was just emptiness. He was dead. It was a revivor.

The car struck him above the knees, and the expression on his face never changed as muscle rippled under the impact and the bones inside snapped. His body pitched forward over the hood as his feet left the ground and one old boot flew off, the rubber heel flapping. His face struck the windshield, and half-rotted teeth shattered against the bulletproof glass.

The car was sliding, and Penny cut the wheel again to compensate as the man's body tumbled past, tearing the side mirror free as he spun like a rag doll in the air. Only a few feet away, two more men stood in the path of our car, and as I heard the shriek of tires cut through the white noise, I screamed.

Past the two men, I saw three more, and then the road curved past a building face to join the main drag, where every car was stopped. Penny cut the wheel again, but it was too late. The car went into a skid, and I felt the two bodies slam against the door. A head struck the window and sprayed blood, but as everything streaked by, I saw nothing but darkness around them. They had no lives to lose. They were all already dead.

They're all revivors, I said to Ai's presence.

We hit the guardrail head-on. The street, the people, and all the cars whipped past the windshield as the rear wheels came up off the ground behind us, and then we were spinning, end over end through the air.

Nico Wachalowski—VA Hospital

It was dark, and they were all around me. Their bellies were swollen, and the meat inside them had begun to rot. They'd dragged me underground into what used to be an old ammo dump, with decaying wooden walls and a ceiling that buckled under the soft earth above it. It was filled with bones and scraps of clothing. They'd used this place before.

Move. You have to move.

I'd relived that day more times than I could count.

Every time I told myself to fight, and every time I didn't until the first set of teeth bit down. No matter how many years passed, I couldn't shake it; from the crooked teeth that punched through first, to the cold tongue that touched the mouthful of skin.

Pain bored into my shoulder as the thing's wet, grimy hair tickled my neck and face. I heard the crunch and screamed. It raised its head with a chunk of my flesh clenched in its teeth, while another one crowded in and bit down where the blood was pumping out. They were eating me. They were eating me alive.

You have to move.

I pushed against them, but the space was too tight. They were too heavy. A knee bashed into my ear. I tried to twist my head, but they had me pinned. A thumb slipped into my eye socket and warmth gushed down my cheek, into my ear. With the eye I had left, I saw one of them pulling a big strip of skin away. In the dim light, I could make out the chest hairs sprouting from it.

I'm going to die, I thought.

I vomited. One of them shoved the eye it had popped free into its mouth. Cold fingers groped at me, holding me. All I saw were sets of teeth stained red. I slipped into shock, and my mind disconnected. The cold feeling turned warm, and something deep inside began to soothe me. It whispered for me to let go.

You've done enough, it said. *It's okay. Don't struggle. Just rest now . . .*

I'd relived this memory again and again, but a part of that day was gone. They told me it might never come back. The next thing I could ever remember was Sean's voice calling my name.

Then there, in a gap between the bodies that crowded around me, I saw a face I couldn't remember ever seeing before.

It was the face of a young boy with black skin and

tangled black hair. He was a native; scrawny, dirty, and out of uniform. He couldn't have been older than twelve. His pulse throbbed at his neck and his eyes were wide.

I wasn't alone down there.

Someone else had been down in that tunnel with me. In the light of the single, swaying overhead bulb, I saw the flash of metal as the boy positioned the tip of the blade behind the closest revivor's neck. How could I have forgotten that?

He pushed the knife into the flesh and twisted it. From the way the revivor dropped, I knew he'd severed the primary nodes at the brain stem. He moved to the next one, the blade shaking and dripping black.

"Wachalowski! Wachalowski, where are you?" A voice was shouting my name, muted, from somewhere up above. Sean's voice. My squad had found me somehow.

I fought them then. My brain seized on the hope that I might still survive, and I fought.

They saw the boy. One of them swung, but he got out of the way as the bayonet tugged at his filthy shirt. With most of my strength gone, the others turned their backs to me and closed on their fresh victim.

He tried for the side tunnel he'd come through, but another one had come in behind him. He was cut off. He scrambled back until he hit one of the makeshift walls. One of the planks was broken, and behind it was a small space that someone had dug out to hide food or munitions.

The boy squeezed through just as they reached him. He retreated back into the cubby as grimy fingers clawed an inch from his face. I pushed myself up and got on my hands and knees next to the revivor that lay facedown in the dirt. I looked for something, anything to stop them with.

"Wachalowski!"

Hands grabbed me from behind and pulled. I tried to

scream, but my throat burned with something salty and warm. I choked, and coughed up blood.

Sean, wait . . .

He pulled me away, away from the backs of the revivors crowded around the broken plank. He thought I was alone. I could just make out the boy's face, terrified, as I was dragged from the room and back up the tunnel.

"Shit! Set up a perimeter!" Sean yelled. I heard gunfire. The trees spun above me as Sean leaned over and shined a light in my one eye.

"Nico, stay with me," he said. I tried to speak, but I was choking. Blood ran from my mouth.

Someone craned back my head, and I felt a tube slide down my throat. I could breathe again. I groped for Sean's sleeve and pointed back down the tunnel.

Sean, wait, I said over the JZI, but I never finished. He leaned in close and stared into my eye. I felt dizzy as his pupils got wider, and as he stared, I felt the pain and the fear ease back. My heart rate went down.

"Sleep, Nico," he said. I felt myself relax. *It's over now. Don't try to talk. Just sleep."*

I wanted to tell him about the boy, but when I tried, I couldn't. The words wouldn't form. He didn't know. None of them knew. He was six feet underneath them, and none of them knew. Why couldn't I respond? What had Sean done to me?

He leaned in until his lips were at my ear.

"You will forget this," he said. *"I can't do anything about the physical scars, but I can do this. I don't know if I can take it away completely, but I'll try. Just forget . . ."*

Forget . . .

". . . forget what happened down there."

The medevac came. They airlifted me out. One of the revivors, its teeth stained red, came back up and watched the chopper. The gunner turned on it and cut it down as we left the boy who'd saved me to his fate, forgotten.

I opened my eyes. I was in a hospital, lying in bed while a doctor stood off to one side, turned away from me to examine an X-ray. I could still picture the boy's face in my mind.

Was it real? Had it been a dream, or had that old memory finally worked its way back to the surface?

Outstanding message: Flax, Calliope.

There were many other beds in the room, all occupied. Off to my left I saw a man with bandages wrapped around his face, and in the bed across from his, another man whose hand was wrapped. At least two of his fingers were missing. A woman on a gurney had been wheeled in and pushed along one wall to wait her turn. Her face was lacerated, and there was a tube down her throat.

Outstanding message: Flax, Calliope.

The words flashed near the corner of my eye. I opened it.

Where the fuck are you?

I smiled, and felt a knot on the right side of my face. The time stamp on the message said it was two hours old. She was alive, or at least she had been two hours ago. I shook off the dream and accessed the Bureau's system to find out what was happening out there.

FBI alerts had piled up, and they were still coming in. All across the city, thousands of people had dropped dead, only to get back up minutes later.

"MacReady was right. . . . We should have listened. . . ." I remembered. The basement caller, maybe Deatherage, had said that. Did he mean Bob MacReady, the same man I knew from Heinlein Industries?

I put in a call to him over the JZI, but he didn't pick up. His communications node was still active, though. Wherever he was, he was alive. I left the channel open and set it aside in case he responded.

Out in the hallway, another patient was trucked by while a man shouted instructions. The hospital was overrun. According to the reports, the revivors had initially shown violent aggression, and riots broke out. Vehicles were abandoned in streets that became gridlocked. Stillwell soldiers had scrambled to assist local police, but before they could get a handle on the situation, the damage had been done.

I closed my eyes and cycled through incident reports. A citizen tip site had been set up, and flooded almost as soon as it came online. The FBI was scrambling to process the incoming information, but phones, data, and even JZI links were getting jammed. The media storm had networks nearly at a standstill.

It was a disaster. The carriers were slipping past perimeters set up after the initial assault, and disappearing. No one could say for sure where they were going or if there was any organization to their movements. The entire city was in a panic.

"He's awake," I heard a voice say. "Call the Agency and get them off our backs."

"Doctor Pellwynne, process him, then get him out of here," another voice said under his breath. "We've had two hacks into our system, looking for info on him, already. And anyway, we need the bed."

Most media reports agreed that the transmission that triggered the carriers had come from Heinlein Industries, and the FBI's information backed that up. There were unconfirmed reports of a security breach over at Heinlein as well. An automated emergency call had gone out, then been cancelled. No one at the campus had called out since, and all incoming calls were being bounced to the messaging system. Even JZI traffic was blocked.

"Agent Wachalowski?" a woman's voice said. A cold hand gently touched my forehead. I opened my eyes and saw a pretty woman with skin the color of chocolate and black hair grouped in short twists. She looked down at me with tired eyes. As the report scrolled by between us, she smiled.

"Welcome back," she said. "I'm Doctor Pellwynne."

"Where am I?"

"The VA Hospital."

I looked around. It was crowded, but the facility was first tier. It was a far cry from Mother of Mercy.

"Why here?"

"You needed some special work done," she said.

"What do you mean?"

She approached the bed and sat down in a chair next to it. I saw an orange flicker inside her pupils.

"What do you remember about the attack?" she asked.

"You don't have time for this," I said, "and neither do I. I'm sorry."

"We have time," she said. "What do you remember?"

"They mobbed us," I said. It was sketchy, but I remembered the room filling up with bodies. They were revivors. "How many of them are out there?"

She kept her face calm, but there was fear there, in her eyes.

"A lot. That's all I know. I haven't had time to think about it; we're running at triple capacity. The hospital is secure—for now."

"I need to get out of here."

"I understand, but I need to speak with you first."

"Why?" I didn't understand.

"What do you remember about the attack?"

"I . . ."

I remembered falling down into the water. I'd been hit in the head. I was disoriented and went down on my back. I fired as one of them lurched toward me.

The ax. It had taken the ax from the wall.

Under the blanket, I'd closed my right fist and felt no pain. I stretched the fingers and made the fist again.

I looked down and saw a crease near the joint of my right shoulder where some kind of major work had been done. It was deep, and the skin there was thick and white. The scar that had been there since my last tour ended abruptly at that crease. I heard the tempo on my vitals monitor pick up.

"Before you look," she said, "I want to prepare you—"

I pulled the blanket away and held up the arm in front of me. It was gray. Under the skin, I could see a network of black veins.

A cold feeling sank in the pit of my stomach. The sound of the heart monitor sounded faraway as it began to blip faster.

"Calm down," Pellwynne said.

I flexed the fingers again. The muscles worked under the skin, but the hand wasn't mine. The arm wasn't mine. My tattoo from the service was gone. The scars, the calluses, even the body hair . . . they were gone. In their place was the smooth, gray limb of a dead man.

"Calm down," she said again. She reached out and took the gray hand in hers, then placed her other over the back of it.

"Feel that," she said. Her hands felt hot, like warm wax.

"They're warm," I said, but it wasn't true. The fingers she had touched my forehead with were cold.

"You'll get used to the temperature difference."

"Who authorized this?" I asked. It was all I could think to say.

"It was at the Agency's discretion," she said.

"Who, specifically, authorized it?"

"I can't tell you that. I'm sorry."

She gave my hand one last squeeze and then let go of it.

"You will get used to it, Agent. I promise."

I checked my JZI, and it had detected the new system. Information regarding the nerve interface and the paper-thin filter that separated the living tissue from the dead popped up and scrolled by. System vitals appeared and provided feedback on the arm's condition, right down to the nanoblood version.

"Where is . . ." I started to ask.

"By the time anyone got there, it was gone," she said. The revivors had taken it.

"You'll have full use of the new arm in two weeks, and it will be stronger than the original," she said. "Until then, you're running at near ninety percent. You can go back in the field, but be careful."

I nodded. I'd seen replacements fitted in the field before. I'd told myself it was the next best thing. The reality of what had happened hadn't hit home yet. It buzzed at the edge of my mind, like a fly at a window that couldn't get in. I felt weirdly distant and calm.

"How long was I out?"

"You've been in surgery for four hours."

Four hours. Fawkes had issued the code four hours ago, and we were still at a standstill. I had to get out of there.

Van Offo was offline. I tapped into the hospital records and checked the inpatient list; he'd been brought in to have the bullet removed from his neck, and was discharged two hours ago.

The man arrested at the site, Rafe Pena, hadn't fared as well; he was still checked in. He'd suffered broken bones, internal injuries, and multiple bite wounds. He was listed as being in serious but stable condition.

I found the FBI records for the lockdown at Mother of Mercy and brought them up. According to them, Van Offo and one SWAT team member were taken out, along with me, by the EMTs. The SWAT officer died in transit. There were no other survivors from the basement.

"Where's Pena?" I asked. Pellwynne frowned.

"He's not ready for transport yet," she said. "His injuries were fairly traumatic. Don't worry about him right now."

I watched one black vein bulge in that gray arm. I tried, but I couldn't look away from it.

"You know, it may not seem that way now," Pellwynne said, "but you're very lucky, Agent Wachalowski."

I cycled through the footage. Bodies lay in a foot of water that had turned red with blood. The cages had been torn open and the captives inside ripped apart. There was blood spatter painted across the walls, punctuated by bullet marks. It had been a slaughter.

"I found you a good match," she said. "The nerve interface . . . it's some of my best work. I know that doesn't make this any easier to swallow. There was enough residual tissue to use with the growth accelerators. The join is solid. The blood is the latest version. It's field upgradable, so you won't have to report to Heinlein for transfusions. You shouldn't experience any of the tingling or phantom muscle ticking usually associated with the older variants, and you'll have full—"

"When can I leave?"

"As soon as you want. I'll be honest, Agent—we could use the room."

I sat up and put a call into the Bureau to let them know I was back on my feet. Fawkes could have played this card at any time—he didn't choose today at random. I had to find out what the reason was.

"You can sign for your weapon when you check out," she said. "I've left my contact information on your JZI, should you have any questions or need anything."

"Thanks," I said, but I barely heard her. She lingered for another minute; then I was vaguely aware of her leaving the room. The fly continued to bounce at the window as I stared at the black vein, following it as it branched out beneath the stranger's cold, dead skin. Though terror was brewing somewhere inside me, I couldn't look away.

4

FIRST STRIKE

Nico Wachalowski—VA Hospital

I left the hospital room in a daze. The circuit request still flashed in the corner of my eye. MacReady hadn't picked up. Maybe he wasn't going to.

Because of the trouble in the streets, the halls were crowded. Patients sat, holding bloodied gauze in place, outside doors while doctors rushed by. People were shouting, but I barely heard it. I felt like I was moving through the chaos in a bubble. Numb. Blood dotted the floor in a wandering line, and I followed it, heading toward the elevators.

I eased relaxant into my system, but even with the drugs I couldn't shake the jitters. One of those things had cut off my arm. While I'd lain there, bleeding to death, they'd carried it away and eaten it. The last man I'd seen with any link to what was happening out there was somewhere in the building right now.

Halfway down the hall, I stopped, and an angry-looking nurse brushed past me. I accessed the hospital's records again.

Rafe Pena. Room 9E-C.

He was on that same floor, being held for questioning. The next time someone in scrubs moved past, I grabbed his arm. He looked irritated, but winced a little when I applied pressure.

"Room 9E-C," I said.

"Back down the hall and to your right," he said, pulling his arm free. Before I could say anything else, he was gone. I turned away from the blood trail and began moving back the way I'd come.

The room had three gurneys, but only one was occupied. The empty ones were still dressed in bloodied sheets, and on the third lay a whip-thin man. His pockmarked face was slack, and there was gauze covering the right side of it. I watched my hand push the door closed and then lock it.

"Wake up, Mr. Pena," I said. He didn't respond right away, and I kicked the gurney. One of his eyes cracked open, and when he saw me, the other one followed suit.

He sat up as I approached him, and when I breathed in, my nose filled with the stink from my clothes: rank blood and sweat, combined with the fouled basement water. I unbuttoned my jacket, the thick, gray fingers tripping me up for a second, then removed it and tossed it onto one of the empty gurneys. Sprouting from the rolled-up sleeve underneath, the thing that took the place of my arm didn't look human. Muscle striations stood out in bands under the gray skin, webbed with a network of black veins. Just the sight of it brought back memories I'd give anything to forget, memories of that damp, dark pit and the cold hands that held me down as they . . .

I overrode the JZI and eased another dose of relaxant into my bloodstream. Warmth and numbness crept through my body as I closed my eyes and counted back from ten. My teeth chattered as I sucked air through my teeth and let it out slowly.

"You can't—" he started to say; then I clamped that gray hand down on his neck. His skin felt hot underneath it, the signals jumping up through the grafted nerves like sparks of electricity. His eyes popped open as the fingers squeezed.

"What was going on in that basement?" I asked him in a low voice.

"Fuck you." He grunted. I willed the dead hand to squeeze tighter, and it responded. His face turned darker, and blood began to bloom through the gauze over his right cheek.

"Tell me," I said.

"Fuck . . ."

He grabbed the forearm and pushed, but I leaned into it. As he struggled, in my head I heard Sean's voice from long ago, back in the grinder. I was underground, where they'd dragged me. Their cold fingers dug into my skin from all around.

"Wachalowski! Wachalowski, where are you?"

In my mind, I heard the crunch as the first set of teeth bit down. I felt the impact of a knee in the side of my head, and that cold hand that clamped down on my face.

"Wachalowski!"

Rafe threw a punch that thumped into my ribs, but there was no power behind it. He threw two more, then tried to kick me, but got tangled in the blanket.

"I want to know what was going on down there," I said. I eased up on his throat, and he gasped in a breath, then coughed through strings of spit.

"I don't know anything," he wheezed.

"You know who you worked for."

He got one leg free from the blanket and thrust his knee into my side, but again, there was no power behind it. He was weak and injured. An IV tube still trailed from one of his arms. I didn't need to strong-arm him, but something was building inside me, out of my control.

Still feeling like I was moving through a haze, I let go of his neck and reared back the fist. I fired it down like a piston, and his teeth broke against the knuckles of the dead hand. A front tooth and canine disappeared into his mouth and he coughed through a spray of blood, both red and black. He held one hand between us as I hammered his face again.

"Hey!" someone shouted from the hall. The person worked the handle and found it locked.

This is wrong, a faint doubt whispered in my ear. *Al can make him talk without hurting him.* Something inside me had tipped over the edge, though, and I was beyond listening to the voice.

I grabbed Pena and hauled him off the gurney, carrying him across the small room before slamming him back into the wall. My fist thudded into his cheek, and the gauze tore away to show a deep bite wound underneath. I fired my other fist into his gut and the breath went out of him. He slid down onto the floor, where he doubled over and vomited.

I raised my foot and stomped down on his left shoulder. He screamed as his collarbone broke and the joint dislocated. Blood was running from his mouth and nose, drops bleeding into the splash of puke in front of him. He put his other hand down in it and slipped forward on the floor.

"Get that door open!" a voice shouted outside.

The dead hand grabbed him under the armpit and I heaved him up until his toes brushed the floor. Red drops pattered down onto my shirt as I flipped him over my shoulder and down onto his back. His head struck the tiles and his eyes swam.

"Wait—" he started to say, but I hit him again. The dead fist went up, leaking black blood, then hammered his face again and again. Even when his hand stopped clawing me and his body went slack, I kept driving that gray fist down. In my mind, I was back in the grinder, back down in that hole, and they were around me, pushing their faces in closer.

"Wachalowski! Wachalowski, where are you?"

Pins and needles pricked through my knuckles, pulsing each time they connected with meat and bone. The sensation was muted and flat, as if the nerves in the skin registered pain, but not like before. It reached my brain through a filter, sanitized and scrubbed.

Distantly, I remembered once telling Faye that revivors didn't feel pain. She hadn't looked sure then. There had been some part of me that was never sure either, but I knew now. I was right.

Faye. I wondered where she was now.

"Stop!" a voice shrieked, a woman's voice.

I felt blood under my fists with each impact. I'd forgotten who Pena even was or what he was. He became the thing that had transformed a piece of me into what I hated and feared more than anything else. Something primal wanted to destroy the thing underneath me, to pull that meat from the bone, like they had done to me.

"Stop!" the woman screamed again.

There was panic in her voice, and it snapped me back. I blinked something salty from my eyes and registered the scene in front of me.

I was kneeling on the floor over Pena, who wasn't moving. His lips were split, and his mouth was filled with blood. His face and the floor around it were a mess of red and black, and I saw thick drops of nanoblood dripping from between the fingers of my closed revivor fist that was still poised for another strike. At some point, they'd gotten the door open and come inside. A crowd of people had gathered to my left.

My jaw was pulled open, teeth bared. A string of drool hung from my lip.

Bite . . .

It was like an itch, deep in my brain. When it registered, I felt my stomach begin to turn. I wiped the drool away and closed my mouth, resisting the urge I couldn't explain. Having a revivor limb didn't make you a revivor. It didn't . . .

Do it . . . bite . . .

I slammed my good fist into the wall, and the people around me jumped. One of Pena's eyes was sealed shut, but the other one moved. He was still conscious, barely. I leaned in close so he could hear me.

"Names," I said in his ear. He gagged and choked up blood onto my collar.

"Deatherage," I heard him whisper.

"Who else?"

"Let him go, Agent!" the woman's voice shouted.

"What were they doing down there?" I said.

"He's . . . going to . . . wake them . . . up . . ."

"What?"

He choked again. He couldn't speak. I scanned through his wrecked face, past hematomas and chips of bone. I was looking for augments—a camera eye, anything that might give me more information. A small object stood out behind two teeth lodged near the back of his throat. He had an implant, some kind of slimmed-down JZI.

I used a 'bot to drill through its security and began pulling data. There wasn't much stored there, but I got three names: Harold Deatherage, Ang Chen, and Dulari Shaddrah.

"Ang Chen," I whispered. I knew that name. Ang Chen was one of the high-level Heinlein researchers that was helping to develop the virus that would hopefully shut down Fawkes's network, when the time came. How did his name end up in Pena's JZI?

"What about Ang Chen?" I said in his ear. He didn't answer. "Who is Shaddrah?"

The connection between us dropped as the implant shut down. Rafe's vitals began to dip.

"Damn it! How are they involved in this?"

Pena's remaining eye closed, and blood bubbled at the corner of his mouth. My fist, still in the air, tightened.

"I said, 'stop'!" the woman's voice screamed again. I turned to my left and saw several men and women dressed in hospital scrubs. In front of them was Doctor Pellwynne, her eyes wide with shock. Her expression was horrified. Tears had formed in her eyes.

A few feet away, I saw my reflection in the side of a polished steel cabinet. My face was as pale as the revivor's arm next to it. My cheeks looked drawn, and there were dark circles under my eyes. My face and neck were spattered with Pena's blood.

"Please," Pellwynne said, holding up her hands. "Please just let him go."

She looked at me like I was some kind of lunatic. She was pleading with me. Behind her, two security guards moved in, and when they looked in the room, their eyes widened. One of them said something into his radio.

"I'm an FBI agent," I said. I reached for my badge, but I'd taken off my jacket.

"Please, Agent," Pellwynne said again. "I am asking you. We can still save him. Please."

My mind buzzed as thoughts crowded in faster than I could process them. I realized what I'd done, and my head began to spin. The whole room felt like it was spinning.

"I . . ."

I lowered the revivor arm and ran the hand over my face, smearing sweat and blood. The fingers and palm felt cold, and I felt myself cringe. This wasn't who I was. What had I done?

The people in the room were saying something, but it was like the voices were coming from someplace far away. For a second, I couldn't remember why I was there or what had happened. My brain was on overload, reaching out for something, anything solid to hold on to until it passed.

I didn't do it consciously. If Faye was still out there she wouldn't answer, and if she did, she couldn't help. It made no sense to send the message to her, but I did, like some involuntary yelp.

I need you.

The message went out, and I killed the connection behind it as a cold drop of sweat rolled down one side of my neck. My stomach clenched, and I thought I might be sick.

Harold Deatherage. Ang Chen. Dulari Shaddrah.

I stood up, unsteady, and grabbed my jacket from the gurney. I looked Pellwynne in the eye, and what I saw there made me feel ashamed. I couldn't explain to her why I'd done what I'd done. I didn't understand it myself. Without looking at the other people, I pushed my way through them and staggered out into the hallway.

Harold Deatherage. Ang Chen. Dulari Shaddrah. I walked, letting the voices fade behind me as I tapped into the FBI's network and began pulling information on the names I'd just obtained. I focused on that.

I knew about Chen, but according to the files, they all worked for Heinlein Industries. Chen was a top-tier nano engineer tied to the Huma project, and currently on loan to the DOD. Shaddrah's specialty was brain work, and she was also tied to the Huma project. Deatherage researched payload and delivery methods for the Huma prototype. How were three high-ranking revivor specialists connected to someone like Pena?

Worse still, Chen was working on what might turn out to be our only viable offense against Fawkes. If he was somehow involved in this . . .

Incoming call. The request flashed in my periphery. It was Van Offo.

I checked the records and found all three of them were all still employed at Heinlein. Whatever the connection was, they were all involved somehow. Fawkes had contacts inside Heinlein Industries and at least one inside the DOD.

Incoming call. I picked up.

Leave the hospital, he said before I could respond. *Someone's on their way to get you. Go to the corner of Tenth Avenue and Park and wait there.*

Van Offo—

Do it, Nico. Your name just lit up the wire. That stunt you pulled is going to disappear, but get out of there.

I glanced back over my shoulder in time to see a group of EMTs push their way into the room. People had stepped out into the hall to see what was going on. I turned away and headed for the elevators.

"Somebody stop him!" a voice shouted, but no one tried.

I don't know what happened in there, I said.

We'll figure it out. For now, just get going. Did you at least get any usable info? Van Offo asked.

Three names: Harold Deatherage, Ang Chen, and Dulari Shaddrah. They're all Heinlein employees, Al, Chen is one of the top researchers on—

I know who he is. Van Offo paused on the other end of the line. *This is bad. You want to get back here right away, Nico.*

Why? What happened?

Word came down while you were under: Fawkes has taken control of Heinlein Industries.

What?

He piped over some video footage that looked like it was taken from a flyby of Heinlein's campus. Below I could see a throng of people crowded at the entrance to the security tarmac. Past them I could see an open flame roar through the empty windshield of a large truck. Smoke rose into the air from several locations in the distance.

This was taken less than an hour ago, he said.

How? I asked. *And why would he do that?*

We don't know how he managed it, but the current assumption is that it was so he could use their link to the defense grid.

They use that to upgrade revivors in the field, I said, *and for the revivor communications bands.*

It's still part of the defense grid. It was a way in. He somehow used it to take control of a satellite armed with twelve nuclear ICBMs less than an hour ago.

What?

Nico, he's threatening to launch if we try to send anyone in after him.

I rounded the corner and found a mob at the elevators. Turning right, I found the stairwell door and pushed it open, leaving a smear of blood behind. It was quieter in there. I started down as the door slammed behind me.

If he's threatening instead of just firing, I said, *then what does he want?*

We don't know yet.

Can we get control of the nukes back?

They're trying, he said. *But like I told you, I think this could be it. The end. It's coming.*

Not if we stop it.

If they could stop it, they—

Never mind that, I said. *Focus. What was going on in that basement? Were we able to figure it out?*

Not yet, he said. *But, Nico, something strange happened down there.*

What?

The people down there, the screaming man in particular—I couldn't control them. I tried to calm him down, but I couldn't. I couldn't influence him.

I remembered the look of fear he'd had on his face when he'd made his way to the cages. Fear and confusion.

Why not? I asked.

You are supposed to be unique, he said. *A lot of the path that we've tried to lay out hinges on that fact; Ai herself predicted it. One man will be beyond our control— one. I don't know why, but I couldn't control those people. Any of them.*

What does it mean?

He was idle for a while. I headed down the stairs to the next landing.

There's more, he said. *I wasn't supposed to live through that attack.*

What?

Mother of Mercy. The dark, the water, and those people ... I was supposed to die down there. Today was supposed to be the day I die. Fawkes was to destroy the city not long after.

You—

Tenth Avenue and Park, he said. *Just get there. We're off the script, Nico. Something's gone very wrong.*

Faye Dasalia—Heinlein Industries, Pratsky Building

A map of the park floated in front of me as the virus I'd planted transferred control of the main computer hub over to Fawkes. He gained access to the transmitter array and connected to the satellite network. Feeds from all over had begun to pour in, and I watched as his forces stormed the campus. Teams I knew nothing about had attacked from along the perimeter. They'd crossed the open tarmac, then struck the facilities at their center. Any remaining security forces were quickly torn to pieces as his soldiers occupied the main buildings.

"What the hell is going on?" someone whispered behind an equipment rack, but nobody answered. A loud thud shook the walls, and the lights flickered. It sparked a quick, hushed murmur that stopped when gunshots boomed through the halls outside. The people with me in the Pratsky Building began to realize the trouble they were in as their phones and computers, even their JZIs, had become useless. All data was rerouted through the transmitter array; everything else was suppressed. Everyone but us was completely cut off. Electricity coursed back through the main fence. The Eye resumed its watch over the tarmac, ready to incinerate anything that moved. No one could get in—or out.

I waited in the lab, not sure what to do as gunfire cracked outside. Heinlein's security team resisted for roughly twenty-five minutes before they finally succumbed. They weren't set up for an attack of that scale, and when they lost the airstrip, and their air support with it, they were quickly overwhelmed. The sounds of destruction from outside faded, until all that was left were quiet whispers and frightened sobs.

"You," a voice whispered. I turned to see a young man crouched in shadow. His eyes were intense as he stared up at me. "Revivor . . . tell me what's happening."

A message from Fawkes appeared in front of me, glowing softly as I stared:

Faye, come here.

His location appeared on the building's map. He was inside the Pratsky facility.

"Stay here," I told the young man. "Whatever they tell you to do, do it."

As I crossed the lab, I heard Dulari's voice come over the intercom. I watched her on one of the feeds as she spoke into a handset:

"Employees of Heinlein Industries, this is Dulari Shaddrah. For those who do not know me, I am a senior engineer in the biotech division. I understand you are anxious about this turn of events, but I urge you to remain calm and at your stations. If the soldiers have not reached you yet, they will shortly. Do not resist them, and I can promise you will not be harmed. Certain employees will have received instructions to assemble in the main hub of the Pratsky Building; make your way there now. If you are—"

She jumped, dropping the handset to the floor, as gunfire erupted through the room. Three of the revivor soldiers lined up near the offices had begun to fire on the row of cubicles. On the feed I saw Dulari's face lit with the flash of sustained gunfire. As I watched, her expression changed to what I thought might be shock, or fear, or both.

The shots covered the sounds of the screams. Bullets riddled flimsy walls and tore the people who cowered inside to shreds as they began to move down the rows. More gunfire echoed down the halls from throughout the building.

A woman ran out from one of the offices and stumbled into the wall. She made it two steps toward the door on the other side of the room before a bullet punched through her neck and her body pitched forward onto the floor. A soldier farther down dropped an expended clip onto the bloodstained carpet and reloaded. When I looked back to the feed, I saw the handset lying on the floor. Dulari was gone.

My job was to hijack Heinlein's transmitter. The others were supposed to smuggle me out. Fawkes was supposed to initiate his code transfer from outside of the campus, but instead he and his men were here, and they were killing everyone.

There's a lot he doesn't tell you, Lev had said. *Remember that.* When I played back the memory, I felt sure Lev knew what the virus was for when he first entered the pipe. Fawkes needed a series-seven revivor to make the jump from the test facility, but something made him doubt me. The operation must have been in the works for several months at least. He had kept me in the dark.

Faye, come here. The message pulsed in the air.

I made my way down through rows of equipment, and saw the processing plant's inventory get called out in a window. More than one thousand revivors were stored there, awaiting shipment abroad. Manifest numbers were being catalogued, as they got ready for reanimation. Fawkes was going to wake them up, all of them.

I pushed open the door and made my way back toward the main offices, where Fawkes was, as the gunfire continued. Debris littered the tarmac, and through one window I saw the fuselage of a downed helicopter as flames spit into the wind.

The processing plant is under our control, someone reported. *Reanimation has begun.*

What about the nuclear satellite? Fawkes asked.

The new targets are locked in.

Keep me informed.

I opened a metal door and stepped through it into a long corridor. Rows of glass panels looked out toward the tarmac where flames rippled off two twisted metal husks, and far off in the distance columns of black smoke rose into the gray sky. Between two of the buildings I saw where one of The Eye's orbital beams had struck. The blacktop had been completely liquefied and blown out to form a wide, blistered crater. Steam drifted from the center while snow streamed down around it.

As I approached the end of the corridor, a brilliant flash from up above threw long shadows across the tarmac. The glass panels tinted darker in response; then the beam arced down like a bolt of lightning. The point of impact rose like a huge bubble, then popped in a cloud of flame as a loud crack, like thunder, split the air. The panels shook in their frames as snow pushed out from the expanding heat wave.

Last hostile Chimera has been destroyed, a report came in. *We control the airstrip and the remaining ten aircraft.*

Roger that.

Across the way, in the adjacent building, I saw figures standing inside and staring in shock. A jeep lay on its roll bar several hundred yards away, flames pouring from one tire. Underneath it, pinned by one leg, a soldier's body lay twisted and broken. Blood ran across the blacktop.

I protected these people once.

I stepped through the door at the end of the hall and left the scene behind me. As the door closed, a man crossed in front of me, backing up with his hands held up as a burst of gunfire tore through his chest. He fell back and crashed to the floor. A moment later, the worst of the noise stopped. Sobs and moans and the occasional scream piped up, along with scattered shots.

Fawkes was close; I could sense him. A glass door led back to the R&D labs, and inside soldiers stood watch as workers were herded into offices. Up ahead of me, a man lay on the floor with blood pooled around his head. Past him, a woman's leg stuck through a doorway, one high heel on its side a few feet away.

Fawkes was set up in the director's office. As I approached, I saw him standing straight in front of a large, wooden desk while the UAC flag hung from a brass pole in a stand over to his left. Ang and Dulari were there. Ang's face looked calm. Dulari's eyes were wide. There were tears in them.

He'd been in stasis too long, and those years in storage had taken their toll. His skin had grown thin and slightly translucent. The black veins underneath were easily seen as they branched along either side of his neck and formed a web across the curve of his scalp. I knew his body was still strong physically, but he appeared almost old and decrepit. He leaned in and spoke to Dulari and Ang. I adjusted my hearing so that I could pick up their conversation.

". . . you found Deatherage?" Fawkes asked.

"No," Chen said. "I think at this point we have to assume he faked the entry log and he's not here."

"I'll handle it."

"What about the other problem?"

"I'll handle that too, Mr. Chen. Leave it alone."

"Gen sevens retain ties to their old identities," Ang said. "You yourself have cited her relationship with the FBI agent more than once."

They were talking about me. It wouldn't be the first time Ang had recommended that I be destroyed. He was clear on where he stood concerning me.

"I don't agree," Dulari managed, her voice shaking. "She can be trusted."

Fawkes looked past them and the two turned and saw me. Ang had a steely look in his eye as he watched me approach them.

"Hello, Faye," Fawkes said. His softly glowing eyes stared back at me like those of an owl. I nodded to him.

"We don't need Mr. Deatherage any longer," Fawkes said. "We have the variant now. Can you proceed?"

A shot went off nearby, and Dulari jumped.

"Y-yes," she said. "The reactivation sequence is complete. Transmission of phase two was completed an hour ago."

"The upgrade was accepted?" Fawkes asked.

"The system shows a failure rate of less than two percent," Ang said. "It worked."

I didn't know what they were referring to. I waited and didn't ask.

"How long will the change take?" Fawkes asked.

"You'll begin to see effects immediately," Ang said. "How long it will take for complete saturation is difficult to say, but the heightened aggression should facilitate that."

"Monitor the situation," Fawkes said. "Let me know if there are any problems."

"Understood," Dulari said. Fawkes turned to Ang.

"Make sure anyone else who can operate that equipment is eliminated," he said. "Take the employees the soldiers have reserved and fit them with the devices."

Ang nodded, and he and Dulari turned and left the room. As they passed by me, Dulari met my eye. She stared at me intently, like there was something she was trying to say. A second later, she sent me a message over a private circuit.

He lied to us. He's going to kill you. I know you can cut his command spoke. Do it. Find Robert MacReady.

The way she stared back at me made me think she'd known for a while about the override I'd discovered, but she hadn't told Fawkes. The words hung there in the air between us; then she nodded and continued on out of the room. As the door closed behind her, I sifted back through my memory and found the override. I didn't execute it, but turned it over in my brain thoughtfully.

He's going to kill you. The message faded away as Fawkes watched me, his expression not changing. I'd known many revivors, but none that were quite like Fawkes. He was from an earlier generation, but his mind was incredibly well preserved. He could track amazing numbers of details, but even more important, he retained a strong capacity to scheme, and unbreakable resolve. He had big plans for the humans of this world, even though he himself was far from human. The years of isolation and obsession had left their mark on him.

"You've kept me in the dark," I said. He started at me, not moving.

"Yes."

"Why?"

"Honestly, because I needed a seventh-generation model to plant the virus, and I wasn't sure you'd help me if you knew what I had planned."

"I thought you needed Heinlein's transmitter array."

"I do."

Another long burst of gunfire drowned him out for a minute. He waited calmly for it to subside.

"Then why take the whole facility?" I asked. "We could have done it remotely. By the time anyone knew, it would have been too late."

"I have my reasons."

"Why kill them all?"

"So that no one can undo what happens today."

He leaned back and sat on the edge of the desk. One thin black vein bulged slightly as it squiggled from his scalp to his temple. His eyes stared at nothing for a few seconds, twitching faintly back and forth.

A second later I felt him creep in over the command spoke, that connection that gave him access to me. It had been there every day since I died, and I knew firsthand it gave him full control. He'd used it once to force me to kill Nico, and though I'd failed, I'd stabbed him through the breastbone. There was nothing he couldn't force me to do, if that's what he decided.

He could even send me down into the void . . . and he was.

"Sleep now," I heard him say, and beneath my memories the void yawned wider. My high-level systems began to wind down. He was in my command node. What I was sensing was my own deanimation.

"What are you doing?" I asked. My vision flickered as I began to sink. In my mind, I fell below my field of thoughts to where the blackness waited. Its threads began to reach for me, pulling me deeper and deeper below.

I tried to force him out, but it was no use. All revivors

had free will, but it wasn't absolute; commands from the spoke overrode everything. I still had access to the override shunt; I could still sense it in my active memory, but . . .

"Sleep now," he said.

Maybe this is for the best, I thought. I'd always feared that darkness, but maybe I didn't need to be afraid. My life had expired a long time ago. Maybe this force that was reaching out to me was something I'd been avoiding for too long.

As my last moments trickled away, the lightless force almost seemed to be alive. It was pulling me deeper down inside it. I thought it would be cold or maybe painful, but instead it was calming.

Time to go, Faye . . .

I resisted once more before relaxing. I was jarred as my knees struck the tiled floor, but barely felt anything.

Yes.

Time to go . . .

Yes. Okay.

Just then, I received a communication. It had come from outside the perimeter. Fawkes's eyes narrowed slightly. He was watching me over the command spoke; he had seen the message too.

The message was from Nico. A single sentence:

I need you.

The blackness recoiled, and the field of memories churned inside my head. The lights swirled and scattered like coals that had been raked as my consciousness rose back through the field, and for a second I was standing with him, back at sea, on the tanker. The rain pounded over me as a tarp cracked in the wind. Nico stood in front of me, a gun smoking in his hand, but the murder had left his eyes. I reached him and grabbed hold of his slick lapel. Before he could move, I pressed my lips to his.

"Good-bye, Faye," I heard Fawkes say, and the memories collapsed.

The rest of my systems began to shut down, rapid-fire, one following another. Before I could even grasp what had happened, half of my modules had winked out. Warnings spilled by through the air in front of me as my awareness began to fade away.

I saw Fawkes's leather shoes, then nothing at all as my visual feed cut out. My balance went next, and I began to fall to one side. There wasn't time to do anything else; before I lost control of my core systems, I launched the override program.

Code flooded past in a stream as the shutdown was halted. The program infected my control nodes and targeted the command spoke. It began to tear it down, and purged all outstanding instructions from Fawkes. . . .

. . . And for just a second, it was wide open. For just a second I could see into him as completely as he could see into me. Unlike Lev, or any of the rest of us, Fawkes maintained a command spoke with all of us. Different ones were active at different times, but they never went away. I could sense his connection to all of them, clustered like individual memories somewhere deep inside his mind. They didn't link to stored information, though. Those portals gave him control over each of the revivors in his network.

Fawkes's mouth parted slightly.

"What did you—"

He was speaking, but I could barely hear him. Everything else fell away as I stared past the collection of command spokes to another construct that hung behind it. There were thousands of portals, hot orange embers that floated in the dark to form a vast, hazy sphere. It emanated a continuous hum, the combination of thousands of voices, and I knew then what it was.

I'd been outfitted with a secondary communications

array that tuned me in to their collective network, so at least on some level, I could sense them. Their constant whispering, like wind or water, had become more pronounced since they'd all been turned and I knew that there were thousands, but to see Fawkes's connection to them all . . . it was hard for me to grasp.

"I can see them—" I whispered.

The words got stuck in my throat as thousands of connections opened at once. A flood of data came crashing down on me, choking my buffers before they adjusted in order to keep pace. I felt the field of my memories recede, the points of light sinking into the darkness as a new field of light appeared above them. The individual points in that new field were sharp and clear, like hot embers in the dark. I could sense them all, and like my memories, I could pull them up individually. Each one was a constant stream of information. I watched the embers as they swirled through the void, around that huge, smoldering mass of white light. I could sense their eyes all over the city. They were still concentrated in several large pockets, but that changed by the second as they spread farther, and farther away. It was amazing he could keep command of so many.

"Faye, stop."

I chose one of the cinders at random and pulled it into the foreground. I was able to coax it open like a portal and look inside. At first, I saw only darkness, but then something moved. Sensations flowed through the connection and into my consciousness. I sensed a bitter cold, and could hear the crackle of ice and grit under many feet as it echoed through the blackness. The unit was underground somewhere. Many more shapes moved through the shadows in front of it.

I reached through the portal and tried to make contact. The images shifted as the revivor turned. When it moved, hundreds of eyes looked back from out of the dark, and each set flashed like those of an animal. They were all together. The sea of eyes flowed by until the revivor stopped moving again, and I caught a glimpse of a tunnel's concrete wall where someone had spray painted graffiti:

ELEVEN FROM ZERO.

"How are you doing this?" I heard Fawkes ask.

ELEVEN FROM ZERO. It looked like it had been painted a long time ago. I wondered what it meant....

The portal closed. The field of cinders faded and disappeared as Fawkes managed to lock me out.

My HUD flickered, and then I could see again. Fawkes's blade was tracing an arc toward my neck. I blocked him, and the point embedded in the wall with a thud. The rest of my systems were coming back. Fawkes's eyes widened slightly as he pulled the bayonet free.

His command spoke had been severed. Orange light burned in Fawkes's pupils as he tried to issue the override code and realized he no longer had control of me.

Before he could swing again, I struck him in the ribs with my palm and fired my own bayonet. His expression didn't change as the blade penetrated him and cool, thick blood oozed between my fingers.

He pulled away and the blade came free. He kicked me in the chest with his heel and drew a pistol from inside his jacket. I swept his legs out from under him, and the shot fired into the ceiling as he fell back. He struck the corner of the desk and spun onto the floor as I pulled open the door and scrambled out into the hall.

"Stop her!" I heard him shout.

I kept low as I ran back the way I'd come. Revivors patrolled between the rows, and as they received the order, I saw their guns come out. Several shots boomed behind me, and I heard screams as glass shattered. I caught a glimpse of a woman in one of the cubes as I passed, her face streaked with tears.

Bullets punched through the drywall next to the door's frame as I reached it and ran through into the hallway beyond.

Zoe Ott—Main Drag

I woke up on my back. It was hot and bright, and right away I knew it wasn't real.

I rolled over and felt warm pavement under my hands. The sun beat down hard, and the dry air had a bitter, smoky smell. Somewhere under that I caught a whiff of gas fumes. When I was caught in a vision, a lot of times sounds and smells from the real world crept in. Those smells weren't good.

When I opened my eyes, I saw I was facedown on a big chunk of blacktop that sat at an angle in the sand. All around were other pieces of what at one point must have been street, but it had all been torn up.

A little ways off, I saw half a body buried in the dirt. A harsh wind peppered my face with grit and made the shredded remains of clothes flap around the corpse so that I could see bones underneath.

This is it, I thought. *The wasteland vision, the vision Ai has been waiting for me to have again.* I was there.

The next time it happens, try to get more information, she had said.

I got my footing and looked around. The city was gone and all that was left were pieces of buildings— jagged walls with burned-out windows and twisted metal beams. The sky was kind of reddish-brown with no clouds, and it was weirdly quiet. A big gust of wind stirred up dust in the distance that formed a big spiral. I watched it get bigger, then blow itself out. There was no sound but the rush of wind.

Something vibrated in my pocket, and I reached in and pulled out my cell phone. It buzzed again in my hand. I shaded the LCD with my hand and squinted at it. The display said Noelle Hyde.

"She had a name!"

I answered the phone, and static crackled in my ear.

"Hello?" I asked. The wind blew again and made my clothes snap.

"We were wrong," a woman's voice said. I could barely hear her over the wind and the static.

"What?"

"If any of this gets through," she said, "you have to do it."

"Do what?"

"We made a mistake. You have to be the one to—"

The line cut out.

"Hello?" The display on my phone said the call was disconnected.

"What mistake?" I wondered out loud. I had to be the one to do what?

I looked out over the wreckage again. Wind kicked up more sand and I saw more bones underneath. More than sixteen million people had lived there once.

We were wrong. What did that mean?

When I tried to call back, the phone wouldn't work. It lost power and went dark.

"Come on . . ."

I shook it and was trying to get it to turn back on when I heard a growl in front of me and looked up. A dog was standing at the base of the blacktop slope. It was a big, black-and-white dog with blue eyes that stared up at me. One of its haunches was shaved, and there was a bite mark on the bare patch.

Standing next to the dog was a woman. She wore combat boots and an army-green T-shirt, and with her almost-shaved head, she looked like a guy. She had on black lipstick, and a spiderweb tattoo covered one side of her neck. A pair of dog tags hung around her neck, and I could just make out the name FLAX, CALLIOPE T.

My face flushed, getting hot as anger surged up from inside me. I knew that woman. I'd never forget that face as long as I lived. That was the bitch that went to Karen's apartment that day, looking for me. Because of her, my best friend was dead.

"It's a bitch, huh?" she asked. The dog let out a low growl, and when I flinched, she smiled to show a missing tooth in the front.

"What the hell do you want?" I asked. She knelt down and pet the dog on the side near the shaved patch. When she looked up at me, I could see there were black spots, like ink, spreading through the white parts of her eyes. It was like the carriers Penny and I had just seen at the Stillwell lab. The Huma carriers got them after they died and came back. She smiled again, and all of a sudden, I understood.

"You're one of them," I whispered.

Ai and the others knew she was still alive. They even knew she was important, important enough that they wouldn't let me or anyone else kill her no matter how many times I asked. She was off-limits, one of the elements that would play a crucial role when the event either did or didn't occur. They didn't know she'd been injected, though. They didn't know she was a carrier. That could be a game changer.

I leaned closer to get a better look. I couldn't see inside her or anything, but somehow I knew. I was sure. How was it that no one had picked her up?

Nico.

I frowned. He knew; he had to. He knew, and he kept it quiet. He was immune to our influence, so he was one of the few people that could keep secrets from Ai. He'd done this.

The dog barked, making me jump.

"Good dog," Calliope said. It bared its teeth and growled again. When it did, I saw its gums were bleeding. A string of rust-colored drool oozed between its fangs and blew in the wind.

My heart started to race, but instead of lunging, the dog turned and ran off. It kicked up sand as it headed toward the remains of the skyline. I let out a breath and looked back at the phone. It was still dark. I stowed it in my pocket. When I looked up, Calliope was gone too.

"Hello?" I called. No one answered.

Carefully, I stepped down the slope. Sand squished under my leather boots as I followed the dog tracks toward the broken wall of a building. The remains of a stairwell there led up to a chunk of what used to be the second floor. I climbed up and stood on the edge, then looked out over the wreckage for anything that seemed like it might be important.

If you stay calm, Ai had told me again and again, *then you'll know what you're looking for when you see it. You'll feel it.*

Ai was, hands down, the strangest person I had ever met in my life. Never mind her stunted body with its baby hands and too-big head; half the time it was hard to understand what she was even talking about. Half the time she wouldn't look at you when she talked to you, and she'd answer things you said like you'd just said something totally different. She spooked me at first, and sometimes, secretly, she frustrated me.

I realized, though, after a while that all of it was because she was like me, only worse. She had visions almost all the time, but she learned to stay at least semilucid during them. When you were with her, a lot of times there were others in the room that only she could see. Sometimes I think they were other versions of people who were already there. I don't know how she kept it all straight. Honestly, I don't know how she didn't kill herself years ago. It was bad enough when it happened on and off. If I had to live in that nightmare full-time, I'd have gone off the deep end before I hit puberty.

She was strange, and she spent half her time floating in an isolation tank, and the other half running on custom-made psychoactive drugs. But she was, in a weird way, almost like a mother to me, which is something I hadn't had in a long time. She taught me more in just a few years than I think I'd ever learned before in my whole life.

I looked out over the ruins and sighed, smelling gas fumes again. If Ai was right, then this place really did exist somewhere, just one version of the city in an endless string of them. The closer that one of them matched ours, the more it bled over for people like me to see. Visions like the wasteland bled over a lot. It meant that's where we were headed.

"We made a mistake. You have to be the one to—"

Me. Element One. I was supposed to somehow help stop all this. But how?

In the distance, more bodies lay half-buried in the sand. The sun glinted off shiny, metallic bits that were scattered around. They were some kind of components that came from revivors. From the amount on the ground, there must have been thousands of them there at one point, but whatever happened, they were long gone, along with everyone else.

Up ahead, I could make out one building that was more intact than the rest. It must have been huge when it was still standing, because what was left looked like it could fill a city block. The wreckage drew my attention. It seemed to vibrate, almost like a tuning fork. I could actually sense a far-off, high-pitched wail. That spot was important.

That's it. That's where it starts, the thing that triggers all this destruction. When I looked at it, something almost pulled me forward. I brushed my hair out of my face and climbed back down the steps.

I hiked toward it while the sun beat down on my scalp and sand got in my boots. The air was so dry, it made my throat hurt. When I finally got close enough, I stepped into the shade of what was left of the building and rested. The base of the building was piled with rubble, and nearby a big metal trash bin lay on its side, scorched and warped. Crushed against the pitted concrete were the remains of a sign that might have been mounted on the side of the building at one point. Sockets for lights were arranged to form big letters, but it was too damaged to tell what it said. Giant metal brackets ran down one edge of the frame, twisted and snapped.

I stared at the sign and let it fill my line of sight like Ai had told me. I stared until it blurred in front of me and the light around me got brighter. Sometimes if you focused just right, you could see not just the possibility being presented in the vision, but all the ones before it too. The farther out you went, the farther ahead the timeline went so if you flipped through them going backwards . . .

The light got brighter and the air rippled in front of me. My vision collapsed to a tunnel, until all I could see was the shape of the ruined sign. The surface of it began to warp. The blackened metal on the sign inverted and the soot began to fall away. The bent brackets straightened and turned shiny again. Powder boiled around it like fog and then formed lights in each empty socket, while pain began to build in my head.

"Zoe," a voice said. It was Ai's voice. The scene in front of me wavered as my concentration threatened to break.

Come on . . .

The building began to reform. Dust and debris and

a zillion glass shards rose and took shape. It was huge. Mirrored glass formed massive sheets that tumbled back up into the air, then back into place as the walls reformed. The structure grew until it would have towered above even the other skyscrapers that once surrounded it. A warm trickle began to creep from one of my nostrils as the pain in my head got worse.

"Zoe, listen to me." Out of the corner of my eye, I could see her. She was standing a few feet away, staring up at me with her large, penetrating eyes.

"Wait," I told her. "I can see it. . . ."

"You're in terrible danger," she said. "You have to wake up now."

The twisted sign broke free of the sand and rose into the air to remount on one side of the building. As it did, it turned slowly, and I saw the lights that spelled out its name flicker on.

ALTO DO MUNDO

I gasped, and the sign fell. A loud boom went off, so loud it made my teeth rattle. The building's glass panels warped and all of them blew into dust. I clamped my hands over my ears as a sound like thunder cracked through the air and the ground shook under my feet. I stumbled and tried not to fall as the dust mushroomed up all around me.

"Zoe, wake up!"

The last thing I saw before I closed my eyes was the silhouette of the building's peak as it sank down into the cloud. The whole building was imploding, crashing down toward the street as voices all around began to scream. . . .

I snapped awake to the sound of a car horn and sirens. Nearby I heard people running, their footsteps crunching on broken glass. Over the racket, someone was screaming.

What the hell?

All the blood had rushed to my face and my head throbbed. I opened my eyes and saw blacktop through the windshield, which had been webbed with cracks. My hair hung down over the blood-spattered dome light, where the neck of a glass bottle lay among broken shards. I was upside-down, hanging from my seat belt. As I watched, more dots of blood appeared to join the others.

"Penny?"

Several pairs of feet ran by the window to my right, and I heard something smash in the distance. A voice was barking over a bullhorn, but I couldn't make out what the man was saying. I could smell smoke and gasoline.

I pawed the deflated skin of the airbag away and looked to my left. Penny's body hung limp from her seat belt, lines of blood painted down one side of her face. Behind her eyelids, I could see her eyes moving back and forth.

"Penny, wake up," I said. "We're in trouble."

A gunshot went off somewhere close by, and people screamed. Penny sucked in a quick breath and her eyes snapped open as two more gunshots went off, their muzzle flashes reflecting off the ice through the window.

"Zoe?" she called.

"I'm right here."

She looked over, and for a second I saw tears shine in her eyes. She reached out and touched my face, turning my head gently so she could see better.

"I'm okay," I said.

She clenched her teeth and held on to the steering wheel with one hand while she reached down and released the latch on her belt. She lowered herself carefully, then crouched on the roof's interior while she twisted around to face me.

The latch on my seat belt was stuck, so she took a thin knife from her boot and cut it. I slipped into her arms and she guided me down.

"Let me see," she said, brushing my hair away from my face. I could feel it was wet with cold blood, and tried to twist away.

"It's fine," I said. "I'm . . . fine. What happened?"

"Fawkes did it," she said. "He sent the trigger code. The Huma carriers, they've all turned."

"I saw her," I said. "That bitch Flax . . . she's one of them."

"The slum rat?" I nodded.

"I saw her. She's a carrier—"

We both jumped as something hit the window next to me hard, and I turned to see a homeless man crouched there with a brick in one dirty hand. Black spots had bled through the whites of his bloodshot eyes, and through the gap in his disgusting beard I could see teeth that were yellow and brown. He stared at us through the glass as he reared back the brick again and smashed it against the glass. If it hadn't been bulletproof, it would have broken for sure.

"Here," Penny said, grabbing my elbow. She pulled me over next to her, away from the window, as a loud boom went off and something left a big divot in the glass right in the middle of a big splash of blood. The homeless man convulsed and went face-first onto the pavement, the brick tumbling out of his hand. A second shot went off and the body twitched. More blood splattered against the outside of the window and began to roll down it.

"Idiots," Penny snapped. She slammed her fist against the car horn and it blared. Through the bloody glass I saw two uniformed soldiers with assault rifles peer toward us. One signaled for the other to hold his fire.

Penny checked the video phone on the dash, but the screen was cracked and it wouldn't come on. She dug her cell phone out of her pocket and made a call while the soldiers approached the car.

"It's me," she said after a second. "Yeah, we're okay. We need a pickup."

The two soldiers came up to the car door, and one of them shoved the homeless man's body out of the way. The other one wiped blood from the window and looked in at us.

"Is there anyone else inside?" he shouted, trying to see into the back. I shook my head.

His partner fired a couple shots at something I couldn't see down the street, as Penny snapped her phone shut. The soldier who had spoken to me tapped the other one on the shoulder and pointed at a woman, wearing a bloodstained nightshirt and nothing else, who was running barefoot down the rows of stopped traffic. One of them held up his hand as she closed the distance between them.

"They're sending a helicopter to pick us up," she said. "We just need to get to—"

A loud, low boom thumped through my chest as the woman in the nightshirt exploded just a few feet from the car. I caught a flash of pieces—an arm and a head—as they blew outward. Then the soldiers crashed back against the glass and everything was covered in blood. The car rocked as shrapnel slammed into it.

"Shit!"

Penny grabbed my arm and heaved the driver's-side door open with a loud groan I could barely hear through the ringing in my ears. She dragged me out into the street and hauled me to my feet as a blast of cold wind blew black, stinking smoke over us.

The street was a mess. As far as I could see, traffic was stopped, and it looked like a lot of the cars had been abandoned. Lights from police cars and a fire truck flashed, and I could hear sirens wail in the distance. Groups of people ran every which way while others lay bleeding in the snow on the sidewalks. Gunshots echoed between the buildings, and I saw them going off down the street in the distance. A chopper banked overhead and shined a floodlight down over the mayhem.

I jumped as a shot went off behind me, and I spun around to see Penny fire a second shot into a shambling homeless man with black spots in his eyes. He staggered back, then turned and ducked behind a box truck that had one wheel up on the curb.

"Come on!" she yelled. She grabbed my hand in her free one and squeezed tight. "Stay close!"

She almost pulled my arm out of the socket as she ran for clear spot between the jammed vehicles and I stumbled after her, holding on. I reached inside my jacket and pulled out my own gun as we ducked down an alleyway and underneath a group of sharp, brown icicles that hung from the grate of a fire escape. We slipped past a row of rusted trash cans and out onto a side street where a stream of people ran down the sloping sidewalk.

We almost got knocked down as she shoved our way in. I hoped she knew where the hell she was going. We went with the flow, while the faster people pushed their way through on either side of us. When we got to a parking garage, she slammed a metal side door open with one shoulder.

"Up!"

She let go of my hand and fired a shot back behind us as I ran up the concrete stairs as fast as I could go. My heart was pounding and my throat was raw from the cold. I thought I might throw up, and I wasn't sure how much farther I'd be able to run. I'd started to slow down when I felt her arm around my waist, pulling me up along with her.

"Faster. Move!"

I don't know how many flights we took. By the time we reached the top and I staggered out onto the roof behind her, my legs were like jelly and I could barely

breathe. Against the lights of the city, I saw bunches of
figures standing near the rails at the roof's edge. Some
looked back at us, while others pointed at a helicopter as
it approached and began to descend.

When they realized it was going to touch down on the
roof, they began to crowd it, and a voice yelled over a bullhorn as a floodlight shone down on them. Penny grabbed
my hand again and weaved through the ring of people as
the wind from the rotors kicked up snow, salt, and sand.

"Back away from the landing area!" the voice from
the helicopter boomed. The helicopter hovered fifteen
feet above the crowd and a door on the side slid open.
Two soldiers with assault rifles were crouched on either
side of it.

We pushed out into the open area in the middle of the
circle, and I shielded my eyes with my gun hand as my
hair whipped around my face. I was going to pass out; I
was sure of it. Other people saw us break the barrier and
started to follow. The helicopter wouldn't be able to land.

"Back away from the landing area or we will open
fire!" the voice echoed over the thump of the rotors.

Penny spun around and fired two shots over the
heads of the crowd. Those in the path ducked down in
a group, and there was a collective gasp before some of
the tougher-looking customers recovered and began to
focus on us. I could feel the minds changing around us
as they began to realize the helicopter was not there to
rescue them. It was there to pick us up, but not them.

I wanted to tell them the helicopter wouldn't take
them, that it wouldn't matter what they did. Even if they
killed us, it wouldn't take them. I tried to focus on them,
to calm them down and ease them back before someone got hurt, but I couldn't. My head was spinning and I
couldn't concentrate on even one of them.

The helicopter managed to touch down, and as the
bodies surged around us, the two soldiers jumped out

and aimed their rifles out over the crowd. One fired a long burst over their heads and didn't let up until they were all crouching. Penny dragged me along with her, out into the clearing and toward a third soldier, who signaled us from inside the helicopter.

"Get down on the ground now!" a voice boomed. The soldier fired another burst, and they started to get down on their knees.

"You can't leave us here!" a man screamed, his voice hoarse. He had gotten back up and started toward us. "Fuck you. You can't just—"

A single shot cracked and the man staggered back before falling to the ground. I saw blood begin to burble out of a hole in his chest. Penny and I marched between the two soldiers as I looked back and saw faces that were full of fear, anger, and hatred.

The man on the ground stared up at me, his breath coming in puffs that were carried off by the freezing wind. The light that swirled around his head was confused and scared in those last moments before his eyes went out of focus and it evaporated into the night air alongside his last breath.

Calliope Flax—FBI Home Office

Cal, are you there? It was Nico.

Nico, I said. *Shit, it's about time. Are you in one piece?*

The whine from the incoming signal had cut out about a mile back. The transfer was done, and the jacks were on the move again. Police and soldiers were trying to keep them in check but there were too many streets not enough bodies to cover them.

I'm okay. Where are you? he asked.

Heading back to base.

Down a slope on the other side of the guardrail, I saw a pair of cops put three jacks against the wall be-

hind a drugstore and shoot them. I cruised behind a strip
mall and saw blues flash between the buildings where a
group of soldiers were moving in. More gunfire cracked
behind us as I squeezed back out into the parking lot,
then back onto the sidewalk. People hugged the store-
fronts as they saw me coming.

"Out of the way!"

Vika bucked on the seat behind me as we hit a ridge
of ice and caught air for a second. The bike fishtailed just
as a man shoved a sheet of plastic out of the way and
jumped out of the alley ahead of us. Vika squeezed my
waist tighter as he grabbed for us and I steered out of his
way. When I blew past him, I caught a flash of light in his
eyes, and the static in my head crackled.

It's nuts out here, Nico.

I know. I'm at the FBI building. Can you get here?

What for?

*I want to run something past you. Off the wire. It's
important.*

I looked down the street. The traffic was jammed as
far as I could see. The Federal Building was a lot closer
than the base, and I could drop the kid off there too.

I'll be there.

Thanks. I cut the line, and called in to get a new route
to the FBI. Dispatch pulled up the traffic reports and
drew one out for me.

Stay off Stark Street; it's gridlocked, the guy said. He
fed me a new route.

Roger that. I changed direction and took us down a
narrow ramp with chain-link on one side and pitted concrete on the other. We passed into the shadows under
the monorail, and a couple pairs of eyes flashed in the
dark. Something knocked over a shopping cart and
stumbled behind a rusted pylon, but I didn't see if it was
human or not.

A shot boomed and more people scattered as I veered past a line of cars stuck behind a crash. Two more went off behind us as we approached a vehicle rolled over on its side, fire and smoke pouring out from the undercarriage. When we passed it, I saw a burned body through the back windshield.

This is fucked.

I took us through an alley to the main drag, where the Federal Building was. Something else scrambled across the street ahead and the static in my head picked up, a spike in the white noise. There was one nearby.

Vika tapped my back. Up ahead the space between the brick walls got narrow and there was a trash bin at the mouth of the alley.

Thrs 1. The message popped up on my JZI. The little shit had some kind of implant. She tapped my back again, and I saw her point from behind me.

Thr.

The crackle got louder. I saw something move from behind the trash bin. In the shadows, a pair of eyes flashed.

I cruised to a stop but kept the engine running. The thing trudged out from behind the box, and I drew my gun.

The static hissed as its feet scraped on the pavement. It was a street guy with a nasty beard and gaps in his teeth. I caught him in the headlight and saw that the whites of his eyes were stained black.

I put one in the guy's forehead. The back of his head blew out, and he fell back against the metal bin. Steam rose off his sticky hair as he slumped over into the snow.

Nice shot.

I glanced back at her. When I scanned her, I found a JZI, or some half-assed version of one. It had a com link, but not much else.

Where'd you get the hardware? I asked.

Army. 2 yrs.

Two years in the army. The kid was sixteen, if that, so it wasn't the UAC army. She had to be a refugee from somewhere in the Slav bloc. Who knew how she ended up here?

I drove past the body and back out onto the street. On the main road, a Stillwell truck used a winch to pull a wreck out of a snowbank. The FBI building was up ahead.

I parked on the sidewalk next to the entrance, and when I stood up my knee buckled for a second. The HUD on my JZI flickered, and a band of static squiggled past.

"You okay?" the kid asked.

"I'm fine. Come on."

I tasted bile in the back of my throat as I headed up the stairs. Fawkes's trigger didn't kill me along with the rest, but something was wrong. I didn't feel right. I was wound up, like I wanted to break something, but I didn't know why. I took a deep breath and blew it out my nose as I pushed open the main door.

Inside I flashed my badge at the guard. He gave a nod and buzzed us in.

"I shouldn't be here," Vika said in the lobby. It was a madhouse in there. Security was doubled and people were backed up coming and going. I shoved my way past them and dragged the kid after me.

"They got better things to care about," I said. "No one cares if you're illegal."

"I'm not illegal."

"Whatever you are, no one cares."

"I'm not a criminal either."

"Shut up."

Nico, I'm here. Where are you?

Fifteenth floor, east wing.

I picked up a kid on the way. Where do you want her?

Put her in Conference Room B and someone will take care of her. Meet me outside the war room.

Got it.

At the fifteenth floor, I took her east and dumped her in the conference room like Nico said.

"Give me five minutes," I told her.

"Wait—"

"Five minutes. Don't wander off."

Vika opened her mouth again, and I shut the door.

Bch.

I made my way down the hall and picked Nico's node out of the mess. When I got close, I tuned in on their chatter.

". . . analysis of the canines recovered at the storage yard is more or less complete. There's no doubt at this point—the nodes we recovered from the animals were created by a version of Heinlein Industries' M10 series, code named Huma. However, after some study, it would appear that there are key differences in the underlying nanotech."

"What differences?" That was Nico.

"We're still trying to determine that," a voice said. "We're working to bring in experts in the field, but without access to Heinlein, there's only so much we can do. All I can say right now is that it's not the original prototype. It's been altered."

I opened the door, and when I stuck my head in, a bunch of suits looked over. A shit-ton of photos were up on the wall in front of the table; I saw a train yard, some burned bodies, and a bunch of wire cages that were ripped open. One was a close-up of wet fur and a shaved patch of gray skin. There was a big bite mark that was puffed and scabby.

"All of the animals we recovered exhibited these wounds," a woman said. "We were able to match at least some to the recovered canines."

"They bit each other?" That was that prick, Van Offo.

"So it would seem. That behavior isn't completely unusual in revivors, but the number of wounds suggests the urge to attack and bite was amped up in these specimens and that would fit with what we're seeing on the streets right now. The shaving of the fur seems to suggest the sites were either being treated or monitored."

"Why reanimate dogs at all?"

"We don't know yet, but those animals appear to have been the main focus of whatever they were doing there."

I saw Nico across the room and snapped my fingers in the air.

Hey, asshole.

He looked over, and when he saw me, he smiled. His face had taken a beating. He had a cut through one eyebrow, and there was a bad bruise around his neck. When he stood up, I saw him wince, but all in all he looked okay.

"The basement caller has been identified as Harold Deatherage," Nico's boss, Hsieh, said. "Agent Wachalowski has provided two other names as well: Ang Chen and Dulari Shaddrah. All three were involved with the M10-series project. And as I'm sure you all know by now, Ang Chen has been assisting directly with the development of the countervirus."

"Where is Chen now?" someone asked.

"Not at his residence or at the Stillwell base. We believe he is most likely somewhere inside Heinlein Industries."

"So Fawkes has him?"

"We now believe he's been working with Fawkes all along. The program responsible for issuing the activation sequence was embedded in the computer systems at the Stillwell compound. They were able to trace it back to his ID."

"He was vetted," Van Offo said. "How was he able to lie to us?"

"We don't know," Alice said. "But it looks like that's what he did."

"What about the other two?"

"Shaddrah is most likely also on the Heinlein campus, but we think Deatherage might be on the run. The statements he made during his call suggested that whatever they were planning he might have gotten cold feet at the last minute and tried to back out. A team hit his residence an hour ago and found the body of a woman identified as his wife, but no one else. We know he bought a plane ticket out of the country, and we're covering the airports, but so far there's no sign of him."

"I might have a lead there," Nico said. "It looks like he had a woman, probably a mistress, set up in an apartment in Palos Verdes. I doubt the wife had that information to give up. Agent Van Offo and I will head over there."

"So we're unable to verify the purpose of either the Mother of Mercy or Black Rock facilities at this point?" a guy asked.

"Not yet," Hsieh answered. "Scans have detected traces of nanostructures inside all of the recovered brain tissue, but nothing resembling revivor nodes in any of the human victims."

"What about the transmission from earlier in the day?" Van Offo asked. "The one that froze them temporarily?"

"I know what that was," I said. Everyone turned around to look at me. Nico grinned just a little.

"Who the hell are you?" some guy in the back asked.

"I've seen it before," I said. "A field upgrade will make them freeze up for a minute."

"What makes you think—" the guy started, but Hsieh cut him off.

"Quiet, Vesco," she said. "Miss Flax is correct. As of twenty minutes ago, our techs were been able to decipher at least a portion of the transmission, and it looks like it was some kind of field upgrade that caused them to reinitialize afterward. Right now, our best theory is that Fawkes somehow enlisted the help of the individuals from Heinlein, Ang Chen in particular, to develop a Huma variant that would not be vulnerable to our countervirus. As of oh-eight-hundred hours this morning, his entire army may or may not be completely protected against that contingency."

That got some fur up. Voices rumbled through the room, until Hsieh shut them up.

"We don't know that for sure!" she snapped. "The current plan is still to attempt to use the virus. We could be wrong. We could be right, but Fawkes's attempt to guard against the virus could have failed. We don't know yet. After the transmission there have been more behavioral changes. So for all we know, that might have been the whole point of the alteration."

"What kind of changes?"

"Heightened aggression, mainly. An increased impulse to attack and bite even without specific direction over the command spoke. Some have begun eating from victims—the ghrelin inhibitor has definitely been switched off since they first went active. For all we know, that was the only purpose behind this. The good news, if you want to call it that, is that this upgrade appears to have affected all M10 nanoblood in the field, including the payloads found in prosthetics. Agent Wachalowski has provided a viable nanoblood sample. Once it's analyzed, we'll know more."

A lot of eyes looked over at Nico.

"Should he be in the field?" someone asked.

"He's fine," Alice said. At least one guy didn't look sure, though.

"That stunt he pulled this morning was a long reach from 'fine,'" he said. "I think we should . . ." He spaced, then, drifting off midrant like he was stoned or something. Hsieh's pupils opened as she stared them down, and the rest shut up.

"Agent Wachalowski is not a revivor," she said, clipped, "and he is vital to this case. Nanoblood from prosthetics doesn't intermingle with a person's organic systems, and he has experienced no symptoms of any kind. Right?" She shot that last bit at Nico.

"Right," he said, but there was something off about the way he said it. Was he lying?

"How'd he manage the code push?" I asked. "Back in the grinder, command used a satellite for that."

Hsieh turned to the wall and a photo popped up of a big cluster of satellite dishes mounted on a frame behind a wall of buildings.

"This is Heinlein Industries' transmitter array," she said. "It's used to communicate with the UAC satellite network for defense, and also for the specific purpose of field upgrades. We've verified the transmission was sourced from this array and bounced back from Heinlein's satellites. This transmitter is also how Fawkes is currently controlling the nuclear satellite, Heinlein's Eye, and his Huma units in the field. It's the lynchpin of his strategy and a high-priority target, but before we can move on it the Department of Defense needs to determine whether or not this might trigger a launch of the ICBMs."

Woah, I said to Nico. *What launch?*

He waved at me to shut up.

"And what if it will?" he asked.

"Osterhagen has a team working on taking control of the grid back," she said. "Stillwell is ready to move on

the facility the second we do. They're doing everything
they can. For now just get over to Palos Verdes. I'll keep
you informed."

Nico signaled to me, and I saw Van Offo watch as he
took me back out the door and into the hall.

"What launch?" I asked. "What was she talking
about?"

"ICBMs. Fawkes has twelve of them pointed at the
city."

ICBMs. That meant nukes.

"Why? What the hell does he want?"

"We don't know for sure," he said, "but the bottom
line is, we have to get to him first. To do that I'm going
to need your help."

"You got it," I said. He waved me into another conference room and shut the door. He turned on the noise
screen and leaned in close.

"When you did your tour, you worked with the M8
series, right?"

"Yeah."

"Did you ever hijack a revivor from an existing command network?"

"Sure."

"Without using some kind of override code?"

"No."

"Never?"

"There's only one way to command a jack," I said,
"and that's over a command spoke. You set up a new
spoke, or you take over one that's there already. You
know that. What are you after?"

"I'm looking for a way to take control of one or more
revivors from an existing command network, without
tipping off the person controlling them."

"Oh," I said. I'd pulled that kind of thing off back in
the grinder. "Sure. You can set that up, but you need to
grab a revivor from the target network."

"These revivors are behind Heinlein's security perimeter, Cal. I won't have physical access to them."

"You need a live command spoke from a jack that can't turn you in to the original commander—Fawkes."

He rubbed his nose, and I saw his right hand. It was gray, like mine. There were black scabs fused over deep gouges in the knuckles. Those came from teeth. He'd bashed someone good.

"Shit, Nico."

I grabbed his sleeve and pushed it up. The gray skin and black veins went up to his elbow.

"It's fine."

"Bullshit."

I put my dead hand on his. The skin was the same color. Usually skin felt hot under it, but now his hand was as cold as mine. He gave my dead fingers a squeeze with his. Then he pulled away. He yanked the sleeve back down.

"I heard what you did down at the VA," I said. "That doesn't sound like you. You okay?"

"I'm fine."

"You don't look fine."

"I'm fine," he said again, looking at the back of his dead hand for a second. "I think I might have some bleed-through, that's all."

He meant nanoblood leaking through the filter that joined a new limb and infecting the real blood on the other side. It happened sometimes with a rush job, or if you stressed a new joint too much, too soon. He said it like it was no big deal, but it was. You could die from that.

"'That's all'?"

"I'll get it looked at," he said. "Never mind me. What about you? The inhibitor worked, then?"

"I'm still here, aren't I?"

He smiled. "I'm just glad you're okay."

"Me too," I said. "I mean, I'm glad you're okay." He looked like he was going to say something else, but before he could I punched him in the arm—his good arm.

"Yeah, yeah," I said. "I know. Me, too. I got to get back to base. Tell me what you need."

"For now, let's say I'm able to get access to one of the revivors without Fawkes knowing," he said. "How would I take control of the rest?"

"Easy. My CO showed me on week one. You keep the one you grab on the command spoke so you don't tip anyone off, then drill into its control center to keep it quiet. Physically drill. After that, you can use a special package to set up your own command net, right on top of the first one."

"That works?"

"Kind of. Any jacks you spoke to will take orders from either person controlling them, so you can still get caught. How many is he running total?"

"Inside Heinlein, probably hundreds."

"Perfect. He can't keep his eye on that many; it's fucking impossible. Pick a few he doesn't move, ones on autopilot, and use those."

"Do you have the modules to do this?"

"I can get them."

"Do it. Keep this quiet."

"I'll need to call in a favor."

"Just keep it off the network. Fawkes had men inside Heinlein. He might have them here too. I'll only have one shot at this."

"Don't worry about—"

I stopped short. A shiver ran down my spine. I heard it before I even knew I heard it.

"What is it?" Wachalowski asked.

The sound came from outside. I'd heard it enough times in the grinder to know you hit the deck when you did. It was the sound of rotors. A Chimera was coming in hot.

"Nico, get—"

The wall to my left blew into a thick cloud of powdered concrete and glass as a Gauss chain gun unloaded on the side of the building. The turret howled as it tore open the conference room around us. I caught a flash of the building across the street through the hole behind me, then hit the floor with my hands over my head.

Dust and grit fell over me as back across the hall, the wall into the war room got carved out. The conference table inside was blown to sawdust, and the people around it popped into clouds of guts. Some guy's arm spun in the air as the wall behind him disappeared.

"Nico!"

I couldn't hear shit. The turret ripped open the floor, and bodies fell through. I saw a bank of screens go down after them, spitting sparks, before a wall of smoke blew over me and the lights went out.

Cal, where are you?

I'm here.

I couldn't see shit either. I could just make out shapes of people as they got back up on either side of the missing floor. The Chimera peeled off, but I heard it bank back to make another pass.

Cold wind blew through from outside and cleared the air at least a little. Wachalowski got up and jumped the gap between us. The tile broke away under his heel, and I grabbed his wrist, then hauled him over.

Street level, he sent, and pointed behind me at the door back out to the hall.

I ran to it and turned the handle, but the wall had shifted and it was stuck. I put my shoulder to it twice and it banged open as the chain gun went off again and the wall across the room exploded.

Wht the fk?
The kid.

Nico slammed into me and shoved me through the doorway and into the hall. He'd made for the stairs when he saw me stop short.

Cal, what are you doing?
The kid.

She was back in the conference room. There was still a clear path to it. I ran for it, Nico on my heels. I cut across the hall and heard him yell, right before the sound of the turret drowned him out. Hot air hit my back, and the floor dropped out from under me. I grabbed the door handle as tiles fell away, hanging on while my boots dangled in the open air. On what was left of the hall in front of the door, I got my footing and climbed back up.

When I pushed open the door I saw her there, up against the far wall. I turned back toward Nico and saw that the hall behind me was gone. He stood on the other side of the gap, ready to jump.

Don't. I'm coming back.

"Kid, come on!" I yelled. I dragged her to the door while she screamed something from behind me. I looked down through the hole and saw a two-story drop to the offices below.

"Hold still!"

"Don't. We'll fall!"

I cinched her around the waist and she screamed as I hoisted her up on my shoulder, then took two steps and jumped.

I cleared it, but when my foot hit the other edge, the floor buckled, and for a second I thought I'd go right through. I didn't. I fell forward on one knee and Nico caught me. He grabbed Vika as she flipped off my shoulder, and dragged her back from the edge.

Back this way, he said. *Hurry.*

Vika stumbled after him, and I kept to the rear to

make sure she didn't fall behind. He took us down another hall to a stairwell. He opened it with his badge and signaled for us to go through.

The stairs shook as we went down. Behind us the wall blew out and sparks sprayed as the metal rails were shredded. Cold air blew in from outside, and as rubble came down, I saw a body fall end over end through the snow.

I hit the floor on the landing and Vika came down on top of me. Nico slammed off one wall and reached for me. A chunk of concrete banged off the wall next to his head. I put my boot on the kid's bony ass and shoved her down the next flight of stairs as the turret turned its fire back the other way.

For the next eight flights we ran, the sounds of the attack slamming through the stairwell from above. Then it stopped. I could barely hear through the ringing in my ears.

Nico cracked open the door and looked through. He signaled it was clear, and we followed. Outside it was a mess. Glass and concrete covered the street where cars were stuck end to end. A desk had come down through the roof of one of them, and I could see bodies in the road. My bike was totaled, crushed under an avalanche of shit. Blood and oil ran down the blacktop.

Everything sounded like I was underwater, but through the ringing, I could make out the sound of rotors. They were pulling up and away. Nico had his gun out as we followed him to the sidewalk. Up in the air I could see the shadow of the Chimera as it banked around the side of a building down the street.

I looked back at the FBI building. Ten floors' worth of the face was gone. Junk had spilled out of the hole, down onto the street. A million papers fell through the snow. Vika watched one of them come down like she was in a trance.

Wind sheared down the street and stirred up a cloud of dust. Orange light sparked in Nico's eyes as he checked for survivors.

"Wachalowski!" The voice came from the gate to the garage. It was Van Offo.

"Come on," he called. "They could be back."

"Come on where?" I asked.

"There's still people in there," Nico said.

"Rescue's on their way," Van Offo said. "We need to go now. We'll take a vehicle from the lot."

"Go where?" I asked.

"Stillwell's got a foothold a few blocks up," he said. "Your squad will meet us there. Come on, we've got to move."

"They're here," Vika said. A burst of static popped in my head.

I turned, and across the street, I caught a flash of moonlight white from a pair of eyes. A jack had been watching us. Behind it, I saw there were more.

Off to the left, another one moved out of an alleyway, then another. The static turned loud and steady.

"Let's go," Nico said.

Paper blew down the street like snow as we made for the garage.

5

EVENT HORIZON

Zoe Ott—Alto Do Mundo

By the time I could see Alto Do Mundo through the helicopter's windshield, I'd thrown up everything there was to throw up. My stomach twisted into a knot, and my throat burned as sweat rolled down my face. I was concentrating, my jaw clenched, on the huge, lit spire at the top of the tower when I heard the pilot shout back at us.

"Hold on!"

I felt Penny's hand on my back as I bit down and held on to the metal rail beside me. Something whipped through the air in front of us, and as it spun back around, the helicopter dropped underneath me.

Spit sprayed from between my teeth, hanging in a long strand. The lights outside spun by the window, and over the rotors I heard a high-pitched whine. There was another helicopter up ahead—no, two—and a huge muzzle flash flickered from underneath one of them. As the pilot spun us around and I slammed into the wall, I saw sparks and shattered glass explode in a trail across the side of a building. It rained down toward the street far below. A huge mob was forming down there around the building.

"They're firing on us! We need support up here now!"

The bottom dropped out from underneath me again and bile crawled up my throat. I hit the wall again as the two helicopters disappeared for a minute behind the spire.

"We're coming in now!"

The engine went up in pitch as the world tilted underneath us. Below, the roof of Alto Do Mundo was coming in very fast. Lights around a helipad began to flash, and I could make out soldiers as they ran past it to set up some kind of rig. One of them began to signal with a glowing baton.

"We're going to return fire," a voice crackled. "Hold your course!"

A flash went off on the rooftop and something hissed past the window next to me, trailing smoke behind it. A whistle sailed off into the distance, then was swallowed by the sound of the rotors.

"Was that a hit?" a voice asked.

"Negative. We missed them, but they're moving off."

I focused on Penny through my wet, tangled hair, and after a second she noticed me and met my eye. I reached out with one hand and groped; she moved closer and put her arm around me. As I shook, I felt her kiss me on top of the head.

A minute later we were on the ground, or the roof anyway. The soldiers flanked Penny and me as she helped me off the helicopter and across the helipad. The air was cold, but having solid ground under my feet and some fresh air made me feel better. I took a deep breath as more armed men arrived through a door about one hundred yards ahead and approached us. In no time, we were surrounded by men with guns.

Inside, the door thudded behind us and closed off the racket from the roof. The air was warm, and I rubbed my hands together, shivering as we followed the group of men to the elevator.

"Ai is waiting for you in the war room," one of the men said. Penny nodded and took a minute to wipe my face as the car went down two floors. In the mirrored interior of the elevator car, I looked horrible; my skin was a pale, sickly gray, and there were dark circles under my eyes. My hair was a mess and caked with dried blood on one side. There was a gash on my forehead that was still wet, with a big knot underneath it.

"Get a doctor to meet us down there," Penny told the man. "I want someone to look at that." He nodded.

"I'm okay," I said. She didn't answer. She was in crisis mode and wouldn't take no for an answer on anything, pretty much until she was out of it, so I just let it go.

The elevator doors opened and we followed the men down a long corridor, then through two doors with keypads to another hall where I could see a set of glass double doors up ahead. Through the glass I could see the room was dimly lit, and light from monitors flickered to make shadows. There was a crowd of people inside, sitting in leather chairs in a tight circle around a giant oval table in the middle of the room.

Ai was inside, I could sense her even though I hadn't seen her yet. I could sense her whenever I was inside the building with her, but right then it was even more intense than usual. Unlike most people, her thoughts were almost fractured, with each shard clicking away, doing its own thing. They were all bound together in a master pattern, like bits of stained glass that formed a picture in a window. They said she was the next step in evolution, and maybe she was but sometimes I secretly thought she was more of an accident. No other mind was quite like hers, not even the other powerhouses that were in there humming around it.

I'd never actually been inside the war room before. Two guards stationed outside opened the doors so that Penny and I could go in. The armed men who'd escorted us down left us at the door, then turned and went back the way they came.

The inside was impressive. All of Ai's top people were there, watching the far side of the room where a giant array of huge monitors were set up, each one displaying something different. In one, I saw General Osterhagen's face looking back at me. Robin Raphael looked out from another one. A third, twice the size of the rest, showed the future model like a gas nebula floating in space.

Some of the other screens had faces I didn't recognize, but most of them showed what I figured were live feeds from throughout the city. In one, I saw helicopters moving in between buildings, while people ran through the streets below. In another, I saw a vehicle on fire in the middle of a traffic jam, while soldiers tried to put it out. Everywhere I looked things were burning or smoking, and people were scared and hurt. It didn't seem real. Less than five hours ago, everything had been normal.

". . . the threat of the nukes is very real," I heard Osterhagen say as we walked in.

"How did this happen?" someone else on one of the other screens snapped.

"Unlike the activation code, this security breach didn't occur at the Stillwell compound. As best we can tell, he used contacts on the inside at Heinlein Industries to access the defense shield," Osterhagen said.

"You're saying this breach came from inside Heinlein Industries itself?"

"Heinlein Industries is connected to several other large military contractors, as well as the Department of Defense," Osterhagen said. "In addition, they have their own defense satellite which is tied to the grid."

"The Eye," a woman said.

"They have the means for sophisticated satellite access from inside Heinlein," Osterhagen said. "Somehow, someone on the inside was able to leverage that to find and exploit and tap into the main defense shield. We don't know exactly how it was done yet, but it would have taken a detailed understanding of the satellite system, and a lot of time to figure out how to crack it. This didn't happen overnight, and it didn't come from Ang Chen. Fawkes had others inside Heinlein helping him. Defense system specialists, with high-level access."

"How many have been compromised?"

"There's no way to know," Osterhagen said. "No one anticipated this move. It's one of the most secure facilities in the UAC, and we weren't watching Heinlein specifically."

"Is this it?" the older man asked. "Is the satellite's payload of ICBMs the catalyst for the event?"

"It's the source of the destruction in the visions," Mr. Raphael said. "It must be."

"But do we know?" someone asked.

"General," Ai said suddenly, and the rest of them stopped talking. "Can you regain control of the satellite?"

"I have a team on it," he said. He nodded offscreen and a window popped up in the corner of the monitor along with him. In the window was the face of a pale, blond man with intense eyes and drawn cheeks.

"This is First Lieutenant Hans Vaggot."

Eyes flashed when he said the name, and I sensed a kind of surge through the room, even from the group at the table who otherwise seemed to be in some kind of trance. The name Vaggot was tied to the very rare visions that took place inside the dark void, where most couldn't see. I knew there were several possibilities who they thought might be the man in question, but it looked like this might be the one.

I watched his face, but it didn't look familiar. In the vision, he was horribly deformed so it was impossible to know for sure if it was him. Those perfect, symmetrical features on the monitor didn't seem like they could belong to the monster I'd seen, but . . .

This can't be coincidence, I thought. *This has to be it. The event they've been talking about is real. It's happening.*

"Regaining control of The Eye would be trickier," Vaggot said calmly, "but we believe we can regain control of the nuclear satellite from here. We don't have a time frame yet, but confidence is high that Fawkes will not be able to hold on to his nuclear option very long."

"He doesn't need very long," someone said.

"Agreed," Vaggot said. "But if he wanted to launch, he'd have launched by now so he's waiting for something. If we can stay under his radar, he may lose this option before he has any kind of warning."

"And if you don't stay under his radar?"

"We'll cross that bridge when we come to it," Osterhagen said. "We cannot leave those nukes under his control. We have to take them back despite the risk. A secondary defense satellite is standing by to take out The Eye once the nukes are off the table, and air teams are ready to scramble and knock out Heinlein's ground defenses. After that, we'll send troops in to mop up what's left."

As I watched Vaggot, I found myself drawn to him. I closed my eyes, and when I reached out, I found it was surprisingly easy to contact him. His presence was very strong to me, and like some I had run into in the past, he was extremely open to my will.

I cracked my eyelids and peered at his face on the screen while I concentrated on his distant little candle flame, the way Ai had helped me master. He wasn't one of us; I could tell right away. He was sharp and intelligent, but not one of us. His mind hummed like an electronic machine, very compartmentalized and focused. He was worried, but he wasn't scared. He believed what he said, that he could take control of the nuclear satellite back from Fawkes and back into our hands at the Stillwell camp.

On the screen, he paused for a second, confused. He sensed me.

"Leave him alone," Ai said without looking at me. I eased off and let his consciousness fade away from me. "Mr. Vaggot, a lot rides on you."

"Yes, ma'am," he said. "I understand."

"I know you will not let us down." The window with his face in it flashed and went out.

"Mr. Raphael," Ai said, "how are efforts on the streets going?"

She sat at the head of the big table that faced the monitors, and unlike the rest, she sat cross-legged in the middle of a large, square pillow that was right up on the table itself. None of the others at the table looked at her or even seemed to know she was there. They stared down at the tabletop, eyelids half-closed. Her face had a slack, distant expression like it did when she was deep in a vision and flying on pentatrosin. She stared off at nothing, aware of the things around her but not seeing them. She didn't see us come in, but she'd known we were coming and knew we were there. One of the many pieces of her aura turned its individual pattern toward me, green light spiking up from out of the blue. With one tiny hand, she waved us over.

"The National Guard is being utilized primarily for humanitarian efforts at this point," Raphael said. His handsome face, young in contrast to Osterhagen's, which scowled from the monitor next to it, looked tired. "They can handle the peacekeeping effort for now. They're in the process of aiding the wounded and transferring them to local medical hubs, but the hospitals inside the hot zones are getting overrun. The streets are impassable along many major routes, though, and that's making transfer to outlying facilities difficult without using air traffic."

"Are the rescue teams encountering any resistance?" Ai asked, her soft, deep voice airy. "Are Fawkes's revivors engaging them?"

"Only as targets of opportunity," he said. "National Guard teams are blockading off areas, courtyards, and buildings to act as sanctuaries to people caught on the street or who can't get home. But they're filling up fast."

"Have there been attempts to run those blockades?" Ai asked.

"Several," Mr. Raphael said, "but not in any concentrated fashion. They haven't found any pattern to it."

"They are looking for us," Ai said, her eyes dreamy. "But they won't stop here, with this city. Before Fawkes destroys it, they will try to leave."

"They're clustered at the three towers," Osterhagen said, "but overall movement suggests that might be the case. They're spreading out to cover a wider area."

"It won't work," someone else said. "All main routes in and out are being locked down. Some will leak through, but not enough to do any real damage."

"They will leave," Ai said, causing some to glance at each other nervously. "What about the virus?"

"We were unable to deploy it successfully," Osterhagen said. "He noticed the breach, and cut off the subject we'd implanted; then, before we could try again, he cut off the lot of them. He must have identified them from the time stamp that keeps track of total reanimation time. He cut off every one of them that was active prior to his sending the code."

"The virus is sent," Ai said. Osterhagen frowned, but didn't contradict her.

"We've tried on several captured revivors, but the initialization time is too long," he said. "He knows what he's looking for now; by the time the virus has gathered the network information from the mesh and is ready to execute, he's already cut off the seed subject."

"A door is open," she said, staring into space. "Somewhere . . . someone he's not expecting and cannot see. The virus is sent."

"Do you know who?" Mr. Raphael asked. But Ai shook her head, just barely.

"I saw it," I said, and all the faces on the screens turned to me. Penny looked at me too.

"What?" Osterhagen asked.

"I saw it," I said. "After we crashed. I know who it is." The room spun a little as I moved toward the screens, but in spite of everything else, I smiled.

"Who?" Penny asked.

"She's one of your people," I said to Osterhagen. "A soldier, the one with the weird name . . . Flax."

"Calliope Flax?" Mr. Raphael offered.

I smiled again, feeling giddy. The night I first met Ai, Calliope went to my best friend's apartment, looking for me. For some reason, she'd beaten the hell out of her piece-of-shit boyfriend, Ted. And for payback, or just because he was pissed, he beat up Karen when she came home. He beat her so bad that time that she died, right in front of me.

I killed him for that. He was the second person I ever killed, and the first one I killed on purpose. I killed Ted, but the bitch who started it never got what was coming to her.

"Calliope Flax," I said, with a firm nod. "That's her. She's a Huma carrier."

"They checked her," Osterhagen said.

"Nico lied," I said. "He covered it up, kept it quiet. He called in a favor, faked it somehow, so we wouldn't find out."

Ai had turned to look at me and I saw her smile, just a tiny bit, as her big, spacey eyes looked into my mind. Osterhagen was saying something offscreen to someone, and I saw people move suddenly behind him.

"If she was infected with the same version and she's not dead yet," Mr. Raphael said, "then that might just be our in."

"Find her," Ai said in her airy voice. It sounded like it came from far away.

Something warm ran down my cheek, and when I wiped it away, I saw blood on my hand. Ai was staring at me, and I felt sweat trickle down my back as she seemed to move away, down a long, dark tunnel.

"Get that doctor down here now," I heard Penny snap at someone.

Good work, Zoe, Ai said, but her mouth hadn't moved. Everyone was talking at once, but I could barely hear them, like they were underwater.

I tried to thank her, but my throat had dried up and nothing came out. At the end of the tunnel, everything began to fall away. I was passing out.

Don't worry, Ai said in my mind, just before everything faded. *We'll find her. . . .*

. . . you're going to get your wish, after all.

Nico Wachalowski—Downtown

The attack had thrown the streets into complete panic. Not long after the first hit, another Chimera appeared and joined the first. They didn't stage another assault, but they prowled above the streets, waiting for something. Reports flooded in from all over as I crept down a narrow lane the guardsmen had set up for emergency traffic. The Chimeras could easily take out the scattered forces on the ground, but so far they hadn't done it. When the rescue choppers approached, they let them pass.

"Metro PD got hit too," Van Offo said from the back. I cut the wheel and felt a jolt go up my dead arm all the way to the shoulder. Some scrambled output trickled by on my HUD off in the corner of my eye.

Van Offo watched me in the rearview mirror.

"Did you hear me?" he asked.

"I heard—"

Pain stabbed into my head, and the gray hand clamped down on the wheel. My foot stomped on the brake, and Calliope jerked in her seat as the car slid to a stop on the wet pavement.

"What the hell?" she snapped.

My head throbbed and light flashed in my eyes. The scene through the windshield flickered, and for a few seconds I was somewhere else; it was a memory, but it was extremely vivid, almost like a hallucination. I was inside the Pleasantview apartment complex for the first time, to visit Zoe. I'd made my way to the seventh floor and had just knocked on her door.

The door opened, and a woman that wasn't Zoe answered. She was stocky and curvy, with a pretty, round face marred by a bad bruise. I didn't know who she was at the time, but I recognized her now as Karen Goncalves, Zoe's friend from downstairs. Behind her, the room was dark except for the flickering light of candles. I flashed my badge and told her who I was.

I remember this. That was the day I dropped off the case photos for Zoe to look at.

Before Karen could answer, another woman appeared. I thought it was Zoe at first, but it wasn't. She was small and skinny like Zoe, but her hair was black and her eyes were blue. Like Karen, I didn't recognize her back then, but I did now.

That's Penny Blount, one of Ai's operatives. Penny wasn't there that day. Karen had gone back inside, and a minute later she left when Zoe came to the door. . . .

"Go back in and tell her he's here," Penny said to Karen. *"Then get lost."*

Karen nodded, eyes dull, and went back inside. Penny looked up at me.

"You're a big one," she said. The pupils of her eyes widened, and I got dizzy. *"Why are you here?"*

I held up the envelope of evidence I'd brought for Zoe to look at. Without thinking, the words came out of my mouth.

"I believe Zoe may have extrasensory abilities. I want her to look at these." Penny smiled, genuinely amused.

"That's rich," she said. *"Okay, sure. Why not?"*

She walked away, down the hall. On the way past Zoe's neighbor's door, she pounded it twice with her fist.

"Stop in later and make sure nothing this guy drops off goes back to Ai," she said through the door. *"And pay more attention next time. She ODs, and you're dead."*

The scene dissolved as more code trickled by and the arm twitched again. The dead hand released its grip on the wheel. Behind us, a horn blared.

"What the fuck was that?" Cal asked. The car behind us blared its horn again as I spun the tires and took us through the gap in traffic ahead.

"Are you all right?" Van Offo asked.

"I'm fine." Sweat had beaded on my brow, and blood was pounding in my head. I clenched my jaw shut, resisting an urge to snap at Van Offo. My shoulder ached like hell. Acid burned in the back of my throat, and bitter saliva formed in my mouth. There was bleed-through, for sure, but I wondered if it wasn't worse than I thought. I needed to get to Heinlein, or at least back to the FBI to have it checked out, but neither one was an option at the moment.

Out of the corner of my eye, I saw Calliope watching me. I sucked my teeth and swallowed as the sudden urge to hit something surged, then faded again.

"You looked like you came off the hook there," she said in a low voice. "You need a tech."

Not in front of Van Offo, I told her.

"I said I'm fine." She looked back out the window.

You sure?

Shock, maybe, I said, but I wasn't convinced. What I'd seen was an old memory that had been wiped, almost like a symptom of Zhang's Syndrome but only revivors experienced that. Nanoblood contamination could cause a lot of problems, but it was rarely fatal, and even when it was, it didn't turn people into revivors.

Did it? I watched the black vein bulge across the back of the dead hand as I gripped the wheel.

Van Offo was watching us. Cal looked back out the window.

I got those mods for you, she sent. *The ones to run the stealth spokes. You still want them?*

Yes. She sent them over. They had military certificates attached, which meant she shouldn't have them, but I didn't ask.

"Vesco is dead," Van Offo said. "I just got confirmation. We lost Pell and Copely too. Noakes is still MIA; he may have been killed in the attack as well."

A row of connection requests flashed in the bottom of my periphery. Three went out. That left seven unaccounted for. A reporter on the radio continued to rattle off details, his voice loud and stressed.

". . . appear to have been a coordinated series of attacks. I repeat, an as-of-yet-unidentified group initiated a coordinated series of air attacks this morning on the six major police precincts, as well as the FBI Federal Building. From what we understand, these attacks were made by at least seven military Chimera assault helicopters. These helicopters are designed for tight maneuvering and urban combat, each one armed with a chain rail gun and a battery of spitfire missiles. . . ."

Seven simultaneous strikes. Fawkes had broken the lines of communication between the local police hubs and the FBI. It would take hours just to pick up the pieces and figure out who was left.

"Those Chimeras are from Heinlein's airfield," I said.

A group of people on foot darted into the street between my vehicle and the one in front of it, trying to cross. The sidewalks on either side were full of people who spilled onto the shoulder. Off to the right, a utility vehicle was stuck while trying to merge onto the main road. The driver honked the horn at a group of people on the crosswalk. The girl, Vika, sat in the back, wedged next to Van Offo. She watched out the window, her eyes sleepy. Her full name was Vika Popik. She turned out to be a refugee of sorts. She served a couple years in the Ukrainian army before her father smuggled her out of the country and paid to have a freighter sneak her into the UAC. That was the last time she'd seen him. She had a surplus communications implant that was at least ten years old, and a rudimentary targeting system. The com system didn't tap the language center, so she had to select letters from a simulated keypad in her HUD, but she was pretty quick at it.

Wachalowski, who's with you? It was Alice.

Van Offo, Flax, and a civilian.

We lost Noakes. We're trying to regroup now. I've got you on the GPS—there should be a roadblock up ahead of you. Can you see it?

I chirped the siren and flashed the blues, nosing out into the breakdown lane, where an officer in a plastic poncho was directing vehicles. I flashed my badge at him as we approached and he waved us through. I could see a roadblock in the distance off to my left.

Calliope snorted from the passenger's seat. "This is fucked."

I see it. Who's left at the FBI building?

A jet whipped by overhead, causing people on the street to jump and look up as it disappeared behind a high-rise.

No one; they're clearing out. It got chewed up pretty bad. Electricity, data, and water are all out. They managed to cut over all network and database connections to the backups, and we're running from there. Just get to the roadblock. Flax's Stillwell unit is there. They're waiting for you.

Understood.

She cut the line.

". . . the MX901 50mm magnetic-rail chain gun is capable of firing more than one thousand rounds a minute," the reporter barked over the radio. "Each round is capable of piercing the armor of most military vehicles, including tanks, which is their primary purpose. As witnessed today, these weapons are also capable of easily penetrating concrete and steel to devastating effect when turned on urban structures. . . ."

People had crowded onto the sidewalks, moving like shadows through steam from sewer grates and car exhaust. The normal flow of foot traffic had stopped. Some were trying to see what was happening. Others wanted to pass but couldn't. People were queued up outside stores. I saw a man squeeze through, carrying a case of bottled water, while another argued loudly with a street vendor in Chinese.

"They're gonna pop," Calliope said.

Every face looked scared. There was no violence yet, but panic simmered just below the surface out there. The military presence on the street helped, but with every media outlet broadcasting the carnage, they could see for themselves how bad it was. We'd been hit hard and were still reeling, and everyone knew it.

Something flickered in the corner of my eye, and it took me a second to realize it was the call request I'd left open to MacReady. He'd just picked up.

Use the new circuit. The message flashed in front of me as he cut the link. A new, encrypted connection appeared. I picked up and applied the provided key.

MacReady, where are you?

Inside the Pratsky Building of Heinlein Industries' campus, he said. *We need to be careful. Fawkes is monitoring communications.*

What does he want?

I haven't been able to determine that. To access the defense grid, and alter the existing revivors using the transmitter array, but I don't know what his ultimate goal is.

What do you know about Harold Deatherage, Ang Chen, and Dulari Shaddrah? There was a brief pause.

I know who they are.

Harold Deatherage called me during a raid of an illegal test facility and he dropped your name.

He paused again, and I was afraid he might break the connection. Several people ran past the front of the car while a police officer shouted after them. One man stopped in front of us, and I honked the horn.

I know them, he said. The man outside changed direction and ran off.

What is their connection to Fawkes?

I don't know.

Don't bullshit me, MacReady. There isn't time.

I'm not, he said. *We worked as a team on a classified project—that's how I know them. But if they're helping Fawkes, then that happened without my knowledge.*

What project?

The study of Zhang's Syndrome.

It was my turn to pause. Years ago, MacReady had been the one who first told me about Zhang's Syndrome. It was believed to be some kind of corruption of revivor memory during reanimation, but Fawkes had identified it for what it really was: erased or manipulated memories that returned to their original state after death. Supposedly, MacReady hadn't believed that.

The four of you worked on Zhang's Syndrome?

Among others.

For how long?

It doesn't matter now, Agent. What matters is that at least part of that team has become convinced that Fawkes is right.

Footage of the attacks was playing across a bank of screens in the window of a nearby electronics store. People were queued up around it as the audio blared through a speaker that sat on the sidewalk outside.

". . . as of yet, no one has claimed responsibility for these attacks, and no demands have been issued," the reporter said. "Several witnesses confirmed, however, that the helicopters that initiated the attacks were sporting the logo of the private military employed by Heinlein Industries. . . ."

So far the FBI had kept Fawkes and the nuclear threat off the radar, but that wouldn't last. Someone would dig it up. In an hour at the most, the media would be saturated with news of twelve ICBMs aimed down on our heads. Then we'd see real panic.

Fawkes has had men watching us from the inside, I said. *I could use a similar advantage right now.*

I'll do what I can.

I need access to a revivor on Fawkes's command network as well. Can you manage that?

What sort of access?

I'll need a control spoke and the ability to install custom packages.

He might notice that.

Can you do it, MacReady?

He understands revivor technology very well, Agent. He'll be scanning for intrusions, but I'll see what I can do. He's bringing online units that were being stored in the processing plant. That might be our best bet.

Good, I said. *Actually, that's perfect. The processing plant is where the Leichenesser stores are kept, right?*

Each revivor that came off Heinlein's line was implanted with a seed of the necrotized, flesh-eating substance in case of emergency. Even trace amounts of it would consume a revivor in seconds.

Yes. It's kept in liquid form in cold storage within the plant itself.

Where is Fawkes based?

Here inside the Pratsky Building.

I want to move some of it from the processing plant to his location.

You'll never get it close to him, Agent.

I won't need to. If it hasn't been gelatinized, it will turn to gas when it hits the air. If I can get it into the climate-control system, will that be enough?

MacReady thought about it for a minute.

That might work, he said.

An alert flashed on the HUD in front of me. The advance team was reporting trouble at Palos Verdes.

"Damn it . . ."

One last thing, MacReady: do you know anything at all about an effort to reanimate animals? Dogs, specifically?

Animals? No. Even for research purposes, we passed the need for animal trials decades ago. Why? What did you find?

More reports were spilling in from Palos Verdes. At

least one revivor had been spotted and was being contained in the building.

"Wachalowski," Van Offo warned from the back.

"I see it."

MacReady, I have to go. Get me access to a revivor and at least five good candidates I can use it to spoke to.

I'll try.

Get back to me as soon as you do.

I cut the connection, trying to find an opening in the lane ahead. Traffic was backed up as far as I could see. We were still blocks away from Palos Verdes.

I nosed into the intersection, where crowds had blocked traffic in both directions, and chirped the siren again. People moved out of the way, scowling and swearing as I inched past. The roadblock was up ahead. Two large military vehicles were wedged there, a gun turret mounted on each with a soldier manning it. A small chopper sat in the middle of a business plaza next to them.

I looked over at Calliope. She had one boot up on the dash and was glaring out the side window.

"You okay?" I asked. She didn't answer.

". . . tally at each of the seven sites places the initial death toll somewhere around three hundred—"

Calliope stabbed the radio button with her finger, switching it off.

"Al," I said over my shoulder. He didn't answer. I checked the rearview mirror. He looked ashen.

"Al, how's the neck?"

"Better than your arm."

Someone nearby leaned on his horn, and a woman screamed back in Spanish. Al rubbed sweat from his face with one hand, and as he took a deep breath, his fingers shook.

Agent Wachalowski, over here.

A man waved from between two trucks off to the

right, where the roadblock was set up. I edged the car down another side street and managed to creep along to where they were stationed. Two military vehicles sporting the Stillwell emblem sat in the street, while groups of soldiers kept the emergency lanes clear and watched for signs of trouble. Several soldiers approached as I pulled in and cut the engine. In front was their sergeant, a man named Ramirez.

I shouldered the door open and the others got out behind me. Rotors approached as I headed for the blockade. I held up my badge. Ramirez stepped forward to meet me.

"Agent Wachalowski," he said, scanning my badge. His eyes flicked to the ashen fingers holding it. "We were told to expect you. I see you brought our soldier back."

Calliope snapped a salute, and he returned it.

"Welcome back, Flax. We could sure use the help. Singh will fill you in."

"Sergeant, I need to get to Palos Verdes Estates immediately," I said. "Can that chopper take me there?"

"Stark Street's inside a hot zone, Agent," he said. "That whole area was overrun when the transmission went out."

"I need to get inside that building."

He nodded. Light flickered behind his eyes and the men near the helicopter began to scramble.

"Have you in the air in one minute," he said. "Watch yourself out there."

Snow, salt, and sand was kicked up, and Vika shielded her face. A soldier inside the chopper gestured for Van Offo and me to get in.

Van Offo, come on. He stood with his back to me.

"Al, we've got to go!" I called.

I can't, Nico. Sorry.

He turned to look at me and swayed on his feet.

Sweat was beaded on his forehead in spite of the cold, and dark circles had formed under his eyes.

"Al—"

A red spot appeared in the middle of the gauze patch on his neck and began to expand.

"Medic!" I shouted. Ramirez signaled, and two men sprinted toward us as Al lost his footing. I got an arm around him as he slumped and guided him down onto the cold blacktop.

Blood seeped through the gauze patch on his neck. As the medic knelt beside him, I used the backscatter filter and saw a big, dark pocket had formed under the skin where the patch was. He'd hemorrhaged, and was bleeding internally.

"Sir, step back," the medic said as a second man joined him. I stood and backed away. Al opened a circuit as his eyelids fluttered and closed.

Get going, he said. *There's no time. I told you, I die today. I already knew that.*

I nodded.

Zoe will stop him.

What?

He reached blindly with one hand as they tried to staunch the blood.

You will kill Fawkes—that's what they think—but Zoe will stop him. That's what she believes.

How? What does that mean?

I pity that girl, he said. *All she ever seems to see is death and destruction, with her at its center. It's too bad.*

Al, how does she stop him? For just a second, his eyes got that amused look they sometimes got.

She's got it bad, for y—

The connection dropped. The medics continued to work on him while the soldier in the chopper signaled to me again. There was nothing I could do. I headed toward them and climbed in.

Cal, I'm going off the grid for a while.
I got it.
Good luck.
You too.

The chopper lifted off, and she scowled up into the wind from the rotors. Off to the side, I saw the medic signal to Ramirez and shake his head. Van Offo had died.

His blank eyes still stared up at the chopper as we lifted off into the air.

Calliope Flax—Avenue De Luz

When the chopper took Nico up, Van Offo bled out and kicked it. I helped wrap him up and get him in the back of the truck, then took the kid to Singh, to see what he wanted to do with her.

"Flax, good to see you in one piece."

"Yeah, you too."

"Sorry about your friend," he said, and jabbed a thumb at the body.

"He wasn't my friend. I hated that asshole."

The wind blew and I smelled blood mixed with those shitty cigarettes he smoked.

"There is no door," a voice said—a girl's voice—right in my ear. I looked around, but no one was there.

Pain throbbed in the back of my head, and everything went blurry for a second. My mouth filled with sour spit. I squeezed my eyes shut and waited for it to pass. When it did, I got a flashback to my old apartment. It was so real, I could smell it.

I was standing in the hall across from the bathroom and I'd pushed aside the flag I took back from Juba. Behind it was a door, and I stood in the open doorway. The room on the other side had walls and floors covered in plastic. There was a gurney and a tray of surgical tools in the middle.

A little, spooky-looking woman stood in front of me, blocking my way. She stared up at me, the middle of her eyes black.

"There is no door," she said.

"You okay?" Singh asked, and when he touched my arm, I jumped. I shook my head to clear it and pushed him away.

"I'm fine, dickhead." I spat on the ground.

"I don't think you are," he said. He leaned a little closer and tapped behind his ear with one finger, right in the spot where I had the scar from the inhibitor implant. "They know."

As the medic slammed the doors to the back of the truck and Ramirez got on the radio, I started to put in a call to Wachalowski, but before I could open the channel, something stopped me and I let it drop.

"Don't call him," Singh said, and for a second, I felt dizzy. "Just relax. Everything is fine."

Ramirez glanced back over his shoulder at me as he stepped toward the jeep. I could just make out his voice over the wind.

"Yeah, she's here," he said, then paused. "We took him out by chopper. Van Offo is down, so we haven't got anyone with him. . . . Yes, he's en route to Palos Verdes."

He was talking about Nico.

We haven't got anyone with him. . . .

"Who the fuck is he talking to?" I asked. "What do you mean, 'they know'?"

Singh acted like he hadn't heard. He looked down at the kid.

"Who's this?"

"My name is Vika," she said.

"Where'd you find her?"

"A fucking stork dropped her off. In Pyt-Yahk, dipshit. Who is Ramirez talking to?"

"No one. Don't worry about it."

Fuck that. I went to call Nico again, but again I fumbled the connection and it dropped.

"I said don't," Singh said. He looked down at the kid and shook his head.

"You shouldn't have brought her here."

"Where the hell was I supposed to bring her?"

Singh leaned in to talk in my ear. I felt dizzy again for a second, as I felt his breath on my neck.

"I can help you," he said.

"Personal space, asshole," I said, but I could see the others looking at me and flags were going up. Singh meant the Huma injection. They knew about the injection.

"However you avoided the kill switch, you're still affected," he said, squeezing my arm. "We need you."

"Fuck off, Singh." I tried to push him away, but he held on.

"Listen. In about two seconds, Ramirez is going to come over here," he said. "He's got orders to take you out of here."

I checked on Ramirez. He was over by the truck, still on the radio, but he kept looking back at me.

"Take me where?"

"The test facility, back at base."

"What test facility?"

"Keep your voice down. You know the one I mean."

"How the hell—" He squeezed my arm.

"I've known for a while," he said. "I didn't say anything. Maybe I should have, but I didn't. I did what I could to keep you out of that place, but they know now. They're taking you. Don't resist them."

I looked at the kid. She wasn't sure what was up, but she knew it was something. She looked at me, not sure what to do.

"What about her?" I asked.

"I don't know," he said. "I can't help her, but I can help—"

I grabbed a fistful of his shirt, and his eyes went weird. The pupils opened all at once. I swayed, and he steadied me. Then it passed.

"Cal, don't resist," he said. "If you do, they'll—"

"Stop talking, Singh." I looked at the kid.

"Cal, I—"

"Shut up."

Vika, I sent. Green light flashed in her pupils.

Whts wrng?

When I say run, you run.

She didn't ask why; she just nodded.

Singh put his face close enough to mine that I could smell his shitty cologne, and his eyes got that weird look again.

"Don't resist," he said, his voice low. "Just relax."

"You relax," I said, and shoved him. He stumbled back, but got his feet under him before he fell. The others looked over. Singh stared back at me, his eyes bugged.

"What the hell?" he said under his breath. Ramirez had put down the radio and was coming over.

"What's the problem?" he asked.

"No problem, sir," Singh said. Ramirez looked down at Vika, then back to me. He had that look on his face he always had when his cock was in a knot.

"Flax, we have orders to take you back to base," he said.

"Why?"

"That's need to know." He held out one hand. "Hand over your weapon."

Over his shoulder, I saw the rest of the squad step in like they were expecting trouble.

"Ramirez, what the hell?" He glared at me, and his

eyes got that same weird look Singh's had. I felt dizzy for a second, then it passed.

"I said, 'Hand over your weapon,' Flax," he said. "Do it. Now."

"Son of a bitch," I said. He stared back with his fucked-up eyes.

"You're with them," I said. I looked to Singh, but his eyes were the same. "Both of you."

They looked at each other, and I knew it was true. They were just like that red-haired bitch, and that other one that rigged me with a bomb and then mind-fucked me. Both of them were in on it. This whole time, they were all in on it.

"Just relax," Ramirez said, and I felt the tension ease out of my body. "Just stand there. Don't move. If you try to move, you will find you can't."

I tried to answer, but nothing came out. I tried to open my mouth, but I couldn't. Ramirez spoke into his radio.

"We've got her," he said. Then he nodded.

Out of the corner of my eye, I saw Vika. She stared straight ahead, still as a statue, like me.

"Everything is still set up and ready to go," he said to Singh.

"Can they do it without killing her?" he asked.

"Maybe."

Slowly, I reached down and took my weapon from its holster. Ramirez snapped his fingers.

"Hey! I told you not to move."

All of a sudden, the wire lit up red and alerts started flashing on the HUD. From the reactions around me, everyone saw them.

"Sir?" someone asked, but Ramirez held up his hand, orange light flickering in his eyes. Something big had just gone down. Everyone was distracted. I handed the gun to the kid, and she took it.

"Holy shit," Singh whispered. He was staring into space, reading something off his JZI, and he looked scared.

I skimmed the stream of alerts that were pouring in as I took a step back, away from the others. I saw a satellite map of the city that showed part of the coastline. Words jumped out at me: "point of impact" and "blast zone." A red marker flashed on the map.

"Jesus, he launched," Singh said. "The crazy son of a bitch launched...."

Something boomed overhead and everyone looked up. High above, against the gray blanket of clouds, a small, dark shape had appeared. A distant shriek swelled as it moved quickly across the sky, leaving a thin contrail behind it.

Run, I told Vika.

"Hey!"

A gun went off near my face and I heard glass explode behind me. I chanced a look back in time to see the kid scoot into an alley. The guy that fired had moved in next to Singh. I grabbed his wrist and twisted hard enough to bring him to his knees. He grunted as I peeled his fingers off the pistol and took it before kicking him down onto the pavement.

"She's not under!" Singh yelled. Ramirez grabbed my collar, his eyes black. The dizzy feeling hit me again.

"Go to sleep," he said. "Now."

Before he could do anything else, I landed a punch right on his ear. He staggered off to one side, drawing his weapon.

"Goddamn it, grab her!"

"How long until impact?"

"Less than ninety seconds!"

"Where? Where?"

I stuck the gun in the face of the soldier closest to me.

"Next one that moves gets his fucking head blown off!" I barked, as two more took aim at me. "Get those guns off me or I will fucking shoot him!"

"Stand down!" Ramirez ordered. "We need her alive!"

They lowered their guns. The guy I had covered glared back at me as the whistle from overhead dropped lower and lower in pitch. It was one of the ICBMs. Fawkes had just dropped one of the twelve nukes.

"We've got to get out of here!" someone yelled, and Ramirez turned on them.

"Get it together, people!" he barked. "We're fine where we are! We have our orders, and I expect you to follow them!"

"You're not taking me," I told him.

"You're making a big mistake, Flax. Singh, get her under control. Now."

"What the hell is this?" Singh whispered. He looked twitchy. "It's not working. . . . Why isn't she under?"

The rest of the squad stood there, guns out, not sure what to do. Ramirez looked pissed.

"You're not getting out of here," he said. He took a step toward me, and I went to hit him again, but when I moved the gun away, a pair of beefy arms grabbed me from behind. They pinned me and squeezed.

"Hold her!"

"You motherfuckers!" I yelled. I stomped Ramirez on the shin with one boot. His face went dark and he grunted.

"Hold her still, goddamn it!"

I got one foot behind the guy who'd grabbed me, then hooked his leg and flipped him. He let go when he started to fall, and I spun around. When he hit the blacktop, I put the heel of my boot down on his face.

Blood squirted from his squashed nose and he stayed down, but two more were right behind him and every time my heart beat, the pressure in my skull got worse. They were all around me and I should have turned on the next-closest one, but I didn't. I dropped to my knees over the guy I just took out and bashed his head into the pavement. Before I knew what I was doing, I felt my mouth open wide and warm spit leaked out.

Do it . . .

His skin was hot under my hand. I could feel the blood pumping under my palm, and something in me wanted to feel that meat between my teeth, even when the gun pressed against the back of my head.

Do it . . .

What the fuck? What the fuck is happening to me?

"Don't shoot! We need her!" Singh yelled. I turned around in time for something to cream me right in the forehead. I saw stars, and my legs went out from under me.

"Watch the head, goddamn it!"

My knees hit the blacktop. I tried to get back up, but my legs wouldn't do it. Everything spun around me, and I felt blood run out of my nose.

Before I went down, someone caught me. Arms held me and lowered me onto my back.

"You're okay," I heard Singh say in my ear as the lights went out. "Don't worry."

"I'll take care of you."

The last thing I heard was the faint roar of the missile, turning from a shriek to a low rumble as it fell down toward the earth.

Faye Dasalia—Heinlein Industries, Pratsky Building

The sounds of gunfire and screams faded behind me. I spotted a stairwell door at the end of the hall and headed for it. To my left, windows looked over the tarmac, off to the distant skyline. As I moved down the

corridor, I saw a door slam open outside and a group
of men and women came running out. They made a
break for the far-off perimeter, but before they made
it a hundred yards, there was a bright flash from the
sky. A beam of energy rippled down through the
clouds and washed over them. In an instant, the tarmac melted underneath them and they were gone in
a cloud of smoke. The thick glass buckled in the heat
and cracked down the center with a thud as wet ash
and tar rained against it. Wind whistled through as I
turned the corner and headed away. I needed to get
out of sight, and soon.

There was no way for me to know where Fawkes was.
I could no longer locate any of them, and it surprised
me how lost that made me feel. I'd come to rely on that
command network, and without it I felt a little bit blind.
I had to watch and listen more carefully. By now Fawkes
was rallying them against me. My former allies were
now my enemies, and that sense of connection I'd felt to
them was gone, leaving a void behind it.

I should have let him kill me, I thought as I ran. *In
another second, it would have been done. Now—*

As I came to a T in the corridor, I almost ran headlong into a soldier who stepped out in front of me. Its
gun, held in one gray hand, hung by its side. It saw me,
but took a second to react.

I rushed it, closing the distance in three strides. My
forearms split apart and I triggered both the bayonets at
once. As it raised its weapon, I knocked it back onto the
floor then thrust both blades down, deep into its neck.
They crossed just in front of its spinal column, and two
spastic jets of black blood painted the walls to either side
of us. I jerked and scissored the two blades together. Its
head nearly severed, the soldier fell back and crashed
down onto the floor.

Faye. It was Fawkes. I could sense him trying to reestablish the command spoke to retake control of me, trying to locate exactly where I was. I stepped through the oily pool growing across the tiles and picked up the soldier's gun.

Faye, answer me, he said. And that's when I saw a second flash out the window, much, much brighter than the first.

It came from somewhere far off, out between Heinlein and the city proper. The source was beyond the mouth of Palm Harbor, maybe ten miles or so from the coastline. The light was so intense, the window tinted and a large, dark spot danced in front of my eyes. A huge dome of flame had begun to expand over the water's surface.

What was that?

The overhead lights flickered and then went out. I heard a collective gasp from back down the way I'd come; then, just as suddenly, the lights came back on. A chest-thumping boom followed, then a low, steady rumbling sound. The wind began to pick up, and snow streaked past the window.

Fawkes, what was that? The ball of light grew larger by the second. There had been a detonation of some kind. Whatever it was, it was huge. . . .

I realized then what I was seeing. A dark cloud began to emerge from the blast and rise into the sky on a column. My heart hadn't beat for years, but still, the cloud's mushroom shape inspired dread.

What did you do? I asked. The words floated in front of the growing cloud, as a huge electrical arc flashed through it.

This is bigger than either one of us, Faye. Come back.

The rumble went on and on, even after the light was gone and the windows cleared. The mushroom cloud continued to grow high into the sky.

This is what we've worked toward, Faye. Your existence no longer matters. I know you believe—

I cut the connection and put a block on his ID. I saw him try to reestablish the link, but I didn't pick up. I checked the pistol's magazine; it was full. For a moment, I stood over the body, not sure what to do next.

Find Robert MacReady, Dulari had said. I wasn't sure who he was, but I scanned the JZI nodes inside the building and found a match for his name. He was inside, then.

I put in a call request, then sprinted to the stairwell door and pushed it open. At the rail, I looked down and saw that it descended several stories. Until then I hadn't realized how deep the structure really went.

I started down. If the revivor I'd just destroyed had a chance to report my location, then there were already more on their way. My best bet was to head down and try to disappear until I could decide what to do next.

I'd descended five flights when my call request was picked up. MacReady was alive.

Faye Dasalia, what do you want? He'd responded, but the circuit hadn't come through the transmitter; Fawkes couldn't monitor the conversation.

Dulari Shaddrah gave me your name, I told him.

Something pricked at my control nodes remotely, some kind of low-level scan. Before I could cut it off, a stream of data went out on the wire.

Your command spoke is locked, he said.

Yes.

That's interesting. Why?

Fawkes meant to kill me. I am no longer part of his network. He paused for a minute, considering or perhaps verifying that, then:

I can help you. Come to the lab.

Help me do what?

Come to the lab, he said. *If you're on the run as you say, you need to get off of Fawkes's radar.*

I took a step down the stairs and then stopped there, uncertain. Fawkes hadn't told me everything, but I'd worked for years to make sure these events could unfold. I still did believe in his ultimate goal. Everything was moving so fast, I hadn't had time to think. Why had I even run from Fawkes? Was the human survival mechanism so ingrained? I had no life to lose. Why did I run? What did I want?

You were a slave for the last part of your life, Faye, I know that, MacReady said. *But ask yourself if what Fawkes offered you was any better. The control that command spoke provided was more absolute than anything you experienced in life. But you're free now. Come to the lab.*

He's luring me, I thought. Some old intuition was bubbling up. There was something too silky about his words.

Is Dulari alive? he asked.

The last time I saw her, she was alive.

And Mr. Chen?

Alive, but they're killing the rest.

I know, he said. *And I know what you are. I know better than you do. I know there are still residual ties to your old identity. Fawkes knows too. It's why even though he needed a seventh-generation to gain access to our systems, he considers you a liability now.*

What he said made sense, but I wasn't sure if he was right about me or not. Some people would die; I'd always known that. But people died all the time.

I need you. Nico's message still floated near the corner of my eye. He'd understood. Not letting anyone get hurt was my ideal in life, but it was unrealistic. He'd known that, believed it. Was he right? I stood on the stairs, not knowing what to do.

Where are you? I asked MacReady. A map of the underground levels appeared in the air in front of me.

I'll direct you. What floor are you on now? I looked up

at the placard tab on the wall next to the gray stairwell door.

Sublevel five, stairwell E3.

Continue down to level eight. I looked over the railing; the stairs wound down into shadows far below. I had no reason to trust this man MacReady, but I didn't have too many options left.

I took another step down and then continued for three flights. Following the path traced on MacReady's map, I opened the stairwell door and into a long, dimly lit corridor.

Follow it to the end, and then through the lab on the other side. Security is down; you'll be able to walk right in.

The hall was strangely quiet, with only the hum from the overhead lights and another, more subtle source of white noise. My footsteps echoed quietly behind me as I approached the heavy metal lab door and gripped its cold steel handle. The scanner mounted there on the wall was dark and inactive.

I pushed, and the door opened with a low thud that turned my skin to gooseflesh. My dead skin never did that unless it was near an electrical field. I traced the thud and the hum that followed it to somewhere over my head, where I saw large coils of thin, shiny wire. Beyond that, the room was dark.

Noise suppressors.

I took a step, and lights snapped on overhead. I was standing on one side of a huge room where rows and rows of figures hung from above, each one covered in thick, clear plastic sheeting. Silhouetted by the light, their feet and toes dangled around head level, where bundles of wires hung down to the floor, then snaked across the tile. Dim light from overhead flickered eerily.

To the other side, MacReady said. *Quickly.*

What is this place? I asked.

It's the culmination of an old experiment, he said. *One your leader started a long time ago.*

I took a step, and something wet touched my cheek. When I wiped it, my fingers came away black. I looked up and saw three small children's corpses tented underneath a single plastic sheet. Two black-skinned boys looked dormant, but the girl's large, glowing eyes stared down at me. On the map MacReady had provided, the chamber I was in was marked as SEMANTIC/EPISODIC MEMORY RECLAMATION FACILITY.

Are you taking their memories?

As I'm sure you know, Faye, revivor memories are much simpler to package and transfer than human memories. They've been known to even share them in the field during long deployments.

Yes.

The light coming from overhead was from them. When I stepped past the door, they'd opened their eyes. Hundreds of them, all staring down to see me. The wires that trailed from them were connected to plugs under the skin. Another black drop dripped down from the end of the girl's toe. More of the eyes looked my way, causing the eerie electric light to shift. The little girl's legs hung still. She stared, conscious, but didn't answer when I tried to contact her.

None of them can respond. Leave them, Faye.

I looked into her eyes a minute longer, then turned back toward the exit MacReady had called out for me. I sprinted between rows of bundled cable, the soft light shifting as their eyes followed me. As I passed between their dangling bodies, I sensed that their signatures were active, but they were cut off from me and each other. Many of their eyes moved around spastically, the way they sometimes did when streaming data.

What do you do with the memories, once you've taken them? I asked.

Come to the lab, he said, *and I'll show you.*

Up ahead of me, several sets of toes twitched as I slipped through a second hanging plastic sheet, down past rows of metal hatches that were covered with thin layers of frost. Light seeped from under a door at the far end.

Without looking back, I opened it and moved on.

6

VEIL

Nico Wachalowski — Palos Verdes Estates

Impact. The word flashed in the air in front of me as the horizon lit up and began to grow brighter.

Satellites had detected the launch and tracked the missile as it entered the atmosphere, but the defense shield wasn't designed to respond to a strike sourced from inside the net itself. There was no way to stop it. The helicopter had just begun its approach to Palos Verdes when the missile detonated above the water, past the mouth of Palm Harbor. A blinding flash lit up the night sky, and spots still swam in front of my eyes as the huge dome of light began to boil into a cloud of radioactive fire. Even at that distance, it was awe inspiring. As the signature cloud rose over the skyline, panic set in for real, and I could see mobs surge through the streets below us. Not even the Guard could control the flow of bodies as they scrambled to clear the area.

I couldn't raise anyone on the JZI. Our people were scattered. Calls were flooding in from all over the city, jamming the switchboards, and it was about to get worse.

You will kill Fawkes—that's what they think—but Zoe will stop him.

I thought about Van Offo's last words as the column of smoke continued to rise above the skyline. I fished the card he'd given me with her number on it out of my jacket pocket. The way things were playing out, I might not get another chance. As we moved over the crowd that had spilled into the street, I dialed it.

It rang several times, but she didn't pick up. When it bounced through to her voice mail, I stared at the mob below and didn't speak.

"We're closing in!" the pilot said.

"Zoe—"

Scrambled code streamed in the corner of my eye and then winked out as the chopper hit turbulence. My stomach rolled, and my dead right arm seized as the scene in front of me changed abruptly.

"*Just tell me what you want,*" I asked. I was sitting in my car, with Zoe next to me. The sign for Pleasantview Apartments shone from across the street through falling snow as I waited for her to answer.

I remember this. It had happened years ago, back before Faye had been killed.

Zoe sat in the passenger's seat, her eyes turned down toward the floor. Her hair covered most of her face, but I saw a tear roll down her cheek.

"*I want you . . . to like me . . .*" she said. Her voice was so soft, I could barely hear her.

"*I do like you, Zoe. I . . .*"

She turned and stared up into my eyes. The color was gone from them, replaced with shiny black. I felt the strength drain out of my body.

"*Don't say anything,*" she said. "*This is hard enough.*" Her eyes returned to normal.

"You really don't get it, do you? You really don't see it." She shook her head. *"You and me . . . there's got to be a reason for it . . . I kept seeing you . . . something made me find you . . . we were supposed to meet. Didn't you feel it too?"*

I didn't answer. I didn't know what to say. Zoe always seemed emotional to me, but I hadn't realized until then just how much she kept buried.

"You mean so much to me . . . don't you see it? You changed my life. . . ."

"Zoe . . . look . . ."

"Am I anything to you at all?"

I realized then that she had feelings for me. More than that, she'd pinned some kind of hope on me. I'd been so caught up in what was happening that I hadn't even noticed.

Zoe was deeply disturbed. She was a late-stage alcoholic, prone to outbursts and paranoia. I thought she might also be critical to my investigation, but she'd asked a straightforward question. Whatever it was she felt, I didn't feel it, but I thought she deserved an answer. Even before I could frame what I was going to say, though, she knew.

"Don't . . . don't say it," she said, shaking her head. She was crying now. *"I don't want to hear you say it."*

"Zoe—"

"Don't!" Her pupils expanded again and her eyes turned coal black. My head began to reel. *"Forget it! Just forget it! Forget this whole thing! We never had this conversation, so forget—"*

The helicopter bucked, and as fast as the vision had come, it was gone. The phone was still in my hand. Zoe wasn't there. I snapped it shut as the pilot began his descent.

I was sure that time; that was a memory. Zoe had wiped my memory, and somehow it had returned.

The dead arm ticked once, and I felt it in my shoulder. The first flash came after Fawkes took over Heinlein Industries, after he sent the transmission to alter the code of the Huma carriers. They had to be connected.

I set up a data miner to dig up instances of revivor bleed-through and memory recall. It began its search, but the networks were jammed and it was slow going. After a minute or two, it had trawled up some garbage, but nothing substantial. There was no tie between nanoblood contamination and memory, at least none on record.

"Hold on!" the pilot said as he brought us in. Maybe Deatherage would have some answers, if he was still alive.

We were closing in on the street below, and the crowd surged beneath the helicopter as people were buffeted by the wind of the rotors. We passed between the buildings and veered down Stark Street, where the traffic was jammed bumper to bumper. As the wire was flooded with warnings about the approaching radiation, people were abandoning their vehicles to escape to anywhere away from the shore. Throngs of bodies shoved their way down the sidewalks on either side. One man trudged along the side of a snowbank with a pistol clenched in his hand. Farther down, two men guarded a storefront with automatic rifles slung over their shoulders.

"It's coming up," the pilot said over the headset. Through the windshield, the building towered above us.

Palos Verdes was a low-rent apartment complex that dominated the block. It was closed off from the main street by a blockade of Stillwell soldiers who kept anyone from entering. On the other side of the cordon it was chaos, but so far the area behind it was clear. One of the soldiers waved the pilot in to a small lot bordered by military vehicles, and he descended into the clearing.

A shot went off down the street and I saw a figure stagger behind a row of cars, but couldn't tell if it was human or not. People on the sidewalk shielded their eyes as the rotors kicked up sand and salt. The pilot brought us down on the icy pavement while soldiers watched from the main entrance.

I climbed out and signaled to the pilot.

Wait here.

Roger that, he said, *but if that cloud blows in they're going to have to try a mass evac. Be ready to move.*

The roar of the crowd rose over the chopper. Another shot went off somewhere as I made for the front entrance. As I approached, one of the officers broke the line and came forward to meet me.

"Agent Wachalowski?"

"Yeah."

"I'm Sergeant Lansky. We heard you were on your way."

"What's going on here?"

"Multiple revivors were spotted inside. We isolated them to the unit you're after."

"Is the target alive?"

"Heat signatures show no one living inside; it looks like we're too late. We secured the site and were waiting for you to arrive."

I looked at the entrance. People stood outside in groups, shivering in the cold. Eyes darted nervously toward the glow out over the water.

"Is the perimeter secure?"

"Yes, sir. No one's come in or out."

"How many revivors?"

"At least two. My men inside can tell you more. Basement level, unit 102. Sir, the launch. Do you know any—"

"Take the rest of your men and cover the street," I told him. "This whole place could be contaminated in an hour; this is only going to get worse."

I climbed the front steps and looked out from the main entrance. Back at the cordon, a soldier stood on top of a truck and barked over a bullhorn while the crowd shoved their way through the street. A mass evacuation would never happen in time. If the wind changed direction, most of the people there were going to be caught in it.

Pain pulsed in my head and I felt my jaw clench, the teeth grinding together. I needed to get back to headquarters to get checked out, but there was no place left to go back to. Even if there had been, there wasn't time.

I pushed open the door. The lobby inside had glass scattered across the floor and I saw shell casings littered in with the debris. Some of the overhead lights were out, and some flickered where the ceiling had taken a stream of gunfire. A handful of tenants sat along one wall, watched by a pair of soldiers.

I drew my weapon and headed down a stairwell with concrete walls. The door clanged shut behind me as I reached the landing and entered the hallway. Following the unit numbers, I turned right, then down a long hallway where two soldiers waited. The younger one's name patch read JIN. The other read ANDERS. When they saw me, they waved me over.

At the door, I switched to the backscatter filter and peered through. I didn't see anyone on the other side. The scanner LED was green; the door was unlocked.

"There's three inside," Jin said. "We got them on camera."

He angled the screen so I could see. From floor level, I saw a crumpled figure, and a woman's face dotted with blood.

"That's your guy's mistress, Panya Garg," the other officer said. "She's confirmed dead. No word yet on whether your guy is in there or not, but we're not picking up any vitals."

"Power's cut," Anders said. "But we've got electrical activity and some light, so they've got some kind of backup."

On the camera I saw a flicker—a flashlight beam, maybe. I heard movement from somewhere on the other side of the door.

"I'm going inside," I said.

They nodded. I pushed open the door, and they took position behind me.

The front entrance opened into a short hallway, and up ahead I could see what looked like the living area. Heavy footsteps moved in one of the rooms nearby. I scanned through the walls on either side of the hall and didn't see anyone.

I approached the woman's body. She was dressed to go out, and there was a suitcase next to the front door. Blood had pooled behind the body from a wound in her back that probably came from a revivor's bayonet. It was the wrong day to be associated with Harold Deatherage.

The living room was small and crowded with old, mismatched furniture. A set of dirty boot tracks crossed the matted carpet, away from the body and through a doorway on the far end of the room. A short connecting hallway extended from there. A flashlight swept through the room on the other side.

I approached, and the soldiers followed. The doorjamb was splintered where the door had been forced, and through the doorway I could see three male figures; two were standing and one was seated. None registered any body heat.

I've got three revivors here.

The room had been converted into some kind of makeshift work area. Two wall racks bordered a workstation, both stacked with equipment that looked out of place in such a run-down unit. Deatherage had been doing more here than just cheating on his wife.

The air inside was hazy, and I smelled smoke. I watched for a minute as one of the revivors rooted through a desk drawer, and the other pushed a collection of data disks from a shelf mounted behind the workstation so that they scattered onto the floor. It moved off to one side, out of my line of sight.

They're looking for something.

The third revivor was seated in a chair in front of the workbench. The monitor glowed softly, silhouetting its face.

The equipment was still running on backup power, but the computer screens were blank. Threads of smoke rose from several chassis mounted in the racks. I zoomed in and pulled any names and model numbers I could read, then handed them off to a data miner to see what it could find.

The revivor in the chair shifted, and I heard a low scrape against the floor as the workstation desk moved. It had one wrist tied to the desk frame with a plastic zip tie. Blood leaked from a gash where it had dug through the skin, but the blood was red; human. A carrier, maybe.

The first revivor gave up on the drawers and looked around the room. After a minute, something sloshed, and the second came back into view, carrying a plastic gas can. It approached the seated revivor, and I smelled fumes as it poured a stream of gasoline down on top of its head. As the liquid splashed down over the desk and floor, I spotted an unlit road flare clenched in the revivor's other hand.

I stepped inside, Jin and Anders moving in behind me. The revivors turned as I fired at the one with the can and caught it in the forehead. Its head pitched back and the can thudded to the floor as Jin fired at the second. The first round tore through its neck, and the second was a clean headshot. It fell back against the bookshelf and crashed to the floor. The second body staggered and left a streak of blood down the wall before it slumped down against the computer table. The road flare rolled behind a chair.

"Hold your fire!" I said.

The third revivor looked up from where it sat, hair plastered to its head. There were black blotches in the whites of its eyes. The first two were dressed in old, dirty clothes, but this one had on a buttoned shirt and a tie. Jin had his gun pointed at the revivor's head, his finger on the trigger.

"Just wait," I said.

I moved closer to the third revivor and scanned its face. The computer pulled up a match.

"It's him," I said. "This is Deatherage. Stand down."

I lowered my gun and removed a penlight from my jacket pocket. I shined it in one of the revivor's eyes. The black hemorrhages branched through the whites.

Alice, I've located Harold Deatherage.

Is he alive?

No. He's been reanimated. It looks like a Huma case. I found some kind of work area here, but it looks like most of it has been destroyed.

The chair creaked under Deatherage's body as he strained against the plastic tie.

"Mr. Deatherage?" I said. He looked up at me, but didn't respond. "Mr. Deatherage, can you understand me?"

I scanned his head and saw a dark blotch inside the brain pan. Revivors relied on existing brain pathways. The kill switch had caused some damage in there.

I looked around the room. The computer equipment was all dark and surrounded by smoke. Cables and wires trailed across the floor.

An icon flashed in my periphery as the data miner came back with its first round of results. Information

began to scroll by in front of me. The model numbers
were getting hits on some very specialized equipment
used to develop and test nanotech code. A high-security
clearance and a federal permit were required to obtain
half the technology on the list.

*Whatever he was working on here, it was something
major,* I told Alice. *The electronics in here are worth
millions.*

Did he get it through Heinlein?

*You need permits for this stuff; they'd never have
signed off on it. This was something he didn't want them
knowing about, or he'd have done it there.*

I looked around the room, waving smoke and gas
fumes away from my face. The revivors had been sent
by Fawkes to destroy evidence, so he knew a place like
this existed. Deatherage's main residence was hit first,
though, which suggested he hadn't known exactly where
it was. Whatever they were doing, the others, Chen and
Shaddrah, had to be in on it, but they hadn't known the
location either, or hadn't told Fawkes.

Their work was tied to Chen's, then. Was there more
to it than just safeguarding against the shutdown virus?

*Wachalowski, a tech team is on its way, but we're
working against the clock here,* Alice said. *Wind patterns
could put fallout over that area in an hour; get what you
can and get out of there.*

Understood.

"Mr. Deatherage?"

He lunged, and the desk jumped an inch as his arm
was pulled taut. Jin and Anders's guns came up, but neither fired. Deatherage bared his teeth and reached with
his free hand to grab me.

"It's okay," I told the two men. "I've got him."

I looked through the musculature of his neck and
was able to make out the nodes that had formed around

the spine. The communications node was active, and I connected.

There wasn't much contained in the memory; Deatherage hadn't been a revivor long. He'd switched over long after the original kill code was sent, so Fawkes must have had him on a separate trigger. A safeguard, maybe. Deatherage was supposed to be in on his plan, but when Fawkes realized he'd been betrayed, he used it to make sure he didn't talk.

"Mr. Deatherage, can you understand me?" I asked. Spittle hung from his lip as he stared at me and strained against the plastic tie. With his free hand, he thumped his palm against his stomach twice.

"Why'd they restrain him?" Anders asked.

"I think he restrained himself," I said.

"Why?"

"Maybe so he wouldn't hurt anyone."

They bite.

The words appeared in front of me, floating in front of Deatherage's face. They'd come over my connection to his revivor node. He was trying to communicate.

What happened here? I asked him. His eyes rolled in their sockets. *What did you do?*

They bite.

What did Fawkes have you working on?

He didn't answer. His brain was scrambled. He used his free hand to thump his belly again.

When I moved my scan away from the revivor nodes around his spine to look down at the hand, I caught a flash of something behind the muscle wall in his abdominal cavity. He was trying to tell me something.

"Hang on. I've got something here," I said. I zoomed in and peered through the soft tissue. Inside his stomach, there was a small piece of plastic with electronics inside.

A data spike.

Deatherage lunged again suddenly, his cold fingers brushing my face before grabbing a fistful of my jacket. Without thinking, I drove my dead fist into the side of his face and his head snapped to one side. A gob of blood splashed the desktop next to him as I pulled back and grabbed his wrist, peeling his fingers away from my lapel.

Do it . . .

I bent his fingers back until I heard a series of dull pops, then twisted his arm around so his broken hand faced the floor. I drove the heel of my palm down onto his elbow, and the bone crunched. Anders took a quick step back.

"Woah!"

Deatherage's arm bent the wrong way, but his face didn't change. He didn't feel it, but I didn't care. The same urge that came over me at the hospital was back, stronger than before, and I fought to control it.

I kicked the chair out from under him, then shoved him face-first down onto the floor. As the chair toppled, the tie twisted his wrist and I heard it snap. Before he could move again, I drew my field knife and stuck the point between two vertebrae just under the revivor nodes. Careful not to damage the nodes themselves, I drove the blade through the spinal cord, and he went limp.

Calm down. My heart rate was spiking. *Just calm down.* The other two officers stood a few feet away, guns still drawn as I took a deep breath and let it out.

Do it . . .

"Wait outside," I said. Anders backed out of the room as I jerked the knife free again.

I flipped Deatherage over, the tie cutting his wrist deeper until the fingers of his hand turned dark and fat. I pulled his shirt open to expose the pale skin underneath, and found the outline of the data spike under the surface. I pushed the knife in below his ribs and cut open his belly.

"Jesus," I heard Jin mutter.

"Wait outside."

I used the backscatter to help guide the knife as I cut through the stomach wall. When the opening was big enough, I pushed my fist through and felt around until I found the edge of the plastic. I grabbed it and pulled it free.

They bite.

"I get it."

I wiped the spike as dry as I could on his shirt before guiding it into the bay of my cell phone. It was loaded with data, some kind of specs, maybe, for the code he'd worked on, but there was a text message included with it:

Fawkes lied. He wasn't supposed to kill them all. What I did, I did for the good of all mankind. It was only supposed to wake them up. No one was supposed to die. That's what I was told.

Ang was just supposed to provide protection for their network, but I found his secret location and now I know what he really worked on. His lab is at Black Rock Yard. He worked on dissemination. I don't know where she worked, but I found out Dulari was one of the Huma payload specialists. She figured out how to make them self-replicate. This kind of research is illegal for a reason. This isn't how it was supposed to be.

None of us knew what the other was doing, or I would never have done it. Alone, any one of these traits could be explained away, but together they could prove unbelievably dangerous. This cannot get out.

If she is still alive, tell my wife I'm sorry—about Panya and everything else. Tell her that no matter what she hears in the days to come, I swear I didn't know.

Included were some images that didn't mean much

at first glance. There were rows of photos, close-up shots of dog bites. There were also rows of X-rays, each panel showing the progress of what looked like revivor nodes growing in the skulls of different dogs. There was a satellite map as well, with The Eye and the nuclear deterrent shield called out. Another map had locations circled and connected with lines, including the Stillwell base, Black Rock train yard, Palos Verdes, and Heinlein Industries.

The last image, though, stopped me cold. I stared at it in the HUD, realization slowly sinking in.

Alice, come in.

Hsieh here.

The image was a satellite photo of the city that included a section of the coast. The image was dotted with tiny red points, and as I watched, more began to appear. As the dots began to bleed together to form clusters, a timer counted off the seconds, minutes, and hours in a fast time-lapse. As days ticked by, the red clusters began to slowly cover the map, then leak out over the bridges, out of the city. At the base of the map were two words:

PROJECTED SPREAD

Alice, I know why Fawkes went back to Heinlein.

What we found at the train yard suddenly made sense. Fawkes didn't care about reanimating animals, and he wasn't testing the new code on them either, not directly.

We already know that, Alice said.

We were wrong, I said. Dissemination, self-replication . . . the simulation wasn't charting the spread of revivors through the city, it was charting the spread of a disease. Fawkes didn't just switch off the ghrelin inhibitors of the people he'd converted, he'd changed them far more fundamentally than that.

No matter what else happens, Alice, we can't allow Heinlein's transmitter to be damaged or destroyed.

It's how he's controlling the satellites, Nico. It's how he's controlling revivors across such a wide radius.

I know, but it's also the only way to introduce any change to their existing systems. It might be the only way to undo what Fawkes has done.

And what is that, Agent? What is it? What did you find?

I think Fawkes knows he can't hold Heinlein forever. He wants to spread the Huma variant to the rest of the city before that happens.

How? I looked over at Deatherage as that bitter taste filled my mouth again. His body was paralyzed but his eyes pleaded as he continued to repeat his message:

They bite.

They bite.

They bite.

Zoe Ott—Alto Do Mundo

When I came to, I was sitting on a hard, uncomfortable chair. The room was quiet, and I could hear the soft buzz of an electric light over my head.

I took a deep breath and opened my eyes. I was sitting on a folding metal chair in front of a table near one end of a small, concrete room whose walls were painted green. A single light flickered overhead, throwing shadows in the dark.

"This place," I whispered. A heavy metal door that led out of the room was open, and the doorway was dark. From outside, I heard footsteps echo, then disappear. My head hurt and my throat hurt. Every time my heart beat, pain went up the back of my neck.

For a long time, the Green Room was just another nightmare place I ended up in when I blacked out, but now I knew it existed, or would exist, and that I was one of only a few people to ever see it, which meant

I was one of the few people who might be around to see it. It was a vision from inside the void, something from the aftermath of the event. I hadn't seen it in a long time.

I looked at the tabletop and thought it wasn't the same one as last time, but I wasn't sure. It was worn, with laminate peeled up in one corner. I thought maybe it was a different shape. Certain things were always the same, like the green paint and the basic layout of the room, but sometimes the details changed. Not enough people had seen it to be sure. No one knew what the room was for.

"It's almost time," a voice said.

I turned around and saw the dead woman, the one with the short blond hair and the nice cheekbones, standing next to a silver metal panel that was fixed to the wall. Her skin looked thinner than the last time I'd seen her, with more of those black veins underneath. She stared at me from near the switchbox, her eyes glowing in the dark like moonlight.

"I know who you are," I said. "Your name is Faye Dasalia."

She was the one Nico used to be in love with. The one he was still in love with. She tried to kill me once, but instead I almost killed her—almost.

"We will meet one last time," she said.

"When?"

She reached over to the electrical box and threw the switch. A spark flashed with a loud bang and fell down onto the floor, where it sputtered out. Two of the lights at the end of the room slowly got a little brighter, while the one in the middle stayed out. Another spark spit from the socket there.

As the lights came up, I saw two figures had appeared, one standing under each of them.

The first one was Nico, and when I saw him, I put

one hand over my mouth. A few years back he'd ditched me and never tried to contact me again, so I had mixed feelings about him, but even so, he looked horrible. He was wearing slacks and a sleeveless undershirt, and the scar that covered his neck and chest ended on his left side at a neat seam where his whole shoulder and arm had turned pale and gray. Black veins stood out over the bicep and down the forearm. There were big, dark bruises on the right side of his body, especially his face. The eyelid that drooped showed only white underneath. He looked half-dead.

"You can help him," the dead woman said, "but you can't save him. He will destroy Fawkes forever."

"I stop Fawkes."

She didn't say anything.

I got up out of the chair, and when I stood, my head pounded. It was all I could do to limp a few steps closer. I couldn't stop shivering. I was almost sure I hated him for turning his back on me, but still, I could barely stand to see him like that.

"He will need you," she said.

"I needed him," I said. My voice was low and hoarse.

The dead woman didn't answer. She pointed to the other figure, Flax, with her short hair and mean face. I felt my face get hot.

"She will bring about destruction," the woman said.

"Yeah," I said. "I know. She's a carrier. They're going to use her as a back door to shut down the rest of them."

She didn't say either way. In the quiet, I could hear the low hum from her chest.

"She will take the last thing that is dear to you," she said.

I clenched my fists, and felt tears well up in my eyes. My hand shook as I pointed one index finger up at her face.

"Enough!" I said. "I've had enough! She's not taking

anything else from me! Nothing else! They're going to kill her, like they should have done a long time ago! The next time I see you, I'll put you down for good. Do you hear me? If I so much as see you I'll—"

Faye moved closer to me. I backed away until I bumped against the concrete wall, and her cold hands grabbed my arms. The cool, lifeless skin of her cheek pressed against the hot red of my own, and she spoke into my ear.

"He will call to you one last time," she said. "If you accept him, you could still—"

"Screw you!" I said, and shoved her back. She staggered into the table and caught herself before she fell, as the chair clattered to the floor. "You're not real!"

I put my hands over my eyes and pressed. My head throbbed so bad it made me feel sick.

"I'm tired of this! All of this! Get out of my head and just leave me alone!"

I took my hands away and opened my eyes. Dark spots swam in front of me. I was still in the Green Room and the chair was still knocked over, but the dead woman was gone. It got quiet, and I could hear myself panting. I wiped my mouth and looked around. No one else was there.

My heart rate started to slow down as I took a deep breath, like Ai had shown me. There was no reason to get upset. The visions weren't something to be afraid of; they were glimpses into a possible future. They provided valuable information, and visions that came from the place even Ai couldn't see into were the most valuable of all. I had to try to calm down and pay attention.

I picked the chair back up and put it in front of the table. I could be pulled back at any time, and with things going the way they were, I might never be back in this place. This might be my last chance to learn something, anything, that could help us. I smoothed down my hair and leaned back against the cool concrete wall, breathing slowly.

"Okay," I said. "Okay . . . pull it together . . ."

As I let my eyes lose focus, the hard lines at the corners of the room seemed to vibrate and hum, like a tuning fork. I forgot about what the dead woman had said and about what was happening back in the real world. I relaxed and let the light get brighter.

Show me . . .

Slowly, an outline, like a ghost, appeared in the room with me. Three more appeared around it, but I couldn't tell who they were. As the color bled away, the outlines of the ghosts got sharper. There were three men. . . .

I brought them into focus. They weren't like my visions of the dead woman or Karen or the others who tried to pass me information. . . . These people had really been here, or would be here, someday. Prior to then, it had been just a location, a staging ground for psionic feedback that I couldn't control. Now I saw the room as it really was and its true occupants. Somewhere, in someone's future, this was happening.

My phone buzzed in my pocket. The ghosts flickered, and I was afraid I might lose them.

Not now . . .

The phone buzzed again. I took it from my pocket but stayed focused on the figures who had appeared in the room. Two of the men were part of a group. They were older, and wore some kind of uniform I didn't recognize, with their names stitched over the front pocket. The first man was a big, blocky guy named Gein. The second guy had very pale skin and an angular face. He had a scar under one eye. He looked different from when I'd last seen him, skinnier and more tired, but I recognized him right away; it was Hans Vaggot. The expression in the men's eyes scared me.

The two of them half dragged a third man to the back of the Green Room and shoved him against the wall.

"Don't move," Gein said. The man looked scared. He stood against the wall under the middle light with his hands held up in front of him.

"I'm okay," he said. His voice was hoarse. "I'm telling you I'm—"

"Shut up," Vaggot said, and right then a woman walked through the door. My eyes widened. The phone buzzed again in my pocket, then stopped, but I barely noticed.

The woman wore the same uniform as the men, with leather jackboots and a pistol that hung from one bony hip. Her red hair was cut short, and I saw the scar from a bite wound on one side of her neck. Her beaky nose had been broken at some point.

It's me, I thought. I checked the name patch to be sure. It read OTT.

I stared, stunned, as she crossed the room to the table and dropped an electronic pad down in front of her. She turned it on and started opening programs with a stylus. Her face looked mean, and unlike me, she was stone cold sober. Her eyes were hard, and focused.

"Hit the lights," she said. Gein went over to the switchbox and threw the switch.

The room got dark except for the single light over the man against the wall. It shone dimly, and made shadows under his brow.

"Starting the scan," she said.

A bright red line flickered across the far wall, near the ceiling. I followed it back and saw a small lens mounted in the cinder block that I'd never noticed before. A light fixed on one side began to flash.

The line began to move down the wall, tracing contours over the man's face and neck before traveling down the rest of his body.

"I have a kid," the man wheezed, as the laser moved down his body. Next to him, I could see divots where bullets had punched into the concrete. I hadn't noticed them before.

"Shut up," she said.

I looked at the screen and saw an outline of the man displayed there. Information was being called out, but the text was too small for me to read. I moved closer and leaned in; then the screen turned red and flashed.

"You've made a mistake," the man said. He looked terrified. The red laser went out. The other me tapped the screen in front of her, and it went dark too.

"I said shut up," she said. She turned to the uniformed men. "Cover him."

Their guns came out and they aimed at the man from halfway down the room. He held up his hands feebly.

"What are we looking at?" Gein asked.

"It changed again," she said. "Goddamn it, it changed again." She crossed to the silver panel on the wall and swiveled it around to reveal a handset. She picked it up and spoke into it.

"We need a containment team down here," she said.

"You've made a mistake," the man whimpered. "You've made a terrible mistake. . . ."

"If he says another word, shoot him," the other me said. Gein and Vaggot glanced at each other nervously.

"You can't stop this," the man said. The other me slammed down the handset.

"Gein, shoot—"

The man seized up all of a sudden, and the cords in his neck stood out. It happened really fast; in a second, the back of his skull melted away under his skin. His neck shriveled and his eye sockets sank until his eyes bugged out of shadows.

"Shit!" Vaggot shouted. He looked ready to piss himself, but stood his ground. The two men stood there, weapons aimed, but not shooting for some reason.

The man's deformed head bobbed at the end of his chicken neck while his clothes draped over a body that wasted away beneath them. He looked around the room like he didn't recognize anything he saw.

"You can't stop this," he gurgled. It looked like his tongue had split down the middle.

"Hold him," the other me said. "The team is on their—"

"You can't stop this!" the man shrieked, and shambled forward, toward the two men. He held out his hands and they were like spindly claws.

The man stumbled, and when the soldiers moved out of the way, he just kept going like they weren't even there. They followed him with their guns as he reached the table and shoved it aside. It flipped and crashed into the wall as he kicked past the folding chair and came right toward me, the real me. It was like he could see me. I backed away, into the wall, and dropped my phone. It clattered to the floor, and I saw the screen light up as a voice came over its speaker.

"If anyone is receiving this message, listen carefully," a woman shouted through the phone, as the thing stopped a few feet from me.

"Wh-what?" I asked. The men in the room were taking aim, ready to fire. When I looked down at the phone, I could just make out the caller's name on the LCD.

Noelle Hyde

"If any of this gets through, then listen. The nukes may be your last chance. . . ."

"What?"

". . . were wrong . . . the missiles don't cause the event;

they stop it," she said, her voice rising in pitch. *"You have to launch . . ."*

My heart skipped a beat and I felt the strength go out of my legs as the guns came up in slow motion behind the man. His mouth stretched open, drooling gray spit, and I saw his teeth were stained red around that horrible, divided tongue.

". . . the detonation overshadowed the rest," the voice shouted from the phone. *"It was all we could see, and we missed the cause behind it. . . . The lines that die out aren't the ones that can't stop the launch; they're the ones that do stop it. . . ."*

Words appeared on the green concrete wall across from me, wet black lines creeping down from the hastily painted letters.

ELEVEN FROM ZERO

The deformed thing's hands grabbed my shoulders, and as the first shot went off behind it, I screamed. The next thing I knew, all I could see was fire swirling all around, throwing hot orange embers up into the night sky like stars. The world was one fire. Everything was burning, and as dark figures lurched blindly through the flames, I heard her voice, low and hoarse, in the back of my head.

"They were wrong," she whispered.

"It was us all along. . . ."

My eyes snapped open and I sat up on the sofa where I'd been lying, knocking something over and sending a metal pan down onto the floor. Penny was there, kneeling next to me, and she reached out to grab me as I started to flail.

"Easy," she said. "Take it easy."

I looked around and saw two armed men and a man in a bloodstained white shirt standing nearby.

"He just stitched you up," Penny said. "You're okay. Take it easy."

Something smelled funny. I looked past them and saw that the sofa I was on was arranged in a big lounge in the middle of a huge condo. Two other sofas and a big love seat all faced in toward a big, heavy wooden table with a thick surface of smoked glass. A bunch of different kinds of glasses, some still half-full, were sitting on the table. There were silver platters of fancy food lined up, half-eaten. Lobster tails and raw oysters on the half shell sat in a crystal serving dish, floating in melted ice. Caviar, pâtés, and leftover hors d'oeuvres were all still sitting out, and it smelled.

"Sorry," one of the men said. "There hasn't been time to clean it up."

"We're all set," Penny said. "Thanks, guys."

My head pounded and my mouth tasted sour. I waited until the nausea passed, then stood up while Penny hovered near me. The room spun a little as I wobbled over to a big serving table where a bunch of food was left out in chafing dishes and serving bowls. I saw ends of rare meat on carving blocks, the edges crusted. Stray flowers of sashimi had shriveled, and raw shrimp lay drowned in a glass bowl of wine. The smell of it all made my stomach turn, but I needed a drink. A bottle of cognac was sitting on the marble tabletop, and I picked it up. I grabbed an empty crystal shot glass from the stack next to it and filled it, my hands shaking so bad I sloshed half of it onto the floor. I gulped it down and poured another one.

"You look like you saw a ghost," Penny said. "What happened?"

I shook my head. Through the cobwebs, I checked my phone to see if Noelle's name was there, but it wasn't. The LCD read WACHALOWSKI.

All at once, my throat burned and my eyes were filled with tears. I half laughed and half cried, spraying spit.

"Now he calls," I sniffed. I wiped my eyes with my sleeve and took another long pull off the bottle.

"You probably shouldn't—" the doctor said, but his voice dribbled off.

"We're good," Penny said again, staring at him. "Thanks. You can go." She stepped closer, carefully. She wanted to touch me, I could tell, but she didn't.

"Zoe, what did you see?"

"Nothing," I said. I could barely form the word.

"That wasn't nothing," she said.

The men left the room, though I noticed the guards stayed outside the door. Penny followed me as I limped over to the wall of glass that looked out over the city below. Off in the distance, a big cloud had risen behind the buildings and begun to lean away from the rush of snow.

"What happened?" I asked.

"Fawkes dropped one of the nukes," she said. "It might have triggered what you saw."

"What?"

"Fawkes's army surrounded the three towers: the CMC, TransTech, and here. Osterhagen ordered a Leichenesser charge dropped in the middle of the blockade outside to try to clear a path out."

She held up a computer tablet so I could see the screen. A feed from somewhere outside looked out onto the front steps of Alto Do Mundo. From where the camera watched, I could see hundreds of people out there, surging shoulder to shoulder. They all had dirty hair and dirty faces. A lot of them bared bad teeth, and their clothes looked like they came from garbage bins. They were all facing up the huge marble stairs at the entrance to our building, staring with wide eyes that were stained black.

"That's when Fawkes dropped the nuke," she said. "It was a warning, I guess."

"There's so many of them," I said. There was only

one spot that was clear, right down the main steps where sets of clothes and shoes were strewn, deflated and empty. They flapped in the wind, and when it blew, it stirred traces of white smoke that lingered around the remains. It looked like hundreds had been wiped out, but hundreds more were taking their places even while I watched. "We're in trouble, Zoe."

"Something's wrong," I said, still staring. The cloud outside was huge. "How long was I out?"

"Not long," Penny said. "They'll have Flax soon if they don't already. With any luck, we can stop him from dropping the rest."

You have to do it. Make sure they launch . . .

My head was still spinning. I took my next swig straight from the bottle and swallowed three big mouthfuls before gasping in a breath.

"What's the matter?" Penny asked.

"What if we're wrong?" I said, looking down at the lights below. Off in the distance, I could see the flashing lights from one of the helicopters as it circled the building.

"Wrong about what?" Her expression changed then. It turned a little hard, and I thought I sensed suspicion coming from her.

"Nothing."

"No, tell me."

"Nothing," I said. "Never mind."

The bottle clinked against the rim of the glass as I poured myself another one and drank it. The hard look in Penny's eyes softened again.

"Okay," she said. "It's okay."

"Thanks, Penny."

On shaky legs I stepped away from her, and turned the cell phone over in my hand as I watched that big, deadly cloud lean closer and closer to the shore. At the window, I looked out onto the city below.

"It was us all along. . . ."

I reached out around me, sensing the others in the room. They had begun to focus on me as something unspoken was passed around between them.

I took one last drink, then returned Nico's call. I held the phone to my ear, my breath fogging the window in front of me as it rang. After three rings, he picked up.

"Wachalowski," he said. And in spite of myself, I began to cry.

"It's me," I said, soft enough so no one else would hear.

"Zoe," he said. "Are you all right?"

"No." I tried to keep the slur and the shaking out of my voice as I spoke. "I'm not supposed to be talking to you."

"But you are."

"She told me you'd call," I said. I felt dizzy and had to put one hand on the window to steady myself. I leaned forward so that my forehead was on the cool glass, and I was staring down into the sea of lights below.

"Who told you?"

I wasn't sure why, but somehow I knew what Noelle had said to me in the Green Room was true. I knew too that no one would listen to me at this point, no matter what I said. As important as I supposedly was, none of them would ever listen to me say that there was no way to get out of this and still stay on top. I knew all that, and I knew that Noelle was right too. She'd been right all along, right from the start. This whole thing was a big, cosmic joke. The city was going to burn. One way or the other, it was all going to burn.

"I want you to get out of the city," I said, wiping my eyes.

"I can't, Zoe."

"Promise me you'll leave. Leave tonight. Right now."

"I can't."

More attention was focusing my way. Any second now, Ai would snap out of it and realize what I'd done. When she did, she'd make me hang up.

"This is the last time we'll talk," I said.

"Zoe—"

"You tried to help me," I whispered. "Please save yourself."

"Why, Zoe?" he asked. "What are they going to do?"

"Nothing," I told him. "But I think I am."

He was still talking when I felt the presence worm its way into my head, gentle but firm. Some small shard of Ai's consciousness had turned its attention to me. I wanted to keep talking to Nico. There were things I wanted to tell him but the presence wouldn't let me.

That's enough, Zoe.

My arm dropped and the phone slid away from my face. I watched his name on the LCD as the phone spun end over end and clattered to the floor.

Calliope Flax—Stillwell Corps Base

I woke up to the sound of static, louder than usual. I couldn't move, and I couldn't see.

"She's prepped," a voice said. *"Are you ready to deploy?"*

"Yes, sir."

I tried to move, but I couldn't. The last thing I remembered, they'd rushed me.

"What was that before?" the first voice asked.

"You mean why didn't she respond to the push?"

"A ten-year-old could control her. Why didn't she stay under?"

"I don't know."

The static in my head cracked. I tried to move again, but my muscles wouldn't respond. I opened my eyes, but it stayed dark. I tried to call Nico, but my JZI's comm link was down.

"It doesn't matter. Let's just do this. Stop her heart," a voice said.

A needle pricked the back of my neck. I felt a cold metal ring push down on my bare back.

"What are you waiting for?"

"Maybe this isn't a good idea," another voice said.

"Fawkes eighty-sixed the test subjects, and every time we grab one off the street, he cuts it loose. It's got to be during the sync-up. She's our last shot at this."

"He just dropped a nuke in the middle of the bay. When he sees what we've done—"

"If this works, he won't be doing anything."

"But if it doesn't—"

"Osterhagen says, 'Risk it.' Now stop her fucking heart; that's an order."

"She can still hear us," I heard Singh say under his breath.

"I don't give a shit. Is the virus ready to go?"

Singh sighed. *"Yes, sir."*

"Then do it. Now."

A hand touched my face. I felt warm breath in my ear.

"Sorry, Cal."

A circuit lit up on my JZI then. I still couldn't call out, but someone on the outside was calling in. It was Singh.

Singh, get me the fuck out of here, or I swear I will—

Don't be afraid, Cal, he said.

I'm not afraid, asshole.

You need to die just long enough for the Huma nodes to finish forming, but I'll make sure you can be resuscitated.

Fuck you. Get me the hell out—

Pay attention. There's no time to get into it, Cal, but we have to do this. If we can get you onto the carriers' network, we can deploy a virus that will shut them all down. This is happening. It might be our only chance, and we have to stop those things. I know you understand that. Do you trust me?

I didn't, but he was right about one thing: I did understand. I was fucked; they knew I was a carrier, and they had me. If there was a way out, Singh was it.

You're a fucking asshole, Singh.

I know. Do you trust me?

What do I have to do?

You don't have to do anything. You're already part of the mesh; that's why you can sense them, but you're not fully synced up. We're hoping Fawkes won't interpret this as a new node joining, just an update of an existing one. . . . If we're right, then you'll be off his radar. When the nodes finish forming, the first thing they'll do is transmit a sync request giving your stats, uptime, location, and so forth. The virus will be attached to the request and propagated. Understand?

No.

All you need to know is that your body will die for about a minute, but I'll bring you back, Cal, I swear. As a human, not a revivor. Are you ready?

I wasn't, but they had me. There was nothing I could do, and even though Singh was a prick, he was a smart prick. If he thought this could work, it might work.

If you fuck up, I told him, *and I turn—*

You won't.

Don't leave me like that.

I won't.

I heard a thud, and pain slammed through my chest. It pulsed down my arms and up my neck, but I couldn't move. The air died in my lungs and every muscle in my body went slack. I heard my vitals tone go flat, then fade out like I'd fallen down a deep tunnel. Everything got quiet. I couldn't move or see or hear. There was just a big, black nothing.

Is this it? Am I dead? I never got to say bye to Nico. I didn't even know where the fuck I was.

Node formation previously interrupted. Continuing . . .

The words popped up in the dark. They came from a JZ implant, so my brain still worked.

Is it alive, though? Was I alive or dead?

I got an itch at the back of my neck, like bugs under the skin. I could at least sense my body again. Just barely, I felt my fingers and toes prick with pins and needles.

Node formation successful. Reinitializing communications network.

In the back of my skull, the white noise streamed in like TV snow. The inhibitor usually stopped it, but not today.

All units clear zone H1B, a message said. As it faded, a shit-ton of them connected all at once and started blasting me with info. The node count kept climbing: a hundred, a thousand, two thousand . . .

Shit . . .

The count passed six thousand. I'd linked with revivors before, but never more than nine. Back in the field, I'd get a feed for each one on my JZI so I could keep an eye on them, but this time there were so many there was no way to show them all. Each feed came up as a point of light on a grid at the bottom of my periphery. They looked like stars.

We are fucked.

I focused on one of those points of light and my receiver called it out. I couldn't control the revivor on the other end, but when I homed in, I could see what it saw. It was looking down at a concrete wall that was covered in graffiti. It was female; I could make out a pair of tits. Strapped between them was some kind of metal casing. A display was fixed there, with an LCD that flashed blue.

It didn't move. It just stared. The display jumped, and the feed fell back on the pile with the rest.

This is what the static was. All this time, I had a link to all of them. At first they must have been dormant, then the inhibitor kept them back, but now I was in it. I was in there with them, up to my neck.

Mesh established. Synchronizing . . .

"The virus is embedded in the synchronization package," Singh said. His voice was muddy, like I was underwater. *"It's going out . . . now."*

The last link lit up, and my node puked data over every one of them. Shit flew back and forth as we all synced up. In seconds, they knew who and where I was. A map of the network formed on the grid in front of me and formed a kind of shape.

"Did it work?" Ramirez asked.

"It's converging," a voice said. That was Singh. He was close by. *"Hold on."*

The Huma node took all the data that came in and used it to make a picture; a map of the city blinked on and an electric inkblot spread over it. Blotches of light spread and bled together.

Synchronization complete. The pattern covered everything; they were all through the city. The light was brightest in shitholes like Pyt-Yahk, and they were clustered around the three towers, but they'd spread all over. They were moving through the whole city, heading out.

All units clear zone H1B. The message popped up again. With the connection to the rest, I saw an area outlined on the city map; the zone surrounded the CMC Tower.

"What's that there?" a voice asked. Ramirez.

"Looks like he's moving them away from Central Media Communications." On the map, the cluster around the tower was thinning out.

"Why?"

I heard fingers tap at a keypad.

"I don't like it. Contact them and let them know."

All units clear zone H—

One signal whined from out of the static, coming through loud and strong.

Initializing command spoke . . .

The link lit up under the rest of them. I knew what that was. Usually I was on the other side of it, but I knew what it was. Whoever was on the other end started to pull data from me. I watched the data stream by; my heart rate and body temp had bottomed, but no revivor signature had formed. Not yet.

"The command spoke is active," a voice said. I barely heard it.

"He's going to cut her off. Did the virus go out?"

"Yes, sir."

Node 5948. Report in. The message came over the command spoke. It was him; it was Fawkes.

"There."

"Are you sure?"

"We've got activity from a remote source. It's trying to assert control. He's seen her."

"Did the virus work?"

"No change in activity yet."

"What about her?"

Commands dropped in. Fawkes had kicked off some kind of diag from the other end. It triggered my systems and code flicked by as my JZI came back online. He connected to it and started to dump its memory.

"He's got her. If she drops off now, it will tip him. Let him have her."

He was pulling data from me. Along with the rest of the shit he was pulling, I packaged up a little something else for him.

A handy 'bot we'd passed around the grinder got pulled back over the link with the rest of it and stuck itself in Fawkes's memory. He might be a smart jack, but he was still a jack, and an old one too.

Respond, Fawkes said. I decided to try to bluff him.

Node 5948. Reporting in.

There was some corruption detected during the synchronization. Stand by.

Understood.

He went idle for a few seconds, then: *You're on the private military base.*

Before I could think of a response, Fawkes tried to pull my signature and didn't find one.

You're not a revivor, he said. He'd started some kind of scan. *Who are you?*

The game was up.

The one who's going to fuck your dead ass.

The goddamned spoke let him pry through into my JZI and before I could stop him, he'd tapped into my systems. In seconds he'd found my communication node and broke in, branching out over every connection he could find.

"He's in our system!" I heard a voice shout. *"Shit! He's in our system!"*

"How is that possible?"

"Cut the link!"

Whatever you're attempting, Calliope T. Flax, it won't work.

Don't be so sure.

As you can see, my army is still online, so whatever you're trying to do, it hasn't worked. The people behind this are going to pay for that, and so will you. My next strike won't be a warning.

Yeah, well none of my strikes are ever warnings. If Nico doesn't get to you first, then you're mine.

That shut him up for a second.

Who are you? he asked. The son of a bitch didn't even remember me.

I set off the remote 'bot, and it started to dump everything in his memory buffers back to my JZI.

You never should have brought me on that boat, fucker.

I found his Leichenesser seed and popped it, but the link stayed up, so he must have had it taken out at some point. I tapped his visual feed, and a window popped up in the dark. Through it, I saw what he saw.

He was at a desk. He looked down at a console that showed a bunch of security feeds, while a figure off to his right reached in front of him and touched one window. It came to the front, and I saw a woman walk through the frame.

I've seen her. . . . It was that creepy revivor bitch, the one Nico locked lips with on the tanker that night.

The image went blank.

"Damn it!" Right behind the visuals, the command spoke went dark.

"He just killed the spoke."

"The virus went out; he's too late."

"She's still tied to the mesh. He still can't trigger the kill switch with the inhibitor in place, but—"

Fawkes was inside Heinlein. I pulled up the stuff I'd grabbed from his buffers. I didn't get it all, but I got enough. I couldn't tell the assholes in the room with me what I had because I couldn't fucking talk, but if Singh came through and got my JZI back online, I might be able to get it to Nico.

"Shit," someone said.

Ramirez answered, *"What?"*

"We just got a surge of activity out there. A lot of it. Look."

On the map, the large blotch changed shape while I watched. It was close to where we were. Slowly, part of the shape began to branch out and move.

It began to creep in our direction.

Zoe Ott—Alto Do Mundo

By the time Penny and I got back to the war room, it was the closest thing to chaos I'd ever seen in front of Ai. She sat there, calm, while voices on the video screens and in the room all tried to talk at the same time.

". . . confirmed, it was one of the ICBMs from the defense satellite," a voice said.

"You get that?" Osterhagen asked.

Ai nodded. "Mr. Vaggot," she asked, "how long until we regain control of those missiles?"

A window with the man's face appeared in one corner of Osterhagen's screen. He looked a little less collected than the last time he'd appeared, but his voice was still strong and confident.

"Not long," he said. "It's taking time for the 'bots to chisel through the defenses he set up, but once they do, control will be transferred here through the Stillwell Corps satellite-communications array. I think we can shunt him out in thirty or forty minutes, maybe less."

"That was a warning shot," Osterhagen said. "He's telling us to stand down."

"A warning shot?" a woman asked, her voice breaking.

"Initial data confirmed all twelve ICBMs were aimed across an even spread of twelve sectors through the city," he said. "In order for him to drop one out in the bay like that, he'd have to have programmed it with a new target. He intentionally fired it outside the city, where it wouldn't cause any structural damage, but where we'd see it. It was a warning shot."

"What about the radiation?" someone asked.

"The explosion created a radioactive cloud of steam and smoke that right now is moving along the shoreline at a distance of ten miles," Mr. Raphael said. "That could change."

"The next launch won't be a warning," Osterhagen said. "What is the situation at Alto Do Mundo?"

"The detonation of a Leichenesser charge cleared a hole," someone said. "But he's streamed in more of them. I'd say we put a weak link in the chain, but it's reforming."

Osterhagen looked offscreen for a second, then nodded and cut back in.

"We just got a report that the revivors in the street are being ordered away from the CMC Tower," he said.

"Why?" Raphael asked. "Moved to where?"

"Outside a five block perimeter around the tower," Osterhagen said. "We have to assume it's to protect them, and that it's a precursor to some kind of strike. Start getting your people out of there."

"How? We're surrounded from the ground and the air—"

"Any way you can, Robin!"

"What about the virus?" Ai asked. "Has it been deployed?"

"Yes," Osterhagen said. "That's how this information was obtained. Ott was right about Flax. We seeded her revivor matrix and transitioned her onto their network. Fawkes cut her off, but not in time. She received the alert along with the rest to clear the CMC Tower."

"How long before the virus will take effect?" she asked.

"It should have worked by now," he said. "It might be taking longer than expected to propagate, but we have to consider the possibility that it failed."

For the first time that day, I saw something like confusion appear on Ai's face before it went back to its drugged-out expression.

"Failed how?" she asked. "The tests were successful."

"Yes," Osterhagen said. "Assuming the Huma version of Fawkes's revivors matches the ones we had in custody, then it should have worked. But as of this morning, that version changed. It could have invalidated the virus partially, or even completely."

"But the virus affects them," she said. "It reaches them, I've seen it."

I closed my eyes and tried to cut through the anxiousness and pressure that emanated from every consciousness in the room, even those piped through remotely. I took a deep breath and focused on Ai.

She was the elephant in the room; her consciousness hung over her tiny body like a small, broken planet whose pieces were carefully held together by gravity. Tentacles of light stretched out from the fragments and connected to the men and women at the table. More tentacles wove through the room to touch Penny and even me. They floated through the walls, ceiling, and floor, across the city, I figured, to reach Raphael, Osterhagen, and the rest. She was amazingly calm in the face of what was going on, her thoughts ticking away beneath the colors of her mind like the tiny pieces of an incredibly complicated clockwork machine. She was tied into the future model that was displayed on the wall, tuned to the smallest change, and looking for some clue, any clue that might tell her what to do as time ran out.

She didn't know, though, and that scared me. Underneath it all, she was confused. Things weren't happening like she expected anymore. With all of her knowledge, she wasn't sure what to do.

Penny was calm, but was ready to physically act. She spent a lot of time like that, and she almost never relaxed, even when she was drunk, but I'd never felt her so alert before. Part of her mind was turned toward me and I sensed a bond there, a protectiveness I'd never quite noticed before. I'd always known she would kill for me, but somehow I'd never seen the devotion that drove it until that moment.

I reached out, following the connections Ai kept with the others at their remote locations, and found Osterhagen and Raphael. Raphael was worried. He was worried for himself and us, but mostly he was worried for the people on the ground; he was afraid for them, and not just our people but the innocent bystanders about to be caught in Fawkes's attack. Osterhagen was angry and frustrated. He was confident he could defeat Fawkes—in fact, he was certain of it—but the nukes had tied his hands, and, yes . . . there . . . buried away deep inside, he was scared too.

The people in the room continued to talk in restrained, clipped tones, and as I took the pulse of their thoughts as a whole, I realized that fear had begun to creep into the entire network. It was fear of the unknown. It was the fear that despite all the manipulation and information tracking and careful planning, they were delving into an unknown where they couldn't see clearly. That scared the hell out of them, all of them.

Even Ai.

They don't know what to do, I thought, and even though I felt like that should make me scared too, it didn't. I thought maybe I knew what they didn't.

There was someone I needed to communicate with. The person who had stood next to me in my vision and the only one in the room I knew would survive along with me if we failed.

". . . the lines that die out aren't the ones that can't stop the launch; they're the ones that do stop it . . ."

Hans Vaggot was isolated, and I could tell that although Ai was watching him, she wouldn't touch him. He was being left alone to retake the satellite, and as soon as I entered his mind, I knew he was getting close. There was a relief there, like a cool undercurrent beneath the hot colors of his mind. He'd recently made some kind of breakthrough and was closing in. I couldn't tell how long it would be, but although he was still focused like a laser, I could sense his hope—he knew he would succeed; he was only worried about the timing. If he knew it and I knew it, then at least Ai and Osterhagen knew it too. Despite their misgivings, they had begun to think that in spite of everything, they still might stop the event from happening.

Except they were wrong.

Mr. Vaggot, I whispered into the back of his mind. I felt the flow of his thoughts hiccup, and I knew he'd sensed me. In a second, Ai would sense me too, and when she did she'd shut me out again. I only had a short time to communicate with him, to plant, maybe, an idea in his mind. It was an idea that I didn't totally understand myself yet, but somehow I knew it was the answer. When I thought back to what I'd learned about Noelle, who came before me and before Penny, it suddenly seemed clear. She'd known. She'd known all along; she just couldn't handle it.

I took a long swallow off the bottle in my hand and wormed my way further into his mind.

When you retake the satellite, don't shut down the launch, I told him. I felt anxiousness in him from somewhere deep inside as the command took root. *Don't shut it down. Wait for my signal. . . .*

I felt Ai then, and my eyes snapped open as the connection was broken. When I looked over at her, her large eyes had narrowed and there was a hard glint in them.

"I told you to leave him," she said in a low voice. "I—"

She stopped short and perked up, as if she'd heard something. The anger went out of her eyes and I felt a spike of alarm from her, licking out of her consciousness like a solar flare.

"Robin, wait," she said.

"Hold on," Mr. Raphael said. He checked something offscreen.

In all the activity, no one else saw Ai sit up straight suddenly. Her eyes looked startled as they opened wide and stared into space. The others around the table jerked in their trances, sitting up straight along with her.

"Mr. Raphael," Ai said, and the voices quieted.

"Yes, Motoko?"

"Abandon the CMC Tower immediately."

"We're organizing the evacuation now—"

"Forget the rest," she snapped. "Use the helipad."

"Motoko, there are sixteen thousand people in this building," he said. "Tell me what you saw. . . ."

On Mr. Raphael's screen, he turned toward a window behind him where something outside had started to glow in the sky above the electric city lights.

"What is that?" he muttered.

The screen flickered and went out. A second later, all of the screens went out and the room went dark.

Nico Wachalowski—Stillwell Corps Base

From the helicopter, I could see fire in the streets below. A car burned in an intersection, flames spraying cinders as the wind howled through the street. Two blocks down, smoke was pouring from the broken window of a residential building.

Alice, we need to start tracking the bites that occurred since the activation code was sent.

We'll coordinate with local hospitals. If this is true, though, Wachalowski, our best bet is going to be stemming it at its source, not chasing thousands of leads.

We need to contain the city. No one in or out.

We're working on it.

The snow began to pick up as the helicopter took us back toward the Stillwell Corps base. Visibility was down and the ride was choppy. The windshield turned black, and a computerized view appeared in its place as the pilot passed between two buildings.

What about you? she asked. *If this really is true, wouldn't you be affected?*

I'm okay.

But have you been affected?

A notification appeared in front of me as my internal diagnostic finished. My JZI called out my new arm on the system tree with a low-level warning. The necrotic bleed-through had been identified. It was true—the altered nanoblood was leaking into my bloodstream.

No, I lied.

The chopper hit a patch of turbulence and bucked underneath me. My stomach dropped. The vectors tilted in the windshield display, and through the side window I watched the buildings below as we banked left and veered over one of the main strips. From our position, I could see the Central Media Communications Tower in the distance, and beyond that, nearly lost in the snow, the UAC TransTech Center.

Keep me informed, she said. *Let me know as soon as you have something we can use against Fawkes.* She broke the connection.

I pulled my collar down to check my shoulder and saw what looked like bruising there. The bleed-through was getting worse. I wondered if the filter was no longer able to screen the altered nanotech at all. I could be running out of time.

I opened a new link over the channel MacReady had provided.

MacReady, this is happening fast. Do you have a revivor I can use?

It's on its way. I will have it shortly.

Let me know the second you do.

Understood, Agent.

In the meantime, I have a question. Something revivor related.

I'll help if I can.

You said you continued the Zhang's Syndrome study?

Yes.

Was the condition ever recorded in a living person?

It's a condition that occurs during reanimation. No, it does not affect living people.

What about a person experiencing necrotic bleed-through?

It doesn't work that way, Agent. Even with the M10 series, the synthetic blood is something wholly separate from the revivor nodes that interface with the brain. Synthetic blood leaking into an organic system does not, and cannot, cause reanimation. If the traces of synthetic blood were to make their way into the brain, they would most likely kill the affected person.

Understood.

Do you know someone who is suffering from this condition? he fished.

What if the nanoblood were altered somehow? I asked. *Could it be changed to that much of a degree?*

You're referring to Fawkes's use of the transmitter earlier.

Is it possible?

I don't know, he said. *In theory . . . at the molecular level, many of the components are generic. They could be recoded to perform different functions, but not easily.*

So it is possible?

I would say yes. Particularly if you had high-ranking scientists like the ones you named on your team. That kind of research would, of course, be highly illegal, but I would say possible, in theory.

Understood.

Are you saying that you're—

*Just get the revivors I asked for. And hurry. There isn't
much time.*

*I understand. I think you should know this before
the time comes, though: you have a relationship to this
revivor.*

What—

It's the revivor of Faye Dasalia, he said.

Even as the storm outside caused the chopper to
buck, I felt a pang in my chest. For a minute, I forgot
about the rest—Fawkes, the arm, everything.

Faye is part of this, I said. *She's with Fawkes now. She's
close to him; you can't use her.*

*Trust with revivors doesn't hold the same connotation
as it does for humans. I believe she was the one who compromised Heinlein's security and allowed Fawkes access,*
he said. *But something has happened since then and she's
no longer part of his network.*

If she's not on his network, then—

*Trust me, Agent. Fawkes is trying very hard to recon-
nect her, and I'll see to it that he succeeds, but only once
we're ready.*

She'll tell him—

*She can't tell him what she doesn't know, and anyway,
at the end of the day, she is a revivor. It doesn't matter
what she did before or why she did it. When I'm finished
with her, you'll have the access you need.*

It was still hard for me to swallow. Everything that
had happened, all those people dead and dying in the
streets, all of it had happened with Faye standing at
Fawkes's side.

Agent?

I'm here, I said. *Set it up.*

Stand by, he said. *I should have access shortly—*

His message clipped off as the helicopter started to
descend toward the building tops. On several of them, I
could see groups of people bundled in coats and scarves

that whipped in the wind. They were looking down at the city, at the streets below.

MacReady?

Down on the street, pedestrians looked up as we approached. Police blues flashed against the white of snowbanks where a group of officers waited, keeping a crowd of people from entering a strip mall whose windows had been smashed in.

The pilot chattered over the radio and was pointing down toward the street, but I didn't hear him. In the corner of my eye, an FBI alert popped up:

IMMINENT ORBITAL STRIKE

The pilot and copilot looked at each other, and the pilot shouted into the radio. Before I could pull up the details, Alice cut back in.

Wachalowski, get out of the area now.

I just got an alert about an orbital strike. Is it an ICBM?

No. The DoD just detected a massive energy buildup in Heinlein's orbital-defense satellite, The Eye. It's going to fire in the next minute.

Fire at what? What kind of buildup?

They're not sure what the target is, but this charge is off the charts. A spy satellite observing it saw it go into targeting mode two minutes ago. It looks like it's focusing every lens it's got on a common target that is outside of Heinlein's security perimeter.

I brought up the specs for the satellite. It had more than one hundred lenses for striking multiple targets such as missiles, aircraft, or ground forces. Any one of them could generate a beam capable of incinerating a large vehicle or even a tank at only half capacity.

Can they stop it? I asked.

Not in time. A communication from Fawkes warned that if The Eye is destroyed, he'll launch another—

The connection skipped, then cut out. A second later, the radio chatter on the helicopter cut out as well.

Something flashed and lit up the sky. A hole appeared in the clouds and a light shone there like a second sun. The hole blew out, until the clouds were gone and a huge, blinding beam of energy arced down toward the ground below.

The helicopter banked hard as I threw my hand in front of my eyes. Everything went white, and a loud thunder crack pounded in my ears. Spots danced in front of me as the white-hot light burned over the skyline and struck the Central Media Communications Tower in the distance.

The pilot screamed to the copilot, but I couldn't hear anything over the racket outside. I stared in shock as a ball of fire engulfed the base of the tower and began to expand.

Clouds of glass blew out and rained down toward the street as the flames began to boil from the windows. The air rippled, and in seconds the base of the tower turned an angry, molten red.

The pilot was screaming to hold on. A blast of hot air rushed in as the beam writhed and arced through the night sky, setting the surrounding building tops ablaze. The helicopter began to shake violently, then fell into a slow spin.

Concrete and glass split under the waves of heat and tumbled down toward the streets below. Over everything else, I heard a low, earsplitting moan echo through the sky as the huge structure started to twist on its failing foundation.

The city reeled through the window as the helicopter's spin got worse. As the remains of the CMC Tower whipped past the windshield, the arc of light flashed and went out, leaving a dark line to float in front of my eyes. The tower was lit up like white phosphorus, while a cloud of black smoke and fire blew out from around it in every direction.

The peak dropped down toward the other buildings it towered above, and then the mighty structure began to implode. As we spun around again, I saw it crumble, and begin a slow collapse down into the debris.

"We're going down! I'm going to try to land her!" the pilot yelled. My stomach rolled as the deck jumped again, but he managed to stop the spin and stabilize us. The street below tilted at a steep angle as we whipped, dangerously close, past a mirrored building face.

"Hang on!"

The buildings tapered off up ahead where a large, flat area was carved out. It was the Stillwell Corps base. Security alerts began flashing as we passed into their airspace. The pilot was barking into the radio, requesting an emergency landing even as we began to drop.

"Negative! Negative!" a voice came back.

"We don't have a choice! We're coming in!"

A helipad was lit up on one of the buildings up ahead. At street level, I caught several bright flashes of gunfire as we banked around and began our descent.

"The security perimeter has been breached!" the voice on the radio said. "Repeat, our security perimeter has been breached!"

As we came back around toward the helipad, I saw more muzzle flashes from below, and when the helicopter's floodlight washed over the street, I saw why: hundreds of bodies surged toward a chain-link fence whose gate had been forced open. Blood sprayed through the air as soldiers on the other side opened fire on them, but there were too many. Already they were breaking their way into the buildings on either side of the street.

The pilot veered off at the last second, struggling to keep control of the helicopter as we passed over the heads of the clawing mob. The copilot pointed out the windshield at another rooftop, farther into the base, past the fence.

The pilot switched off the radio, cutting off the screaming voice on the other end as he began to take us down.

7

OUROBUROS

Zoe Ott—Alto Do Mundo Penthouse

The silence that came after the lights went out was worse than all the chaos that went on before it. I stood in the dark with the others for what felt like a long time before the overheads flickered back on, but even once they did, the screens on the wall stayed dark. The feeds were all dead.

"What happened?" I asked. Ai was staring into space, not moving or saying anything. At first she looked like she had a seizure or something, but when I focused on her, I saw her mind was still working; she was just in some kind of trance. None of the others at the table moved either.

The armed guards were all alert but weren't sure what to do. One of them called on his radio to see about the power, while the noise outside rumbled off into the distance. No one approached the table or Ai.

"What happened?" I asked again.

"It was the CMC Tower," Penny said. Her face was

lit by the glow from her computer tablet. "Fawkes just destroyed it."

"What?"

She turned the tablet toward me, and on it I could see a video feed from somewhere in the city across town. Someone was filming from the window of a building that would have looked out at the spot where the Central Media Communications Tower would have been, if it had been there.

"Oh . . ." It was all that came out. I stared at the image as thick black smoke billowed up from flames that had spread through the surrounding blocks. The CMC Tower was gone. It just . . . wasn't there anymore. I couldn't get my brain around it.

"That's why we lost all the feeds," Penny said, her voice flat. "It was all going through a hub at the CMC Tower."

"Mr. Raphael—"

"He's dead, Zoe."

I just stared. I liked Mr. Raphael. He was always nice to me, and whenever we'd met face-to-face, he'd always brought me a little gift of some kind. The last thing he'd gotten me had been my little diamond solitaire. I put my hand to my throat without thinking, but I wasn't wearing it.

"He blew up the CMC?" I asked. My voice seemed to be acting independently from my brain, which was still trying to take in the size of the wreckage I was seeing on the screen. The fire blazed as waves of smoke and dust several stories high boiled down the surrounding streets, swallowing up the cars and streetlamps as they went. Pieces of debris were still falling down through the air, raining down into the expanding cloud below. The CMC Tower had been almost as big as Alto Do Mundo, and now it was just gone.

"Zoe, snap out of it," I heard Penny say.

I felt her hands grab my elbows as I looked around. No one else in the room was moving.

"What's wrong with them?" I asked.

"I don't know," Penny said. The guards had left the room to secure the floor and try to get back communications with the others. Except for the distant rumble, it was completely quiet. It was almost like Penny and I were alone together.

Penny started to get up, but I stopped her by grabbing her sleeve. She looked back at me, confused.

"Wait," I said.

"I need to check on Ai—"

"Wait. I . . ."

"What?"

"Something happened," I told her. "I saw something. Something important."

"What did you see?"

"The Green Room," I said. "I saw inside the void again. I think . . . Noelle tried to contact me there."

Penny's face changed when I said her name. I felt a distant spike of emotion that she stifled just as quickly, a red flare that arced up out of the aura surrounding her.

"Did she say anything to you?" she asked. I nodded.

"I think we've been wrong this whole time."

"Wrong about what?"

I glanced past her at Ai. Her consciousness had taken the form of a dense, white sphere. The connections had all been withdrawn. She was experiencing an intense vision, and wasn't watching either of us. Still, I leaned close to Penny and whispered in her ear.

"Penny, I think I'm Element Zero," I whispered. She tried to pull away, but I held on to her sleeve.

"Fawkes is Element Zero," she whispered back. "Fawkes drops the nukes. You stop him."

"She's been trying to tell me something. . . . I think we're wrong."

"We're not."

"What if we are? She said the blast doesn't cause the event; it stops it. I think Noelle knew that. I think she knew Ai was wrong and that she'd have to be the one to kill all these people, to stop something worse from happening. She knew—"

"It was one vision," Penny said, raising her voice. "That's not enough to—"

"But it's the only one that matters," I said. "It came from the void after the event . . . isn't that why Ai tracked us down? Maybe she is some 'next step in evolution' but even if it's true she can't see past that point—she doesn't survive whatever happens, she knows that. We ran out of time, and even with everything she did, she wasn't able to figure it out."

"Zoe—"

"I'm telling you I saw something, something important. Noelle tried to reach me there. . . . I think she's alive."

"She's not alive."

"The database says she's dead, but how can we really—"

"Because I killed her, Zoe."

I felt the vibe again, like a spike. Her face didn't change, but I felt it, and I remembered something she'd said to me a long time ago:

"*This can be a good gig,*" she'd said, and her voice had been serious. "*It can also be a bad one . . .*"

"I thought they had her killed," I said.

"They did."

"Ai made you do it?"

She shook her head. "Osterhagen," she said. "Things were different then. Noelle was . . ."

"Was what?"

"She was amazing," she said. "She was better than I ever was. Ai sent her to go get me and bring me in. She took me under her wing. She took care of me and protected me."

One of the screens flickered, but didn't make it back on. Ai's consciousness pulsed, but she stayed withdrawn.

"Like you did with me," I said.

"Yeah."

"Then why did you do it?"

"She had a bad vision one day," she said, looking down. "Like the ones you've been having . . . the deformities and all that. She started talking dangerous talk."

"Like what?"

"You're right about one thing," she said. "Noelle was afraid. She did think we had it all wrong. One day, she saw something she wouldn't talk about, and she changed after that . . . she lost her appetite, stopped smiling. Something was really wrong, but she wouldn't tell me what she'd seen."

"She knew. She knew what she'd have to do."

"Maybe," Penny said. "She decided at the time that the only way out of this was for us, everyone like us, to be destroyed. Maybe that was the alternative . . . maybe it was one or the other. Either way, she believed it. She got this idea that we were wrong about everything. She sounded a lot like you, but she just . . . wouldn't let it go."

"How did Ai react?"

"How do you think she reacted? We're the greatest human breakthrough the world's ever known. Even if it was as simple as flipping a switch and getting rid of us, no one's going to listen to that."

"So what did she do?"

"Even back then, the model was crystal clear," she said. "Whatever other factors might or might not be in play, Fawkes triggers the event. When she realized no one would listen to her, she pushed to take out Fawkes early, to kill him. He was just an engineer at Heinlein back then. He had no idea any of this was going to happen, but she didn't want to wait. She wanted to cut the line there."

"But why not? Why not do that?"

"Ai can see how all the pieces fit together in a way no one else can. She knew killing Fawkes was a mistake even if Noelle couldn't see it. She knew he'd be more dangerous dead than alive, and she was right, but Noelle was off on her own by then, and she tried to kill him anyway. She jumped him on the street and stabbed him. He lived, but they all knew she'd done it. By that point they'd begun to think she was some kind of 'rogue element', and that she had the potential to cause the very outcome she'd seen ... the one where the people with our abilities are wiped out. Osterhagen wanted her dead. . . ."

"What about Ai?" I asked.

"She didn't," she said. "But Osterhagen was so sure she was going to end up causing the holocaust that even when Ai refused to authorize it, he came to me."

"And you—"

"I was different then, Zoe," she said. "Osterhagen convinced me it was the only way to stop things. He promised me the number-two slot if I did the right thing."

She shook her head.

"And here I am, like he promised."

She got quiet. The longer she talked, the deeper I could see the pain inside her went. I couldn't think of anything to say.

"It was quick," she said. "I watched her bleed out. But I stuck around too long, and someone saw me. I could have wiped his memory, but I gave him the knife and made him believe he'd done it. He copped to the murder and went down for it."

"You just made some random guy do life in prison?"

"He didn't do life. He got killed in jail before his first year was up. He ended up at Heinlein."

She smiled a bitter smile.

"The guy heard our last conversation before I wiped his memory. We didn't know about Zhang's Syndrome at the time . . . in Fawkes's lab, his revivor remembers everything. With what he must have heard, Fawkes finds out who tried to kill him and why. He learns Ai's identity. For all I know, that's what sent him down the path he chose. How's that for irony?"

I focused on her . . . not too hard, not enough to get her attention. Just enough to let her colors fade into view so I could see them. Under her calm exterior, her thoughts buzzed like bees in a hive. There was almost more going on in there than I could make sense of. I saw fear, like a cold, white cloth that rippled in the wind. . . . You'd never know it to look at her face, but she was afraid. I saw concern, confusion, and uncertainty, but underneath it all, shifting slowly like a gray mist, was guilt. When I concentrated on it, I could see how deep it ran.

"I'm not a good person, Zoe," she said.

"That's not true."

"You don't have any idea."

"Yes, I do." I looked deeper . . . there were a lot of things she carried around, but one thing in particular was tucked away. Something she'd barely admit even to herself.

What is that? I couldn't read her mind. I couldn't know what caused it, just that it was there, but it was something I'd never known about her. She'd never let me look that far. I looked deeper and still didn't find an end to it.

She put one arm around me and held me to her. I kind of tensed up at first, but she was gentler than she usually was. I rested my forehead on her bony chest, and she stroked my hair. It reminded me of how my father used to be, back when I was little. I let out a big sigh into her shirt.

"You'll get through this," she whispered.

She put her cheek against the top of my head and squeezed me a little tighter. It was the longest we'd ever touched. It was the longest I'd ever touched anyone in years and years.

"Do you remember when we first met?" she asked. She smoothed my hair with one hand.

I didn't. I didn't want to admit it, but it was lost along with so many other things over the years.

"It was in the subway," she said. "Raphael sent me to make contact with you. I caught you near one of the sake stands. You looked like you really wanted one."

I still didn't remember, but it sounded like me. She laughed just a little.

"You thought you dreamed me."

"I used to get confused about that."

"I know. Back then, I approached you because they told me to," she said. "I didn't want to. I didn't want anything to do with you, Zoe, but . . ."

"It doesn't matter," I said. I pulled away so I could see her face, and for the first time ever, I saw she was crying. She didn't make any noise. Her face didn't even really change except her eyes. Tears just came out, and the colors swirled around her head like a tiny storm, with something dark just under the surface. I saw a glimpse of it just before the halo brightened and pushed me away.

There was something else; something she wanted to say. There was something she needed to say but it wouldn't come out.

"I threw Karen out the first time she showed up at my door," I said. "It doesn't matter how it started."

She said something then, that, unlike most things, I always remembered.

"When this is over," she said, "I'm going to save you, Zoe. If we're both still alive, I'm going to save you."

"What—"

"He's going to destroy us all," a voice whispered in the dark. I thought it was in my head, but Penny perked up too. We both turned and saw that Ai had lifted her head. Her eyes were still closed and sweat ran down her face as her mouth hung partway open.

The others at the table snapped awake as her eyes opened. Her eyes wandered for a second before they found Penny and me.

"We need to evacuate," she told her.

Penny nodded.

"But they have the outside completely surrounded," I said.

"Have the soldiers secure the roof, whatever it takes," Ai said. "We'll take the chopper."

"But the chopper will only hold—" Before I could finish, I felt a numbness seep through me. My head spun a little, and the words fizzled out.

"We're too late," Ai said calmly. "This city will be gone within the hour. We're leaving. Now."

Calliope Flax — Stillwell Corps Base

I felt a rumble through the floor, and the map that floated in the dark warped. A band of static flicked in front of me, and the light came back. I could see.

"Shit, we lost it!"

Everything was a blur. I blinked, and saw the floor down below me. I was facedown, with my forehead pressed into a rubber pad. My body hurt, and there was pressure in the back of my skull. The floor shook again.

I looked to my left and saw Ramirez and Singh humped over a terminal. There was a window behind them, and I saw a big flash of light there. The two looked up.

"Goddamn it!" Ramirez shouted, slamming his fist on the desk. Something out there blew up. Something big.

"I told you!" a voice said. "I warned you he'd—"

"Shut your mouth, soldier!"

Everything went black again. The map blinked a few times, then came back. The points of light began to pop back up.

Synchronizing . . .

"It's the shockwave," Singh said. They were quiet for a minute. *"We've got it back."*

"Shit! What was the target?"

"The CMC building."

"How much dam—"

"It was completely destroyed, sir."

The room got quiet after that. The CMC . . . that was one of the big three. Did he just say Fawkes had destroyed it?

The radio squawked, and I heard Ramirez pick up. A voice babbled on the other side.

"Understood." I heard the handset click back into its cradle. *"Vaggot's team hasn't been able to get control of the satellite back. Will the virus work or not?"*

"It should have stopped them. They—"

"We are running out of options, damn it! Did it work or not?"

The shape on the map bled closer to us. A shot went off somewhere outside, then a bunch more on top of it. Another voice piped up.

"Sir, the hostiles are continuing to move. They're definitely heading for this location."

"It's her," Singh said. *"She pulled something over the command spoke just before it dropped. Fawkes traced her when the link was active."*

"Then unplug her!" Ramirez snapped.

"It's too late! He already got the location!" The arm that broke off from the main shape got closer.

"Then shoot her!"

"It won't matter! He used her to jump into our systems! He knows about Vaggot, he knows everything!"

"Is this base secure or not?" a voice shouted. *"Stop them at the perimeter, goddamn it!"*

"They were overwhelmed, sir. There's too many of them!"

"They're in. Perimeter has been breached in sections three and four . . ."

"Sir, if they take this base before Vaggot's team succeeds, that will be the end of it. Never mind her. We have to concentrate on holding them back."

There was a loud snap, and the map cut out. The static stopped. Light flashed in the dark, and I could see again. I heard machines wind down, and pain throbbed down my arms.

"They cut the power," someone said.

My JZI picked back up and threw up a bunch of warning messages.

Heart function ceased.

Blood-oxygen levels below threshold.

Body temperature below threshold.

It kicked off the emergency resus. I seized as the wire to my heart lit up. Oxygen and adrenaline pumped into my bloodstream.

"Where are they now?" Ramirez asked.

"I don't know. We lost the uplink. Security's down."

My body seized again, and this time the vitals picked back up. My heart thumped. I clenched my fists and heard the knuckles crack.

Heart function resumed.

I grabbed the edges of the gurney and pushed myself up. Wires around my body stretched tight, and I felt pressure at my neck.

The lights were out and the room was full of guys, some in uniform, some in suits. There was equipment set up, but all the screens were blank.

Cn u rd me?

The message popped up just as the emergency lights

kicked in and the computers turned over. I could make
out Singh and Ramirez. Some of the rest were guys from
my squad. Some I'd never seen before. They were pack-
ing shit up, getting ready to move out.

That you, kid?

Ys. I ct pwr. I c u. U c me?

I brought up the GPS and found her signal. She was
in the building, to the south.

How the hell did you get on the base?

Ur dfnses r trshd. U gys r fckd.

She followed us. The little shit actually staged a rescue.

You armed?

Y.

You got a vehicle?

Y.

Then get in it and be ready. I'll come to you.

"She's up!" someone barked. I turned and saw Ramirez
point at me.

"Singh, take care of it!"

Singh drew his gun, but he didn't aim it.

"Singh!" Ramirez yelled.

"I took something Fawkes doesn't want getting out,"
I told Singh. "The ones in the building are here for me.
I'll draw them off."

Ramirez stepped in and pointed his gun. I grabbed his
wrist and twisted as the shot went off and metal sparked
next to my face. The pressure behind my neck built as
I got up, then the wires came loose and snapped away.

I twisted his wrist and he hollered. When his fingers
went limp, I took the gun.

"Cal, wait!"

I bit him on the hand. I bit him so hard that for a second I felt the bones between my teeth. He screamed as
salty blood filled my mouth.

I pulled back. He stood there, one hand bent the

wrong way and the other one bloody. I could see the teeth marks in the meat of his palm. They were deep.

I looked at the rest. There were two grunts left; the remainder were suits. I sucked the salt off my teeth and spit a red gob onto the floor.

"Shoot her!" one of the suits ordered, but no one else would do it. The grunts ignored them and filed out. The last one to go turned back to them.

"If you're coming, then fall in."

He left, and they followed. I spit on the floor again, trying to get the taste out of my mouth. I'd never bitten anyone in my life, no matter how dirty the fight got. The mark on Ramirez's hand was brutal. I don't know why the hell I did it.

Singh was still standing there staring at me as I wiped blood off my chin.

"I'll draw them off," I told him. He nodded.

Vika, which way?

Sth ext.

My shirt was folded next to the gurney. I slipped it back on and buttoned up as I ran after them. From the sound of it, they were headed for the main lot at the north side of the building. Before I lost the feed, it looked like the revivors were moving in from the south.

You're about to get a shitload of company. Keep the engine running; this might be tight.

Rgr.

Down the hall, I saw the last of the suits peel off and head toward the main entrance. I got a fix on Vika and tracked her as she made a beeline for the back lot.

Wachalowski, pick up. It took him a few seconds, but he answered.

Cal, where are you?

Long story. What the fuck is going on out there?

Fawkes just took out the CMC building. Where are you?

*I'm on the base. Look, never mind how, but I was
just on Fawkes's command spoke. Not for long, but long
enough to dump his buffers. I'm sending them to you
now.*

I compressed everything I got and fired it over the
JZI.

Got it. I'm coming in by air now. I'll meet you—

*Don't come after me. Go to the command center. I'll
get back to you.*

I cut the line as something crashed through a window
down the hall. Back behind me, a couple shots went off.

As I passed an open door, I caught a flash of moonlit eyes and heard the crunch of feet as they shuffled
through broken glass up ahead.

Faye Dasalia—Heinlein Industries, Test Facility Five

At the end of a remote corridor, I pushed open a heavy
steel door and felt cold air pass over me. The other side
was dark, but when I adjusted my optical filters I could
make out a heavy sheet of plastic with a slit in the middle hanging from the ceiling ahead. The flaps rippled
gently as fog swirled around my ankles, carrying a smell
that seemed vaguely familiar. I slipped through as the
door thumped shut behind me.

As I moved through the dark, an encrypted call came
in from somewhere inside the building. Someone who
wasn't MacReady was attempting to contact me in secret. I accepted the key and opened the link.

Faye, you escaped. It was Dulari.

Yes.

*Don't tell me where you are. Fawkes got an approxi-
mate location on you during his last communication.
He's sent Ang to find you.*

I stood at one end of a room whose other side I
couldn't see. It was lit from above by some kind of very

dim, pale green glow. The room was a maze of tubes, pipes and wires. Wires trailed from somewhere overhead to connections in steel trays that were assembled in stacks. Slick, creviced gray membrane covered each one, and I sensed electric current humming through it.

I recognized the smell then. It was the greasy, bitter tar smell of heated revivor blood.

Faye, Dulari said. *Fawkes dropped one of the nukes. He used The Eye to destroy the CMC Tower. I didn't realize. I didn't know how far he'd go.*

The route that MacReady had laid out for me took me through the strange room, and as I began to make my way though, other details began to jump out at me: long needles and hairless flesh, miles of squiggling black veins pulsing under thin, wet sheets of gelatin. The low hum of air circulators and liquid coursing through pipes filled my ears, stirring memories from deep, deep inside.

Faye, he's not finished. He's going to destroy everything. I don't think we can stop him.

We can't, I told her. *Be very careful around Fawkes.*

Believe me, I am.

Thank you for the warning. Keep off this line, or he'll catch you.

Faye—

I cut off the connection, and her words faded as I breathed in the smell of the room through my nose.

It was one of the few times that a physical place had affected me since my reanimation. For some reason, standing there in that strange place was comforting. I'd never been there, but it reminded me somehow of my return back into this world. The sound and the smells were imprinted on my brain, like I'd felt them before during my long sleep after my life was taken. In a way, I found difficult to explain that it felt safe and familiar, like being home.

Something was being born, there. I caught myself

wishing Lev was with me so that we could compare that strange perception. I wondered what he would have made of it.

Follow the path, MacReady interrupted. *Hurry.*

What is this?

The future, he said. *The next step. Revivors without human limitations, that don't require second-tier benefits. No human can get through there without requisitioning a biohazard suit. It will buy you some extra time, but you have to move quickly.*

I continued on, picking out organic shapes in the dark. I saw fat squiggles of tissue I didn't recognize, bones that seemed almost but not quite human, and then eventually muscles, joints, fingers and toes. At the opposite end of the chamber was a door, and I pushed it open, leaving the web of disconnected pieces behind me.

It's just up ahead, MacReady said. Ahead was a single, gray metal door.

I see it.

I turned the handle and pulled open the door. The room was in the shape of a large circle, the curves of its wall covered ceiling to floor with microthin display screens. The center of the circle was dominated by a large, round table, six workstations arranged around its circumference. Only one of the stations was occupied. A man in a suit sat there. He didn't turn when I stepped into the room, and the door clicked shut behind me. He just stared at the screen closest to where he sat, while it displayed footage of a large explosion.

"Mr. MacReady?" He nodded.

The electronic screens that covered the wall displayed a dizzying amount of data. I scanned it, picking out code mixed with complex mathematical equations littered between more familiar items: media clips, handwritten notes, and photos. On the screen he was watching, a large structure was collapsing into flames.

"That's the CMC Tower," he said quietly. He rubbed at his brow, and I saw his hand shake. "That was the CMC Tower."

I realized the feed was live. That hole was forming in the skyline right now. Over MacReady's shoulder, I watched the last of the Central Media Communications Tower crumble into the cloud of smoke and fire.

Memories were rising out of the darkness, points of light expanding to display visions of that structure as it loomed in the distance. The morning it all started, as I rode the monorail on my way to the scene of Mae Zhu's murder, I'd watched the tower's shadow loom off in the distance through the haze of snow. I'd seen it nearly every day of my life.

I made this possible.

The blocks around the blast lost power, the buildings and neon lights going dark to form a black hole in the bright cityscape. A smaller building nearby began to fall. I'd always known this was part of Fawkes' plan. I knew he would destroy the three towers, but it seemed that knowing it and seeing it with my own eyes were two different things, even now. For the first time in a long time, I wondered if I hadn't placed my trust in the wrong man.

"You may not have much time, Mr. MacReady."

He turned then, and looked at me. He was an older man with thick, wavy hair that had turned completely gray. He smiled, showing unnaturally white teeth, but he couldn't maintain it. He stood and approached me.

"You've held up remarkably well," he said.

"That isn't Fawkes' only target."

"I know. Did Fawkes remove the Leichenesser seed, or was it Agent Wachalowski?"

"It was Nico." My eyes moved over the screens, following the trees of data mapped out there. On some level, the patterns were familiar. I saw profiles of individuals, lines tracing associations between them.

"It reminds me of the precinct," I told him. "When we'd try to chart organized crime or gang associations."

That caused him to grin weakly. He followed me as I passed by him and stepped toward the screens.

"That's not too far off," he said.

A high-pitched whine filled my head as something cold pierced the skin behind my ear. Immediately, I felt my muscles seize. I opened my mouth to speak, but before I could, my jaw locked in place.

"I'm sorry, Faye," he said. He guided me down into the chair he'd been sitting in, and reflected in the screen I saw that he had some sort of handheld tool pressed near the base of my skull. He disconnected something at its tip and moved it away, placing it on the table behind him. A long, metallic rod was left behind, sticking several inches out of the back of my head. He guided a wire into the rod and fastened it there.

I tried to move, but I was completely paralyzed. When I tried to access my communications node, I found I was cut off. He moved back around to where I could see him and tapped a stylus to an electronic pad he held in one hand. My jaw unlocked.

"What did you do?" I asked.

"I've frozen your primary systems. I've cut off most of your motor functions, and outgoing communications will be monitored and controlled from here on out."

I triggered the injector, but my arm didn't respond. In my system tree, everything was locked down. My core functions still ran, but electrical impulses had been cut off at the C3 vertebrae.

"I will need to disable your control shunt as well," he said.

"If you do, Fawkes will reestablish his command spoke."

"I know, but he won't be able to do much with you now."

"He'll be able to track me and come here."

"I know," MacReady said, "but there's no other option; Fawkes has to be stopped. Your friend needs your help, and I can't leave this to chance."

"My friend?"

"Agent Wachalowski," he said. "He needs your help, and so do I."

He pointed to the screens of data.

"This is where we continued Fawkes's work," he said, "after he was gone. This is where we continued his work studying Zhang's Syndrome. There were six of us at first. Heinser, Cross, Deatherage, Dulari, Chen . . . and myself. We kept it quiet, but believe me, I understand, and I know what Fawkes is trying to do."

"You may not know as much as you think," I told him.

"Every second-tier citizen who dies comes through here," he said. "We've had access to all of them, along with every scrapped generation-seven model we've been able to get back in here. As you saw on your way in, reclaiming their memories has gotten much more efficient since Fawkes's day. That's a lot of data points. These people manipulate things in a very-well-thought-out way to influence policy and politics on governmental, corporate, and even social levels. Right now, their most powerful organization is based in the UAC, and the UAC dominates the globe both militarily and economically. But there are others like them, and over time other seats of power will rise in other parts of the world, if they haven't already. What we will ultimately end up with is a group of powerful countries that follow the UAC model."

What he said surprised me. I'd heard this before, but I didn't expect to hear it from him.

"You sound like Fawkes," I said.

"Fawkes's data was irrefutable," he said quietly, looking back to the destruction on the screen. "When I realized what we had, I knew no one could know. When your friend Wachalowski came sniffing around, I threw him a bone, hoping he'd track down Fawkes on his own without leading anyone back to us. But it was a mistake. Both sides figured out someone was watching them from here. Cross was killed and Heinser disappeared overseas after the Second Chance incident. Two years ago someone— Ang, I think—took matters into his own hands and used a rail-gun sniper to try to assassinate their leader, Motoko Ai, when she came out into the open to meet with Agent Wachalowski. I should have known then. I should have kept a closer eye on him. When Ang and Dulari truly understood what was at stake, data gathering wasn't enough. They wanted action."

"They were right," I said. "Fawkes has a plan to stop them, not study them."

"There are things Fawkes doesn't know," he said, "things he never bothered to learn. He was obsessed with proving their existence and eliminating them. He never dug into those lost memories to understand what drove these people. They are afraid of something, Faye. Something much bigger than Fawkes himself."

His words triggered something inside. Memories swirled over the void below them, and one small cluster disengaged from the rest. As one ember broke orbit, a portal opened to the contents inside.

"What you did was attempted murder, Noelle," I said. *"You're going to jail."*

In the memory, I sat in an interrogation room. A gaunt, wasted woman sat across the table from me. This was the memory Fawkes didn't want to hear.

"I wish I was," she said. *"They might not be able to get to me there. That's why I'll never go."*

"Who is 'they'?"

"I was supposed to stop him," she said. *"I just wanted to stop him. Samuel Fawkes is a dangerous man."*

"He's some engineer at Heinlein Industries. The man is not dangerous."

"Things change," she whispered.

MacReady's brow creased as he watched the tablet in front of him. He tapped at it with his stylus, and memory addresses began to appear in the HUD in front of me.

"That's a suppressed segment you're replaying," he said. "Reclaimed information."

"A woman," I told him, "long ago. Fawkes was still alive, but she was afraid of him even then. Afraid enough that she had tried to kill him."

"Did she say why?"

"No," I said. "She never did, not directly, but I got the impression it was to avoid something much larger."

"Did you relate these memories to Fawkes?"

"I tried. He didn't agree."

"Well, your instincts were right, I'm afraid. What they fear is much larger than anything we've seen so far, and it begins with the destruction of this city."

"Fawkes has specific targets. He won't destroy the city. He's trying to save it."

"Fawkes will destroy the city," MacReady said. "He knows that killing hundreds or even thousands of them is futile. If you remove the human equation, then the only efficient way to stop this is genocide. He's been lying to you, Faye. He plans to wipe the slate clean, and start fresh. These people, these mutations, they don't just envision the city's destruction; they've seen a nuclear annihilation specifically. They foresee eleven nuclear devices—specifically eleven—that will cause it, and after dropping one in the bay as a warning, that is exactly the number Fawkes currently has pointed at the city from the orbiting missile shield. Fawkes will destroy this city and with control of the nuclear defense shield I don't think he'll stop there. These people have foreseen a world-ending event, Faye. Total annihilation of society as we know it."

He stepped closer, and I could see the bands of orange heat that ran up either side of his neck beneath the skin. The core in his chest pulsed. He believed it too.

"Fawkes will strike another target, probably soon, and I think you know that," he said. "You've been dead a long time, but I don't think you're ready to write off the world you knew as an acceptable loss, not yet. Please. Help your friend."

Orange flickered behind MacReady's pupils. Shortly after, he forwarded a link to my communications node. It was him. It was Nico.

"I'm putting him through," MacReady said.

The channel opened, and Nico was there.

Faye, he said. *It's me.*

Hello, Nico.

It's been a long time.

Yes.

I know a lot has happened, but I need you now, Faye. Will you help me?

Do I have a choice?

You know me well enough to know the answer to that. There's too much at stake.

Fawkes could be the only chance we ever have to stop them, I told him.

I know. And they might be the only chance we have to stop Fawkes. That's what I'm left with. That's what we're all left with.

So you've chosen them?

I'm not looking out for either side. I'm trying to look out for the people stuck in the middle of all this. No matter what you think of his motives, Fawkes set something in motion today. He killed thousands of people who aren't even part of the thing he's trying to stop, and he's used Heinlein to alter the revivor technology inside them.

That stopped me. He was referring to Fawkes' transmission.

Alter it? Alter it how?

It's spreading on its own. Jumping from host to host.

That's impossible, I said, but even as I said it I began to wonder. It would explain why he needed to occupy Heinlein Industries. It would explain how he intended to keep up his resistance, even after he was gone.

It's happening, Faye. It's already out of his control.

A virus. An engineered virus. Was this what the woman, Noelle Hyde, feared all those years ago when she'd sat across from me in the interrogation room? Had her abilities allowed her to see what Fawkes would someday unleash on the world?

If it was true, and she had, then had she witnessed the end of humankind? Or only the end of her kind?

Faye?

I'm here.

Something has to be done. I've made my choice. You have to make yours. Who will you trust? Me, or Fawkes?

In my mind, I could almost picture Nico's eyes. I could almost see the ruthlessness in them, and that certainty in his soul that he was right. I remembered the way he was, long ago, when he put everything he knew on the line because of that certainty. I had envied him that, but in some ways, to truly see in terms of pure right and wrong—Fawkes's way—was what he railed against hardest.

I'm reactivating your command spoke, he said. I felt him intrude into my systems, and begin some kind of transfer.

When you do, he'll track me down, I said.

I know. This is going to be close. You know Fawkes better than me at this point. You could make the difference.

Nico—

I know you don't love me, he said. *I know you can't, not anymore, but you can still trust me. You can still do that.*

The locks I'd placed on the command connection

began to break down, and fall away. Immediately I could feel Fawkes there, finding footholds in those new openings, and forcing his way in.

We're out of time, Nico said. *Make your choice.*

Nico Wachalowski—Stillwell Corps Base

Stillwell soldiers flanked us, escorting us down the hall after an armed garrison unit met us on the helipad. The northern section of the base, where we were, was still secure, but the numbers outside were rising.

The connection to Faye flashed on the HUD. Through her, I would be able to direct a team of five revivors to move a payload of Leichenesser from the processing plant into the atmosphere control center for the Pratsky Building. It was a total distance of roughly a quarter mile, and the clock would begin ticking the second I reactivated her command spoke.

"It's down!" someone shouted in a room as we passed. "The entire structure is down. Communications are out all over the city—"

Military channels were still functioning, though, and the footage coming in from the street was devastating. Smoke drifted between the buildings below like a gray fog. The Central Media Communications Tower, the second-tallest structure in the city, had been razed in less than a minute. A hollow pit formed in my gut. Not even anger had filled it yet.

"I need to talk to Osterhagen," I said to one of the guards. "Is he here?"

"He'd just arrived back at the UTTC when the attack began," he said. "We can put you in touch with him."

As we walked, I cycled through the data Cal had sent just moments before the explosion—the only lead I had on Fawkes. In it I found lot numbers and stats for the units under his control, circuit information for the revivor network ... even override codes for the sixth-gen-and-up revivors on his command spokes.

Good work, Cal.

He'd flushed his visual data regularly, but the last segment was still in there. In the playback window, I watched as he addressed an Asian man and a dark-skinned woman that I recognized from the FBI records as Chen and Shaddrah.

There was no audio, but after a minute Shaddrah nodded and left the room. Chen began to follow her, then turned back as what must have been a private message to him flashed on the screen.

Watch her.

Chen nodded.

The next strike will come soon. If she becomes a problem, you know what to do.

The soldiers led me into a war room where engineers were hunched over terminals in rows. Mounted on one wall was a screen that lit up as we entered, and I recognized the face that appeared as Osterhagen's.

"You're on," the soldier said.

"General, my name is Agent Wachalowski," I said.

His face was calm, but fury brewed behind his eyes. "I know who you are," he said. "I'm told you're recommending we leave Heinlein's transmitter intact."

"Yes, sir. Hear me out. I think I know what's going on."

"Motoko puts a lot of faith in you," he said, "but there are millions of lives at stake here, and a preliminary analysis of the data you recovered from Palos Verdes doesn't prove your suspicions that we're dealing with some kind of outbreak. The threat of the nukes is real and immediate."

"With respect, sir, we'll never be able to analyze that data in the time frame we have."

Osterhagen thought for a minute, then turned to the men in the room.

"Mr. Vaggot?" One of the engineers glanced up at the screen. His eyes were wide but focused. His fingers moved over a keypad like they acted on their own. "Can you retake control of the satellites or not?"

"I can, sir."

"In the time frame we discussed?"

Vaggot hesitated. "I can, but not in that time frame."

"And if we destroy the transmitter?" he asked.

"If Mr. Fawkes had rigged the satellite to launch already," he said, "meaning, if it was set to launch at a preset time, then the launch sequence would be, in effect, already active. If that were true and we destroyed the transmitter currently controlling it, then it would assume an enemy infiltration, and the launch sequence would be locked down; we wouldn't be able to stop it. If the launch sequence was not active, then the satellite will be receptive to our control, as long as the proper security codes are presented. At this point, we are confident that the launch code is not currently active."

"You're sure?"

"We won't know with one-hundred percent accuracy until the 'bot reasserts full control, but we've got hooks into most of its systems now. I'm sure."

"Agent Wachalowski," Osterhagen said. "Fawkes is no doubt gearing up The Eye to fire again."

"I know."

"Without that transmitter, he'll lose control of both satellites, and his ground forces too."

"I know," I said, "but I'm telling you—Fawkes used contacts inside Heinlein Industries to develop a Huma variant off the grid. The transmission that halted the revivors earlier fundamentally changed the behavior of the nanotech. He repurposed it."

"Repurposed it for what?"

"With the help of Heinlein's engineers, he's found a way to administer the Huma payload without an injection. They're spreading it through saliva, through bites." The Stillwell engineers were listening now. Even Osterhagen's face changed.

"You think he's trying to create more revivors?"

"No," I said. "The dogs we recovered at the train yard had standard M10 revivor nodes, but the engineers worked on different components of Fawkes's variant. At Black Rock, they were testing the ability to disseminate it through bite wounds. Another engineer designed it to self-replicate so it could be transmitted over and over, but I think the experiment in the Mother of Mercy's basement was the key. We found evidence of nanotech in their brains, but no revivor nodes. When Van Offo tried to influence the prisoners down there, to calm them down, he couldn't. Fawkes has been experimenting in secret for years now, trying to figure out what makes you guys tick, and I think he finally did it. He's repurposed Huma not to make more revivors, but to switch off your influence. To trigger Zhang's Syndrome in the general population and give them their memories back. That's what this is about. He is trying to wipe you out, but not in the way you think."

"How can you—" Osterhagen started, but I cut him off.

"I can't prove it, but I'm telling you I'm right. It's affected me as well. I know it's true. At this rate it will spread beyond the city in hours and we have no idea what it will do. If you destroy that transmitter, you'll never—"

On Cal's recording I saw Chen nod, then turn and leave the room. The angle of the feed changed as Fawkes returned his attention to a console in front of him. Data streamed across the screen. His hands, almost skeletal now, moved quickly over the keypad. An image I recognized as a map of satellite positions hung at the top of the screen. He was inputting coordinates.

"What is it?" Osterhagen asked. I checked the time stamp on Cal's recording.

"Sir, how long would it take The Eye to spool up for another shot?" I asked.

"We predict thirty minutes," Vaggot said.

According to the time stamp on Cal's footage, the satellite had to have already been aimed at the CMC Tower and was preparing to fire when it was recorded. That meant that on the recording he was entering in the data for a different target; his next target.

While I watched, a list appeared in Fawkes's HUD, mapping over the recording. There were several more sets of coordinates there in a column. When I ran them through the GPS, I found the location of the target he'd just entered.

"General, I know what Fawkes's next target is. He's going to fire on the UTTC."

"How—"

"I'm forwarding the data to you now, but get out of that building."

"Sir," Vaggot said. "In a worst-case scenario, you have maybe twenty minutes. We will not have control of the satellite by then."

"The UTTC is under siege at the moment," Osterhagen said. "We can push our way out but it will be a bloodbath, and it will take hours."

"Can we destroy The Eye?" I asked.

"Fawkes has threatened to launch if we try." He looked thoughtful for a minute.

"Sir, I have a contact inside Heinlein Industries," I told him. "I may be able to take Fawkes out from the inside."

"We can have a short-range missile in the air in five minutes," one of the soldiers said, "and destroy that transmitter in seven."

Osterhagen nodded. He didn't say anything for several seconds.

"Sir, what do you want us to do?" the soldier asked.

"Ready the missiles," Osterhagen said, "but don't launch without my order."

"Yes, sir."

"No matter what, you do not fire those missiles without a direct order from me."

Two men snapped a salute and rushed out of the room.

"Alto Do Mundo is next on the list after the UTTC," Vaggot said, looking at Cal's data. "Then a list of major utilities; water, power, and transportation."

Osterhagen nodded again and met my eye.

"She believes in you," he said.

"I know."

"You've got five minutes," he said, and his image winked out.

MacReady, we need to go now.

I understand.

Faye, will you help me?

She didn't answer right away, but she did answer.

Yes.

I cycled through the list of override codes that Cal pulled from Fawkes's memory, and queued up Faye's, just in case.

We'll have one chance, Faye.

I have shared Fawkes' security information with Mr. MacReady. He's found five revivors that can form a chain without leaving their individual security zones, but it won't take Fawkes long to realize something is wrong.

Understood. Get ready.

I hope you're doing the right thing, Nico.

Me too.

I pushed down the packages that Calliope had given me over the circuit, and they began to install themselves.

Her command spoke back to Fawkes went live, and I saw him try to take control. He tried to issue her override code, but it wasn't accepted. After that, he began to run a trace on her physical location. It wouldn't take them long to reach her.

Calliope's shunt initialized and created the virtual command hub inside Faye's system. Stealth connections began to open, riding on an unused portion of the command matrix. They made the five connections, and five remote feeds appeared on my JZI. I was inside Heinlein.

The five units I selected form a relay starting in the processing plant and ending in Central Atmosphere Control, MacReady said. *Use them to move the Leichenesser payload between zones.*

Two of the feeds came from the processing plant; through a set of doors, I could make out rows of bodies that hung from the ceiling. The other three waited outside in different parts of the campus, staring through the snow at the plant in the distance.

I sent the virus, and it replicated over each channel. It dropped into the primary node of each revivor and began to worm its way into their systems. In less than a minute, the mirror-spoke endpoints went active.

I'm taking control of them now.

One by one, I issued the overrides and took remote control of the revivors. Their systems were reflected back, giving me full access.

"Four minutes, Agent," a voice said.

I scanned the layout of the processing plant and located the Leichenesser stores that MacReady had called out. I sent one unit to retrieve the payload from storage. The automated system responded and retrieved a single crate containing a series of pressurized metal tanks.

One will be enough, MacReady said. *The Leichenesser is in liquid form, and highly concentrated.*

Understood.

I sent the target revivor the route to take, making sure to keep it inside its designated security zone. I kept the feeds open to monitor them, and waited as the first revivor moved to the storage locker.

None of the others seemed to pay it any notice as its black hand gripped the handle and pulled open the heavy steel door. Mist drifted out of the gap as it slipped through the fog and into the freezer chamber.

The rows were filled with stores of chemicals. The revivor passed by them as it followed the location on the manifest and found a single rack of thin, glossy black canisters. Each one was labeled with multiple warnings and marked with a biohazard trefoil.

The revivor removed a single tank from the container and headed back through the mist toward the freezer door. It pushed it open, and kept an even pace as it headed for the plant's western exit.

How long will it take the gas to saturate the sublevels? I asked MacReady.

Not long, he said. *I've shut off the blowers to the lab, but they don't need to stay that way. The gas won't affect me.*

On the feed, the revivor's optics isolated a figure through the snow. It waited near a fence at the processing plant's perimeter. The feed bobbled rhythmically as the revivor began to run the canister over to it.

Agent Wachalowski, I understand your feelings in this matter, MacReady said, *but I think it's time to let her go.*

My fingers curled into a fist, tendons crackling.

I know.

It would be safer to—

I know. We still might need her.

Is that the reason?

This has to work, no matter what the cost. But do what you can to save her.

I will.

The revivor on the feed reached the second one in the chain and handed off the canister. I switched over the active feed and watched through its eyes as it turned back to the metal door behind it, where a sign was mounted:

PRATSKY WEST

Over the feed, I saw an incoming call request appear on Faye's system. It was flagged urgent.

Faye?

That's Fawkes, she said. *He's looking for me.*

Stall him. The payload will be positioned soon. How long will it take once you start the air circulators?

Five minutes to get the Leichenesser into position; another ten for the saturation to reach critical.

MacReady's estimate would put me past Osterhagen's deadline, but still inside the window before The Eye could fire a second shot. If the Leichenesser was already released, I might be able to convince Osterhagen to wait.

The revivor on the tarmac moved quickly as it clutched the canister to its chest. Up ahead, through the snow, the third revivor in the chain waited.

Let me know the second the reaction starts. If we can retake control of the facility and the transmitter, we might still be able to stop this.

Faye's connection turned from green to red. It went out. The link dropped.

Faye?

"Three minutes, Agent."

On the tarmac, I saw the revivor stop short in the snow. A second later, the feed went dark.

8

REVENANT

Calliope Flax—Stillwell Corps Base

A door to my right bashed open as they shoved their way into the hall behind me. I picked up speed and put some distance between us, but got stopped at the end of the hall by a metal door with panes of safety glass. I put two slugs into one of them and kicked out a hole, then squeezed through as they rushed in behind me. Palms slammed against the glass, and one grabbed at my boot as I started to run.

Vika, you ready?

Rdy.

It's going to be close.

Behind me I heard them smash out the rest of the glass. Down the main hall I could see the back exit, with a guard station between walls of bulletproof glass. Past that was the back lot, and outside the bodies were already piling up. They'd mobbed the door, beating on it with their palms and fists.

I'm not getting out this way, kid.

They surged against the wall, and the metal frame

squealed on its hinges. Back behind me, they were closing in. I aimed my pistol and put down the two in front, but it didn't slow them down much.

Kid—

A crash came from the lot, and I turned to see an armored military truck plow into the crowd on its way to the back exit. It didn't slow down as revivors were smashed against the grille and dragged underneath. Up in the cab, I saw the kid grip the wheel as she braced for the impact.

The glass caved in and the metal frame broke loose from the concrete as the truck smashed through the guard station and into the back lobby. Glass sprayed down the hall and cold air blew through the gap.

The kid revved the engine and waved me in. I fired a couple more rounds into the crowd behind me, then jumped through the wreckage toward the cab. A hand grabbed my boot as I pulled the passenger's door, and I turned and shot a woman in the face between her black eyes. I threw myself in the seat and slammed the door behind me. There was a rifle propped against the dash inside.

"Can you shoot?" I asked.

"Yes."

"Switch places!"

She squirmed past me and grabbed the rifle as I got behind the wheel. They pulled her door open, and she fired three quick shots. An expended shell burned the back of my hand as bodies fell into the snow, and she pulled the door shut again and pounded the lock.

Gears ground as I slammed the truck into reverse and stomped on the gas. Bodies thumped against the rear of the truck as I cut the wheel and hit the brakes. Outside, one of them smashed a trash can against Vika's window, but it held. She cracked it open and fired out the slit. Shells trailed smoke as they pinged off the dash and onto the floor.

"Hold on!"

The back lot led to a side street through a short connector, and I aimed for it. Tires spun in the snow, then we lurched forward. Faces flashed in the headlights before they got creamed against the grille and went under.

Metal and glass popped as we clipped a parked car and pushed out onto the street. There were more of them out there, maybe hundreds. They swarmed us, piling up as we smashed through. At the main road, I smashed the nose of a passing car, and bodies tumbled into the street as I hit the brakes.

They climbed over the grille and onto the hood. Vika fired the rifle again as I picked up speed and rolled over them. A few slipped off, but one hung on the driver's-side mirror. I jerked the wheel, and it was scraped off as I swiped a parked car.

"Shit!"

Horns blared, and I felt the rifle's muzzle flash on the side of my face. Tires squealed and the truck started to slide. We spun out, and metal and glass crunched as we hit something hard.

"Goddamn it!"

Something hit the driver's-side window. Bodies slammed against the truck and hands tried to pull the doors open. Another one jumped on the hood and stomped down on the windshield. I punched the gas again and broke out of the snowbank. Bodies thumped under the tires as I gunned it down the street. Soldiers scrambled, firing into the crowd but there were too many of them.

Up ahead, way in the distance, I saw the smoke. The spot where the CMC Tower used to be was nothing but black smoke that rolled down the streets and swallowed up everything. Mobs of people ran to try to get out of the way of it, and more revivors were coming. The CMC was southwest of the Stillwell compound. I pulled up the GPS and plotted a route to the north gate.

"They'll try and follow," I said. "I'm going to lead them off the base!"

I cut the wheel again and took a side street toward the compound's main strip. With the smoke in our rear-view mirror I watched as the bodies fell off behind us, still running in our direction.

Faye Dasalia—Heinlein Industries, Test Facility Five

The revivor stood stone still, the metal canister clutched to its body. Wind sheared across the tarmac, whipping its clothes around it.

"Faye, what are you doing?" MacReady asked.

"It wasn't me," I said. Someone else was in my head. They'd shunted their way into my command node and put a hold on my communications.

"Faye—"

"I fucking knew it," a voice said. Out of the corner of my eye I saw Ang Chen step through the doorway, a pistol clutched in one hand. His eyes moved from me to MacReady, then back.

MacReady held up his hands and stepped forward, but stopped when Ang pointed the gun at his chest.

"Ang—"

"You were overruled, Bob. You should have stayed out of it."

"Chen, he destroyed the CMC Tower," MacReady said. "He's going to—"

"You don't know what's at stake," Ang said. His voice was still calm, but his eyes had grown wide. The hot mass of his heart thudded in his chest.

"Ang, please," MacReady said, as he took another step. "Think about—"

The gun boomed as Ang fired a single shot. Mac-Ready staggered back and dropped the electronic pad to the floor. He stared down at his side, where blood had begun to spread through his shirt.

Ang aimed to fire again, and MacReady lunged. Not toward Ang, but toward me. His fingers, warm with blood, touched my neck, and I felt the metal rod slide out of the back of my head. The control lock winked out, and impulses began to flow back down the length of my spine. My system tree reestablished. I could move again.

Ang fired. The bullet shattered through MacReady's front teeth, then exploded out through the back of his neck. His body fell against the wall behind him, then collapsed onto the floor. Chen stood, still pointing the gun, as smoke drifted slowly out of the barrel.

"I know what's at stake," I told him.

Chen's eyes flicked to me and stared. "Shut up," he said.

"I know what they did to me—"

"So do I!" he barked. "They got to me too, and I know it now! I know everything! Every goddamned thing!"

The gun shook in his fist as he held it out. The network of veins stood out under his skin, like spiderwebs of warm light, and I knew he was very close to the edge. I realized then that when he said he knew, he meant he really did know; his memories had returned. Somehow, Fawkes had found a way to return them while still leaving him alive.

Whatever happened to him, whatever he'd done and been made to forget, he'd come face-to-face with it. Whatever it was, he couldn't accept it. Without a revivor's disconnectedness, he was losing control.

"Fawkes woke you," I said, and I could see it was true. "How—"

"Shut up!" He stepped forward and stuck the gun in my face. He took two steps toward me, and the end of the barrel pushed into my cheek.

I fired the bayonet and struck Ang's gun hand with it.

The pistol went off near my ear, as blood spurted from the notch cut in his wrist. He staggered back, blood seeping through his shirt cuff. Blood dripped down onto the floor as he clutched his wounded arm. He raised the gun again, but he couldn't hold it straight.

Suddenly, something forced him out of my head, and the communications block was released. The revivor connections came back online. When he realized what happened, Ang's eyes widened.

"Who did that?" he whispered. "Who else is helping you?"

Faye? Faye, are you reading me? It was Nico.

I'm here. I checked the revivor feeds and saw the units perk up as the command spokes reformed. They found me.

Ang transferred the gun to his left hand and took aim. He followed me as I circled the table and fired a single shot that went wild. I could sense him digging into my systems, trying to reestablish the override. I pointed my own gun in his direction.

"Drop that connection," he said.

The remote unit carried the canister across the Pratsky Building, where the last revivor in the chain waited down in a darkened stairwell. I watched them make eye contact with each other, meeting halfway on the stairs. The last unit accepted the canister, then turned and made its way down.

Both guns went off, and a bullet struck my chest. I grazed Ang's shoulder as he fired again, punching through my right elbow. It triggered the mechanics in my forearm, causing it to split apart. The pistol flipped free from my hand and spun across the floor.

I ducked under the table as the final revivor picked up speed down a long corridor and into the main climate-control center. I swung the bayonet and slashed Ang's hamstring. He screamed, and I heard his gun thump down onto the table above me.

I stood and saw him reel, hopping on one foot. He lunged for his weapon but stumbled and fell. I pulled the bayonet back, preparing to deliver the killing blow, when Samuel Fawkes appeared in the doorway.

Two soldiers followed him in. They aimed their rifles at me.

"Stop," Fawkes said. His eyes glowed flatly in the dim light. Ang looked back, his face dark. A vein pulsed at his neck. Three more revivors filed in from behind Fawkes and took positions around him. They all had automatic rifles at the ready.

"Pick up your gun, Mr. Chen."

He reached across the table, smearing blood, and recovered the weapon. He hopped back, and one of the revivors held him steady.

I felt Fawkes connect, and he began to scan my systems. He poked around, looking for a way in. His owl's eyes didn't change expression.

"Who is controlling you?" he asked.

"She's running some kind of virtual command connections," Ang said. "I tried to shut her down when someone blocked me, someone from inside. Someone besides MacReady is helping her."

"Virtual command connections to where?"

"I wasn't able to trace them before I got kicked off."

In the feed, I saw a pair of hands place the tank on the concrete floor as the revivor scanned the room. A huge turbine of some kind took up most of the space there, surrounded by smaller blocks of machinery and rows of metal ductwork. The main pipe stood higher than a man. According to the building's schematic, that was the main outflow pipe.

All nodes, report in. Fawkes's eyes looked distant as the responses began to pour in. It would take time to process them all, but not much.

On the feed, the revivor grabbed the tank and approached the pipe. Using a cutter, it opened a hole large enough to squeeze through, leaving one corner attached. It peeled back the lid, and I could see its uniform begin to ripple madly as the air escaped. From far off, I heard a low whistle moan through the halls.

Fawkes looked back through the doorway.

"What is that?"

The revivor passed the tank through the hole, then climbed in after it. Inside the pipe it was dark, but its night vision allowed me to see the interior as it reached back through, grabbed the metal lid, and pulled it back. The whistle went up in pitch as the revivor held the metal in place, its fingers stuck through the seam.

Fawkes began issuing orders over the command spokes. In minutes, a squad of revivors would be down there, and he'd know.

Faye, I'm shutting down the circulation to T5. The message came not from Nico, but from Dulari. She'd been monitoring us. I tried to respond, to tell her that Fawkes was here with me, but the circuit was one-way, so it couldn't be traced back.

A low thud came from somewhere in the building. The airflow to the room we were in stopped. Fawkes continued to watch me impassively as he ran a trace on the override circuit.

The revivor in the pipe gripped the tank between its legs, still holding the pipe lid shut with one hand. It used its free hand to open the tank, and icy mist began to drift from the mouth. It pushed the tank over with one foot and liquid gushed out, down the pipe. When it hit the air, it exploded in a cloud of gas. I caught a glimpse of the revivor's arm and hand as they bubbled and dissolved away. I saw the mechanism that held the blade inside the forearm as the muscle and flesh melted; then the feed warped and went black.

It's away, Dulari said. *Critical saturation should occur within minutes.*

Fawkes looked down at MacReady's body, then back to me. "What did he tell you, Faye?"

"He said you're going to destroy the city."

"That's bullshit," Chen said. "She—"

"Take Mr. Chen to be treated, please."

The revivor that was holding him up steered him toward the doorway and began half dragging him out. Over his shoulder, Chen glared at me, red-faced.

"What else did he say?" he asked.

"Just do it," I said. "Kill me." He stepped closer, and his soldiers crowded in behind him.

"Not until I've had a chance to look through your memory core," he said. "Something's going on here. What else did Mr. MacReady tell you?"

"He said you'd destroy the city no matter what anyone did."

"If I wanted to destroy the city, then I'd do it. I have the capability to do it right now. I could issue one order and it would be done. I have no intention of destroying the entire city."

Fawkes stopped short. Orange light glowed in the darks of his eyes.

"One of the gen-eight nodes just dropped off," one of the soldiers said.

A message came in over the command network, instructing all revivors inside the missing unit's patrol perimeter to report the location of the missing node. One by one the responses would be coming back.

"Faye, what did you do?"

Faye, Nico sent, *get him out of there. He needs to be inside the dispersion area.*

There wasn't any other option. I opened a channel to Dulari and tried to warn her, even as Fawkes began tracing it.

Dulari, open the blowers to this room, I said, but she didn't respond.

Fawkes came farther into the room. Through the open doorway I could see down the corridor to the other end, where two guards stood in the main corridor. He stepped past the body on the floor and stopped in front of me.

"You still belong to me."

He finally broke through, then, and released the locks on my systems. He reestablished the command spoke and tapped into my nodes.

"Now tell me: what did you do?" Data spilled by in front of me as he accessed everything. He found the packages Nico had installed. He found the virtual command network hidden inside his own. He identified the end nodes, and his eyes widened just a fraction.

Something clattered in the hall outside the room, and he turned suddenly. Through the doorway, I saw the guards sway on their feet as white smoke began to stream from their flesh. A crackling sound filled the air, and both figures collapsed inside their uniforms. Their remains splashed to the floor, dissolving away to nothing.

The guard closest to the door slammed it shut. Fawkes turned back to me and stared. It was one of the few times I saw anything resembling emotion in his eyes. He tried to shut down the virtual links and found that they wouldn't respond.

"Kill her!" he barked. One of his guards took a step, then all at once they seized and fell to the floor. The Leichenesser hadn't made its way into the room; someone had hijacked them and shut them down remotely.

"Dulari," Fawkes hissed.

Faye, Nico sent. *Get him out into that corridor. It's the last chance you'll have.*

Orange light flickered in Fawkes's eyes, and a moment later a thud drummed through the floor as the air circulators shut down. The others must have reached the control center.

Fawkes issued a broadcast and pulled a node count. Already it had dropped to a third of his original forces. He slammed one fist down on the table.

Faye, take him now. Fawkes stepped closer and looked into my eyes, like he was staring through a window at something, or someone else.

Wachalowski, he sent.

He grabbed my throat with one hand and squeezed.

Nico Wachalowski—Stillwell Corps Base

I was almost out of time. In the confusion I couldn't see what happened to MacReady, but his link had dropped. I still had a connection to Faye, but she'd lost her weapon. On her feed I could see Fawkes. He had leaned close and was staring into her eyes, at me.

You're too late, Agent.

"He's not waiting for a full charge," I heard Vaggot say. "He's preparing to fire."

Fawkes, don't do this.

Orange light began to flicker behind the soft glow of his eyes. There was only one way left to stop him from issuing the command.

I sent Faye's override code over the command spoke and her system tree appeared in front of me. In seconds, direct control of everything was switched over to me.

Nico, what—

Her message was cut short as the override completed. All she could do now was watch. Her targeting system called out the carotid arteries on either side of Fawkes's neck and the nodes clustered at the base of his skull. I triggered the attack, and her POV feed lurched as she swung.

Fawkes was just fast enough; he got his own blade in

the path of the strike, and the two crashed together an inch from his neck. The feed jerked again as he shoved her back.

An alert flashed in my own display. The Eye was almost ready. In minutes, we'd lose our window to sever the connection to it.

Fawkes, stop, goddamn it—

The screen in front of me flickered and Osterhagen's face appeared.

"Agent Wachalowski, what is our status?" he asked.

Fawkes, they're going to destroy the transmitter if you try to fire, I told him. *Don't do it—*

Is that supposed to be a threat? Fawkes asked. *If they don't destroy it then, before this is over, I will.*

"Agent Wachalowski," Osterhagen said again, "what is our status?"

I threw Faye at Fawkes again. Her second blade deployed as she closed in on him again and thrust it toward the middle of his chest. He managed to deflect the strike, and instead it thudded into his shoulder. Black blood came out in a glut as she jerked out the blade.

Two guard revivors closed in, and in the chaos of movement I began to lose track of where they all were. Faye's POV spun around as warnings began to spill past indicating trauma to her torso and right leg. Muzzle flashes lit up the room, and I saw sparks fly from a console in front of her.

"Wachalowski, answer me!"

One of the revivors appeared to Faye's right, and I sent the bayonet flying. I caught a glimpse of a gray, waxy face tilting off at an unnatural angle as the edge of the blade chopped deep into the flesh of its neck. Several more figures scrambled past; then the computer isolated Fawkes ahead in the fray. I sent her after him again. Another body stepped in front of him. On the feed, I saw Fawkes duck back out the way he'd come in as the remaining guards mobbed Faye. I couldn't get her past them.

"Damn it!"

Faye, did he move into the dispersion area?

The sublevels aren't completely saturated. He's still active. I can't tell where he went.

I'm too late, I thought. Fawkes had escaped. Osterhagen was going to order the missile strike. We'd lost everything.

"General—" I started.

"Were you successful or not?" he asked.

On Faye's feed, I saw a splash of black appear on the wall to her left. Through the struggling bodies in front of her, I saw someone appear in the doorway for just a second. A severe-looking, dark-skinned woman. It was Dulari Shaddrah. There was a gun in her hand.

I turned to answer the general, when the image on the screen warped. A second later, it went dark.

"Get him back on the line," a voice said.

"There's too much interference," another voice answered. "Let me try—"

"Fire the missiles," someone snapped.

"Not without authorization from the general," Vaggot said.

"The general could be dead!"

"You don't know that," I said. The faces in the room turned to me. "Who here knows the name Motoko Ai?"

Most of them looked confused, including Vaggot. One woman on the team met my eye and signaled with one hand.

"Do whatever you have to do to contact her," I told her. "Tell her Nico Wachalowski said not to fire those missiles. She'll know who I am."

She nodded.

"Don't let anyone here initiate the launch until you've given her that message. Can you stop them from doing that?"

"I can."

"Can you get me to Heinlein Industries?"

"Key monorail routes are being kept active to move military personnel only. The southern sector of the base is still secure. You can access the rail from there."

"Do it. In the meantime, hold the base and wait."

"And if Ai asks why we shouldn't launch, what am I supposed to tell her?"

A route to the bases' monorail platform appeared on my HUD as I pushed my way past the soldiers and toward the door.

"That her prediction was right," I said. "Tell her I'm going to kill Fawkes."

Calliope Flax—Avenida De Luz

Helicopters swarmed around the base far behind us when I saw a small light appear up in the sky behind the clouds. The way ahead was blocked by cars stuck on the main drag, and there were too many people moving in between them to just bash my way through. The light disappeared behind a building as I ducked down a narrow side road.

Tires and hydraulics squealed as I punched the brakes and slowed down, and people turned and scrambled to get out of the way. I took us over the sidewalk and squeezed down the strip, blaring the horn. Hands pawed at the truck. Bloody fingers pulled at the door and left greasy smears along the jagged edge of the missing window. Alerts had begun to pour in over the JZI as the clouds overhead started to move.

"What the hell is that?" Vika asked. The light in the sky had come back into view, and it was getting brighter.

Cal, this is Nico. The satellite is going to fire again. The target is the UTTC. How close are you?

I couldn't see the tower from where I was, but it wasn't more than ten blocks away.

Closer than I want to be, but out of the blast zone, I said. *Where are you?*

I'm headed toward Heinlein. Find a metro stop. The military has control of the railways. They're shut down to civilians, but they're moving military personnel. You need to get off the street.

Something thumped into the door on my side and I jumped. Bodies were shoving their way between the stuck vehicles as people scattered. One had reached the truck and had its hands on the edge of the open window.

"Goddamn it!"

I took aim and pulled the trigger. The jack stumbled back and went down on the ground. Another one crunched under the front wheel as I lurched forward, and I heard one climb up on top of the truck. I hit a parked car and set the alarm off while the revivor fell down onto the hood.

Two military helicopters blew by overhead. A second later, something exploded on the sidewalk off to our right, and the pavement shook underneath us. Glass and debris blew over the street and banged off the side of the truck. Something bashed through the back windshield of a parked car. I checked the mirrors and saw the shadows of the revivors fade behind us.

"We need to get off the street. Hang on."

Something whistled overhead then and creamed the building to our right about twenty stories up. Light flared through the smoke, and everyone around us stopped and turned. A wall of warm air huffed down through the swirling snow and dust as a twisted fire escape crashed down from above.

A chunk of concrete pounded the road next to us. Another one flattened the roof of a cab; then what looked like part of a fucking gargoyle whipped past and bowled through the crowd, spraying blood across the driver's-side window.

People dove out of the way as I jerked the wheel and took us down a side street. In the rearview mirror I saw something big fall through the smoke, and the impact made the ground buck underneath us.

I blew through a pile of trash bags on the corner at the end of the street and caught air for a second as the road dipped. The undercarriage scraped a speed bump, and we fishtailed on a patch of ice. I spun the wheel and got us under control, then made a break for the subway stop at the end of the block as a cluster of broken bricks flew by in front of us, trailing smoke.

Other people had the same idea. A hundred yards away, the crowd got too thick to move the truck through. I killed the engine.

"Come on!" Vika held the rifle in a death grip as we opened the doors and got out. I shoved my way around the back and hauled the doors open.

The back of the truck was full of equipment. I climbed up the rear bumper and pulled the closest locker open; it was loaded with guns and ammo. I traded my pistol for a better one and grabbed a few clips and stuffed them in my pockets.

"What are you doing?" Vika called. I climbed out, then jumped back down onto the pavement.

"Stick close, no matter what!" I said. I dragged her toward the metro entrance and muscled our way into the flow. People pushed and shoved as we made our way down the stairs into the station.

Most people just wanted to get off the street and away from the worst of the crowd. I took us through, then down onto the nearest platform. The tracks were empty, but down the tunnel I saw the lights from a train that was parked there, not moving. In the other direction, the tunnel was clear. I sent our location back to Nico.

Back the way we came, there were screams. I looked back and saw that a group of revivors had come down after us. People tripped over each other as they tried to get away. Somebody got bitten and blood squirted from his neck. Another guy got dragged off the platform and into the dark.

Vika jerked her hand away and tried to run, but they'd reached us. I fired, and one of them fell, but the rest just went right over it.

"Vika, get behind me!"

I tried to block them, but an elbow thumped into my chest and I was knocked back as feet stomped the floor around my face.

"Vika!"

I flipped over, and a boot came down on my back. I slammed onto the concrete as two of them grabbed Vika by her shirt. She screamed and tried to get the rifle around, but she was pinned. I shot one in the knee and it fell, but more hands grabbed her. They pulled her away from me, down the tunnel.

Something hit my head hard. Spots swam in front of my eyes as one of them bit down on her arm and she screamed again. I tried to bring the gun around again, but my arm didn't move. The platform started to tilt.

Vika . . .

A band of static flicked in front of me and the JZI puked out a stream of errors. I heard Vika yell something, but I couldn't see her. Feet stomped down around me as more of them ran to join the fray.

My eyes rolled and another band of static rippled by before the lights went out. The last thing I heard was Vika's high-pitched scream as it echoed from somewhere down the tunnel.

Zoe Ott—Alto Do Mundo

The tromping of boots echoed down the hall as we headed toward the stairwell at the far end. The hall ended in a giant pane of glass that looked out over the city, and through it I could see the TransTech Center, lit up and towering above the surrounding buildings. Osterhagen was still inside; I could sense him. I couldn't make out what he was thinking, but something was very wrong.

This city will be gone within the hour. . . .

We walked as fast as Ai could manage. I watched the back of her large head as we went, and saw sweat roll down her thin neck. One of the guards should have just carried her, but even under the circumstances, no one dared suggest it.

"Is the roof secure?" one of the men said into his radio.

"The Chimeras are still active," the reply came. "But we've got surface-to-air missile capability set up on all—"

Something flashed outside the window at the end of the hall, and something rumbled up above us, loud enough to shake the floor. The lights flickered as the sound of helicopter rotors got louder.

"Come back," the guard said into the radio. "Is the roof secure?"

The rotors thumped louder, then something big flew past the window. A loud shriek rose over the drumming sound, and three bright lights whipped by after it. A shadow banked past one of the buildings below, and I saw three thin smoke trails spin toward it. They hit the building face and exploded, sending a big, bright cloud of fire into the night air.

"We'll keep them off you, but—"

The rest of the reply got cut off by another crash from overhead. Chunks of metal and glass fell past the window, and I saw a flailing body tumble down along with it. Another loud shriek sounded, followed by a thud.

When we got to the stairwell, one of the guards opened it while another signaled for us to go through, but I was pretty sure I didn't want to go up there. Penny didn't seem too sure either.

"Come on!" the guard said. "We're going up—"

Light flashed at the end of the hall, through the window. It tinted in response, but even so, it was so bright I had to shield my eyes. Through the glare, I saw the window glass warp and then blow out into the open air. The sky outside was filled with a cloud of pulverized glass as the other windows on the building face, and those of the buildings around it, all exploded with an earsplitting crash.

A wave of hot air blasted down the hallway, stinging my hands and face. Through my fingers, I saw a huge arc of light pass over the buildings below and hit the Trans-Tech Center.

No . . .

People were screaming, but I couldn't hear them over the sound of the beam sizzling through the air. Energy arced off and struck buildings nearby as it rippled over the city like a huge, electric worm. Shards of glass jumped and danced on the tiled floor as the building shook.

My clothes flapped around me as I gaped, unable to register what I was seeing. All I could do was stare out through the snow as a huge cloud of fire boiled up from the base of the tower. Fear pulsed outward from inside the building, like streams of raw, white adrenaline. They hit me like a truck, and before I could push them out I'd slipped and almost fallen to the floor. In front of me, Ai staggered, and Penny caught her. The rush left me feeling sick, pain burning in my chest.

One of the guards was barking into the radio, but I couldn't hear him. The TransTech Center was crumbling, collapsing down in a cloud of smoke and fire. The threads of fear began to fall off and go dark. They were dying. I felt Osterhagen's consciousness wink out, along with the rest of the thousands of others. They were dying. They were all dying.

"Get back!" one of the guards shouted into my ear as cold wind blew through the opening and peppered us with powdered glass. "Back away from the window!"

I couldn't move. The light outside just kept getting brighter and brighter. It washed everything out, until it forced my eyes shut and I screamed. Distantly, I felt a hand grab my arm and pull me back. . . .

The noise stopped.

Not just the racket outside, but the voices, the screaming, the wind, everything. In the quiet, my ears rang.

I opened my eyes. I was outside, on the street. There was no explosion and no falling debris. Snow fell gently through the night sky.

Where am I?

Neon lit up the dark. I was on a sidewalk, with my back to a parked car. There was snow piled up along the curb between the walkway and the street. The street was full of cars, and people streamed by all around me. None of them even seemed to notice I was there.

I stood up and brushed myself off. My breath trailed as I looked across the street and saw the towering face of Alto Do Mundo, all glass and neon. It was completely intact. The UTTC still stood in the distance, and far off, I could see the third needle of the CMC Tower.

Is this real?

I shook my head, and snow went down the back of my neck. No one looked at me, and no cars honked, even when I wandered out into the road.

They can't see me. This isn't real.

From the dark mouth of an alley I saw a pair of eyes flash, low to the ground. They stared up at me, and I heard a low growl.

I took a step back as a dog moved out onto the sidewalk to face me. It was big, with matted, mangy fur. A patch was shaved on one side and I could see an ugly, scabby bite mark on the bare skin there.

"You again," I said. It stopped a few feet away and bared its teeth. Its gums were black, and its fangs were stained red.

"You were in my dream—"

The dog jumped. I slipped and fell back onto the sidewalk with it on top of me. I could feel its breath on my face as it snapped, and I crossed my arms between us.

Its jaws clamped down on my wrist and I screamed. Blood gushed out of the wound, and my hand went numb as the dog huffed out a breath through its cold nose. I tried to kick away, but it wouldn't let go.

A warm feeling crept up my arm from the spot where it had me. The warmth moved up to my shoulder, into my chest, into my heart. My body began to feel relaxed and a little numb. It was a little like being drunk.

The dog let me go. It barked once, then turned and ran off.

"Son of a bitch . . ."

I rolled over and got on my knees. None of the people on the street even glanced at me. When I held up my forearm, I could see muscle through the tear in the skin. It looked like it should hurt, but it didn't. It didn't hurt at all.

The weird heat coursed through my whole body, and my body relaxed. I looked around, but the dog was gone.

The neon lights flickered. I felt sick for a second, and then out of nowhere, words appeared in the air in front of me. They were like words on a computer terminal, but they just hung there in the air, like they were floating in space a few inches from my face.

Control node initialized (103.9 seconds).

"What the hell?" someone next to me asked.

I turned and saw a man standing on the sidewalk. He was staring at the air in front of him with his brow scrunched, like he was reading something.

When I looked around, I saw the others, all around me, doing the same thing. Some rubbed their eyes. They all looked confused and afraid.

"They see the words too," a voice said. I turned and saw a woman standing a few feet away from me, her stringy black hair whipping in the wind. She had a tattoo of a snake that swallowed its own tail around her neck, just like me and just like Penny.

"You're Noelle," I said. Her shirt was stained with blood around a slit in the fabric. Through the hole, I could see a deep stab wound.

"They all have it," she said.

"Have what?"

She waved for me to follow, and I did as she limped down the sidewalk to a rusted metal door just inside a nearby alley. Men bundled under dirty blankets watched us from the shadows as she pulled the door open. She waved again and stepped through.

As soon as I was through the door, it slammed behind me and everything went black. As I turned back, though, a light came on from overhead and I saw Noelle standing near an electrical switchbox on one wall. The light flickered across concrete walls that were painted green. Three electric lights, all dark, hung near the far wall. There were no bodies, and this time the table and chair were missing. When I looked around, I saw a series of wire cages along the back wall. Inside each one was a dirty-looking bedroll.

The floor was littered with trash, and the air smelled like BO and piss. In with the empty food containers and cardboard cups were torn white wrappers marked STERILE. In one corner was a used syringe with a broken needle. Noelle looked at the mess sadly.

"It's almost time," she said.

"I don't understand," I said, but she didn't seem to hear me.

"You see your mind's interpretation of the quantum

data streams it receives," she said. "Information can only be sent back."

"What information? What are you talking about?"

"By now, Fawkes has released the nanovirus," she said. "He does this in an attempt to end our influence over the rest of them."

"Maybe he should," I said.

"His plan will fail," she said. "It was only supposed to replicate a set number of times. Enough to spread throughout the world, and then degenerate of its own accord. The violence of the spread would stop, leaving the world free from us, but something went wrong. Something alters the virus. The replication never stops. It can't be allowed to spread beyond the city."

"The bombs," I said.

"The city's destruction overshadowed and hid the real disaster. We couldn't see past it. Fawkes never intended to destroy the city, but because of him, because of us, someone will have to. It will come down to the city, or the world."

My throat burned, and I felt tears in my eyes as I leaned back against the cold concrete wall. I wanted to cry, but I didn't have the strength. Was what she was saying true? Was any of this even real at all?

"What is this place?" I asked. "Why do I keep coming here?"

"The green zones are all that is left."

Green zones. It was true, then; there was more than one. The Green Room changed from vision to vision because at some point in the future, there would be more than one of them.

"What are they for?"

"Refugees are brought here to see if they can be saved. This is all that's left of humanity."

My forearm itched. When I scratched at it, I saw the scab from the dog bite there.

"That's how it spreads," Noelle said, "at least at first.

People without our abilities will begin to realize that we're among them. They'll wake up and regain their memories, but the mechanism to wake them up was fashioned on revivor technology. We didn't know what we were dealing with until it was too late. We now believe the countervirus we developed corrupted the original variant somehow and caused the mutation. Pushed past the limits of its design, Fawkes's variant eventually remembers its original purpose."

"And what's that?"

"To make revivors," she said. "And that is what it tries to do."

The ceiling spun over my head and a high-pitched whine filled both my ears. Pressure built up in my head and behind my eyes until every time my heart beat, pain throbbed through my skull. I felt like I was going to be sick.

What's happening? The whine got louder, until it was all I could hear.

"Noelle, help me . . . I can't do this. . . ."

I couldn't hear my own words. The whine got louder and louder, and the room spun faster and faster.

The lights went out, and it all stopped. The tone in my ears was gone and I could hear the hum of the air system again. I opened my eyes, and the ceiling had stopped moving, for the most part.

Huma variant 34000174T initialization complete.

The words appeared and floated in front of me.

Initialization successful.

The headache was gone. The tremors were gone. I looked around. Noelle still stood there watching me.

"What happened?" I asked. She didn't answer.

"Hello?" My voice echoed in the room.

I didn't feel drunk anymore, which was weird. I didn't have the shakes anymore either. Instead I felt clear, clearer than I had in a long time, and maybe even ever.

It was so quiet, a quiet like I'd never known before, and after a minute, I realized why. That constant stream of sensation that always lingered in the back of my mind was gone. Noelle was standing a few feet away, but I couldn't sense her. I couldn't sense any of the stray thoughts that were always there, like white noise in the background. The sensation was gone altogether. It was as if I'd suddenly woken up blind and deaf.

For a second I felt panic, but then, just like that, it vanished and instead I felt something else: relief. I felt profound relief.

It's gone. The thing people called my gift, the ability I never asked for and that had haunted me my entire life was gone. It was gone, and it took the visions and the nightmares and that horrible, crushing weight of responsibility away with it.

"It's gone," I whispered. Noelle smiled a little, but she didn't look happy.

I took a deep breath and let it out slowly. It felt good. I remembered once, years ago, the first time I'd come face-to-face with a revivor and I realized I couldn't sense or control it. I remembered how scared it had made me feel, how lost I felt without that ability. It was different now. Now it felt liberating. If I didn't know the future, then I was under no obligation to try to change it. I didn't have to feel any guilt for not being able to change the things that couldn't be changed. I didn't have to live in fear.

"It's gone," I whispered again; then something moved under the skin in back of my neck. Phantom fingers wormed into the muscle and sent a shiver down my spine.

Error. The word appeared in front of me and flashed. *Error.*

Something shocked me. My whole body jerked, and I almost fell to the floor. Before I could wonder what happened, the skin on my face felt tight all of a sudden. My lips peeled back and pain pricked at my gums.

What's happening?

Something was wrong. Inside me, something was very wrong. The scratching in the back of my neck started to burn. I reached back, and when my hands touched the back of my head, I felt the skull melt away under the skin and hair there. Heat trickled down into my stomach, and under my fingers the skin pulled tight across the knobs of my spine.

Error.

Pain pricked my gums like needles and I felt my tongue peel down the middle into two pieces. My cheeks collapsed as the skin pulled taut around my neck, and the walls around me shifted from green to a colorless gray.

The word flashed more urgently, then winked out. The crawling under my skin stopped.

Primary node network construction failed. The new words floated under the first ones. A few seconds later, they both faded.

My head felt big and heavy. It wobbled as I turned, and when I did, I noticed a strand of drool had oozed down from my lower lip. When I wiped it with my hand, I saw something black in it.

I turned again and caught my reflection in the steel of the headset panel. I tried to scream, but nothing came out.

"This is how it begins," Noelle said.

I stared at my face, distorted in the polished metal of the switchbox. My neck was shriveled to a bent stick, and my head bobbed at the end. I could barely support it. The back of my skull had melted away under the skin. My lips were pulled back to show my teeth. The gums pulled away and there was blood there, and saliva that drooled from the end of my chin. It was what Ai and the others had termed the Vaggot Deformation.

My eyes stared out of sunken sockets, the whites spotted with broken black veins. I turned back to Noelle and tried to speak, but I couldn't form the sounds. All that came out was a guttural wheeze.

"Without the building blocks it requires, it tries to use the tissue around it," she said. "It fails, but drags its victims into a state between life and death, and the spread never stops."

I got a flash of streets full of surging bodies, eyes blank and staring, and deformed heads that shook at the end of crooked necks. They moved through the wreckage of an abandoned city, not understanding the things around them.

"The living are forced underground," she said. "You are seeing the last remnants of humanity."

My reflection worked the swollen halves of its black tongue as I tried to speak. Noelle stepped close to me and looked into my eyes.

She leaned in and put her arms around me. I felt her cold hand on the back of my vulture's neck, and rested my chin on her bony shoulder. I felt her breath in my ear as she whispered one last time.

"Someone has to do it," she said. "You know in your heart this is true. Destroy the city, and you can stop this. It's the only thing that can stop this. You have to—"

The room warped in front of me. I staggered forward as Noelle disappeared. The green concrete walls faded and I was back at Alto Do Mundo, in the war room, where Penny stood shaking me.

"Zoe!"

I touched my face. It was normal. I ran my hands over the back of my neck. I was okay. It wasn't real. None of it was real, but . . .

"What happened?" Penny asked. "What did you see?"

I turned and vomited onto the tiled floor. Even as I

retched, I couldn't shake the horrible feeling of being trapped in that deformed body.

"Zoe, come on. We're leaving."

I looked around and saw that men in black body armor had surrounded us. They all had automatic rifles and were standing at attention. Ai had approached us, her face pale as she stared into my eyes.

"What did you see?" she asked.

"I . . ."

"They're swarming out there," one of the guards said. "We're not going to be able to get past them!"

"The blockades are to keep us in until he can destroy the towers," Penny said. "Heinlein's satellite is recharging to fire again right now. We don't have a choice. We have to leave now."

"What did you see?" Ai asked again.

"I know what I have to do," I told them, trying to spit the puke taste out of my mouth.

"We don't have time for this," Penny said. "We're going to the roof. Come on." No one moved.

"Tell me what you saw," Ai said.

"You were right," I told her. "The city is going to burn . . . it will be gone in an hour."

Ai didn't answer. She didn't push any further. She didn't make me say the last part of what was going through my mind, the part I didn't want to think about.

Penny put one of her arms around my waist. She pulled me along as we began to move again.

"Is that true?" she whispered in my ear. "Are we too late? Is this it?"

"Yeah," I said. I saw the mistake we'd made, the same mistake made over and over, but I'd seen it way too late.

It was true.

9

WORMWOOD STAR

Faye Dasalia—Heinlein Industries Perimeter

I awoke into darkness, at the thin edge of the void. There was no light and no sound as I hung suspended over the abyss.

It's time, Faye, it seemed to say.

I know.

Primary systems initializing.

The words floated in the dark as energy collected in my cold chest. My physical body was awakening, but I felt disconnected. The synthetic blood that had gelatinized in its web of veins warmed. It thinned and began to flow as the low vibration of my heart began.

Never mind that, the presence soothed. *It's time to sleep now.*

Secondary systems initializing.

Distantly, I picked up sounds. I heard the whistle of wind and the low creak of metal. I was sitting on a hard, rough surface that was cold to the touch.

Tertiary systems initializing.

Faye . . .

Not yet, I thought. *Soon. Not quite yet.*

I opened my eyes and a dim light seeped in. I sat inside a small space with humid air and dirty metallic walls. Just ahead was the opening of a large steel duct. Thick frost had formed around its lip. It was quiet, except for the sound of breathing. There was someone behind me.

What happened? How did I get here?

I searched, and found my last coherent memories. I focused in on that section of the field until a bright point of light rose from out of the rest to present itself to me.

Faye, take him now.

I had been standing inside the hidden lab, its walls covered with data. MacReady lay on his back, still-warm blood pooling around his dead body. Fawkes had one hand on my throat, his lifeless eyes locked on mine. I was under the control of someone else.

Nico.

I wasn't sure what he'd done. Somehow he'd managed to assert full control. He used me to target Fawkes's spinal cord, and fired my bayonet. . . .

The image flickered and the memory collapsed. It shrank to a point of light and receded into the sea of others. It was the last in the chain. After that there was nothing until I'd awoken here, inside the room.

I put one hand on the floor. Black blood had congealed there, and I felt it squish in between my fingers.

"Hold on," a voice said. I recognized it as Dulari's. Something probed at the back of my neck.

Calibrating . . .

"Okay," she said. Her breath blew like smoke through the cold air.

Warmth tingled down my spine, and I turned my head. Dulari Shaddrah crawled across the floor from behind me, her right sleeve soaked through with blood. Her red fingers were curled around the grip of a pistol.

"Where are we?" I asked. My voice reverberated in the small space.

"One of the cooling ducts," she said. "The inflow is from outside; the air here is safe for you." She turned the dimmer on a small electric lamp she'd placed in one corner, and the room got brighter. I could see a film of sweat on her face and neck despite the fact that she shivered in the cold.

"How did I get here?"

"You walked," she said. "I took you offline for a while. Any memories that hadn't been committed to longer term got lost. Sorry."

Breath blew from her nostrils as she winced. I checked the temperature in the room and realized it was just below freezing. She wouldn't stop shaking.

"What about Fawkes?"

"He got away," she said. "He made it outside the building and he's heading for the transmitter. He's going to try to destroy it."

"Why?"

"Because he knows it's over. He lost control of the nukes. The military is on its way. He set something in motion today, and he wants to make sure no one stops it, even after he's destroyed."

Tears brimmed in her eyes and her nose ran. She rapped out her words as she tried to keep her teeth from chattering. I wanted to offer her some kind of warmth, but I didn't have any to give.

"What did he do?"

"It's what we did," she said. "Me and the others. I thought we could stop them, but what we created—what I created—wasn't fully tested before Fawkes released it. It's out there now, Faye. I don't know what will happen, but it scares me. . . ."

She reached behind me and dragged over a large metallic case. Her fingers could barely work the security latch, but she got it open. Inside, there was a small box and some kind of folded material.

"Fawkes destroyed any stores of the original Huma product," she said. "He knows that if anyone gets access to the transmitter array, they can initiate another code change, but to do that they'll need something to fall back on."

She opened the small box. The inside was lined with foam, and two clear cylinders were nestled there. Each was filled with black fluid.

"These are the last samples of the current gen-M10 blood inside the country," she said, holding the box out to me. "You have to get it to the soldiers who come and tell them what to do. They can still stop this."

I took the box. She patted the bundle of cloth inside the case, leaving bloodstains.

"You'll have to cut through the middle of Pratsky to get there, but the air is still saturated with Leichenesser," she said. "This suit will protect you. Fawkes will be forced to go around the building's perimeter to get to the transmitter. You can beat him there if you go now."

"What about you?"

She shook her head. "I'm not going," she said. "I'm sorry . . . I can't . . . reconcile what I did."

"You didn't know," I said.

"This is still our fault."

I nodded. She lifted the gun and put the barrel against her temple. She took a deep breath and frowned, trying to hold it steady. A tear rolled down one cheek.

"We were wrong to do what we did," she said. "Get that sample to the soldiers. Promise me."

Her blood coursed hot beneath her skin. The mass of heat in the middle of her chest pulsed quickly now.

"I will."

"You're more human than some humans, Faye," she said, and her lips twitched into a crooked smile as she squeezed her eyes closed. As I watched, her finger tightened on the trigger and the pistol went off two feet away from my face. The report boomed down the duct as Dulari's body jerked, and the gun clattered next to her as she fell to the floor with a thud. Blood burbled from the hole in an arc before subsiding to a steady stream that trickled through her thick hair. Steam began to rise from the pool as it slowly expanded.

I removed the suit from the case and managed to climb into it. By the time I formed the seals and straightened the hood's mask, Dulari's body was cold.

Nico, I called, *are you there?* After a minute, he picked up.

I'm here.

Where are you now?

Approaching Heinlein's perimeter.

Are you coming for Fawkes? I asked.

Yes.

I picked up the box containing the samples and snapped it shut before stowing it in one of the suit's pockets. I picked up Dulari's gun from the floor next to her body.

Then meet me at the transmitter.

Zoe Ott—Alto Do Mundo

We had reached the stairwell when Ai's phone rang inside her jacket. She took out the phone and answered it, signaling for the guards to wait. She listened without speaking for a few seconds; then I saw her face change.

"Are you certain?" she asked. She nodded, then said, "I see. Thank you."

She snapped the phone shut and put it back in her pocket.

"Mr. Vaggot has succeeded in regaining control of the nuclear satellite," she said. My heart jumped in my chest.

"Are we sure?" Penny asked.

Ai nodded. She looked confused. "It has been confirmed," she said. "A superorbital strike is being levied against The Eye now."

"That's good, right?" Penny asked, but Ai shook her head.

I took a long drink off the bottle and let the warmth seep down into my belly. Osterhagen would never have let the nukes launch once he got control of them back, but Osterhagen was dead now. He and all the rest of his men in the UTTC. They were all dead.

But Vaggot wasn't. He wasn't inside TransTech; he was off on the Stillwell base. If Vaggot had just retaken control of the nukes, then he'd still be inside the system. There was still time.

"Someone has to do it . . . it's the only thing that can stop this . . ."

The visions had been telling me what had to be done all along. I just didn't want to listen. Like Noelle, I didn't want to believe it, I didn't want to face it, but that was before everything else. That was before Nico and Karen, and all the people I'd killed and would probably end up killing later. The city was a pit, full of bad people. Was it really worth saving anyway?

Blocking out the chaos around me, I reached out for Vaggot. I found his consciousness and eased my way into it. The relief he was feeling washed over me and actually made me feel calmer.

Mr. Vaggot, I said, and I sensed him stiffen at the intrusion.

Who is this? he wondered, still doubting if what he was experiencing was real. I eased in further, through the cloud of his consciousness to the sharp, defined map of colors beneath. He stiffened again when I made contact, and then I felt him begin to give himself over to me without even knowing it.

Leave the satellite as it is, I told him. He resisted that, but he didn't move.

What?

Can that satellite really destroy the entire city? I asked.

Easily. I felt fear. A cold, white membrane, like a sheet, began to ripple in an unseen wind beneath the rest of the colors of his mind.

All of it? He knew something was wrong. He sensed, I think, what might ride on his answer, and I could feel that he didn't want to tell me, but he did.

Ten times over, he said.

The image of those collapsed faces staring back at me filled my mind. The feeling of my own skull as it melted away, and the feeling of my own tongue as it divided in my mouth had wormed their way into my brain. Even as the explosion across the city grew, I couldn't shake the alien thoughts that took over in the vision as everything that was me slipped away. Whatever the nature of Noelle's image when it came to me, I knew she was right. Ai had been wrong all this time: Fawkes wasn't Element Zero at all. Element Zero was something else completely. It was the person Ai had been searching for, the person who was supposed to stop the disaster, what she first saw in Noelle and then Penny and then me. The one that would save the world from not only Fawkes but also from them, and with the same fire they'd been so desperate to avoid.

Are they disarmed? I asked him. Again he resisted me, but again, he answered.

Yes.

Rearm them.

All along we'd been waiting for some key event to make the star and the void disappear, but now I saw that we couldn't have both. There was no way to stop both. Stopping one meant letting the other happen. To save the world, the city had to burn. To save the city, the world had to end. Someone had to choose.

Fear and anxiety began to course through Vaggot's mind again as he did what I wanted.

"Wait," I heard one of the men in the hallway say. "Wait. The launch sequence just initiated."

"What?" someone else asked.

"The ICBMs just went active again."

"Is it Fawkes?"

I felt Ai's attention turn to me. "Zoe, what are you doing?"

When I opened my eyes, I saw her standing in front of me as the wind from outside whipped through her hair. The fragments of her consciousness were gathering focus, and turning that focus onto me. She knew, but she was too late.

Mr. Vaggot, I said. *Launch the missiles.*

Nico Wachalowski — Heinlein Industries' Perimeter

Snow streaked past the window of the monorail car as it bulleted toward Heinlein's main campus. Off in the distance, the last of the UTTC had crumbled into the angry glow lighting up the skyline. If they'd destroyed the transmitter like they'd wanted to, it might have been avoided.

My hands shook, and I felt sweat roll down the back of my neck in spite of the cold. The sickness was getting worse. I stared at the glow in the distance until it blurred, then closed my eyes.

Death tolls and damage assessments were all queuing up behind the block I'd put down. Carriers were being spotted closer and closer to the city limits. Time was running out. This had to work.

Wachalowski, pick up. It was Alice.

Tell me you have good news, I said.

Not exactly. Osterhagen's team at Stillwell cracked the satellite. They took back control of the nukes just minutes ago.

And The Eye?

A superorbital EMP was standing by and has been launched. It won't get a chance to fire again.

Then what's the bad news?

The launch sequence was initiated on the nuclear satellite shortly after control was reestablished.

Alice, that doesn't make sense. Who issued the code?

The only one that could have done it is Hans Vaggot, the engineer who retook control of the satellite in the first place.

Why would he do that? Is he alone in there?

Yes, she said. *In fact, the security feeds inside the base show that as of a few minutes ago, Hans Vaggot inexplicably drew his weapon and shot to death the other engineers who were with him.*

An image appeared in my HUD. Vaggot was seated at the control console with a bullet wound in one arm, the sleeve wet with blood. He stared at the screen intently, without expression.

He's sealed himself into the room, Alice said. *They're attempting to gain entry now.*

Alice, why would he do this? Why now?

She hesitated briefly.

We have reason to think that he might be under Ai's direct control, she said.

What?

There's evidence that his actions are actually being forced.

Ai's devoted all of her time and effort obsessing over this possibility so that she could stop it, I said. *Why the hell would she—*

I don't know, Agent. But when our people tried to

contact him remotely, they found someone already had control of him. Someone else is in his head, someone powerful enough to keep anyone else out. We've traced the connections back, and we believe they're coming from Alto Do Mundo.

Damn it . . .

Destroy the satellite, I said. *Before it can launch.*

Destroying The Eye was one thing; it was essentially privately owned. This is the UAC defense grid; we could trigger some kind of all-out response.

Then destroy the tower itself.

The Eye was knocked out. We'll never organize another strike large enough in time.

This doesn't make any sense! Why would she . . .

Before I could finish, though, it hit me. I remembered what Van Offo had told me shortly before he died.

"Zoe will stop him. . . . You will kill Fawkes—that's what they think—but Zoe will stop him. That's what she believes."

"I pity that girl. All she ever seems to see is death and destruction, with her at its center."

Zoe, I said.

What?

Alice, I think Zoe is behind this.

Why?

Because I think she believes, for whatever reason, that it might be the only thing she can do. To stop the spread. To stop Fawkes.

Look, even if there was anything to that, she's in the Alto Do Mundo penthouse with Motoko Ai and the rest of the top brass. She doesn't make a move that Ai doesn't want her to. She's powerful, but she's not that powerful.

I rubbed my eyes. The truth was that Zoe was unstable. She was an extremely powerful, emotionally stunted, late-stage alcoholic, and she was a very mean drunk. If half the visions she described to me were true, then she lived her life in an almost schizophrenic state, and there was some part of her that hated the world she lived in. Part of her saw all those visions of destruction as inevitable.

Send a team in, I said. *If you use the monorail, you can get a squad in there fast.*

To do what?

To stop her.

She hesitated again, but again, not for long.

It will have to be Stillwell. We have a team nearby; we might be able to get them there in time. It has to be manned by our people. Anyone we've got up there will make mincemeat of them otherwise.

Understood. Just get someone up there.

Where are you now?

On the rail, approaching Heinlein.

A team is infiltrating Stillwell's base to take out Vaggot, but we're not going to be able to contain Fawkes' ground forces much longer. After losing the UTTC and most of the Stillwell compound, the military is gearing up to come down hard on Heinlein and I'm not going to be able to stop them. An airstrike will be ordered just in front of them to knock out that transmitter and cut Fawkes off from his forces. You'll be about ten minutes ahead of them. There will be a vehicle waiting for you at the platform. It's the best I can do.

Understood.

Kill Fawkes. Get control of that transmitter back. Our best bet might end up being a good reason not to launch in the first place. Got it?

I got it.

Last chance—anything else?

Snow whipped by the window as wind whistled on the other side.

Yeah, one thing, I said.

Go ahead.

Can you direct a metro car to the city limits? Could you get someone through the blockade?

Why?

I'd like to get someone out of the city. It would be a favor.

Flax?

Yes. There were a bunch of reasons why she'd say no, but in the end, she surprised me.

I'll see what I can do, she said. *Good luck, Agent.* She cut the connection.

The black disc of Heinlein's tarmac loomed as the rail car glided closer.

Calliope Flax—Underground Metro

I came to on the tail end of a bad dream.

In it, I was back at my place in Wilamil Court, where I shoved open the door, then kicked it shut behind me. I'd scored some Zombie Makers from Al back at the Porco Rojo. The old man, Buckster, would be by later, and he had some kind of intel Nico wanted. I figured I'd loosen his tongue a little.

Two steps in, I stopped short. Some scrawny, spooky chick was parked in front of the TV. She had a cartoon on with the sound down low.

"Who the fuck are you?" I asked. She looked up over her shoulder at me.

"I didn't think you were ever coming back," she said. *"Where the hell did you go?"*

My dead hand ticked like crazy and I was in no mood for bullshit. I clomped across the floor toward her, my other fist clenched.

"How the fuck did you get in here?"

She rolled her eyes, and I lost it. I took one more step and got ready to plant the toe of my boot in her ass when her eyes changed.

She had blue eyes; I remembered that. She stared up from under a wool cap, and the blue parts turned black. When that happened, I got dizzy. I slowed down and stopped a foot away from her.

"That's just your answer to everything, isn't it?" she asked. She got up. I heard more people in the next room and a jingle, like metal. It came from behind the flag I'd hung on one wall. It was the flag I'd used to carry that girl out of Juba.

The spooky chick followed my eyes and looked back at it.

"Yeah, sad story," she said. *"You could have washed the blood out anyway."*

"I don't want to wash it."

"Keeping it real, huh?" she said. *"What's the point? You didn't save her; you just put off the inevitable."*

"I saved her life."

"A single life doesn't mean much."

"Fuck you."

The girl smirked. *"Can't argue with that,"* she said. She yelled over her shoulder. *"You guys ready for her?"*

"Yes."

It was a guy's voice. It came from the wall behind the flag.

"What the hell?"

She stared at me and stepped closer. The dizziness got worse. I felt drunk.

"How about you follow me into the next room?" she asked. I felt myself nod.

"Sure."

She stepped around the corner, across from the bathroom, and moved the flag out of the way. There was a door back there, behind it. I remembered I thought that was wrong. There was no door back there. I wouldn't have put the flag up in front of a goddamned door. If I had an extra room, I'd use the damned thing.

The girl smirked again.

"Don't worry," she said. *"There's no door. This door isn't here."*

There were a few padlocks on it, but they were all open. She turned the handle and pushed it open. When she did, it pushed a sheet of clear plastic out of the way in front of it.

"Inside," she said. I felt myself nod again.

My feet moved like they were on their own. I walked up to the door and when I got close, I saw a bunch of guys in white coats in there.

"In."

My feet moved again. I stepped through the slit in the plastic, into a room I'd never seen. It didn't make sense. I'd moved in and set the whole place up. I'd have known if there was a room there. . . .

The walls and floor were covered in clear plastic. There was a gurney in the middle with an IV rack next to it. There were three guys inside. They all wore white and had on face masks.

My eyes moved to a tray next to the gurney. There were scalpels lined up on it, and a needle. The spooky girl followed me in and walked up to the gurney. She patted it with one hand.

"Hop up," she said. *"Let's get this party started."*

My eyes opened and I woke with a start. It was cold, and I was facedown on the hard ground. Off in the dark somewhere, a bottle skittered across concrete, then popped against a wall. My head throbbed.

Goddamn it . . .

I pushed myself up off the ground and saw a palm-sized pool of blood around a squashed piece of gum. I wiped at my forehead and it came away red. My dead hand felt like it had pins and needles. At some point, someone put a coat over me. I let it hang off my shoulders.

1 message(s) outstanding.

The words floated over the stained concrete. I pulled the message and opened it. It was from Nico.

Cal, in case we don't talk again, I want you to know I'm glad we met. Neither one of us is good at this kind of thing, but you mean a lot to me.

My head was still spinning, but a knot formed in my throat.

"You're such a fucking sap," I muttered. I kept reading.

I have your location, and I'm sending a metro car to pick you up. This is over, Cal. I don't want you to get caught up in it. The car will take you to a platform across the river. I hope I'll see you on the other side.

"Son of a bitch . . ."

Back on the platform, people were huddled up. The revivors were gone, but they'd drawn some blood. One guy lay on his back, alone and not moving. The rest licked their wounds. One woman had a bite mark on her face, and a fat man had a scarf wrapped around his bloody hand. It looked like he might have lost a finger.

I heaved myself back up on my feet and took a second to let the head rush pass.

"You okay?" The voice echoed in the dark, and I turned to see a gray-haired man in the shadows nearby.

"Yeah," I said. Something banged down in the tunnel. The old man pointed toward the sound, and I saw a nasty bite on his hand.

"They went that way," he said. I nodded.

"This your coat?"

"You looked like you could use it," he said. I shrugged it off and handed it back.

"Thanks."

"Don't mention it. You with the military?"

"Kind of."

I looked around and saw a couple bodies down next

to the tracks. There were a few more on the platform where the concrete was splattered with blood. I didn't see the kid.

"How long was I out?" I asked the old man.

"Not long. Few minutes."

"The kid I was with," I said. "Where'd she go?"

"She got dragged that way," he said, pointing down the track. "I didn't see. Things got pretty crazy."

Down on the tracks a guy lay on his back, not breathing. I could see the black spots in his eyes, and blood was smeared around his mouth, which still hung open.

"This is fucked," I said under my breath. Pain drilled into my head as I got back up on my feet. I didn't get bitten, and I still had my gun, and my knife.

"Never seen ones like that before," the old man said. I ran a check on my JZI and eased some painkiller into my bloodstream. A map of the tunnels was there, with the platform called out where the car would be waiting, and something else . . . orders for my squad—Singh, Ramirez, and the rest. I was still on the roster, it looked like. The ones that were left all got regrouped and sent to Alto Do Mundo on some kind of extraction mission.

"Thanks for the coat," I said to the old man. I drew my gun and jumped down next to the track. "Watch yourself."

I turned up the light filter so I could see where I was going and started down the track in the direction the old man had pointed. I stepped over a couple more bodies, both male. When the tunnel curved and the platform was out of sight back behind me, I layered a thermal filter over the night vision and saw a thin trail. Someone came down this way alive. My boot splashed into a puddle of cold, dirty water as I followed it.

It had gotten quiet. The sounds from the platform back down the tunnel echoed a little, and somewhere up ahead, in the dark, I could hear far-off movement. I scanned the tracks, but all I could see were bottles, a couple syringes, and an old sneaker next to a tipped-over shopping cart. The trail of heat was starting to spread out, specks scattered over the floor and the concrete wall next to me. Blood.

As I walked, I repositioned the subway map to show where I was. I packed up the feed from my Stillwell squad and got ready to shut it down when a name jumped out at me.

ZOE OTT

"What the fuck?" My voice echoed down the tunnel as I stopped short. I rechecked the orders, and I hadn't read them wrong. My squad had been sent to Alto Do Mundo, up to the penthouse, to "incapacitate or kill Zoe Ott, along with anyone else who might be tied to the launch."

"Too much," I muttered. Singh was one of them, for fuck's sake, and so were the rest. Were they turning on each other now?

It wasn't my problem. I shut down the feed and looked around, picking up the heat signatures again. If Nico said go, it was time to go, but I wasn't going alone. I had one more thing to do.

The blobs on the thermal scan got bright just around the corner, and I could see it spread all over. There were boot tracks going around and through it. In the middle, there was a small body.

"Kid?" My voice echoed down the tunnel.

I moved closer and stepped on something soft. When I looked down, I saw it was Vika's coat. A few feet from that was a boot, then a torn shirt.

"Kid?"

The toe of my boot hit something, and I stumbled toward the body. It was still warm. I couldn't tell if the heart was still beating or not. When I got close, I shut off the thermal display and opened the light filter until I could make out a face.

It was hers. Half of it anyway. The other half was chewed off.

"Kid?" I said, but she was dead. I could see she was dead. I shook her anyway and felt sticky blood under my palms. They'd stripped her down so they could get to the skin. The meat had been pulled away from one shoulder and arm so I could see the bone. The one eye she had left was stuck open in shock.

Vika's body blurred in front of me, and I felt tears in my eyes. I slammed my fist against the cold ground next to her so hard I saw stars.

"Goddamn it!" I screamed, and my voice echoed down the tunnel.

10

APPROACH

Nico Wachalowski — Heinlein Industries, Pratsky Building

Cracks in the tarmac thumped under the tires as I picked up speed, easing around a large, glassy crater. Snow accumulated on the wiper blades as I huffed past the burned-out husk of a jeep that lay on its side.

Heinlein proper was mostly dark, but I could make out the red lights that ran up the length of the transmitter. The huge curve of the dish was just visible against the moonlight. They hadn't destroyed it yet.

Normally Heinlein's security deactivated any non-registered JZIs inside the perimeter, but it looked like the field was down with the rest of their systems. I pulled up an aerial view and began scanning for revivor signatures.

There were hundreds of them clustered inside the processing plant and some of the surrounding buildings as well. Pratsky was empty, though; the Leichenesser had worked. Signatures clung to the outside of the building where the ones that made it were forced to retreat. It was possible they hadn't detected me.

I had the computer sift through the signatures and start pulling IDs. Most of them either weren't on file or had been moved over from the processing plant earlier. I didn't care about them.

"Come on . . ." The filter flagged an entry and brought it to the front as a ragged shelf of blacktop appeared in front of the car. I cut the wheel, fishtailing on the wet snow.

Fawkes, Samuel.

He was there, outside Pratsky. There were three other revivors with him. They were separated from the bulk of them, who looked like they were beginning to crowd around the entrances. They were preparing for the coming assault, but not Fawkes. He was moving away from the rest, following the building's perimeter back toward the rear of the facility.

The transmitter. He was heading for the dish.

I pulled up the layout of the Pratsky Building. Like the other structures at Heinlein, it was built low to the ground. A lot of it was underground, but it still covered a significant area; it would take him a while to make it all the way around. The transmitter could be accessed from the southern side of the building, which was a straight shot from an underground entrance in the northwestern parking garage. Fawkes couldn't cut through because of the Leichenesser, but I could.

I veered around another huge scar burned into the tarmac's surface. The guard posts were dark and the floodlights were out, but with the help of the computer I was able to call out the ramp up ahead. A group of signatures had massed down there, but they hadn't organized in force yet.

A concrete pylon whipped past on the driver's side as I aimed for the garage entrance and gunned it. Through the snow, I made out a pair of eyes as they flashed in the dark up ahead, then a second pair.

Gunfire punched through the car's side, but I didn't see the source. Before the revivor in front of me could take aim, it was crushed against the grille. I saw it tumble across the hood, and its head left a divot in the windshield before it spun past the passenger's window. The car caught air for a second as the ramp descended, then the undercarriage scraped the concrete and the car lurched toward the guardrail.

The right headlight popped out as I glanced the rail. I hit the brakes and turned as the ramp circled around, tires shrieking as I flew out between two rows of parked cars. More eyes stared from the darkness ahead. The computer put three of them at the entrance.

One of them fired, and a bullet punched through the windshield a foot to my left. I accelerated, bearing down on the two I could see as car alarms squealed behind me. When I hit the first one, I stomped on the brake. The momentum carried us into the second one before the car slammed into the pylons in front of the entrance. I felt the rear tires come up off the ground and the seatbelt dig hard into my chest as I was thrown forward.

A spray of black splashed across the windshield as the rear tires crashed down. I could hear footsteps moving outside the car as I groped for the seat belt and released the catch. Fingers had already begun to claw at the door when I pushed it open and drew my gun, sticking the nose through the crack and pulling the trigger three times. A dark shape fell back, but more footsteps were close behind it.

The entrance was up ahead. I climbed over the body crumpled between the pylons and ran. The glass door was shut, the scanner dark. I pulled it open as several figures darted from between the vehicles parked to my left and began to run toward me. An organic smell blew over me as I ran through.

Halfway through the small lobby, I heard something slam into the door behind me. I turned and saw several figures at the door, eyes glowing in the darkness. I caught the rustle of cloth as a cold hand clamped down on my wrist and something big crashed into me.

I fell back onto the floor as fingers pawed at my face. I managed to land two shots but it didn't stop. Teeth flashed as the body pushed down, forcing its way closer.

Something began to hiss, and I felt cold air with the stench of decomposition blow into my face. Through our tangled arms I saw white mist bubbling from the skin of the revivor's face. The door slammed behind it.

It leaned back, holding up one hand and watching as the fingers shriveled, then dissolved to expose the yellowed bone underneath. There was no comprehension on its face.

Before it could react, I slammed my fist into its chest. The softened tissue underneath gave way and a jagged edge of bone cut into my knuckle. It tipped back, the shirt collapsing around the dark pocket in its torso. Kicking back, I broke free and climbed back up on my feet. The hiss had gotten loud as the revivor was consumed, disappearing into the mist.

I ducked through the doorway and into the building. A small fire smoldered in the far corner, throwing shadows between rows of cubicles where shell casings were littered. Shapes were sprawled across the floor.

I approached the closest figure. It looked like a body in uniform, but when I nudged it with my toe, I found the clothes were empty. The shirt and pants were still in the shape of a man, pant cuffs still tucked into the boots, but the only things left inside were pieces of metal. A mechanism that housed a long bayonet poked from the end of one sleeve. There were more uniforms crumpled on the floor ahead. It looked like they were headed farther into the building when it happened.

A gun went off somewhere up ahead, and I ducked through the office door next to me. A bullet punched through the cubicle wall on the other side and into the computer monitor on the desk behind it. Two more shots went off; then I heard someone mutter something.

"Hold your fire. I'm a Federal Agent!" I yelled.

The office window exploded and the cubicle across from me was riddled with bullets. I spotted the shooter, a young male, taking cover behind a support column. I fired and clipped his arm. Blood dotted the drywall as he pulled back, but not fast enough. I put the next bullet in his head, and he staggered back against the wall before crumpling to the ground.

I darted out of the office and stepped through the scattered clothing toward the figure. The young man made a choking sound, and red blood ran from his mouth. He'd been human.

Reloading, I stepped past the body. An exit on the far side of the room was the most direct route to the transmitter. That's where Fawkes would be.

My footsteps echoed down the long, dark corridor in front of me as I moved farther into the building.

Calliope Flax—Third Street Station

When I came out of the tunnel and saw lights again, the railcar was there, like Nico said it would be. There were other people on the platform, some lined up by the wall, others hanging around the train looking for a way on. I showed them my gun and they got out of the way. The scanner turned from red to green when I showed it my military ID tag, and the doors opened to let me on. Some of the seats still had people's coats and bags on them from when they ran, and there was an open suitcase in the row to my right with most of the clothes pulled out.

I stepped through then turned and stood just inside the doorway looking out. One guy looked like he might try to push his way past me, but he didn't. The doors closed, and the staring faces on the platform fell away as the train took off. The last thing I saw before disappearing back into the tunnel was two guys on their knees, robbing a dead body.

To hell with this place.

"Confirm military ID," the computer croaked. I rattled it off.

"Flax, Calliope," the computer said. "Citizen First Class. Decorated Emet Corporal. Your destination has been preprogrammed. Do you wish to override?"

"No."

"Please enjoy your trip."

I hung on to the pole as the train took off down the tunnel, and stood there like a zombie until the dark of the tunnel fell away and the city lights filled up the windows. I watched Alto Do Mundo, that big, fucking tower of rich assholes, get closer as the slums flew past. It made me think about Luis, that kid I met in the tank a million years ago. He used to live there. I wondered if the rest of my squad was there and if they managed to get in. I wondered if it would still even be there when the sun came back up.

Why do they always die?

Luis died hard. The old man who looked after me when I came back from my tour, Buckster, died hard too, but I was just a dreg back then. I was a soldier now. That kid was right next to me. I could have reached out and grabbed her. I was armed and I knew it was coming. She'd saved my life. We were supposed to get out of there together.

Pain drilled into my head and my knees gave out for

just a second. A scramble of code streamed by in front of me, as I grabbed the pole next to me and held on. Spit filled my mouth, and my eyes burned. Everything inside me felt fucked up. I checked my wrist and saw two big, dark veins creeping down my forearm, right across the join where the dead hand was grafted on.

Necrotic bleed-through. I had it too. Between that and the revivor nodes that had formed I wondered if they could even fix me, if it even mattered whether I got out of the city or not.

"You could be a champ," a voice said. I thought someone said it anyway. When I turned around, no one was there.

The car phased out for a second and I was somewhere else. I was back at the Porco Rojo, in the locker room. It was postfight, and I had a butterfly clip over a cut on one cheek. There was a knot on my right wrist and a nasty purple bruise was forming there. It throbbed, but I felt good. I fought hard and I won. The air smelled like a mixture of BO and soap, along with fifty different de-odorants and colognes. The smell took me back, and on the train, I smiled.

I remember this.

"I am a champ," I said. Leaning against the lockers across from me was Tito Gantz, a fight scout. Getting noticed by Tito was a good thing. I was psyched, but I still had my guard up. I didn't expect to find him back there waiting, and definitely not for me.

"You're a good fighter," he said, *"but you're not a champ."*

"I'm on TV."

Tito snorted. *"TV,"* he spat out. *"Where your show is so deep in the muck, even the fucking data miners can't find you."*

"You found me."

"I'm paid to find you," he said. *"That's my job. I take people like you and put them in front of actual viewers,*

on actual networks with actual advertisers. You want to knock heads in this hellhole until you finally burn out? Or do you want to at least have a shot?"

"A shot at the big time, huh?" I sneered.

"I'm not psychic," he said. *"I wouldn't call it the big time, and it's a shot—that's all. Maybe you can hold your own and maybe you can't. You want to find out or not?"*

He didn't oversell. I liked that. It was a rung, just a bottom rung, but sometimes that's all you needed. It was the first step up, out of the pit, maybe. I grinned and held out my hand, still with the tape on it.

"I—"

Before I could get an answer out, the word fizzled in my mouth. Three guys I'd never seen before came walking into the locker room like they owned the place; two big guys in suits and one smaller guy in a tight silk shirt. He was lean and looked like he spent way too much time in front of a mirror. His duds looked like they cost a fortune, and I'd have bet money the diamond in his ear was real. He had ice-blue eyes, real light, almost gray. When he came closer to us, he smiled, and I saw he was wearing eyeliner.

"Who the fuck are you?" Tito asked. He was pissed, but when the little guy looked over at him, he just shut up and got real interested in the floor.

"Quiet," he said. *"I'm a fan."*

"I got a lot of fans," Tito said.

"Not of yours," the guy said. *"Of hers. I like to come here. I like to mingle with the thirds. I like to bet on Flax, here, and I almost always win."*

He smiled, looking into my eyes, and I saw his pupils get big.

"Even when I don't," he said, *"it's always entertaining."*

He turned to Tito, who was still looking down at the floor.

"She's not interested," the little guy said. *"Just forget*

this ever happened, and go back to your business. Both of you."

Tito looked like he was on dope or something, but even so, he didn't look sure.

"*But I could book her in the Capital,*" he said. "*I mean, the suburbs, but still, the Capital, man. . . .*"

The little guy with the eyeliner looked annoyed.

"*I'm not driving all the way out there,*" he said.

The locker room faded, and I was back on the train. All of a sudden, Alto Do Mundo was practically on top of us. How long had I been zoned out?

What the hell was that?

I didn't remember ever getting a meeting with Tito Gantz. If you'd asked me yesterday, I'd have said you were crazy, but I knew what I'd just remembered was real. It was real. It happened, then it got wiped out. . . .

"Wait," I said. The train kept moving.

"Wait," I said again. "This is Flax. I changed my mind. I want to change my destination."

"State your override destination," the computer said. I thought for a second. My heart rate was starting to pick up again, cutting through the fog.

"Voodoo Proper," I said. "Heinlein Industries."

"Destination is blocked," the computer said. "Would you like to choose another?"

"Piece of shit . . ."

"Would you like to choose ano—"

"Alto Do Mundo Station," I said, pointing out the window. "There. Pull in there."

The car veered so suddenly, I almost lost my footing. It went down into the nearest tunnel and picked up speed.

I chewed the inside of my lip until I tasted blood. I wanted to bite something. I wanted to sink my teeth into something so bad, I wondered if maybe I had turned.

Maybe the inhibitor died, and I was one of them and I didn't even know it.

The train evened out and air whooshed as it came out of the tunnel and into the station. Lights popped up outside the windows again and I saw a wall decorated with little, fancy colored tiles that spelled out the station name.

Alto Do Mundo Central Station

Sorry, Nico.

As the platform flew past, I saw a few bodies facedown among the trash. A bench was knocked over on its back, and glass was scattered across the tiled floor. Black stains trailed along one walkway, and I saw spent shells. No revivors, though. The underground looked secure.

The train slowed, then stopped. The doors opened, and I drew my pistol and stepped out onto the platform. Voices echoed through the station from back up at street level, a dull roar over the pop of gunshots. The toe of my boot scattered shell casings that jingled off across the floor as I started to move toward the closest stairwell. There'd been a major firefight down there as well.

ADM Station looked to me like some third-world thug's palace. Even the stations I'd seen in what I'd call the good parts of town were nothing like it; before the fighting it must have looked like the inside of a fucking five-star hotel. Instead of pizza joints and food carts there were fancy restaurants, and bars. There was no graffiti, and the floor was tiled and shiny. There were green plants arranged to make the inside look like a park, and water ran down the walls at either end into a pair of big fountains. Right in the middle, under the huge vaulted ceiling, was a bronze statue of a huge, ripped dude with a giant globe on his back. It was hard to believe I was still in the same city.

The place had seen fighting, though. From the look of it, revivors must have pushed their way down to

try to get in from underneath, then been forced back.
There'd been a lot of gunfire, and blood, both human
and revivor, ran across the stone-tile floor. Up ahead,
divots were dug out of the sides of a fountain where a
body lay facedown in the rubble. Glass from the store-
fronts had been blasted out and covered the floor. I
counted more than twenty bodies before I got halfway
across.

I didn't see any sign of Singh or the others. Check-
ing through the squad's last orders, it looked like they
were tracking their target using a GPS signal in one of
their phones up in the penthouse. I punched in the ID
and picked up the signal. According to the map, it was
close, maybe half a block from where I was, but the signal strength put it high up above me.

Past the statue, I saw a wall of elevators and a big,
fancy sign that said LOBBY ACCESS. The call lights were
lit, so it looked like they were still running.

I punched up the closest one and the doors opened
into a car big enough to hold fifty people. There was
only one in there at the time, though. It was Ramirez,
sitting on his ass, leaning into the corner of the elevator
with a hole in his head. The mirrored wall behind him
was shattered and specked with blood.

Stepping through broken glass, I leaned down and
pulled his ID off his belt. It looked like the elevator only
went to ground level. I hit the button and rode it up.

As it rose, I could hear the racket above get louder:
gunfire, screaming, and someone yelling over a bullhorn.
The doors opened onto a landing where all the gold,
marble, and crystal was still in one piece, but across the
lobby on the other side was the main entrance, and outside it was chaos.

The entryway was all bulletproof glass, scarred with
gunshots where bodies lay slumped on the other side.
It looked out over that huge, semicircular stone stair-

way I'd only ever seen from the other side, where bodies clashed in a huge, sprawling mass.

There were hundreds of revivors out there. They'd surged through the streets from all sides. The square was completely mobbed, and they pushed toward the building front where Stillwell had set up a makeshift military barricade. Bodies thrashed on the other side of a row of military trucks and a wall of soldiers holding up riot shields. Flood lamps shone down over the crowd as the revivors tried to break through, fingers clawing through gaps in the line. Shots cracked through the night air, but there were too many of them. Even as I watched, a group of revivors shoved their way through the gap in the shields and made a run for the line of vehicles. A turret opened up and an arm flipped back into the crowd in an explosion of gray meat. Across the square, another group managed to get over the trucks, and I saw a body throw itself against the glass before it was pounded with gunfire. A thick, black streak was smeared down the surface as it slumped to join the other bodies.

On the other side of the lobby was the main elevator hub, and I ran to it. At the far right end was an express that went up to the penthouse. According to the last reports, that's where she'd be.

The doors had a security scanner. I put Ramirez's ID to it and the light flashed.

"Ramirez, Edward," the door said. "First-Class Citizen. First Sergeant. State the nature of your business."

"It's an emergency."

"State the nature of the emer—"

"National security. Open the fuck up."

Outside, more revivors had pushed through. One jumped over a fallen body, and when its coat opened, I saw black wiring bundled around a blue LCD readout. It pitched forward as automatic gunfire tracked across its back. It hit a pane of glass and began to go down onto the concrete. I saw the detonator flash in its hand.

"Open the doors!" I barked.

The blast shook the floor, and the glass panel exploded through the entryway on a blast of hot air as more bodies began to storm past the barricade. One of the vehicle-mounted turrets spun around and opened up, cutting two revivors in half as they approached the hole but it was no use. I saw more of them climb up the side of the vehicle and grab the gunner from behind. They were through.

The elevator doors opened, and as the jacks began to fill the lobby, I jumped in.

"Destination?" the car asked.

"Penthouse!"

Through the doors I saw another explosion go off, and there was a surge of screams as another turret opened up. More revivors had made it to the lobby and begun to scatter. Figures broke off in every direction. A stairwell door banged open and some of them crowded through. Others were heading in my direction, toward the elevators, and a bullet whined past my ear, punching into the glass behind me.

"Can you shut down all elevators but this one?" I asked the computer.

"I am unable to complete your req—"

"Just go!"

Bodies scrambled across the lobby toward me, while the soldiers fired after them. The last thing I saw before the doors slid shut was a strung-out-looking female with black gums breaking through the pack. I heard her body slam against the other side.

My gut dropped as the elevator launched like a rocket, and the number on the LCD above the door began to count up.

Faye Dasalia—Heinlein Industries, Pratsky Building

Once out of the cooling ducts, I moved quickly through a large metal locker whose walls were covered in frost. At the far end, I pushed open the heavy door, and fog blew out into the corridor after me. As I made my way down, I heard a loud boom from somewhere in the building and felt a tremor through the floor. The lights overhead flickered.

Nico was inside the building now, and he'd begun tracking my signal. As I reached the end of the hall, he opened a channel. I wiped the suit's faceplate and picked up.

Faye, how are you able to be in here?

I have an environmental suit. Be careful; there are still living people inside.

Fawkes is heading for the transmitter.

I know. He's going to destroy it.

I'm going to try to head him off.

He's destroyed the original Huma stores. You won't be able to revert the units in the field to their original state without them, but a member of his team held on to a single sample without his knowing. I have it with me now.

Is anyone left there who knows how to set up the code transfer and issue it?

My foot kicked through a pile of revivor components bundled inside empty clothes. A bayonet clattered across the floor and struck another pile. As I began to run, I saw there were remains everywhere; boots, clothes, and wires all crumpled in the shapes of shriveled bodies. In the offices and cubicles I saw more remains, dissolved away so that even the blood was gone.

When he first arrived, Fawkes made sure there would be no one left who could operate the transmitter, I told him. *Dulari Shaddrah and Robert MacReady are dead.*

What about Ang Chen?

He can work the transmitter, but even if he's alive and

you can find him, he won't. Dulari provided me with in-structions when she gave me the sample.

Can you set it up?

I can try.

As I passed by one of the offices, I saw a woman in-side. She sat, wearing a vest that was strapped with ex-plosive bricks over a white silk blouse, behind the desk. She didn't look up as I passed. Even when my move-ment caused the device to begin emitting a shrill beep, she stared at the desktop, mascara dried in lines down both cheeks.

I picked up speed and ran through a doorway at the end of the row. The device went off, and light flashed bright enough to cast a long shadow in front of me be-fore I felt air rush over my back. I stumbled forward as something flew past me and crashed through a window to my left. Glass rained against the wall next to me.

Faye? Are you there?

A shape ran through the smoke. I couldn't make out who it was. He struck me with his shoulder as he passed and spun me around.

Faye?

I'm here.

I ran past another series of cubicles. Down the row, I saw a man sitting in a swivel chair, staring sadly at the stump of his forearm. A prosthetic, maybe, that had been dissolved away. I could make out wires around a flashing LCD, but I seemed to be out of range of the mo-tion detector. I kept my head down as I passed by him. One tear in the suit is all it would take. If enough of the Leichenesser got inside to begin the reaction, nothing would stop it.

The ones he left alive are dangerous, I told Nico. *They're rigged with explosives. The devices are motion sensitive.*

Got it, Nico said. *I'm going to head off Fawkes and*

his men. Get to the control room and get ready to send on my mark.

Understood.

And thank you, Faye.

Another shape darted across the hallway in front of me as I picked up speed. Somewhere outside, I could make out the high-pitched whine of approaching jets.

Good luck, Nico.

Revivors don't believe in luck.

No, I said, *but you do.*

When this is over, Faye, wait for me. I'll find you.

And when you find me, what will you do then?

He didn't answer. After enough seconds had passed, I answered for him.

I'll wait for you, Nico.

You will?

Yes, I said.

It wasn't the first lie I had ever told him, but I knew that it would at least be the last.

Zoe Ott—Alto Do Mundo

"Zoe, what are you doing?" Ai asked. As Vaggot struggled against me, I felt another mind intrude and break my connection.

"Let him go," I said.

Ai's tiny hands spread their fingers wide as her stare intensified. I felt the armed guards around us move all at the same time, and their attention turned to me.

"No, Zoe," she said, and their guns began to take aim.

When the first gun was pointed at me, Penny reacted. I heard a sharp chirping sound over the wind and the rumbling from outside, then the guard screamed as she shattered his elbow with a collapsible metal baton. The gun slipped out of his hand and clattered to the floor as he clutched his arm and staggered back.

Some of the men turned, unsure for a second, before they all pricked up again and pointed their guns back at me.

"Penny, stop it," Ai said. She stared up at me, and I could feel her reaching through my defenses, into my mind.

"Zoe, do as I say," she said.

Penny looked confused, but she didn't back off. She had a second baton in the other hand now, and was looking over the guards like she might spring at any second. I could feel her, and her fear, as I tried to push Ai back. It was one of the only times I'd ever felt such panic from her. She was scared right then, scared to death. She was scared those men were going to shoot me and that she wouldn't be able to stop them.

"Get those guns off her," Penny said to the guards, her voice stressed. There were five left, two of them between me and her. They looked at each other, then at Ai. No one moved.

I heard the chirp again, and this time the nose of the man next to me seemed to explode, spraying warm blood across my cheek. He stumbled back, then grunted as Penny struck him in the chest.

Her hand grabbed my arm, and before I knew what happened, she pulled me away and shoved me back behind her. She squared off against the remaining four men as the one with the broken nose slumped back against the wall. As he slowly slid down to the floor, I saw the hilt of a knife sticking out from over the edge of his body armor. His consciousness dimmed, then winked out. Penny had killed him.

"Penny!" Ai snapped.

"The blockade has tripled in size and closed in," one of the men said to Ai. "It's an all-out rush. They're inside the building."

"Hold Zoe under guard," she said. But when they approached, Penny tensed again.

"Penny, let them take her," Ai said, but Penny shook her head.

"You heard them," Ai said, calmer. "Fawkes's army has breached the perimeter and is inside the building. They are coming for us. We need to leave now."

"Can we shut down the elevators?" someone asked.

"Not from here," a voice answered over the radio. "We'd need to get to the maintenance—" The voice was cut off.

"We've got movement in all wings," one of the guards said, shaking his head as he looked at a computer tablet in his palm.

"How long?" Ai asked.

"At their current rate? Not long. Five minutes."

"Take them both under guard," Ai said. "Right now."

"Next one that moves—" Penny started to say, but Ai turned on her and she stopped short. To concentrate on Penny, though, she took some of her focus off me. I saw the cords in Penny's neck stand out as she tried to hold her ground.

"How dare you resist me?" Ai asked.

A shot rang out, and Penny jerked back. Blood spattered across the floor. One of the men lunged past her and grabbed me.

"Penny!"

I could sense the consciousness of each of the soldiers as they surrounded me. I could feel them trying to gang up on me and push their will on me. I even felt my body start to relax.

Before they could worm their way in any further, I pushed them all back. I locked on to each of their patterns and found the hot, white band that fed them.

I severed them all, and the lights went out. A gun clunked onto the floor, then another, as their bodies crumpled and fell where they stood.

"Zoe, stop!" Ai snapped from behind me as I ran to Penny.

"Penny!"

I knelt down next to her. She lay there, beads of red scattered on the tile around her, but her mind was strong. I sensed pain and worry but not panic. I didn't sense that slow euphoria and disconnect people got when they slipped away. She wasn't dying, at least not yet.

"Penny . . . Penny, are you okay?"

She lifted her head, then propped herself up on one elbow.

"Hold on. Don't try to move."

"I'm okay. Don't turn your back on her."

I turned as the colors in the hallway washed out and the lights turned bright. As another blast of freezing wind whipped through my hair, I saw the pattern appear around Ai's large head, bright orange, and red, like molten pieces of a broken planet.

"You have to let Vaggot go," I said. "You were wrong about everything." Ai shook her head.

"I have seen more clearly than you are capable of."

"The end is coming," I told her. "This has to happen. Fawkes doesn't destroy the city, and he was never going to. It's something else, something you didn't see—"

"Thousands of visions from thousands of people have been catalogued over the course of years and studied by the best minds—"

"None of them live—"

"Don't you dare interrupt me!"

"None of you survive," I said. "You can't see what's really going on because none of you live. You see these . . . snippets of what happens beforehand, but it's useless because you can't see past it to what really happens. This is the only way to stop it—"

"Who do you think you are?"

I felt her punch through my defenses and grab hold of me. A jolt went down my spine and my whole body started to wind down. She'd found that stem of white light at the base of my consciousness and was trying to pinch it off. My heart skipped a beat and fluttered in my chest as I started to sag.

"We have control of the satellite back," Ai said. "Heinlein Industries will be reoccupied, and Fawkes will be destroyed very soon. His army on the street will be shut down and then collected and destroyed. Fawkes has lost, and we've won. All we need to do is survive until they retake control of Heinlein's transmitter; then it will be over."

"It won't be over," I gasped. "It's already too late. . . ."

My vision blurred as I pushed back, trying to force her out of my head.

"Penny, kill her," she said.

Penny got back up onto her feet, and turned toward me. Distantly, I could feel the conflict in her mind; she was my friend, but she'd belonged to Ai for a long time. At some point over the years, Penny had learned to kill without thinking about it, either before or afterwards. I looked into her eyes but it took everything I had to keep Ai from killing me herself, and I couldn't tell what she was thinking.

"Don't," I whispered to her. "Please."

"I said, 'kill her.'"

Slowly, Penny turned away from me and faced Ai. Red dots appeared on the tile near her feet as she straightened her back.

"Penny, you know you can trust me," Ai told her. "She is wrong. She dies here in this building; you know that. You both die here."

"Then so do you," I said, and as the light got so bright that it stung my eyes, I pushed her away and out of my head.

11

SACRIFICE

Nico Wachalowski—Heinlein Industries

The four revivor signatures moved around the western face of the Pratsky Building, heading for the transmitter hub. The one in the lead was Fawkes. With his head start, it was going to be close.

I skirted past several more piles of clothing strewn on the floor. The toe of my boot hit a stray pistol and sent it spinning down the hall, where it struck an empty helmet. Somewhere else in the building, several shots went off.

Faye, I called. She didn't respond.

The corridor opened into a large area with cubicles set up in the center. Offices ran the length of the wall to my right, and across the room, a huge window looked into a dark laboratory. The glass had been punched through with a long row of bullet holes, and through the web of fractures I could make out hulking machinery. According to the map, I could cut through there on my way to the dish.

The door was jammed. I kicked through the damaged

glass and climbed over the edge, dropping to the floor. Back the way I'd come, I heard more gunfire.

Faye, are you receiving me? She didn't answer, but someone else did.

You're too late, Agent. It was Fawkes.

A large tank along one wall had ruptured, and the air in the lab had a chemical smell. Fog had formed over the wet floor, where several sets of clothing were bunched. The smell got worse as I headed down a row of equipment, my sleeve pressed over my nose and mouth.

Fawkes, you cannot destroy that transmitter. The variant is spreading out of control.

That's the point.

Past the racks of dark equipment were three bodies lying facedown in the chemical spill. The lab must have been sectioned off from the main climate system, and Leichenesser had dissipated before it made it this far in. All three of them looked human, and were dressed in lab coats. One of them had been shot in the throat.

Something's wrong, Fawkes. They're going to nuke the city anyway.

You're lying.

I'm not lying. The launch has been initialized.

If that's true, then it doesn't matter if I destroy the transmitter or not.

They're trying to stop the spread. If it can't be stopped using the transmitter, then those nukes are going to fall, Fawkes. I believe you; I don't think you ever had any intention of destroying this city. Don't let this happen—

Fawkes broke the connection.

A heavy, temperature-controlled vat sat in the wreckage ahead, and I saw that a gray hand had broken the surface. A series of glass jars connected with chrome tubes had been shattered, the sharp edges stained black. Inside one I saw the slick lump of a human liver trailing wires. Another had spilled out a long coil of intestine that hung from the glass edge down to the floor, where black blood had pooled. I stepped in something soft as I banked left around the equipment, toward the exit.

As I shoved open the door, something lunged out in front of me. I ran headlong into a large figure, almost bowling us both over as I grabbed a fistful of shirt collar and spun the man around. I slammed his back into the wall and pressed the barrel of my gun to his forehead.

"Don't shoot!" he yelled. Pale-skinned, he was a man I didn't recognize. He was wearing a long coat that was wrapped tightly around him. He brought his hands up where I could see them, his eyes wide. His face was covered in sweat. "I'm not armed! Don't shoot!"

A high-pitched whine began to sound. It was coming from the man.

"Get this thing off me," he said. His eyes were wild. "Get this thing off me. . . ."

He grabbed my lapels and pulled me toward him. I stumbled, shoving him back.

The man's coat fell open, and I saw a light flash underneath through a nest of wires.

"Help me!" he screamed. "I don't want to die!"

Energy was building up fast in the device. There wasn't time to stop it from detonating. I knocked his hands away from my jacket, and the material tore free from his fingers. He tried to grab me again, and I put one heel in his chest, kicking him back through the office doorway. He crashed against the desk behind him as smoke began to trail between the wires of the device strapped to his chest.

"I don't want to—"

I spun to the left, around the corner, as the air thumped and the bomb went off. Overhead lights rained glass and sparks down over me as fire boiled down the corridor, throwing me to the floor as the wall in front of me flew into pieces.

I reeled, my ears ringing, and static flickered across my HUD as a message came through from the outside.

Wachalowski, this is Alice. The first nuke is set to launch in six minutes. Where are you?

Inside Heinlein.

Stopping the launch from this end might not happen. If you stick to the lower levels over there, you stand a good chance of surviving any blast.

What about the control center at Stillwell?

They're cutting their way in, but it's going to take time.

You don't think they'll make it in before the launch?

I don't know, Wachalowski.

What about Motoko? I asked. *What did your team find at Alto Do Mundo?*

The first team never made it. They got swarmed at the station, and we lost contact. No word back from teams two or three, either. Motoko isn't responding, and neither is any of her personal guard.

If someone there is influencing Vaggot, I said, *what happens if they die?*

I can't—

Alice, answer me. If I'm right and the one doing it is killed, will Vaggot stop the launch on his own?

I don't know. Maybe.

Then you have to try to—

I know, Agent, believe me. Additional teams are moving in, and Chimeras are en route to the penthouse, but I can't guarantee they'll get there in time.

I checked Fawkes's signature again. He was almost at the transmitter.

Stopping him was beginning to look like the only option left, and I was running out of time.

Faye Dasalia—Satellite-Dish Control Tower

The entrance to the transmitter's control room required security clearance, but Heinlein's systems were still offline and the scanner was dark. I pulled it open, and lights flickered on overhead as I stepped inside. The room was situated off the northern face of the building, with a huge, wide window that looked out onto the base of the transmitter itself. The outer rim of the main dish formed an arc across the sky far above.

There were many sets of clothes strewn throughout the room. Empty shirts lay against the backs of several chairs, still situated inside suit coats, neckties still in place. Pants legs dangled over empty shoes. Fawkes had forced them to initiate the first code transfer, then he'd had them killed at their workstations.

I've accessed the control room, I told Nico.

I pulled up the instructions that Dulari had given me, along with the sample. The dish should still be aligned with the geosynchronous satellite in orbit above from the previous transmission, but I had to make sure. I tapped into the system and began the verification as I scanned the room. There were arrays of panels covered in minute controls and readouts, none of which I recognized or understood.

Using the included map of the consoles, my computer was able to identify both the main control station and also the image reader that would analyze and queue the sample for transmission. After that, I had no choice but to take Dulari's instructions on faith.

Queuing up the current version requires two keys, the instructions indicated. *They may still be in place. If not, use the provided override code.*

I found the console and checked it. She was right; each panel was fitted with a large metal key with a thin hanging chain. Each was turned to the ON position.

Fixed beneath them was a thin metal door with a turn latch. With a twist, I pulled it open, and cold mist drifted out.

Satellite alignment verified.

Reaching through the mist, my fingers found the edge of the sample container, and I pulled it out of the bay. Carefully, I removed the sample Dulari had given me from its case and slid it into the slot. I shut the door and when I turned the latch, several lights on the console lit up. Messages began to scroll across one of the screens there.

Sample inserted.

Verifying version stamp . . .

Verifying authentication code . . .

Verifying certificate . . .

Green lights pulsed in response to each, and something thumped in the floor. The hum of electricity filled the room.

Validating sample . . .

Another screen blinked on and began cascading messages faster than I could read. A percentage appeared in one corner and began to creep up from 0 toward 100.

The door crashed open behind me and I turned in time to see a figure in a suit step through. The man leaned heavily on a crutch and held a pistol out in one hand. When he limped into the light, I recognized him immediately.

"Ang—"

He fired, and the bullet struck me in the left shoulder. Air from inside the suit began to leak through the hole as I staggered and fell back onto my side. Two more shots went off and struck the floor near my head as I kicked away, pushing myself behind one of the consoles.

Blood began to run down my arm as air blew through

the hole in the suit. As soon as the pressure let up, air from the outside would make its way in.

As I heard Ang limp toward the console to shut down the sequence, I turned my gun on the window that overlooked the dish and fired. The glass stopped some, but not all, of the rounds.

I grabbed the nearest chair and gripped it by one metal leg. Pushing myself up off the floor, I spun it around and struck the broken glass.

Two more bullets struck me from behind as a spiderweb of cracks gave way in the observatory window and the chair sailed out into the dark in a shower of glass. Wind and snow shrieked through the jagged opening as I turned and aimed the gun at Ang.

He tried to dart away, but his injured leg gave out from underneath him. As he fell, the bullet punched through the wall behind him. I pulled the trigger again, but the hammer just clicked.

Something behind the row of consoles crashed, and I saw him get back to his feet, a vein bulging in his neck and his face red. He fired again as I began to barrel toward him. There was no way to know if the air was safe, but the seal on the suit was already broken.

I triggered the bayonet, and it sliced through the palm of the glove as I closed the gap between us.

Zoe Ott—Alto Do Mundo

As I focused on Ai, the halo appeared around her head like a thin laser and tried to push me back. She had turned all of her energy onto me, but I wasn't afraid. Suddenly the air was as cold as ice and everything was crystal clear. Something warm ran from one of my nostrils and tickled my upper lip before dripping off the end of my chin.

"Zoe . . ." Ai gasped, and the halo warped. I pushed my way closer, and her eyes widened.

"Zoe, stop."

Something slammed down the hall, and Penny turned. Behind her, I saw one of the smoked-glass doors open, and a woman in uniform stalked through. Her black hair was short, and there were tattoos on her neck. As her boots tromped down the hall, I could feel the anger radiate from her.

You. It was Flax, the one who'd killed Karen.

Penny flicked out both batons, extending them as she marched down the hall to meet her. She was strong, but she was in pain, and I could see her limp just a little as she walked. Behind her, she left a trail of dots on the tile.

I felt Ai worm her way into my brain and I turned back to her, struggling to push her back as I remembered the dead woman's words in my last vision. The words she'd said when she showed me that woman marching toward Penny with death in her eyes.

"She will take away the last thing that is dear to you."

"Penny, wait!" Ai was overwhelming me. I could feel her beginning to take control. Penny was going to die. She was going to die right in front of me.

"Stop!"

I turned on Ai, and everything, all the fear and the hate and the desperation, came out at once. I smashed through the barrier she'd thrown up, and emerged on the other side like a missile entering the atmosphere. The fragments of color below were like a work of art, an intricate field of stained glass that contained more knowledge than I would ever know in my lifetime. They floated above a storm of emotion that no one ever saw; the loss of everything she ever cared about, the knowledge that she would never reach old age, fear for the future that would unfold when she was gone . . . and throughout it all, guilt. Deep inside, buried under layers and layers of duty and discipline and justification, was a remorse so intense it was almost blinding.

I saw remorse for everything she had done—every person she had killed or allowed to die, every life she'd destroyed or allowed to be destroyed. She carried it all deep within, even a truth that Penny had known all along: she'd let Karen be taken away, because she knew that without her I would find solace in them. She knew. She knew everything and she did it anyway.

The only thing I hadn't expected was the remorse, made all the worse by the one, childlike fear that she kept as a secret in her heart of hearts.

I don't think I can stop it.

"You don't kill me," I heard her whisper as I reached for the white band from which all the other light sprang. "I die from—"

Something in her brain burst. The halo disappeared and she twitched in shock. One hand desperately reached out at nothing, and the tiny fingers closed around a fistful of air.

"Don't..."

Her colors didn't disappear, but they shifted suddenly. The stained glass of her mind melted and skewed. All the beauty went out of it. In an instant, it turned to something jumbled and meaningless.

One of her eyelids drooped. Her eyes rolled back, and then the colors faded and scattered.

She fell, and her large head struck the tile with a heavy thud.

I swayed on my feet, smearing something wet from under my nose and across my cheek. Ai's little body lay on the floor, her clothes fluttering in the wind as it blew down the hall. A little speck of hot blue that reminded me of a pilot light fluttered above her head. I stared at it, pawing at the inside of my jacket until I found the flask there. I took off the cap and dropped it on the floor as I took a long swallow. The last splash ran down the side of my mouth; then it was empty.

I looked at the big Z monogram etched in the smoked glass and felt my throat burn. Ai had given that to me. Tears blurred in my eyes as that little pilot light went out, and Ai was gone.

I tossed the flask and heard it smash on the floor. It didn't matter. There wouldn't be any tomorrow. Not for me, or any of us.

Reaching back out into the night, I found Vaggot again as my last vision began to seep into my mind. For a minute I was in the dark, and a rolling field began to form: dark hills covered in wet grass and fog. Wind rushed over me, moaning through trees somewhere far away, where there were no buildings and you could see the stars and the moon. The ground began to move, and I saw that the field in front of me was crowded with figures. A mob of misshapen heads bobbed and swayed against the moonlit sky like boiling, black water, and thousands of eyes stared back at me.

Mr. Vaggot, how soon?

Less than five minutes.

Five minutes. In five minutes, it would all be over.

I don't want to die. That was the last thing I sensed from him.

I've seen your future, I assured him. *Believe me, you don't want it.*

Calliope Flax—Alto Do Mundo Penthouse

At the penthouse, I'd followed the signal until I came to a glass door in a long hall where a bunch of bodies sprawled out on the floor. They were decked out in body armor, weapons scattered around them where they fell, along with big chunks of safety glass that had been blown out behind them. The glass panel was gone, and the hall opened right out into open air where shredded drapes flapped in the wind. Snow blew in on a rush of cold air.

Past the bodies, I saw her; I knew that beak nose and bony neck the second I saw them. Her long, red hair blew in the breeze as she stared at some other little twerp with her, some freaky-looking Asian chick with a big head. They didn't even look like they heard me as I picked up the pace and started toward them.

Halfway there, I heard something behind me. I stopped and spun around in time to see a small figure lunge. It was a spooky-looking girl with black hair and blue eyes. She had a metal baton in each hand.

You . . .

The bitch was fast. The air chirped and one of the batons hit my gun hand hard. Black blood popped from the back of it as the skin split open. I fired two rounds, but they went wild.

Error.

The word flashed as warnings scrolled about the damage to the dead hand. A piece of yellow bone stuck through the skin where she hit it, but there was no pain. Pins and needles ticked down my arm as I squeezed the grip harder and tried to steady the gun. She moved in again.

"I know you," I said. Her eyes were focused and intense, but there was pain there too. Her shirt was stained with blood, and when I scanned into the meat behind it, I saw a small, bright bullet lodged there. She was hurt.

"You should have done your job on the tanker," she said. Her pupils opened up, and I felt a little dizzy. "This would all be over."

It was her. That bitch who stopped me at the train station when I got back from my tour. The one who took my memories. She had me cut open right inside my own apartment and wired a bomb through my guts, then made sure I ended up on that boat so they could blow it up. She'd fixed it so I never knew. I remembered that dizziness now. It was the same as when Singh tried to tweak me back at the roadblock. It was the same every time one of them fucked with my head, but this time the feeling passed.

"What's the matter?" I said. "Your little ace in the hole not working any—"

She moved fast. At the last second, I leaned back as the baton whipped past my face and I aimed the gun. Something hissed in front of me and I saw a puff of white mist as I squeezed the trigger. The gun boomed, but she'd ducked down again and was gone.

Warning. Warning. Warning.

Messages flew past as white mist began to boil from the back of my dead hand. Before I knew what happened, the skin melted away and I was looking at the meat and bone underneath.

Leichenesser. The bitch had a little key-chain canister hidden on her somewhere. She tossed it aside and picked up the baton she'd dropped on the floor as she closed in again.

The bone melted like wax as muscle sprang free and began to dissolve. I tried to fire again, but what was left of the hand wouldn't respond. The gun fell to the ground, trailing smoke, and she stomped on it with one foot before kicking it back down the hall behind her.

"You fucking—"

She spun around again as the last of the hand sizzled away, leaving a clean stump where the filter and nerve interface was. Pain blasted through my ribs as the baton hit home.

"I won't let you near her," she said.

"She's going to launch the nukes, you stupid bitch," I gasped.

My right hand wasn't half as good, but in a straight-up

brawl, it wouldn't matter. I reached back and pulled my field knife out of its sheath. She saw it and came around for another attack, but I closed the distance between us before she could strike.

"You're dead," I told her, and swung the knife.

12

ATROPOS

Zoe Ott—Alto Do Mundo Penthouse

Something crashed back out in the hallway, and the dark field scattered. I was back in the hallway with the bodies, and . . .

Penny. Penny was in trouble. She needed me.

Cold air rushed over me from the empty window. Snow blew against the back of my neck as I turned to see Penny and Flax fighting. Both of them were bleeding, and the floor around them was smeared with blood. Penny had one baton still clenched in her fist. Flax was missing one hand, but had a knife in the other one.

"Penny!"

"Go to the roof," she grunted without looking back. "Get out of here."

Flax lunged, but Penny ducked under the blade and darted in close, to strike again. Before she could land the blow, Flax grabbed her by the wrist and head-butted her in the face with a loud crack of bone. Blood gushed from Penny's nostrils as she staggered back.

I started to run toward them, not sure what I'd do when I got there. All I knew what that this woman had killed the first real friend I'd ever had, and she was about to kill the only one I had left. Before Penny could do anything else, Flax swung back around. The edge of her knife slashed Penny's arm open, and blood splashed onto the floor.

"Penny!"

I ran. One of the batons was on the floor, and I went to scoop it up and fell. I slid across the tiles, then managed to pick myself up and stumble toward them.

Penny turned and saw me at the last minute. I flew past her and brought the baton down on the tattooed woman's neck, but it didn't stop her. I lost my footing, and the knife whipped over my head as I fell onto my butt.

Penny stood, rearing back to deliver a strike, when Flax stabbed her in the chest.

It was the most horrible sound I'd ever heard. The blade went in right at the base of her throat, and the hilt struck so hard it forced the air out of her mouth in a spray of blood. She jerked once, and the baton clattered onto the floor.

"No!"

Flax wrenched the knife out, and Penny choked. Blood was pumping out of the gash. Her eyes rolled and she fell to the floor.

"No! Penny, no!"

I scrambled beside her. A pool of blood was growing around her head. I put my hands over the hole, but it kept coming. I couldn't make it stop.

The room got bright around me as I stared down at her. I looked for her colors, to try to soothe them, to try to stop any pain she might have, but I couldn't find them. They were already gone. Penny was dead.

Penny, no . . . this can't be happening . . .

I let go of her and held my head. It felt like it was going to explode. I couldn't hear anything or feel anything. I was still staring down at her when I felt Flax's hand grab my arm.

"Zoe Ott?" she growled.

I jerked away and ran. My foot slipped in Penny's blood and I went down on one knee, then bolted back toward the stairwell as the woman's footsteps closed in behind me.

I made it to the stairwell door and pulled it open. When I was through, I turned and tried to slam it shut, but I was too late. A tattooed hand clamped down on the edge of the door and held it. I backpedaled as Flax shoved it open and stepped onto the landing.

"Get away from me!"

I ran for the stairs, but she cut me off and backed me into the corner, up against the concrete wall.

"You're too late," I gasped. I could barely breathe. I could feel hatred pour off her as she walked right up to me. She was going to kill me too, but I didn't care. In less than a minute, the missiles would fall.

"You're too late," I whispered.

Calliope Flax—Alto Do Mundo Penthouse

The red-haired bitch flinched when I grabbed a fistful of her shirt and pulled her up onto her toes. In the corner of my eye, I saw the launch countdown drop below three minutes.

"How are you doing it?" I asked. "How are you controlling the satellite?" She just smiled, blood running from one nostril.

"Goddamn it, make it stop!" I screamed in her face.

"You're going to die," she said. "You're all going to die now."

"You'll die too."

"I don't care," she said. She'd started to cry. "I don't care anymore. You killed my friend . . . my best . . ."

"Your friend had me cut open and tried to kill me," I said. "Fuck her. However you're doing it, stop the launch."

"You killed—"

I slammed her back against the wall, and that woke her up a little.

"You're going to kill everyone in this fucking city?" I said. My breath was coming fast now. The blood felt hot in my veins, and I felt a string of drool start to run over my bottom lip. The JZI flashed warnings as whatever it was inside me twisted in the back of my head. The counter was getting too low.

"Yes . . ."

My fingers squeezed on her throat, and another fat drop of blood came out of her nostril.

"I don't know how you're doing it," I said, "but I know you are."

The bitch's eyes started to roll as I kept up the pressure on her throat. Her pupils dilated, then relaxed.

"Last chance," I said.

"Go to hell," she gasped.

Bite . . .

I let go of her neck and put my palm over her mouth. Before I knew what I was doing, I leaned in and felt her scrawny neck under my lips. I could feel the big vein there throbbing, then the salt of her sweat on my tongue. My mouth opened, my lips peeling back like it was out of my control.

Do it . . .

I bit down, and she screamed. Greasy blood filled my mouth, and the warmth ran down my neck. Something inside me drove me, telling me to bite harder, deeper. It was all I could do to stop with that vein still pulsing under my tongue.

Do it . . .

I squeezed my eyes shut and shoved her away, down on her back onto the floor. Blood was running out of the bite mark on her neck, flowing down her chest and seeping into the dress she wore. She tried to say something but couldn't, as she stared up at me in horror. She held out her hands, and they started to shake.

"N . . . no . . ." she gasped. I stomped her bony chest with the heel of my boot, knocking her back. I drew the knife again and took a step toward her. I swallowed blood, and even though it made me sick, my teeth still itched to bite again. Drool leaked out of the corners of my mouth.

"You ruined me," I heaved. I closed the gap between us. "You motherfuckers ruined me. . . ."

"I . . . lost him . . ." she whispered. "I lost . . . him . . ."

Kneeling down over her, I put the point of the blade under her chin. She didn't react when it touched her. She didn't look like she was seeing me anymore.

"You . . . will bring about . . . destruction . . ." she wheezed. Her head lolled, and she fell back onto the concrete. I spit on the floor next to me and wiped my mouth.

In the corner of my eye, I saw the launch countdown had frozen.

Blood began to pool around the little bitch's head. Her eyes went out of focus.

"You . . . save . . . my . . . life . . ." she whispered. Then she let out a long breath and went still.

I moved the knife away and pushed myself back up onto my feet. My head spun and I leaned against the wall, leaving a smear of blood.

I turned and left the stairwell, letting the door slam shut behind me.

Nico Wachalowski—Heinlein Industries

An alarm bell went off as I shoved open a fire door and came out into the cold night air where the transmitter dish towered above me. In the distance, over the howl of the wind, I could hear the scream of jets. Shielding my face against the snow, I scanned the tarmac. Fawkes's signature was close.

Wachalowski, this is Alice. The launch has been aborted. Repeat: the launch has been aborted. What's your status?

I checked the countdown and saw it had stopped.

How?

They never reached Vaggot. He manually disarmed the satellite from inside on his own.

What about Zoe?

Unknown. What is your status?

I'm at the transmitter.

I squinted through the storm and switched to night vision. Sweeping the area, I spotted a group of figures in the distance. Two of them were carrying some kind of crate between them.

I've got Fawkes, I told her.

Something hit me from my left, lifting my feet up off the ground. A large, meaty shoulder knocked the wind out of me, and I felt a big hand on my chest before I was shoved back. I landed on my side on the blacktop and slid a couple feet as a large figure moved toward me, its moonlit eyes glaring down.

I got my gun between us and fired a burst that tore across its chest. It staggered back a step, then recovered and reached down to grab me. I heard a loud snap over the sound of the wind and saw its hand split apart. The long blade thrust out from the gap, and it lunged.

I rolled as the tip of the blade thudded down onto the tarmac next to me, then stomped down on the side of the thing's knee. Cartilage crunched as the joint bent at an odd angle and the revivor began to fall. It hit the ground, and I fired another burst into the back of its head, spraying black across the snow.

"Fawkes!" I shouted. One of the shapes in the distance turned.

Zooming in, I saw two of the remaining revivors with him quickly assembling some kind of tripod, while the third heaved a large, heavy cylinder from inside the crate, which was now open. I scanned the cylinder, and the computer isolated its shape through the snow. It was a surface-to-surface missile. He was going to try to blow the dish.

"Fawkes!"

I got to my feet and ran as the wind sheared over me, stinging my face and hands. I fired, and a bullet sparked off the launcher assembly.

One of the two at the launcher returned fire, while the second joined the third to help load the missile.

Faye, do you read me?

Yes.

I'm feeding you three revivor signatures; can you pull their IDs and connect to them from where you are?

Stand by.

Something struck the armor plate on my chest and knocked the breath out of me. I stumbled as I fired again, straining to spot Fawkes through the snow.

Nico, I'm in, Faye sent.

I hooked into the stealth command-spoke package still resident in Faye's system, and used it to open command links to all three of the remaining revivors. For a second, they were all being controlled by both Fawkes and me, but a second was all I needed. Before he could react to lock them down, I triggered the Leichenesser capsules in all of them.

The one carrying the missile dropped it and it hit

the tarmac with a metallic thud before rolling in a slow semicircle. White mist began to shoot from the back of its neck, and it stumbled to one side.

The other two revivors tried to keep their footing as the flesh and bone inside began to dissolve. One fell back against the launcher's tripod before it lost integrity, and I saw one arm slide from its sleeve and fall onto the ground next to it. The other went down on its hands and knees, then collapsed.

Fawkes saw what had happened and bolted away from them to avoid getting caught in the smoke himself.

Nico, Faye sent, *the transfer has been initialized. The dish is sending.*

I fired another burst at Fawkes and caught him in the leg. He lost his balance and fell, crashing down onto his side as I approached.

The lights from the transmitter lit his otherworldly face as he stared up at me. I took aim and was about to put a bullet in the side of his head when he pulled his shirt aside to show the mechanism strapped to his chest.

"Stop the transmission," he shouted. "Or I will."

I scanned the device. The explosives rigged to it were extremely powerful. They wouldn't destroy the entire dish, but they'd knock it down, out of alignment.

"It's a dead man's switch," he said. "If my signature ceases, it will go off."

"It's over, Fawkes."

He lifted one hand and I saw the detonator. I fired a burst into his forearm and the flesh erupted in a splash of black blood. Sparks sprayed as the hand snapped apart to reveal the bayonet tucked inside, and the trigger spun off into the dark.

He recovered quickly; he got to his feet to go after it, but I'd closed the distance. I struck him in the chest with one shoulder and he pitched back down onto the ground.

He'd deteriorated a lot over the years, but he still had the strength of a revivor. He didn't know pain or fear. He recovered and sprang back up from the ground. His moonlit eyes locked on me as he lunged with the bayonet.

I fired, and the bullet punched through one side of his neck. Blood pumped from the hole, but he kept coming. His cold left hand grabbed my shoulder as he thrust the blade into my gut. The armored weave took the brunt of it, but I felt the point bite through and warmth seep into the fabric.

I knocked his leg out from under him and shoved him back down onto the blacktop, coming down on top of him. He tried to stab at me with the bayonet again, but I pinned his arm under one knee and shoved the gun in his face. He tried to say something, but nothing came out. His teeth were stained black.

Agent, wait.

I shot him in the shoulder twice, and the arm stopped moving.

Agent, this is the only chance we will ever have to stop them forever. You've seen what I've done.

I saw it.

No one else needs to be hurt. No one else needs to die. This will level the playing field—nothing more. No more control; no more lies. People will be free, free to walk their own path. Free to govern themselves. Free to wake up each day and know that the events of the previous day were real, that they were true, and that their will and their consciousness are their own.

Vibrations sparked from the shoulder of my dead arm to its fingertips, and messages began to stream past in front of me. The nanoblood inside was responding to the transmission. Fawkes's alien eyes widened as he realized it too.

You've doomed them all, he said.

I took a sample of his signature and re-created the waveform on my JZI. When they synchronized, I used my field knife to slice through the straps of his vest. I pulled it off of him, and the LED began to flash an urgent red.

Before it could explode, I slipped it on and pulled it taut around my chest. The mechanism homed in on the signature I'd cloned, and the LED turned blue again.

You've doomed them all, he said again.

I knelt down in front of him and grabbed his tie. I twisted it under his throat and forced him back onto the tarmac. The blade of my field knife flashed as I aimed the point at an angle toward his neck.

I guess the little mutant was right, he said.

I jammed the blade in and twisted. The edge severed the connections between the revivor nodes and the brain stem.

His signature warbled, then snapped out of existence, and the moonlit glow faded from his eyes.

13

AFTERMATH

Zoe Ott—Heinlein Industries

The next thing I remembered, I was outside.

The city was gone, but it wasn't destroyed. Instead of
the wasteland, I was sitting on a blanket that was spread
out over thick, green grass. The blanket was on a hill that
looked out over a big, open space that was covered in
patches of yellow flowers. The sun was low in the sky,
and it was shady and cool.

"What do you want to do tonight?" Karen asked. She
was lying on her back, looking up at me. Her face was
clear and smooth. There were no bruises or scars. All
of her teeth were still there. She looked happy as she
closed her eyes and stretched.

"I don't know," I said. "Watch a movie?"

I pressed my hand into the grass. It was soft, and cool.
I liked the way it smelled.

I'd never really seen grass before, not like that. Somehow, though, I knew what I was seeing wasn't a vision.
The thing Karen used to call my gift was gone, and I

knew it would never come back again. I'd never have to see another vision. I'd never sense anybody's consciousness or be able to change it. That thing that had haunted me my whole life . . . it was finally over. This was just a regular, run-of-the-mill dream.

Karen smiled and looked out over the field.

"We should probably get going," she said. "It will be dark soon."

"Just a little longer."

We watched the sky turn dark blue, then shift to a mixture of orange and pink.

"Will it be okay?" she asked. "Being like the rest of us?"

"Yes."

"Really?"

I felt like losing that part of me should scare me, but it didn't—it felt like a terrible weight was lifted. The knowing had been awful, but trying to change those things had been much worse. I didn't want to know those things anymore. They had never once helped me. The money and the power—none of it made anything any better. It was all gone now, but I think it was the first time I'd ever really known peace.

"Better than okay."

"Good," she said. "It's all over, then."

A nagging doubt crept in when she said that. I couldn't know, not like I used to, but I did remember certain things from before.

"One thing still kind of bothers me," I told her.

"What?"

"A woman used to come to me in my visions," I said. "I only met her twice in real life."

"So?"

"She said we'd meet three times."

Karen shrugged in the growing dark. I scratched the side of my neck.

"Maybe she was wrong."

"Maybe."

I scratched the side of my neck again, and felt a ring-shaped scar there. That's where that woman, Flax, bit me. I could remember her lips on my neck, then terrible, blinding pain. I'd fallen as hot blood pumped out of the wound. It spread out across the floor, and I'd lain there in it as the puddle grew. She'd walked off and left me, and as she turned the corner the world faded to black.

"She was a carrier," I said.

Karen raised her eyebrows. "A what?"

"She bit me," I said, half to myself. "She was a carrier."

Karen didn't answer. When I turned to look at her, she was gone and I was alone. The wind picked up and blew across the field, making the grass and flowers ripple, almost like water.

"Karen?"

System initialization complete.

The words appeared in the dark. I rubbed my eyes, but they didn't go away. They floated in front of me for a minute and then they faded away.

"Karen?"

Are you awake? The words appeared in front of me, then faded.

"What?"

Are you awake?

The air flickered in front of me and the field warped. The air turned cold for a second, and I felt it rush over bare skin.

Are you—

I opened my eyes. The field disappeared. I was staring down at my flat, bare chest, and my legs dangled beneath me. Wires or tubes were draped down the front and back of me, and I could feel other bodies close to mine. A large man's hand with a vein that bulged across the back hung next to mine. Our fingers were touching.

Beginning system analysis . . . The words appeared, then blinked out as random characters started to flow top to bottom in the corner of each eye.

What's happening? I tried to say the words, but nothing came out. Instead, they appeared in front of me, like the others.

You're back.

I looked around to see who was sending the messages. I was hanging from somewhere near the ceiling of a large room, surrounded by other hanging bodies. Clusters of wires ran from the backs of their heads and down their spines. Many pairs of eyes stared into the darkness that surrounded us, casting a soft glow that created shadows. There must have been hundreds of us there. The wires trailed down like vines or webbing to the floor down below, which was covered with black splotches.

What is this place? I asked. I waited for the fear to come, but it didn't.

Here. The message pulsed, then faded.

I looked between two of the hanging bodies and saw a nude woman maybe ten feet in front of me. Her body was scarred, and I could see the dark veins beneath her pale skin. Her hair and eyebrows were gone, and wires sprouted from her skull and spine, like the rest. Behind her, and between the bodies to her left, I could make out a sign mounted on the far wall:

SEMANTIC/EPISODIC MEMORY RECLAMATION FACILITY

Beginning memory analysis . . . a new message said.

The dead woman's eyes stared back at me. I knew her face. I'd seen it years ago, down in the old storage facility where Nico had brought me. Years later, I shot her in an alley and hoped that she was gone for good. But now I was no longer afraid. I didn't feel any fear or jealousy or hatred.

What's happening to me? I asked her. The many eyes

around us jittered, like they were all stuck in a dream. In the dim light they created, they seemed to sparkle.

As I watched them, I sensed another light. It was like a little star, or an ember that floated up from the dark. Below it was something like a field of lights, pinpricks in the dark that hung over a void. Instinctively, I knew they were my memories and that beneath them waited oblivion. It wasn't like my visions. This was something different.

I focused on that single glowing ember, and when I did, it opened, like a portal. It showed me a memory, as crisp and clear as if it were on TV. Not a dream; not a vision. Just a memory.

I was sitting in a warm car with Nico. Snow was drifting down past the windshield outside. He was smiling at me from the driver's seat, and the way he looked at me made me feel good. It seemed impossible that we were sitting there and he wanted to be there. He looked at me like I really was someone, not a weird curiosity or a joke. When he watched me, those pretty, iridescent lights shone from behind his eyes, like he was something out of one of my dreams.

"This is a lot," I said. My heart raced, like it had then. The whole thing had been overwhelming to me, but that smile of his helped put me at ease.

"I know."

"Half the time I'm not even sure how much of it's real."

"It's real," he said. *"The information the suspect provided was accurate, and after going over everything, I believe it's real. I believe in you."*

And when he said the words, they had made me cry. But not anymore.

"I believe in you."

The dead woman continued to stare at me, and I felt a connection form between us. An energy, almost, began to flow back and forth, and the scene in front of me blurred as my eyes began to move in time with hers.

"... we will meet three times, before this is all over ..."

I remembered her words, and as I began to feel a strange sense of calm, the other shoe dropped.

". . . your chances of successfully navigating these encounters are, in percentages, respectively thirty, one hundred ..."

My time had come. The end was here. I watched her through the maze of wires, and felt those embers of memory begin to separate from the field of lights and stream into the void. They trickled away, down the hanging wires, and away.

"... and zero ..."

Nico Wachalowski—The Shit Pit

I never understood what Cal saw in that bar, and I guess I never will. It was loud and full of smoke. The air reeked of sweat and too much perfume and cologne. Everyone there was covered in tattoos, and they all looked like trouble.

Maybe that's what she liked about it. She never did feel completely at ease with first-tier status. She hated places like Bullrich, but even after she got out and moved on, it's what she knew.

Whatever the reason, it was as good a place as any to go and get lost in. People drank, gambled, and argued, and no one paid any attention to two soldiers in the corner, or the flicker of orange light in their eyes as they sat and appeared to never speak.

She stared into her shot glass. It was half full, and surrounded by three empty ones. She was a woman of few words, and she never said much about what happened. Her occasional call and the odd night out were as close

as either one of us got to saying it meant a lot that the
other made it. Maybe it didn't need to be said.

Before she did her run into Alto Do Mundo, she'd
returned the message I'd left for her. By the time I read
it the whole thing was over and I thought she might have
said something she'd regret since she'd lived, but there
was no epiphany or soul baring. Just three words: *Back
at you.*

When I saw the words, I realized I hadn't expected
her to live through Fawkes's attack. That fact cut me almost as deep as losing Faye. Calliope Flax had gotten
under my skin at some point.

You had enough? I asked. She lifted one battered
brow.

I'm just getting started.

The city wasn't the same since the attacks a month
back. We'd dealt with terrorist attacks before, but nothing on the scale of what happened that day. The loss of
the CMC and TransTech towers was a blow that everyone felt, and would feel for years to come, but that
wasn't why it was different. People had learned who
Samuel Fawkes was, and that he was behind the assault,
and that he was gone. They got their closure, at least on
that front, but the attack wasn't the only shock they'd
received.

Fawkes's variants were shut down in due time. The
revivors in the streets were rounded up on command
spokes and filed back to Heinlein for study. The Huma
blood was no longer contagious, and the spread had
been stopped. Eventually, the nanos would be flushed
from everyone's systems, but those who were bitten had
been changed. Like me and like Cal, the upgraded nanos
had entered their brains and constructed the shunt that
Fawkes had so carefully designed. It blocked any interference from psionic control, and unlocked any memories that had previously been buried. The true fallout of

that day was just beginning to gain traction, and no one knew where it would lead.

A month ago, very few people had ever heard of Samuel Fawkes. They would have had no reason to know how or why he would orchestrate such a terrible assault on his own country. Everyone who was infected that day, though, woke up to a truth they could barely believe. Everyone who received the shunt also received a single, simple message that was encoded in the nano-machines and imprinted on the host's brain:

I have awoken you.

It was like an itch you couldn't reach. Even I felt it; Fawkes's final vindication of himself, like a bad memory that you couldn't forget.

Some even believed it.

I was still sorting through my own memories as they came back to me. They'd taken an interest in me a long time ago, back to the grinder, and even before that. I had never completely understood how Faye could turn on her own kind like she did until I began to experience those alien memories for myself. It was hard to know just how those violations felt, how complete they were, until you felt them firsthand.

There were times I could almost understand Fawkes's drive to stop them, until I looked to the skyline.

They ever find your girl? Cal asked. Neither of us had brought up Faye in weeks.

No, they never found her.

And the stick? Ott?

When the cleanup crews finally made it up to the Alto Do Mundo penthouse, they found the place mostly cleared out. They recovered the bodies of several soldiers up there, along with Zoe's friend, Penny Blount, and Motoko Ai, but Zoe was never found. A large patch of blood spatter was identified as hers, but according to the reports her body wasn't up there.

Cal saw my look and nudged me under the table with her boot.

She was breathing when I left. I swear, she said.

I know. I didn't want to talk about Zoe. *You decided if you're going to stay with Stillwell yet?*

I'm staying.

Good. Despite what had happened, Stillwell had proven committed to serving in the aftermath of the attacks. Like everywhere else, they'd had a reckoning, but also like everywhere else, things were slowly returning to normal, if the word still applied.

I'm glad you didn't listen to me. You saved a lot of lives that day, I told her. She nodded.

You too. It looks like your girl came through in the end, at least.

Maybe.

It was time to let that go anyway, she said. *Find yourself a new girl. One that's alive this time.*

Maybe.

I finished my drink and signaled for another. The bartender nodded and sent one over, along with another shot for Cal.

How about you? she asked. *What are you going to do now?*

Maybe I'll retire.

Yeah, right.

She pushed her shot glass to one side and grabbed the next. She held it up and smiled, showing the gap in her teeth.

To better days.

I clinked the glass.

Better days, I said, and that's where it ended.

Well, more or less.

ABOUT THE AUTHOR

James Knapp grew up in New England and currently lives in Massachusetts with his wife, Kim. He is at work on his next novel. Visit him at www.zombie0.com.

STATE OF DECAY

They're called revivors—technologically reanimated
corpses—and away from the public eye they do
humanity's dirtiest work. But FBI agent Nico
Wachalowski has stumbled upon a conspiracy
involving revivors being custom made to kill—and
a startling truth about the existence of these
undead slaves.

**"Knapp's writing is sharp and his fast and furious
plot twists keep the pages turning."**
—*Publishers Weekly*

R0055

THE ULTIMATE IN
SCIENCE FICTION AND FANTASY!

From magical tales of distant worlds to stories of
technological advances beyond the grasp of man, Penguin has
everything you need to stretch your imagination to its limits.

penguin.com

ACE
Get the latest information on favorites like
William Gibson, Ilona Andrews, Jack Campbell,
Ursula K. Le Guin, Sharon Shinn, Charlaine Harris,
Patricia Briggs, and Marjorie M. Liu,
as well as updates on the best new authors.

ROC
Escape with Jim Butcher, Harry Turtledove, Anne Bishop,
S.M. Stirling, Simon R. Green, E.E. Knight, Kat Richardson,
Rachel Caine, and many others—plus news on the
latest and hottest in science fiction and fantasy.

DAW
Patrick Rothfuss, Seanan McGuire, Mercedes Lackey,
Kristen Britain, Tanya Huff, Tad Williams, C.J. Cherryh,
and many more—DAW has something to satisfy the
cravings of any science fiction and fantasy lover.

*Get the best of science fiction and fantasy
at your fingertips!*

R0064-111510